D0578061

You are always in my heart,

Even though you're far away . . .

—ERNESTO LECUONA
(Cuba, 1895—Canary Islands, 1963)

THE

ISLAND

of

ETERNAL LOVE

THE

ISLAND

of

ETERNAL LOVE

DAÍNA CHAVIANO

Translated from the Spanish by
ANDREA G. LABINGER

RIVERHEAD BOOKS
a member of Penguin Group (USA) Inc.
New York
2008

RIVERHEAD BOOKS
Published by the Penguin Group
Penguin Group (USA) Inc., 375 Hudson Street, New York, New York 10014,
USA · Penguin Group (Canada), 90 Eglinton Avenue East, Suite 700, Toronto,
Ontario M4P 2Y3, Canada (a division of Pearson Canada Inc.) · Penguin Books Ltd,
80 Strand, London WC2R 0RL, England · Penguin Ireland, 25 St Stephen's Green,
Dublin 2, Ireland (a division of Penguin Books Ltd) · Penguin Group (Australia),
250 Camberwell Road, Camberwell, Victoria 3124, Australia (a division of
Pearson Australia Group Pty Ltd) · Penguin Books India Pvt Ltd,
11 Community Centre, Panchsheel Park, New Delhi–110 017, India ·
Penguin Group (NZ), 67 Apollo Drive, Rosedale, North Shore 0632,
New Zealand (a division of Pearson New Zealand Ltd) ·
Penguin Books (South Africa) (Pty) Ltd, 24 Sturdee Avenue,
Rosebank, Johannesburg 2196, South Africa

Penguin Books Ltd, Registered Offices:
80 Strand, London WC2R 0RL, England

First published in Spanish by Grijalbo,
an editorial group of Random House Mondadori, S.L.
Copyright © 2006 by Daína Chaviano
English translation copyright © 2008 by Andrea G. Labinger
All rights reserved. No part of this book may be reproduced, scanned,
or distributed in any printed or electronic form without permission.
Please do not participate in or encourage piracy of copyrighted materials
in violation of the author's rights. Purchase only authorized editions.
Published simultaneously in Canada

Library of Congress Cataloging-in-Publication Data

Chaviano, Daína, date.
[Isla de los amores infinitos. English]
The island of eternal love/Daína Chaviano ;
translated from the Spanish by Andrea G. Labinger.
p. cm.
ISBN 978-1-59448-992-1
I. Labinger, Andrea G. II. Title.
PQ7390.C52I7513 2008 2008004331
813'.64—dc22

Printed in the United States of America
1 3 5 7 9 10 8 6 4 2

BOOK DESIGN BY AMANDA DEWEY

To my parents

Contents

· PART ONE ·

THE THREE ORIGINS

Blue Night   5
Wait for Me in Heaven   12
I Know of a Woman   21
Burning for You   29
Dust and Foam   36
Black Tears   41

· PART TWO ·

GODS WHO SPEAK A HONEYED TONGUE

Why I Feel So Alone   63
Weeping Moon   66
I Hate You, and Yet I Love You   74
Soul of My Soul   82
Destiny Proposes   94
Forgive Me, Conscience   99

· PART THREE ·

CITY OF ORACLES

Cuban Night 111

If Only You Understood Me 118

Wounded by Shadows 128

A Tempest Going Nowhere 132

Don't Ask Me Why I'm Sad 148

Like a Miracle 156

· PART FOUR ·

PASSION AND DEATH IN THE
YEAR OF THE TIGER

Ah, Life! 165

Very Close to My Heart 173

Love Me Deeply 178

I'll Remember Your Lips 188

I Can't Find Happiness 194

You, My Delirium 209

· PART FIVE ·

THE SEASON OF THE RED WARRIORS

My Only Love 217

Absence 227

Sweet Enchantment 233

Matters of the Heart 243

I Was Missing You 247

Havana of My Heart 259

· PART SIX ·

CHINESE PUZZLE

I Should Have Cried   271

Defeated Heart   285

Twenty Years   290

Free of Sin   294

You Got Me in the Habit   301

Today, as Yesterday   308

Acknowledgments   317

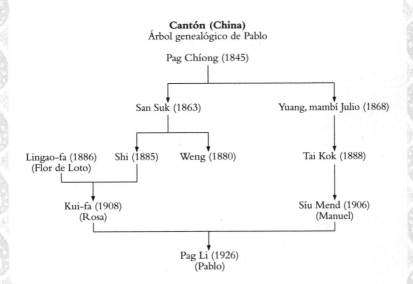

Cantón (China)
Árbol genealógico de Pablo

Pag Chíong (1845)

San Suk (1863)   Yuang, mambí Julio (1868)

Lingao-fa (1886)   Shi (1885)   Weng (1880)   Tai Kok (1888)
(Flor de Loto)

Kui-fa (1908)   Síu Mend (1906)
(Rosa)   (Manuel)

Pag Li (1926)
(Pablo)

Reino de Ifé, actual Nigeria (África) – Cuenca (España)
Árbol genealógico de Amalia

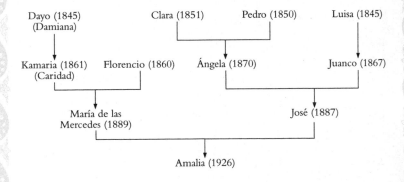

Part One

THE THREE

ORIGINS

From Miguel's Notebook

Mi chino . . . mi china:

 A term of endearment used by Cubans among themselves without any implication of Asiatic blood on the part of the person so addressed.

 The same can be said of the expression mi negro *or* mi negra, *which is not necessarily applied only to those with black skin.*

 These are simple expressions of friendship or love, whose origin dates back to when first the three principal ethnicities that make up the Cuban nation—Spanish, African, and Chinese—began to blend.

BLUE NIGHT

It was so dark that Cecilia could hardly see her. Rather, she intuited her silhouette behind the small table next to the wall, beside the photos of the sacred dead: Bcny Moré, the genius of the bolero; Rita Montaner, adored diva of Cuban composers; the night-black chansonnier Bola de Nieve, with his smile, white and sweet as sugar. . . . The dimness of the place, nearly empty at that time of night, was already becoming contaminated by the smoke of Marlboros, Dunhills, and the occasional Cohiba cigar.

The girl paid no attention to her friends' chatter. It was the first time she'd ever been there, and while she recognized a certain charm to the place, her own stubbornness—or perhaps skepticism—would not yet let her admit what she knew was true. A sort of energy floated in the bar, a whiff of enchantment, as if the door to another universe had opened. In any case, she resolved to determine for herself whether or not the rumors circulating in Miami about the hangout were true. She sat down with her friends near the bar, one of the few places with any light. The other illuminated space was a screen across which scenes of an antiquated Cuba, resplendent and colorful, paraded.

It was then that she saw her. At first Cecilia thought she was an outline of a shadow amid the surrounding darkness. A reflection led her to believe that the woman was bringing a glass to her lips, but the gesture was so fleeting that she questioned whether she had really seen it. Why had Cecilia fixated on this woman? Perhaps because of the strange solitude that seemed to settle over her. . . . But Cecilia hadn't gone there to feed on new suffering. She decided to forget about the woman and order a drink. That would help her probe the enigma her spirit had recently become—a region of herself she'd always believed she knew, but one that had, of late, turned into a labyrinth.

She had left her country escaping many things, so many that there was no longer any value in remembering them. And as she watched the crumbling buildings along the Malecón disappear into the horizon—in that strange summer of 1994 when so many fled the island on rafts in broad daylight—she swore she would never return. Now, four years later, she was still afloat. She wanted nothing to do with the country she'd left behind, but she still felt like a stranger in the city that housed the largest number of Cubans in the world after Havana.

She tasted her martini. She could almost see her own reflection in the glass and in the swaying clear, vaporous liquid penetrating her nostrils. She tried to concentrate on the miniature ocean rocking between her fingers, and on that other sensation creeping in as well. What was it? She had felt it as soon as she entered the bar, noticed the musicians' photos, and gazed at the images of a bygone Havana. Her glance once again rested on the motionless silhouette in the corner.

Her eyes returned to the screen, where a suicidal sea crashed against the Havana seawall, the Malecón, while Beny Moré sang: " . . . and when I kissed your lips, my soul was at peace." But the melody evoked a feeling contrary to his declaration. Cecilia sought refuge in her martini. In spite of her desire to forget, she was overcome by embarrassing emotions, like that quavering in her heart she preferred to dismiss. It was a terrifying feeling. She didn't identify with those painful heartbeats stirred by the bolero. She realized she was beginning to miss the gestures and sayings, even certain expressions she had detested when she lived on the island, an entire lexicon of murky neighborhoods that she was now dying to hear in this city full of *Hi, sweetie*s or *Excuse me*s, where all blended into a Spanish that came from many different places but belonged to none.

"My God!" she thought, plucking the olive from her glass. "To think I actually studied English over there!" She hesitated for a moment, unsure whether to eat the olive or leave it until she had finished her drink. "And all because of my obsession to read Shakespeare in the original," she recalled, biting down. Now she hated all that. Not the bald poet of the

Globe Theatre, of course; *him* she still loved. But she was tired of hearing a language that wasn't her own.

She regretted gulping down the olive in a fit of anger. Now her martini no longer looked like a martini. Again, she turned her head toward the corner. The old woman was still there, her glass practically untouched, mesmerized by the images on the screen. A solemn, warm voice, a vestige of another era, spilled from the speakers: *"It hurts so much, it hurts, to feel so alone. . . ."* Oh, God, what a sappy song. Like all boleros. But Cecilia could identify. She was so ashamed that she gulped down half her drink, and it launched her into a coughing fit.

"Don't drink so fast, girl. I'm not in the mood to play nursemaid today," said Freddy, whose name wasn't actually Freddy but Facundo.

"Don't tell her what to do," murmured Lauro, alias La Lupe, but really Laureano. "Let her drown her sorrows."

Cecilia shifted her eyes from her glass, feeling the weight of a silent summons. She sensed that the old woman was watching her, but the smoke obscured her line of sight. Was the woman really looking at the table where Cecilia and her two friends sat, or was she gazing beyond them toward the dance floor, at the musicians who were beginning to arrive? The images vanished, and the screen rose like a heavenly bird, disappearing into the ceiling's framework. There was a barely discernible pause, and suddenly the musicians let loose with a feverish passion capable of unleashing the soul. That rhythm infused her with an indescribable sadness. She felt the pang of memory.

She noticed the astonishment of a group of Nordic-type tourists. They must have found it very strange to see a young man with the profile of Lord Byron playing drums as if possessed by the devil, standing next to an Asian-featured mulatto woman who was shaking her braids to the beat of the *claves;* and that prodigious-voiced black man, like an African king—a silver hoop in his ear—singing a range of cadences, from an operatic baritone to the nasality of the *son.*

Cecilia scanned her companions' faces and realized what it was that made them so attractive. It was the unawareness of their own mixture, their inability to acknowledge (or their indifference to) their diverse origins. She looked toward the other table, feeling sorry for those Vikings, trapped in their bland monotony.

"Let's dance," Freddy said, tugging at her.

"Are you crazy? I've never danced to this in my life."

As an adolescent she had devoted herself to listening to songs about stairways reaching to heaven and trains that passed through graveyards. Rock music was subversive then, and it had filled her with passion. But her adolescence was long gone, and now she would have given anything to dance this *guaracha* that was lifting everyone from their chairs. How she envied those dancers, gyrating, pausing, entangling, and disentangling themselves without losing their rhythm.

Freddy got tired of begging, so he grabbed La Lupe instead. And off they went toward the dance floor, amid the chaos. Cecilia took another sip of her ancient martini, by now on the brink of extinction. Only she and the old woman remained at their tables. Even the descendants of Erik the Red had joined the revelry.

She finished her drink, and without any affectation, sought out the old woman. It made her feel slightly uneasy to see her so alone, so removed from the general commotion. The smoke had cleared, almost as if by magic, and she could distinguish the old woman more clearly. She was watching the dance floor with an amused expression, and her eyes sparkled. Suddenly she did something unexpected: she turned her head and smiled at Cecilia. When Cecilia returned the smile, the old woman pulled out a chair, in invitation. Without a moment's hesitation, Cecilia went to join her.

"Why aren't you dancing with your friends?"

The woman's voice was tremulous, but clear.

"I never learned," Cecilia replied, "and now I'm too old."

"What would you know about being old?" the woman muttered, her smile fading slightly. "You still have half your life in front of you."

Cecilia didn't respond, her interest caught by something that hung from a chain around the old woman's neck: a little hand clasping a dark stone.

"What's that?"

"Oh!" The woman suddenly emerged from her reverie. "A gift from my mother. It's against the Evil Eye."

The lights began to spin in all directions, vaguely illuminating her face. She was a mulatto, nearly white, although her features revealed her mixed race. And she didn't appear as old as Cecilia had first guessed. Or did she? The fleeting reflections seemed to change her moment by moment.

"My name's Amalia. What's yours?"

"Cecilia."

"Is this your first time here?"

"Yes."

"Do you like it?"

Cecilia hesitated. "I don't know."

"I can see it's hard for you to admit it."

The young woman fell silent, while Amalia rubbed her amulet.

The *guaracha* ended with three strikes of the *güiro,* and the soft trill of a flute introduced another number. No one wanted to sit down. The old woman watched the dancers take up the beat again, as if enchanted by the music of the Pied Piper of Hamelin.

"Do you come here often?" Cecilia ventured to ask.

"Almost every night. . . . I'm waiting for someone."

"Why don't you make a date with them? That way you wouldn't have to wait alone."

"I enjoy the atmosphere," the woman admitted, and her glance lingered on the dance floor. "It reminds me of another time."

"And who are you waiting for, if I might ask?"

"It's quite a long story, although I could tell you the short version." She paused to stroke her amulet. "Which one do you prefer?"

"The interesting one," Cecilia said without hesitation.

Amalia smiled.

"It all started more than a century ago. I'd like to tell you from the beginning, but it's getting late."

Cecilia nervously gripped the table, not knowing if the comment was a refusal or a promise. Classic images of an antique Havana overcame her: women with pale faces and thick brows, wearing flowered hats; shimmering signs on a commercial street; Chinese greengrocers hawking their wares on every corner . . .

"That came afterward," the woman whispered. "What I want to tell you took place long before that, on the other side of the world."

Cecilia was startled by the way the old woman had intuited her daydream, but she tried to control herself as the woman began to tell her a story unlike anything she had ever read or heard. It was a story of fiery landscapes and creatures that spoke an incomprehensible dialect, of superstitions and ethereal ships that sailed for the unknown. She barely remembered that the musicians were still playing and the couples still danced endlessly. It was as if some sort of pact existed between the band, the dancers, and the old woman, allowing her and Cecilia to converse alone.

Amalia's tale was more of an incantation than a story. The wind blew menacingly through the tall sugarcane in a distant country, rife with beauty and violence. There were celebrations and deaths, weddings and killings. The scenes were peeled from some corner of the universe as though someone had made a hole through which memories of a forgotten world could escape. When Cecilia once again became aware of her surroundings, the old woman was gone, and the dancers had returned to their tables.

"Ay, I've had enough," sighed La Lupe, falling into a chair. "I think I'm gonna pass out."

"You don't know what you missed, girl." Freddy quaffed the rest of his drink. "That's what you get for acting like a *gringa.*"

"With that ghost-white face she doesn't need to act like anything. She's in another world, can't you see?"

"Shall we order another round?"

"It's late," she said. "We should go."

"Ceci, excuse me for saying so, but you've been acting like a snowman: a-bom-i-na-ble."

"Sorry, Laureano, but I'm starting to get a headache."

"Girl, lower your voice," he said. "Don't call me that, or pretty soon people will start asking questions."

Cecilia stood up, rooting in the bottom of her purse for some money, but Freddy stopped her.

"No, tonight it's on us. That's why we asked you to come out."

Kisses as insubstantial as butterflies. In the darkness, Cecilia verified once more that the old woman had gone. She didn't understand why, but she was reluctant to leave. She walked slowly, bumping into chairs, without taking her eyes from the screen, where a couple from another era was dancing a *son* as no one of her own generation could. Finally, she stepped out into the sultry night.

The visions conjured from the old woman's tale—the evocation of a Havana filled with music and life—had left her with an odd sensation of dislocation. She felt like one of those saints that can be in two places at the same time.

"I'm here, now," she assured herself.

She glanced at her watch. It was so late that there wasn't a doorman in sight. It was so late that there wasn't a soul in sight. Knowing she'd have to walk alone to the corner brought her fully back to the present.

The clouds had swallowed the moon, pierced here and there by milky rays. Two penetrating eyes opened next to a wall. A cat moved among the shrubbery, alert to her presence. As if on cue, the lunar disk escaped its cloudy eclipse, illuminating the feline and its silvery body. Cecilia studied the shadows: hers and the cat's. It was a blue night, like the one in the bolero. Perhaps that was why it reminded her of Amalia's story.

WAIT FOR ME IN HEAVEN

Lingao-fa decided it was a good night to die. A warm wind blew between the reeds rising timidly from the water. Perhaps it was the breeze, its spirit fingers caressing her clothing, that filled her with a sense of the inevitable.

She stood on tiptoe, the better to breathe the clouds. She was still slender, like the lotus adorning the pond, with its gauzy-tailed fishes. Her mother would sometimes sit alone by the pond and contemplate the bulbous stalks that disappeared into the quagmire, often stooping to touch them. And this would fill her with peace. She always suspected that her own contact with the flowers had endowed her daughter with the delicate features so many had admired since her birth: smooth, creamy skin; feet as soft as petals; straight, shiny hair. So, when it came time to celebrate her arrival—one month after her delivery—she decided on her name: Lotus Blossom.

She regarded the humid fields that seemed to swell on that afternoon just like her breasts when she had nursed her rosebud, little Kui-fa. The child was now eleven years old, and soon a husband would have to be found for her; but that task would fall to her brother-in-law Weng, her closest male relative.

With hesitant steps Lingao-fa headed inside. She owed her unstable gait to the size of her feet. To prevent their growth, her mother had bound them for years. It was an important requirement if she wanted to make a good marriage. That's why she, in turn, now bound the feet of little Kui-fa, despite the child's tearful protestations. It was an agonizing process: all the toes, except the big one, had to be bent toward the ground; then, a stone would be placed in the arch and held down by bandages. Although she herself had abandoned the custom since her husband's death, a few broken, badly healed little bones had left a permanent mark on the way she moved.

She reached the kitchen, where Mei Lei was cutting vegetables, and she noticed her daughter playing by the fire. Mei Lei wasn't any ordinary servant. She had been born to a wealthy household and had even learned to read, but by a series of misfortunes she ended up a landlord's concubine. Only her master's death had freed her from such affliction. Alone and with no resources, she offered her services to the Wongs.

"Did you get the cabbage, Mei Lei?"

"Yes, Madame."

"And the salt?"

"Everything you ordered." And she added timidly, "Madame mustn't worry."

"I don't want the same thing to happen as last year."

Mei Lei blushed with shame. Although her mistress never scolded her for anything, she knew that the last flood had been her fault. She was old now and forgot certain things.

"This year we won't have any problems," she said brightly. "The temple lords are elegantly robed."

"I know, but sometimes the gods are vengeful. It's good to have extra, just in case."

Lingao-fa went to the bedroom, and the aroma of the simmering soup followed after her. Early widowhood had awakened the greed of several esteemed landowners, not just because of her beauty, but also because the late Shi had left her many fields where rice and vegetables grew, in addition to some cattle. Modestly but firmly, she had rejected all their proposals, until her brother-in-law suggested that she marry a Macao businessman. He was the owner of a bank that managed the clan's finances, and their union would ensure the safety of the family fortune. She didn't know what to do or from whom to seek counsel. Her parents were dead, and she had to obey her deceased husband's older brother. One day she realized the decision could no longer be postponed. Weng presented himself at her door and told her, without preamble, that the wedding would take place on the third day of the fifth moon.

On the table was the silver comb her mother had given her. With a mechanical gesture she caressed the mother-of-pearl inlay, and after untangling her hair, she dampened it to refresh herself and then she stepped outside the front door. The moon emerged from behind the clouds.

"It's your fault, damned old man," she muttered angrily, looking at the brilliant disc that housed the capricious old man in the moon. He was the one who tied together the feet of those destined to marry—and few escaped his plan. He was why she had become Shi's wife, and why she now had to face her troubling destiny.

It was the last time she would see that bluish light over the countryside, but she didn't care. Anything was better than bearing an endless torment. She cared nothing for Weng's mockery. He had often ridiculed her beliefs. She knew that her husband's spirit would tear her to shreds in the next life if she ever were to remarry. A woman can only be the property of one man, and that conviction certainly bore down on her more than never seeing her loved ones again.

That night she dined early, tucked in Kui-fa, and remained at her bedside longer than usual. Afterward she said good night to Mei Lei, who was about to go to sleep at the foot of the child's bed, and quietly went out to the patio, where she remained for hours contemplating the constellations. . . . It was the cook who discovered her hanging from the tree the following morning, next to the pond of golden fishes.

Lingao-fa was buried with great honors on a foggy dawn in 1919. Her death, however, was not totally useless to Weng. In spite of the fact that the merchant had lost all possibility of a business relationship, the family's prestige grew, thanks to her display of conjugal fidelity. Besides, as the relative charged with the future upbringing of Kui-fa, his capital grew with the riches that passed into his hands. Of course, the money and jewels that were part of Kui-fa's dowry remained in chests in the bank in Macao. And as far as the cattle and crops were concerned, the businessman resolved to multiply—as long as he could—whatever he was now charged with administering.

Weng felt great respect for his ancestors, and although he wasn't superstitious—unlike some other villagers—he did nothing to avoid the honors accorded him by the interminable line of dead relatives that accumulated from one generation to the next. Because he felt such loyalty to his dead, Weng resolved immediately that his niece should be treated like one of his own children, a very uncommon decision in a place where girls were seen as a burden. But in truth, all obligations aside, the businessman understood the practical side of his tutelage. Kui-fa was as pretty as her mother, and she possessed a dowry with no shortage of relics and family jewels, in addition to the lands that would be turned over to her husband as soon as she married. Three years before, Weng had taken as his charge the son of Tai Kok, a cousin who had died under somewhat unclear circumstances on an island in the Caribbean Sea where he had gone seeking his fortune, following in his father's footsteps. Siu Mend was a quiet child, gifted in mathematics, whom Weng wished to initiate into his business affairs. There was no one better than that boy, he thought, as a husband for his niece. She would soon be of age to negotiate a marriage.

For the moment, little Kui-fa would remain in the care of Mei Lei, who would be responsible for ensuring her virtue. The nursemaid would sleep on the floor at her mistress's feet, as she had always done, which might ease Kui-fa's sadness at her mother's absence.

In any case, her new home was a noisy place where all sorts of people freely came and went. Apart from Uncle Weng and his wife, in the house also lived Grandfather San Suk, who almost never left his room; two married cousins, the sons of his uncle, with their wives and children; the boy called Siu Mend, who spent his days studying or reading; and five or six servants. But it wasn't her cluster of relatives that most aroused her curiosity. Occasionally she spied some pale visitors with round, washed-out eyes, wrapped in dark, tight-fitting clothing and speaking a barely comprehensible Cantonese. The first time Kui-fa saw one of those creatures, she ran into the house screaming that there was a demon in the garden. Mei Lei calmed her after going out to investigate, reassuring her that it was just a *lou-fan,* a white foreigner. From that time on, the child devoted herself to the comings and goings of those luminous beings that her uncle treated with special reverence. They were tall, like the giants in stories, and they spoke with strange music in their throats. On one occasion, one of them surprised her while she was spying on him. He smiled at her, but she took off in a flash, looking for Mei Lei, and didn't return until the voices had faded into the distance.

During the day, Kui-fa spent hours by the fire, listening to stories from the old woman's youth. That was how she learned of the existence of the God of Wind, the Goddess of the North Star, the God of the Hearth, the God of Wealth, and many others. She loved to hear about the Great Flood, caused by a lord who, filled with shame at having been defeated by a warrior queen, banged his forehead against a gigantic bamboo tree that punctured the clouds. But her favorite was the story of the Eight Immortals who attended the birthday party of the Queen Mother of the West, by the Lake of Jewels, and who, to the rhythm of music played by invisible instruments, participated in a feast where the most exquisite dishes were served in abundance: monkey tongue, dragon liver, bear paws, phoenix marrow, and other delicacies. The climax of the banquet was dessert: peaches fresh from a tree that blooms only once every three thousand years.

Mei Lei dug deep into her memory to satisfy the child's curiosity. Those were peaceful years, like only those lived unreflectively can be, years that, at life's end, are recalled as the happiest. Only once did something happen to interrupt their monotonous existence. Kui-fa fell gravely ill. Fever raged through her body, as if an evil spirit was trying to steal her young life away. No doctor could find the cause of her illness, but Mei Lei didn't lose her head. She went to the Temple of the Three Origins with three paper banners on which she had written the characters for *heaven, earth,* and *water.* In the tower of the temple, she offered the first banner to heaven; then she buried the one belonging to the earth beneath a little pile of dirt; and finally she plunged the last scroll deep into a stream. A few days later the child began to recover.

Mei Lei dedicated a corner of her room to the adoration of the Three Origins, sources of happiness, forgiveness, and protection. And she taught Kui-fa always to keep in harmony with those three powers. From that time on, heaven, earth, and water were the three kingdoms to which Kui-fa directed her thoughts, knowing that in them, she would always find protection.

The rainy months passed, and the time arrived when the God of the Hearth would rise to the celestial regions to take note of the people's actions below. Later on, the harvest season began, and after that came the gusts of the typhoon season. The months passed, and again the God of the Hearth began his ascent, carrying with him divine gossip that mortals attempted to sweeten by smearing the statue's lips with honey. And the peasants went back to their planting, and the rains returned, as did the season of one thousand winds that shredded the paper kites. And amid the kitchen aromas and the god-plagued legends, Kui-fa became a young woman.

At an age when many young girls were already nursing children of their own, Kui-fa still clung to Mei Lei's braid, but Weng didn't seem to take note. His head was filled with the counting of numbers and projects, like grains of rice, and that feverish activity had postponed his niece's wedding indefinitely.

But one afternoon, as they were chatting in one of the teahouses (where the men went only to make deals or find prostitutes), he overheard some neighbors commenting on a young woman of marriageable age and with a good dowry, who was nonetheless condemned to an undeserved spinsterhood by a greedy uncle. Weng pretended he hadn't heard a thing, but he blushed to his roots, already tinged with gray. When he returned home, he called Siu Mend on some pretext and watched the boy as he went over some papers. The adolescent had become a robust young man, decidedly handsome. That same night, when the family gathered for dinner, he decided to announce the news:

"I've been thinking Kui-fa should get married."

Everyone, including Kui-fa herself, raised their eyes from their plates.

"We will have to find her a husband," his wife ventured.

"It's not necessary," Weng said, fishing for a piece of bamboo shoot. "Siu Mend will make a good husband."

Now all eyes were directed toward the astonished Siu Mend and then toward Kui-fa, who fixed her gaze on the platter of meat.

"It would be good to celebrate the wedding during the kite festival."

It was a propitious date. On the ninth day of the ninth moon, it was customary to climb to a high place, either a hill or a temple tower, in order to commemorate an event from the Han dynasty, when a teacher saved his pupil's life by warning him that a terrible flood would demolish the earth. The youth fled toward the mountain, and on his return, he discovered that all his animals had drowned. That commemorative festival heralded the season when the winds howled fiercely and endlessly, with the promise of future storms. Then, from the mountaintop, hundreds of paper animals were launched into the air with their gaily colored forms: pink dragons, butterflies that fluttered furiously, birds with moving eyes, warrior insects . . . Each year, an entire assortment of impossible beings fought eternal, legendary battles for the dominion of the skies.

On the very day of her wedding, from behind the curtains of her sedan chair, Kui-fa could discern the distant silhouette of a phoenix. She couldn't quite distinguish its colors because a red veil covered her face. And when she walked, she needed to look steadily down at her feet if she didn't want to trip and fall.

The young woman had not seen Siu Mend again since the night when her uncle had announced their betrothal. Mei Lei was charged with keeping her hidden. Wary of the man's imprudence at declaring their engagement with both parties present at the table, the servant decided to counteract his carelessness. Taking advantage of a moment when everyone was busy, she approached the altar of the Goddess of Love and removed one of her tiny porcelain hands.

"Lady," she beseeched, bowing before the statue while clutching the extremity between her own hands, "bring good fortune to my little girl and keep the evil spirits away from her. I promise you a fine gift if the wedding goes off without any problems and an even finer one when their first son is born." She hesitated for a moment, adding, "But only if mother and child are in good health."

She bowed three more times and kept the porcelain hand in one corner of the kitchen. Of course, no one thought of asking about the missing extremity. It would resurface when the supplicant's prayer was answered.

A few weeks after the wedding, the rivers overflowed their banks, and many people died. The poorest suffered famines, and the rich, looting. The epidemic was one of the few things that affected everyone equally. The water level of the rice paddies rose quickly, only to recede lazily, and the rice stalks peeked out from the murky waters. The first little south wind blew through the region, frigid and mocking, in time for another festival. . . . But Kui-fa still showed no signs of pregnancy. Mei Lei went again to visit the goddess.

"Try to grant what I ask, or you'll end up in a rat's nest in some corner," she threatened, turning her back on the statue.

The warning worked. A few weeks later Kui-fa's belly began to swell, and Mei Lei placed a basket of fruit at the altar. Months later, when the rains had once more reached their peak, Pag Li was born, in the middle of the Year of the Tiger. He screamed like a demon and latched onto his mother's nipple right away.

"So small, and already he has the nature of a wild beast," his father predicted when he heard him shriek.

Siu Mend had awaited the birth of his son with joy and concern, after he learned that the delivery was prelude to a long voyage, a journey to the island where his father had died and where his grandfather Yuang, whom he had never met, still lived. He owed this decision to Weng, who was working to establish business contacts for a store there.

"I'd go myself," the man had said, "but I'm too old for such a long crossing."

Distant memories of his father's departure crossed Siu Mend's mind: the confusing news, his mother's sobs . . . And now would history repeat itself? What if he never returned?

"Things have changed in Cuba," Weng assured him, noticing the young man's anxiety. "They don't hire the Chinese as coolies anymore."

He said that because his own grandfather, the venerable Pag Chiong, had for seven years worked twelve hours a day, bound by a contract he had signed, unaware of its weight. Until one afternoon he dropped dead on a pile of sugarcane he was trying to carry. In spite of all that, Yuang followed in his father's footsteps and also left for the island. Years later, his son Tai Kok, Siu Mend's father, decided to rejoin him, leaving his wife and son in Weng's hands. Although he didn't work as a day laborer, he became involved in a complicated web of debts that, in a quarrel, cost him his life. The following year Siu Mend's mother died of fever, and the child was left in the care of the man whom he always called uncle, although he was really his father's cousin.

"But what are things like there?" Siu Mend insisted, pouring more tea into his cup.

"Different," Weng said. "The Chinese are doing well on the island. . . . They do good business. At least that's what Uncle Yuang tells me."

He was referring to Siu Mend's grandfather, the only survivor of the family migration to Cuba. He had lived on the island for more than three decades.

"Tell me about Havana, Uncle."

"Yuang claims that the climate is like ours," the merchant responded laconically, because he had no more information to give.

The following week, during his usual trip to Macao, Siu Mend bought a map in an import-export store. Back home, he spread it on the floor and with his finger traced the line of the Tropic of Cancer, through his province, across the Pacific, and all across America, finally arriving in Havana. Siu Mend had just discovered something else. It wasn't a mere coincidence that the climate of both cities was similar: Canton and Havana were at exactly the same latitude. And that clean, straight voyage struck him as a good omen. One month after the birth of his son, Siu Mend left for the other side of the world.

I KNOW OF A WOMAN

She sighed as she started the motor. The morning shimmered with sleep, and she was dying of exhaustion. Maybe it was premature old age. Lately she'd been forgetting everything. She suspected her blood carried the genes of her grandmother Rosa, who had ended her days confusing everyone and everything. If she had taken after her grandmother Delfina instead, she might have been a clairvoyant, knowing beforehand who was going to die, which airplane would fall from the skies, who would marry whom, and what the dead had to say. But Cecilia had never seen or heard anything that other people couldn't also perceive. And thus she was condemned. Her birthright would be premature senility, not the powers of an oracle.

The blare of a car horn jarred her from her reverie. She had stopped at a tollbooth, and the line of vehicles behind her was impatiently waiting for her to pay. She threw the money into the metal basket that swallowed it up immediately, and the barrier lifted. One more car among hundreds, thousands, millions of others. Before exiting the highway and pulling into the parking lot, she drove automatically for another ten minutes, like someone who had done this many times before. It would be another morning of riding the same elevator, walking down the long corridor to the editor's office to turn in some article about things that didn't interest her. But, as she entered the office, she noticed there was more commotion than usual.

"What's going on?" she asked Laureano, who was walking toward her with papers in his hand.

"This thing is red-hot."

"What happened?"

"It's not what happened, it's what's about to happen," he replied as she turned on her computer. "They say the Pope is going to Cuba."

"So?"

Her friend stared at her, mouth agape.

"But don't you understand?" he said at last. "It'll be the end of the world there."

"C'mon, Lauro, it's not going to be the end of anything."

"Ceci, I'm telling you! Every time the Pope sets foot in a communist country, it's kaput! *Arriverderci, Roma! Ciao, ciao, bambino!*"

"No way . . ." Cecilia muttered, picking up a pile of old notes to toss into the trash.

"Too bad for you if you don't believe me," Lauro said, leaving the papers on his desk. "Fine, here are the pages you asked for."

Cecilia glanced at them. It was the article she had requested the day before, when someone suggested that she take another look at that story of the phantom house that appeared and disappeared all over Miami. She didn't know if her boss would like the subject, but she had been racking her brain for two days now, trying to come up with something new, and that was all she had.

"I don't like it much," her boss said after listening to the idea.

Cecilia was about to reply, but he interrupted her.

"I'm not saying that because of the subject matter. It might be interesting if you could find a different angle. But why don't you keep working on the other stories as well? If you manage to find some more interesting stuff about your phantom house, we'll schedule it for one of the Sunday supplements, even if it takes six months. But don't rush it—just think of it as something extra."

And so she finished up two pieces she had begun weeks earlier, then immersed herself in the article about the house, making note of the names she would use later for possible interviews.

Toward the end of the day, she stopped to reread a certain paragraph. Maybe it was a coincidence, but when she was still living in Havana, she had known a girl by that name. Could this be the same person? Cecilia had never met anyone else with that name. She couldn't recall her surname, so no help there. She could remember only the girl's first name. Gaia. A goddess in a Greek myth.

Gaia lived in one of those bungalows hidden by trees that cover a large portion of Coconut Grove. Cecilia crossed the yard to the little house, painted a deep, ocean blue. The door and the windows were an even more luminous shade, like a delectable confection, like meringue on a birthday cake. A wind chime dangled from one side of the doorway, filling the afternoon with its lonely tinkling.

The neighboring flame tree drizzled orange-colored petals all over her. Cecilia shook the flowers from her hair before knocking, but her knuckles barely produced a sound against that solid antique door. At last she noticed the crude copper bell, like something a goat would wear, and she tugged on the cord that was tied to the clapper.

After a brief silence, she heard a voice on the other side of the door.

"Who is it?"

Someone was watching her through a tiny, eye-shaped peephole.

"My name is Cecilia. I'm a reporter from—"

The door swung open before she could finish the sentence.

"Hi!" exclaimed the same young woman she remembered from college. "What are you doing here?"

"Do you remember me?"

"Of course!" the other woman replied with what seemed a sincere smile.

Cecilia got the feeling that she was very lonely.

"Come on in—you don't have to stand outside."

Two cats nestled on the sofa. One of them, white with a golden spot on its forehead, scrutinized her through half-closed eyes. The other, multicolored as only she-cats can be, shot off into the other room.

"Circe's very shy," the young woman explained. "Have a seat."

Cecilia stood beside the sofa, unable to make up her mind.

"Beat it, Poli!" Gaia shooed the animal away.

At last she sat down, after the second cat had hidden beneath a table.

"What are you doing here?" Gaia asked, settling into an armchair by the window. "I didn't even know you were in Miami."

"I came four years ago."

"My God! Eight years ago, for me. How time flies!"

"I'm writing a piece for the newspaper I work for, and I found your name in an article. The reporter still had your address, but I tried the phone number and it wasn't the same. That's why I couldn't call before I came."

"What's the story about?"

"It's about that apparition, the phantom house. . . ."

Gaia's expression grew dark.

"Yes, I remember. It was about two years ago. But I don't want to talk about that anymore."

"Why not?"

Gaia started playing with the hem of her dress.

"It's not the first time I've seen a phantom house."

She sighed, almost painfully. "I saw another one in Cuba. Or, rather, I visited it."

"That's interesting."

"It had nothing to do with this one," Gaia hastened to add. "That one was an evil house, terrible. . . . This one's different. I don't know what it means."

"Ghosts don't mean anything. They're there or they're not. People see them or they don't. They believe in them or they make fun of those who see them. I've never heard that they mean anything."

"Because no one knows."

"I don't understand."

"Ghosts houses hold secrets."

"What kind of secrets?"

"It depends. The one I visited in Havana held the greatest evils on the island. The one that shows up here is different. I don't exactly know what it is, but I'm not interested in finding out. Seeing it was enough. I don't want to know anything more about ghosts."

"Gaia, if you don't help me with this article, I'm screwed. My boss wants an angle, something more interesting than just an apparition."

"Ask someone else."

"They've all changed jobs or addresses. You're the only one left. And it just so happens you're the only one I know. . . . If ghosts bring meaning to things, as you say, then this meeting means something."

Gaia cast her glance down to the rug that covered the floor.

"I'm not asking you for anything impossible," Cecilia insisted. "I just want you to tell me what you saw."

"Read the article."

"I did, but I want you to tell me again." As she spoke, she pulled a tape recorder the size of a pack of cigarettes from her bag. "Pretend I don't know anything about it."

Gaia watched as the tape began to roll.

"All right," she said grudgingly. "The first time I saw it was around midnight. I was coming home from the movies, and everything was very dark. I hadn't walked very far when the lights in *that* house suddenly all went on."

"Where was it?"

Gaia stood up, went toward the door, opened it, and walked a few steps among the trees, followed by Cecilia with her tape recorder.

"Here," she pointed, stopping in a strange clearing that interrupted the vegetation.

It looked like one of those circles attributed to fairy dances in Celtic lands. Cecilia looked around, uneasily. Was she afraid, or did she want the vision to reappear? Maybe both.

"What was the house like?"

"Ancient, wooden. But not like mine. It was much larger, two stories. It looked like it had been built to face the sea. The top floor had a balcony all around."

"Did you see anyone?"

"No, but all the lights were on."

"And what did you do?"

"I turned around, got into my car, and went to a hotel, knowing that it couldn't have been real." She glanced around again before retracing her steps back to her own house. "I stayed there for two days, because I didn't dare return alone. I didn't even go to work. Finally I called a friend and lied to him so he'd take me back home. I told him someone had tried to hold me up and I was afraid to go back by myself. He tried to convince me to call the police, but I claimed it had been an isolated episode; besides, I hadn't been robbed. Anyway, he insisted on coming inside with me to make sure everything was in order. While he was checking the rooms, I made the mistake of playing my answering machine. . . . What I'm about to tell you is off the record." She bent down and turned off the tape recorder, which Cecilia had again placed on the table. "I didn't mention it then, and it can't appear now, either."

"Why not?"

"While I was at the hotel, my boss got tired of trying to reach me by phone. Since I didn't answer, she went to visit me. In the message, she said she had spoken to my cousin when she arrived. My cousin told her that I was very sick with the flu and had been recovering in her house. My boss was afraid of catching it and apologized for not going inside to say hello. In the message, she wished me the best and sent regards to my cousin."

"What cousin is that?"

"No one. I have no cousins."

"Maybe she went to the wrong house and someone played a prank on her."

"My boss has been here several times; she certainly knows where I live. You can imagine how shocked my friend was when he heard the message, which sounded pretty strange after my story about the holdup. I had to tell him the truth."

"And did he believe you?"

"He had no choice, but he forbade me to mention his name if I ever told that story. He's a very well-regarded lawyer."

"What happened the second time you saw the house?"

"I never said I saw it again."

"You spoke of the first time. So there must've been a second time. . . . If you don't remember, I can replay the tape."

For a moment it seemed as if Gaia were going to reveal something else, but then she changed her mind.

"It's better for you to look for other eyewitnesses. I don't want to talk about this anymore."

"I've already told you I don't know where they are."

"Look in occult shops."

"What would I find out there?"

"You always hear stories in those places, and the people are always ready to talk."

Cecilia nodded silently before packing up her tape recorder. And while

Gaia watched her, she felt something like pity seize her chest without really knowing why.

Yet again Cecilia faced the commotion of the traffic, drivers desperate to move forward. . . . She would have to do something, something to shake up her daily routine. The worst part was that feeling of perpetual loneliness. Her scant family, except for a great-aunt who had arrived thirty years earlier, still remained on the island; the rest of her companions—with whom she had grown up, laughed, and suffered—were scattered throughout the world.

Now, whenever she thought about her friends, she referred only to Freddy and Lauro, two boys who were as different as they were alike. Lauro was slim, with huge, tubercular eyes, very much like the legendary bolero singer whose nickname he bore. And just like that other vibrant La Lupe, he was a real ham. Freddy, on the other hand, was chubby, with Asian eyes. That face, together with his contralto voice, earned him the nickname Freddy, in honor of the fattest bolero singer in history. If Lauro was like a moody diva, Freddy displayed great poise and control. They were like the reincarnations of both singers, and both took pride in that similarity. For Cecilia, they were like two petulant brothers whom she had to scold and advise continuously. She loved them very much, but the realization that they were her only companions couldn't help but make her feel a little depressed.

As soon as she opened her apartment door, she took off her clothes and climbed into the shower. The warm water splashed over her face. With pleasure she inhaled the rosy fragrance of foam left by the sponge on her body. An exorcism. A cleansing. A conjuring to relieve her soul. She sprinkled her head with a few drops of the holy water she bought every month at the Shrine of Our Lady of Charity.

She enjoyed those moments devoted to her bath. There she could commune with her grief and her woes before the One who cast his powers on everybody, no matter what its name: Olofi or Yahweh, He or She. Both or All. As a matter of principle, she didn't attend Mass. She had no confidence in any authority, spiritual or otherwise. She preferred speaking privately with God.

As she looked in the mirror, she wondered if the bar would be open yet, remembering her encounter with the old woman. Even the old lady seemed a phantom now. Maybe she'd been drunk and had dreamed the whole thing. Well, she said to herself, if martinis can produce such interesting visions, tonight she'd have a few more. Should she phone Freddy or Lauro? She decided to go alone.

Half an hour later she pulled up to the sidewalk. She paid her entrance fee and crossed the threshold. At that early hour, almost all the tables were empty. On the screen, the divine Rita crooned: "In Cuba each merry maid wakes up with this serenade . . . Peanuts! They're nice and hot. Peanuts! He sells a lot . . ." And she stretched out the *u* in "Peanu-u-u-ts." Cecilia was fascinated by the grace with which the mulatto woman rolled her eyes, offering the peanuts, then withdrawing them with a feline gesture, as if she'd changed her mind and decided to keep the bounty for herself.

"In the old days people moved differently."

Cecilia was startled. The comment came from a dark corner to her right, but she didn't need to see in order to guess who had made it.

"And they talked differently too," the girl responded, groping her way toward the voice.

"I didn't think you'd come back."

"And miss the rest of your story?" Cecilia replied, feeling her way into a seat. "It's obvious you don't know me."

A smile gleamed in Amalia's eyes, although the girl couldn't see it.

"You have time to tell me some more, yes?" she pressed, impatiently.

"All the time in the world."

And she took a sip of her drink before beginning to speak.

BURNING FOR YOU

"This girl's got the Evil Eye."

In the middle of the room, the Priestess watched the three drops of oil spread and disappear in the bowl of water: an undeniable sign of the curse.

"Jesus!" muttered Doña Clara, crossing herself. "What do we do now?"

"Calm down, woman," the Priestess murmured, giving her helper a sign. "You've brought your daughter to me; that's what's important."

Angela suffered through the ritual of her diagnosis indifferently, too immersed in the incendiary heat bubbling through all of her body's inner crevices. There was a chill that bathed her in sweat, an inferno that destroyed her with breaths of hot air, a chaotic vortex that pinned her wherever she lay, unable to move or speak. Unmoved by the diagnosis, she clutched the bowl of water just as the woman had instructed her to do. Above her head, a flickering oil lamp spewed shadows everywhere, perhaps attracting more spirits than the old woman had intended to summon.

The assistant, who had left the room moments before, now returned with a kettle that emitted an almost appetizing vapor: rue and coriander boiled in wine.

Two have cursed you,
Three will cure you,
The Virgin Mary and the Holy Trinity . . .

The Priestess made the sign of the cross over Angela, following the prayer's commands.

If your head should ache you,
Saint Helen won't forsake you.
If your brow is sweaty,
Saint Vincent's at the ready.
If your eyes should ail you,
Saint Ambrose will not fail you.
Saint Apollonia can, forsooth,
heal a sore or abscessed tooth.
Blessed Saint Urbain is the man
to cure your rough and callused hands.
If your trunk with toil is bent,
pray to the Blessed Sacrament.
And if you suffer on your feet,
invoke Saint Andrew, then repeat.

Upon offering the prayer, she snatched the bowl from Angela's hands, hurling it into the corner. The water left a trail of darkness on the wood.

"That's all, child. Now go with God."

Angela stood up with her mother's help.

"No! Not through there!" The Priestess blocked her way. "You mustn't step in that water or the curse will return."

It was already pitch-black outside when they left the house. Don Pedro had been waiting for them at the rock that stood some thirty paces away, at the edge of the village that rose beside the frozen mountain range of Cuenca.

"What happened?" he whispered anxiously.

Doña Clara made a slight gesture. Many years of life beside the same woman allowed him to understand: "Everything is resolved, but let's talk about it later." For months neither he nor Clara had been able to sleep in peace. Their daughter, a girl who until recently had run happily through the fields, chasing after all sorts of beasts and birds, had turned into another person entirely.

First came the visions. Although Don Pedro had been forewarned, he still couldn't conceal his surprise. His own wife had alerted him the very afternoon he proposed to her: all the women in her family, since time imme-morial, had been shadowed by a certain impish creature named Martinico.

"I started seeing him when I was a girl," Clara told him. "And so did my mother and all the women in my family."

"And if we don't have any girls?" he asked skeptically.

"The wife of the firstborn son inherits it. That's what happened to my great-grandmother, who was born in Puertollano and married my great-great-grandmother's only son. She wanted to move to Priego, so she wouldn't owe her family any explanations."

The man didn't know whether to laugh at her or get angry with her, but his fiancée's face reflected the gravity of the matter.

"It doesn't matter," he said at last, when he finally became convinced that she was serious. "Martinico or no Martinico, you and I are getting married."

Although his wife would complain about the invisible presence, he always thought it was a product of her imagination. He suspected that the story, so deeply rooted in her family, made her see something that didn't really exist. And in order to avoid what she called "the contagion," he made her swear that she'd never speak to the child of her visionary inheri-tance, much less tell her tales of imps or any other supernatural creatures. That's why he nearly died of fright the day that Angelita, barely twelve years old, stared fixedly at the shelf where he used to put his vases to dry and whispered with an air of surprise, "What's that dwarf doing there?"

"What dwarf?" her father replied, casting a quick glance at the shelf.

"There's a little man dressed like a priest, sitting on that pile of dishes," the girl responded, lowering her voice even more. Noticing her father's expression, she added, "Don't you see him?"

Pedro felt all the hair on his body stand on end. This was the confirma-tion that, despite his precautions, his daughter's blood was contaminated with the family's supernatural curse. Frightened, he grabbed her by the arm and dragged her out of the shop.

"She's seen him," he whispered into his wife's ear.

But Clara received the news joyfully.

"The girl's a young lady now," she said.

It wasn't easy living with two women who saw and heard what he could not, no matter how he tried. Most of all, it was difficult for him to accept the change in his daughter. His wife was already suffering from that mania when they met. Angela, on the other hand, had been a normal little girl who preferred chasing birds or climbing trees. She had never paid any attention to the stories of apparitions or enchanted nymphs that sometimes made their way through the town. And now this.

Clara had a long conversation with Angela to explain who the visitor was and why they were the only two who saw him. It wasn't necessary to ask her to keep the secret. Her daughter had always been a prudent child.

Only Pedro seemed defeated. Several times his daughter caught him watching her with a dismayed expression. Instinctively she understood what was happening and tried to be more affectionate with him to prove how little she had changed. In time, the man's anxiety began to fade. He had almost grown accustomed to the idea of Martinico the imp just when everything else started happening.

One fine day, when Angela was about to turn sixteen, she awoke pale and weeping. She refused to speak or eat. She remained as still as a statue, indifferent to the world, feeling like her heart was about to burst like ripe fruit falling from a tree.

Her parents catered to her at first, offering sweets, but they ended up shouting and locking her in her room. They weren't angry, only frightened, and they didn't know how to make her respond.

When they had exhausted all their resources, Clara decided to take her to the Priestess, a wise woman who was imbued with a certain power because her brother was a bishop in Toledo. He cured souls with the word of God, while she cured bodies with a little help from the saints.

The Priestess's diagnosis confirmed what Clara already suspected: her daughter was the victim of the Evil Eye. But the Priestess had remedies for any eventuality, and after the exorcism the mother felt calmer, confident that the prayers would work. Pedro would have liked to feel her same confidence. When they returned, he kept furtive watch over his daughter, waiting for some sign of improvement. The girl walked with her head bowed, looking at the ground as if she had never trodden the damp, cold paths of the mountains, which, during that tranquil year of 1886, appeared more desolate than usual.

"We'll have to wait and see," he said to himself.

. . .

The wind smelled of blood, and the raindrops stuck to her skin like thorny fingers. Every sunbeam was a dart piercing her pupils. Each glint of moonlight was a tongue licking her shoulders. Three months after the exorcism, Angela still suffered from these and other symptoms.

"She doesn't have the Evil Eye," the Priestess proclaimed when Clara called on her again. "Your daughter has the Mother's Curse."

"What's that?" Doña Clara asked from deep within her terror.

"The uterus, the place of origin, has become detached and is now traveling through her entire body. This causes pain in women's souls. At least she bears it quietly. Other women howl like banshees in heat."

"What should we do?"

"It's a serious case. The only thing I can recommend is prayer. . . . Come here, Angela."

The three women knelt around a candle:

"In the name of the Trinity,
and of the daily mass,
and the Gospel of Saint John,
Mater Dolorosa,
go back to where you came from. "

But the prayer was useless. Dawn came, and Angela wept in every corner. The sun rose to its height, and Angela stared at her food without touching it. The sun set, and Angela remained by her front door while Martinico played his tricks. . . . And the most terrible thing of all: the Mother's Curse had struck Angela dumb, but the imp's behavior was growing more and more troublesome.

Every afternoon, when the girl sat down to watch the growing shadows, stones flew over the heads of the passersby who led their cattle to graze or drink, or else they attacked merchants as they returned from selling their wares. The villagers complained to Pedro, who had no choice but to reveal the family secret.

"Imp or spirit, all we ask is that he doesn't knock our blocks off" was their general plea when they learned the news.

"I'll talk to Angela," the father said with a lump in his throat, knowing beforehand that the imp's behavior depended on his daughter's frame of mind but, at the same time, realizing that his antics were completely his own.

"Angela, you have to convince him. That goblin can't keep on bothering people or they'll throw us out of here."

"You tell him, Father," she replied. "Maybe he'll listen to you."

"Don't you think I've asked him before? But he doesn't seem to hear me. I suspect he's never around when I talk to him."

"Today he is."

"Is he nearby?"

"Right there."

Pedro nearly knocked over a pot of jam.

"I can't see him."

"If you speak to him, he'll hear you."

"Sir Martinico . . ."

He began this most respectful dialogue just as he had done on other occasions, always followed by an explanation of the problems his behavior could cause for Angelita herself. He wasn't begging him on his own behalf, for he was a poor, unworthy potter, but rather for the sake of his wife and little girl, thanks to whom Martinico was able to live among human beings.

It was obvious that Martinico was listening. During the conversation, everything around was completely still. Two neighbors passed by and heard the peroration, during which the man seemed to be addressing the air, but since they were already eminently aware of Martinico's existence, they guessed what was occurring and hurried along their way before they were clobbered by one of the goblin's projectiles.

Pedro finished his speech and, satisfied with his performance, turned around to resume the task at hand. Immediately the stones began raining down once more from all directions until one of them hit him in the head. Angela ran to his aid and received a wallop right in the buttocks. Both of them had to hide in the workshop, but the stones kept pounding the hut, threatening to knock it down. For the first time in many months, Angela seemed to emerge from her stupor.

"You're a horrible little creature!" she shouted as she cleaned her father's bloodied face. "I hate you. I never want to see you again!"

All grew quiet, as if by magic. The squawking of a few birds, frightened by the noisy storm of rocks, could still be heard. Angela was so furious, she paid no attention to her father's pleas for her not to leave the refuge.

"If you strike my father again, or my mother, or me, I swear I'll throw you off a cliff!" she shouted at the top of her lungs.

Even the wind seemed to stop blowing. Pedro felt a wave of fear penetrate him to his core, and he suspected that the imp shared his terror.

The family went to bed early after applying poultices to Pedro's head. Pedro swore he'd never speak to Martinico again, leaving the stonings for the others. Besides, he didn't know if his daughter's words would have a permanent effect, and he didn't want to suffer the imp's wrath again. In any case, he needed to rest. He had been working for two days on an order of vases that he planned to decorate the next morning.

In the middle of the night, a frightful din awakened them, as if a chunk of the moon had come crashing to earth. Pedro lit a candle and left the house, shivering, followed by his wife and daughter. The countryside was like a blind cavern.

In the pottery workshop, pandemonium reigned: vases flew in all directions, shattering into a thousand pieces as they hit the walls; tables trembled on their legs; the pottery wheel spun around, an unstoppable windmill. . . . Pedro helplessly watched the disaster, blinded by despair. With Martinico around, his life as a potter was destined for ruin.

"Woman, start gathering our things," he muttered. "We're going to Torrelila."

"What?"

"We're going to Uncle Paco's. The pottery business is finished."

Clara burst into tears.

"With all the work you've put into it . . ."

"Tomorrow I'll sell whatever I can. We'll go to Uncle's place with the money, since he's asked me so many times." And, trusting that the imp wouldn't hear him over the destructive din, he added, "From now on, that Martinico will live on saffron."

DUST AND FOAM

The sea snaked up to the shore, spilling its load of algae and kissing the feet of those who dozed nearby. Then it curled back on itself like a furtive feline, only to resume its ceaseless rhythms.

"No, I've never gone back," Gaia said. "And I don't think I ever will."

"Why not?"

"Too many memories."

"We all have them."

"Not as awful as mine."

The sun was setting over South Beach, and droves of young, golden bodies began shedding their casual clothes for something more appropriate to the sophisticated Miami night. The girls had been sitting by the sea for hours, with time to chat about their shared experiences on the island, although not about the particulars of their individual affairs. Cecilia had made an attempt, but the other woman stubbornly maintained a strange silence.

"It's because of that house, isn't it?" Cecilia ventured to ask.

"What?"

"You don't want to return to Cuba because of that house you told me about."

Gaia nodded. "I have a theory," she murmured after a moment. "I think those sorts of houses, which change appearance or location, represent the souls of certain places."

"But what if two or more of them were wandering around the same area?" Cecilia asked. "Would they all be souls of the same city?"

"A place can have more than one soul. Or, rather, different aspects of a single soul. Places are like people. They have many faces."

"Truth is, I've never heard of phantom houses that change the way you describe."

"Neither have I, but I assure you that in Havana there's a mansion that transforms itself every time you go inside. And now, in Miami, there's another one that wanders the city."

Cecilia dug her fingers in the sand and found a snail.

"What was the Havana house like?" she asked.

"A place of illusion, a monster created only to confuse. There, nothing is what it seems, and what seems to be never is. I don't believe the human spirit is equipped to live in such uncertainty."

"But we can never be sure of anything."

"In life there are always accidents and events unforeseen; that's a dose of insecurity we can accept. But if something happens to loosen the foundations of our everyday lives, our mistrust takes on distorted proportions. That's when it becomes dangerous to one's sanity. We can withstand our individual fears if we know that the rest of society still operates within normal boundaries, because deep down we hope that those fears are only a small, individual aberration that won't appear on the outside. But as soon as fear affects their greater environment, people lose their natural system of support; they lose the possibility of going to others for help or comfort. . . . That was what the phantom house in Havana was like: a dark, bottomless well."

Cecilia watched her out of the corner of her eye.

"Do you think the Miami house is like that other one?"

"Of course not," Gaia replied brightly.

"Then why don't you want to talk about it?"

"I've already told you: those apparitions contain bits of a city's soul. There are dark ones and bright ones. I don't want to find out what kind this one is. Just in case."

"It's a shame you've never told me about the second time you saw the house," Cecilia ventured, not hoping for too much.

"It was at the beach."

Cecilia reacted, startled.

"Here?"

"No, at the little beach in Hammock Park, near Old Cutler Road. You've never been there?"

"Truth is, I don't go out much," Cecilia admitted, somewhat ashamed. "There's not much to see in Miami."

Now it was Gaia who gave Cecilia a curious glance, but she didn't pursue it further.

"And what happened?" Cecilia pressed on.

"Late one afternoon I went to the restaurant across from that beach. I like to eat and look out at the sea. When I finished, I decided to take a little walk through the park, and I amused myself watching a possum and her baby. They had climbed down a coconut tree and were about to enter the little grove when the mother stopped, lifted her tail, and fled into the weeds with her child. At first I didn't know what had frightened them. The only thing around was a house that appeared empty. It was partially hidden by weeds, which is why I didn't notice it until I was close by. Then the door swung open and I saw a woman dressed in clothes from another era."

"A long dress?" Cecilia interrupted, reminded of the phantom maidens she had seen in books.

"No, nothing like that. It was a lady in a flowered dress, like an outfit from the forties or fifties. The woman smiled at me very sweetly. Behind her, an old man came out but didn't pay me the slightest attention. He was carrying an empty cage, which he hung from a hook. I moved in closer, and then I discovered there was a second story, with a balcony all around. That's when I recognized the house: it was the same one I had seen next to mine that night."

"And did the woman speak to you?"

"I think she was about to tell me something, but I didn't give her time. I took off running."

"May I include it in my article?"

"No."

"But this is new. It doesn't appear in the earlier story."

"Because it happened later."

"I have only one interview," Cecilia complained, "and yet, I can't include any part of what you're saying."

Gaia bit her nail.

"Go ask at the restaurant by the little beach. One of the workers there may have seen something."

Cecilia shook her head.

"I don't think I can find a better witness."

"Do you know where Atlantis is?"

"The bookstore in Coral Gables?"

"It belongs to a friend of mine who can give you information. Her name's Lisa."

"Did she see the house too?"

"No, but she knows people who have seen it."

Darkness fell upon the sand, and Gaia had long since gone, but Cecilia lingered, listening to the music coming from the open-air cafés behind her. For some reason the tale of the second sighting had saddened her. Why hadn't Gaia come to the beach with a friend? Was she as lonely as Cecilia herself?

Her gaze slipped to the increasingly turbulent sea as night descended. She thought about how different her life would have been if her parents had given her a brother. Long before she ever thought of leaving Cuba, both of them had died, a few months apart, leaving her alone in a big house in El Vedado, until she finally decided to escape during the days when thousands of people took to the streets, shouting, "Freedom, freedom!" an insane mob. . . .

Overcome with solitude, she picked up her towel and stuck it in her bag. She'd take a shower before going to the bar. Around her people were leaving for parties, getting together with friends, making plans with their partners, but she seemed to have only one routine . . . if you could even claim a couple of conversations with the same old woman as a routine. But she had nothing else to do. She needed only half an hour to get to her apartment, and another to eat and get dressed.

When she arrived at the bar, it was already full of partiers and smoke: a fog as asphyxiating as it was toxic. She could barely breathe in that atmosphere, which was like the waiting room of a cancer ward. She sneezed a few times before her lungs gradually grew accustomed to the high concentration of poison in the air.

"Man can adapt to any kind of shit," she thought. "That's why he can survive all the catastrophes he causes."

People were crowded together on the dance floor, lulled by the singer's voice. At the bar, a couple gazed lovingly at each other in the tomblike blackness. There was no one else at the tables.

Cecilia sat down at the other end, but there wasn't even a waiter around to serve her. Maybe she'd escape to the dance floor, too, and sway to the ancient bolero: "I suffer the unbearable pain of your leaving, and I cry bitterly at your departure, but you'll never know that I weep black tears, tears as black as my life. . . ." Suddenly the bolero abandoned its plaint and became a merry rumba: "You want to leave me; I don't want to suffer; I'll go with you, my angel, even if I die trying. . . ." The couples broke their embraces, deliciously shaking hips and shoulders, oblivious to the funereal message of the song. "These are my people," Cecilia thought, "filled with life and joy even in tragedy."

"That was always one of my favorite songs," said a voice behind her.

Cecilia startled, turning toward the woman who seemed to have crept in.

"And it was my mother's favorite too," she added. "Every time I hear it, I remember her."

Cecilia noticed her face. The darkness must have deceived her before. The woman couldn't have been more than fifty.

"You never told me what happened to Kui-fa when her husband left for Cuba, or what became of the half-crazy girl."

"Which girl?"

"That one who had visions . . . the one who thought she saw an imp."

"Angela wasn't crazy," the woman assured her. "Having visions doesn't necessarily mean someone is out of their mind. You should know that better than anyone."

"Why?"

"Do you think your grandmother was crazy?"

"Who told you she had visions?"

"You did."

Cecilia was sure she had never mentioned her grandmother's abilities. Or had she said something that first night? She *had* been a little woozy. . . .

"I just wanted to know how your story turned out," Cecilia said, glossing over the incident, "but I still can't see what connection there is between a Cantonese family and a Spanish girl who talks to goblins."

"That's because the third part of the story is still missing," the woman replied.

BLACK TEARS

The road leading to the country house was surrounded by all sorts of fruit trees. Orange and lemon trees perfumed the air. Ripe guavas burst as they fell, tired of waiting for someone to pick them from the branches. In farther rows, the cornstalks pierced the afternoon with their pointed sheaths.

Although she still hadn't stopped crying, Caridad observed the landscape with a mixture of curiosity and wonder. She and several other slaves had covered the distance that separated Jagüey Grande from this spot. The girl didn't cry for her old master, but rather because the remains of her mother had been left behind at the sugar plantation.

Dayo—as she was known among her people—was kidnapped by white men long ago while she was still living on the distant jungle coast of her beloved Ifé, a place the whites called Africa. And so Caridad never knew who her father was; even her own mother didn't know. Her mother had serviced three of the men during the crossing to Cuba. Then she was sold to a plantation owner on the island, where she gave birth to a strange creature with milky skin.

Shortly before the delivery, Dayo was baptized with the name Damiana. Years later she explained to her daughter that her real name meant "joy arrives," because that is what she had meant to her parents: great happiness after many petitions to Oshún Fumiké, who grants children to sterile women. Damiana had wanted to give her own daughter an African name as well, to remind her of her roots, but her masters wouldn't allow it.

Nevertheless, the child's beauty was so great that she decided secretly to call her Kamaria, which means "like the moon," because of the way her baby looked: radiant. But she used that name only when they were alone together. For her masters, the child was known as Caridad.

Mother and daughter were lucky: they were never sent to the plantation. Since Damiana had plenty of milk, she was a perfect nurse to the master's newborn daughter. And when Caridad grew a little older, she began to serve in the private quarters of the mistress, a smiling woman who gave her coins for no reason at all. And so mother and daughter began to make plans to buy their freedom. Unfortunately, destiny changed their course.

An epidemic laid waste to the area during the summer of 1876, killing dozens of the region's inhabitants, blacks and whites alike. Herbal concoctions, fumigations with medicinal incense, and the secret ceremonies performed by the blacks all proved useless: masters and slaves succumbed to the fever. Caridad lost her mother, and the master lost his wife. Unable to bear the sight of the little slave girl who reminded him of his deceased wife, the man decided to give her to a cousin who lived on an estate in the newly developed Havana neighborhood of El Cerro.

The little girl prepared herself for the worst. She had never served outside the house before, and she wasn't sure she would have the same privileges now. She imagined herself working from dawn to dusk, filthy and sunburned, with no energy left at night for anything but singing or getting drunk.

Caridad didn't know that she was going to a vacation country home, a place dedicated to rest and contemplation. She cautiously observed the haciendas by the roads along which her covered wagon passed: dream mansions surrounded by gardens and sheltered by fruit trees. For a moment she forgot her fears and listened in on the conversation between two overseers driving the wagon.

"That's where Doña Luisa Herrera lived before she married the Count of Jibacoa," one of them said. "And over there is the Count of Fernandina's house," he indicated, pointing to another mansion, graced with a side garden and an imposing front door, "famous for the statues of two lions in the entryway."

"What happened to them?"

"The Marquis of Pinar del Río copied them in order to put them on one side of his house, and so the count went into a snit and ordered the originals removed. Look, there are the Marquis's lions. . . ."

Even if her life had depended on it, Caridad would never have been able to describe the majesty of the portico flanked by those two stone animals—one of them asleep, its head resting on its paws, and the other still drowsy—nor would she have known precisely how to describe the elaborate stained-glass windows with their bloody reds, deep blues, and mythical greens, or the lacy grillwork protecting the windows, or the splendid Roman columns bordering the front door. She lacked the words to do so, but her breath caught before such beauty.

"That's the Count of Santovenia's estate," the man said, moving slightly to one side so that his companion could see more clearly.

Caridad nearly let out a gasp. The mansion was a dream, sculpted in marble and crystal, where the light and the colors of the tropics were multiplied. It had marvelous gardens that blended into the horizon, with their jets of water shushing in the fountains and the whitest of statues gleaming like pearls beneath the sun. She had never seen anything so lovely, not even in dreams where she wandered alongside stone walls and mysterious labyrinths, lost in the jungle homeland of her mother, who had told her of her own meanderings among the ruins when she was a girl.

They soon lost sight of the mansion and headed for another one with a more austere façade. Like many other wealthy families, the Melgares-Herreras had constructed a manor house in the hope of escaping city life, which was becoming more frenetic and promiscuous. The city was teeming with commerce: vendors hawking their wares at all hours, with guesthouses for travelers or merchants from the provinces; a place rife with corruption, where crimes of passion darkened the headlines.

José Melgares's country estate was famous for its parties, like the one celebrated years before in honor of the wedding of Missy Teresa, fruit of his union with María Teresa Herrera, daughter of the second Marquis of Almendares. None other than Alexei, grand duke of Russia himself, had been among the guests.

Now the covered wagon was entering the hacienda with its cargo of slaves, some of them frightened, others resigned to their fates. The group immediately was brought before Doña Marité, as the lady was known to her associates. The woman emerged at the doorway while the slaves maintained a certain distance. After observing them for a few seconds, she advanced toward them. With each step her dress rustled with a distracting swish that did nothing to calm the captives' nerves.

"What's your name?" she asked the only adolescent girl in the group.

"Kamaria."

"What kind of name is that?"

"It's the one my mother gave me."

Doña Marité studied the girl, intuiting the pain behind that defiant reply.

"Where is she?"

"Dead."

The tremor in her voice did not go unnoticed by Doña Marité.

"What did they call you at the other hacienda?"

"Caridad."

"Well, Caridad, I think I'll keep you for myself." And, waving her lace fan, she pointed it at two boys who hadn't let go of each other's hands throughout the entire trip. "Tomás," she addressed one of the men who had driven them there, "don't we need more gardeners and someone else in the kitchen?"

"I think so, ma'am."

"All right, take care of that. You three," she said to the young woman and the boys, "come along."

She turned around and started walking. The girl took the little ones by the hand and led them behind the woman.

The house had been built around a central patio surrounded by walkways. But unlike similar manor houses, these walkways were enclosed corridors, not passages opening onto the patio. Nevertheless, the geometric designs of the wide French blinds and picture windows allowed light and air to penetrate, illuminating and freshening the rooms.

"Josefa," the mistress said to a black woman, "make sure they bathe and eat something."

The old slave woman made them bathe and dress in clean clothing before leading them into the kitchen. Born on the island, none of the younger servants understood their native tongue very well. Therefore, the old woman felt obliged to admonish them in her broken patois: "When bell ring, is time for slave eatin'. . . . Master don't like his boots be even li'l bit dirty, so mornin' come, you shine good." She looked at the boys. "That your job."

Caridad understood that she was to be a sort of lady's maid. She had to iron, do her mistress's hair, polish her shoes, perfume her, bring her cold drinks, or fan her. Josefa would take charge of training her in all the chores because, although the young woman already had some experience, the sophisticated life beyond Havana's walls demanded more refined skills.

Occasionally the girl would accompany Doña Marité on her trips to other estates. There was one especially beautiful hacienda they visited from time to time. It belonged to Don Carlos de Zaldo and Doña Caridad Lamar, who had inherited the property after its previous owner died.

The first time the girl arrived at the villa with her mistress, three slaves were busily watering and pruning a garden crowded with rosebushes and jasmine. One of them, a mulatto with skin like her own, took off his hat as she passed by, but Caridad keenly felt he hadn't done so out of respect for the white mistress. She could have sworn the servant's eyes were fixed on her. That was the first time she saw Florencio, but it wasn't until three months later that he dared speak to her.

One afternoon, taking advantage of Caridad's moment alone in the kitchen as she prepared a beverage for the ladies, Florencio approached her. And so she learned that he, like her, was the son of a white man and a black slave.

His mother had managed to buy her freedom after her previous owner sold her to Don Carlos, but the woman preferred to stay on in the new mansion with her son. Caridad thought it a strange situation, but Florencio assured her that there were similar cases. Sometimes house slaves were better fed and dressed under the tutelage of a gentleman than working on their own, and for that reason some blacks thought of freedom as a responsibility they weren't ready to face. They preferred a master who gave them a little food to a life of aimless wandering and indecision. Florencio had received a careful education: he could read and write, and he expressed himself with an extremely educated accent, a consequence of his master's desire to have a well-trained slave who could carry out fairly complex tasks. But unlike his mother, who had died two years earlier, Florencio wanted to earn his freedom and start a business. He was no longer tied to the estate. Besides, for him and the majority of his brothers, a risky freedom was better than degrading enslavement. And with his goal in mind, he had been saving up for a while. . . . Another slave walked into the kitchen and cut short the conversation. Caridad wasn't able to tell him that she too was saving up for the same reason.

Sometimes Doña Marité would go to Doña Caridad's house; other times, the Zaldo-Lamars visited their neighbors. As coachman, Florencio accompanied the lady and gentleman of the house on these expeditions, which gave him the opportunity to exchange a few words with the girl when she came outside to serve drinks.

Months passed with the lovers unaware. Then two, three, four years, and the love affair between the mulatto woman and the elegant slave was secret only from their masters.

"When are you going to talk to Doña Marité?" Florencio asked as soon as they determined that both of them had saved enough to buy their freedom.

"Next week," she said. "Give me time to prepare her."

"Time?"

"She's been very good to me. At the very least, I owe her . . ."

"You don't owe her anything," he protested. "It seems like you don't want to have a life with me. . . ."

She went over to him tenderly.

"It's not that, Flor. Of course I want to be with you."

"What's the problem, then?"

Caridad shook her head. She didn't want to admit it, but she suddenly felt the same fear that had seemed so ridiculous to her before. She'd grown accustomed to having a roof over her head and a well-stocked kitchen. She was terrified at the idea of landing on the street with only the sky overhead for protection, exposed to all of life's cruelties. This thought anchored itself within her, as the spirit remains buried when it has long lived in the shadow of its master. She was left without the courage to fend for herself, terrified at the prospect of a world she didn't know, a world that would never ask her if she was ready to live in it, a world whose laws no one had ever taught her. . . . She thought of those fledglings she had seen so many times balancing timorously on the branches, clamoring for their parents on some nearby branch, and she realized she would have to do what they did: attempt to fly by hurling herself into the abyss. Surely she would crash to the ground.

"All right," she said firmly. "I'll do it tomorrow."

But she let days and weeks go by without resolving to speak to Doña Marité. Florencio languished as he pruned the rosebushes, more from the desire to be with his beloved than from his stalled plan for freedom.

One afternoon he overheard a conversation that alarmed him. Don Carlos had summoned Florencio to the front door where the master and mistress were drinking *champola*, enjoying the afternoon breeze.

"It's the end!" Don Carlos was saying as he waved a newspaper before his wife's pale face. "We won't be able to keep this estate. Do you realize we have twenty slaves just taking care of the house and the garden alone?"

"What will we do?"

"We have no choice but to sell."

Florencio felt the blood drain from his face. Sell! Sell what? The house? The stock of slaves? They'd separate him from Caridad. He'd never see her again. . . . Don Carlos noticed the mulatto waiting at the head of the gate.

"Florencio, get the carriage ready. We're going to Don José's."

The young man obeyed, a whirlwind of ideas frustrating his hands as they struggled to harness the horses. Then he went back to the house and put on his boots, cassock, and gloves. He nearly forgot his top hat. Don Carlos bolted from the house like a tornado, newspaper in hand, followed by his beleaguered wife. They whispered to each other during the entire brief journey to the other villa, but Florencio didn't pay attention to their murmurings. In his head there was just enough room for only one decision.

The couple exited the carriage without giving him time to do anything. Still seated inside the coach, he could hear their agitated voices, the exclamations of Don José and his master. He waited a few seconds before entering. As he was crossing the patio, Caridad blocked his way.

"What are you going to do?"

"What we decided a while ago."

"It's not a good time," she whispered. "I don't know what's happening, but it doesn't look good. . . . I'm scared."

Florencio kept on walking, ignoring her pleas. His appearance in the parlor was so striking that both men halted their discussion and turned to him. Doña Marité fanned herself nervously in her seat, her face whiter than the lace on her fan.

"What's going on?" Don Carlos asked, with a sour expression.

"Master . . . excuse me, sir, but I need to say something, now that you're all together here . . ."

"Can't it wait?"

"Let him speak," his wife implored.

"All right," huffed Don Carlos, burying his face once more in the newspaper as if he had already dismissed the matter.

Florencio thought his heart would leave his chest.

"Cachita and I . . ." He stopped as he realized he had never before used that nickname in front of anyone. "Caridad and I want to get married. We have the money to buy our freedom."

Don Carlos raised his eyes from the newspaper.

"It's too late, my boy."

"Too late?" Florencio felt his knees tremble. "What do you mean, sir? Too late for what?"

"Too late to buy anyone's freedom."

Behind him, Florencio heard the rustle of starched petticoats. Caridad collapsed against the wall, paler than her mistress. He rushed to her side, while Doña Marité shouted for the other slaves to hurry with the smelling salts.

"Why is it too late, sir?" Florencio asked, his eyes threatening tears. "Why can't we buy our freedom?"

"Because from today on, you are all free," the man replied, throwing the newspaper into a corner. "Slavery has just been abolished."

Caridad and Florencio moved to the part of the capital that twenty years before had been within the city walls. The Creole nobility still occupied huge manor houses near the cathedral and its surrounding plaza, but business of all sorts were opening. They belonged to enterprising working-class folks without much of anything, many of them former slaves who, like the young couple, had saved a bit of money.

Florencio had searched throughout the Montserrat area, predicting the exodus to new neighborhoods beyond the city walls. He bought a two-story property near the plaza. The couple set up house on the upper floor, and converted the ground floor into a tavern, the Flower of Montserrat, where they would also sell goods from across the sea.

Nothing seemed to mar their newfound peace, but time passed and Caridad was increasingly distressed by her lack of a child. Year after year she tried all the recommended methods for getting pregnant, without result. But she didn't give up. In any case, those were good years but difficult, prosperous but painful. Nothing seemed certain. Caridad's patience overflowed as she awaited her long-desired maternity, and Florencio had to expend both charm and energy in the business. More and more often he would sit and drink with his countrymen.

"Flor, could you come here for a moment?" Caridad called, pretending to look for something behind the counter, and when he came over, she warned him: "You're on your third drink already."

Sometimes Florencio heeded her call, but other times he made excuses.

"Don Herminio is an important customer," he would tell her. "Let me finish this drink and I'll be right back."

But the important clients kept growing in number, as did the quantity of drinks that Florencio took each day. Caridad watched, and sometimes she let him . . . until one day when her belly finally began to swell. She could no longer watch over her husband so closely, occupied as she was with embroidering diapers and mantillas for their unborn child. When she went downstairs to the main room, she could never tell how many drinks the man had had.

"Flor," she called out, massaging her belly.

He rose from the table, already annoyed.

"Can't you just calm down?" he yelled at her through the curtain that separated the storeroom from the tavern filled with customers.

"I just wanted to tell you that you've already had—"

"I know!" he shouted. "Just let me take care of the customers properly."

And he left with a broad smile to serve himself the next shot. Caridad returned to her room with a heavy expression, unable to understand why her husband's good nature had grown sour just when business was going so well. Their clientele became more and more distinguished, because Florencio knew how to attend to his countrymen's requests, even when they asked for things he didn't have: black stockings from Berlin, Helmerich soap for rashes and ringworm, Viennese raw piqué, tolu syrup, harnesses for horse buggies, dental elixirs, Vichy water. . . . But the anxiety these tasks produced in him was beyond his wife's comprehension.

"As luck would have it, I'm about to receive a shipment," he would lie, flashing his best smile. "Where would your grace like for me to contact him?"

He'd jot down the address and, leaving the shop in his wife's hands, he'd scour all the businesses in the city in search of something similar. Once he had found the merchandise, he would buy a few samples in order to negotiate a discount, and the next day he'd notify his customer. From that day on, he would display the new product, and if it sold well, he would order more.

His establishment's fame spread beyond the neighborhood and expanded in both directions, even reaching the plaza around the Cathedral—the eastern core of the central city—and beyond the partially destroyed walls, in pursuit of the estates to the west. From time to time some count or marquis would show up, wishing to present his sweetheart with a few yards of Oriental fabric or a Manila shawl.

Florencio's ill humor grew along with the business. Caridad wondered if her man's spirit had been adequately prepared for so much activity and wistfully recalled their life at the country house, when she was the only thing that mattered to him. He hardly cast his gaze in her direction anymore. Every night he climbed the stairs, heavily dragging his feet and collapsing on the bed, almost always drunk. She stroked her belly, and her tears flowed silently.

One morning while returning from the market, she decided to enter the house through the tavern instead of using the side staircase. Florencio was sitting at a table, egged on by the din of several men who cheered as he downed glass after glass of whiskey. With each new glass, more coins piled up in front of him.

"Well! I can see that people around here really know how to have a good time!" remarked a pleasant voice behind her. "That's something no one ever told me before!"

Caridad turned around. A mulatto woman, so fair-skinned she could have passed for white, observed the scene from the street. She had apparently just stepped down from a small carriage whose driver awaited her. Caridad only had time to glance quickly at the stranger. Although age had left traces on her face, the curves of her scarlet dress revealed a surprisingly lithe young body.

"Did you come to have fun too?" asked the stranger.

"He's my husband," Caridad replied with a lump in her throat, pointing to Florencio.

"Ah! You've come looking for the turtledove who left the nest. . . ."

"No. This is my house. This is our tavern."

The mulatto woman regarded Caridad and, for the first time, noticed her condition.

"How much longer?" she asked, gesturing vaguely toward her belly.

"Not much."

"Well, since you're the owner and your husband is so busy, I imagine you can help me. . . . I need carbolic soap. Someone told me you carried it here."

"I don't know. My husband's the one in charge of the merchandise, but I can take a look."

Caridad crossed the room and disappeared into the grocery at the rear. After a few moments she poked her head out from behind the burlap curtain and asked the stranger: "How many do you need?"

"Five dozen."

"So many?" she replied ingenuously. "They aren't for daily use—just for epidemics."

"I know."

Caridad stared at her as if trying to remember something, but finally she slipped back behind the curtain. From the sidewalk, the woman motioned to the driver to bring the carriage closer while she fanned herself vigorously. Caridad emerged from the interior, struggling to drag a box, but she didn't get too far. She felt a stitch in her lower belly that made her jump as if she'd been whipped. She looked out toward the street, but the woman appeared distracted, watching something that was happening on the corner. She turned to her husband, who remained oblivious to her existence. With difficulty she made her way through the crowd.

"Flor, you need to help me."

Hardly looking at her, the man grabbed another glass from the table.

"Flor . . ."

There were six empty glasses before him. One more now. Seven.

"Flor . . ." She touched his arm just as he was about to lift the eighth one to his lips.

With an impressive shove, he knocked her to the floor. She screamed out in pain while the men's commotion subsided as they realized what had happened. The stranger went to her aid.

"Are you all right?"

Caridad shook her head. Fat tears slipped down her cheeks. She stood up, assisted by the woman and one of the men.

"Leave it." The stranger blocked her way when she saw Caridad trying to drag the box once more. "I'll get the driver to do it. How much is everything?"

The woman paid the amount she was told and left, although not without casting an expression of pity in Caridad's direction. The shouting had died down after the altercation, and many customers had walked away, but Caridad couldn't focus on anything else. She headed for the second floor, leaning on the banister.

That night, Florencio stumbled up the stairs and entered the bedroom. A dense, heavy odor assaulted his nostrils.

"Dammit, woman, can't you open the windows?"

A strange cry filled the room. Florencio went over to the corner, where a candle gave a tenuous light. His wife was in bed, with a bundle pressed against her breast. Only then did Florencio realize that the smell was blood.

"Cachita?" he called, for the first time in ages.

"It's a girl," she whispered in a thread of a voice.

Florencio approached the bed. The candle trembled so much that Caridad took it from his hands, placing it on the night table. Slowly, the man leaned over the bed and looked at the sleeping infant, still latched onto her mother's breast. The fog that had been clouding his brain lifted. He vaguely recalled the terms of a wager, glasses being filled, jokes, the moan of a woman . . .

"You didn't call. You didn't . . ." He began to cry.

Caridad stroked his head. And she didn't stop for the entire two hours he knelt there, asking her forgiveness.

The next day he refused to drink, and the day after that, and the third day, even though several habitués brought over a contender ready to defeat the most famous "glass guzzler" in those parts. Despite his sudden teetotaling, the nickname he had earned from the neighborhood boys didn't disappear. No one believed his resolution to reform, but Florencio decided to ignore everyone. His mind was filled with more important matters.

With María de las Mercedes' arrival, he would now have more mouths to feed. He knew that the reputation of his business had declined due to his continuous binges, and he resolved to earn it back. In the months that followed, he worked harder than ever. Although he had first sought to provide his business with a good selection of merchandise, now he decided it would be the best. He hired a worker to tend store while he went to the port in search of unusual or curious goods. La Flor de Montserrat once more became a reference point for travelers and wanderers seeking directions. The place held such a reputation that soon it earned its place as a guidepost in the city.

But as the city grew, so did the number of shops and businesses. New families and new neighborhoods sprang up on the outskirts of the city walls. Florencio suspected he wouldn't be able to compete with those more prosperous establishments on the other side of the ancient barriers. After thinking hard about a strategy for reaching his most distant customers, he realized that his helper could peddle merchandise from door to door, with a big sign displaying the name and address of his store. It wasn't his idea, of course. Weeks before he had seen Torcuato, an old calèche driver with a troublemaker's reputation and the nickname Green Jug, driving his carriage with a sign that read:

MISSIU TORCUATO
FINE WINES SIDER AND VIRMUTH

He ordered his clerk to take Calzada del Monte to the far-off country estates of El Cerro with samples of cloth and other similar articles. Soon he began to receive orders that he filled himself. For the next four years, there were constant dealings through those neighborhoods that kept growing before one's very eyes. The city lost the remainder of its walls and expanded like a wondrous, living monster. Florencio could have traversed it with his eyes closed while reciting the details of its social life to any passerby.

"I'll bet you can't guess who's moved to the Cathedral Plaza," he said to his wife one day.

"Who?"

"Don José and Doña Marité."

"Are you sure?"

Her husband nodded without a pause in his eating.

"In what palace?" she insisted, recalling her days in service to the Melgares-Herreras.

"Where the Marquis of Aguas Claras used to live," he explained, swallowing.

"And the country estate?"

"It's up for sale."

"Why would they do that? It can't be for lack of money, if they moved to that place. . . ."

"They say the Count of Fernandina wants to buy their hacienda."

"And what about his own?"

"I think he doesn't want to see Don Leopoldo's mug anymore. Ever since the Marquis copied his lions, he's had him stuck in his craw like a chicken bone."

"That was years ago."

"Rich people don't forgive certain things."

"Well, now Doña Marité will be closer. Do you think she'll buy something from us?"

"I'm going to bring her a sample of the French piqué."

It was then that his only clerk decided to leave. Instead of hiring someone else, Caridad told her husband she would take care of the place, and despite Florencio's resistance she finally convinced him. Little Meche was already old enough to keep her company.

"This place always surprises me," said a voice from the doorway, one week after Caridad began working there. "I see Miz Caridad has decided to get busy."

She raised her eyes and saw a familiar face.

"Do you have any carbolic soap?" the woman asked, coming in from the street.

In spite of the time that had passed since their first and only meeting, Caridad recognized the stranger who had come to the store with such an odd request on the afternoon her daughter was born.

"I need five dozen," the woman said, without waiting for a reply. "But

I won't take them with me now. Tell Don Floro to send them to Miz Cecilia, to the usual address. . . . I'll pay when they're delivered."

The woman turned to leave, but she bumped into a sour-faced black man who was just entering.

"Florencio here?" he asked in such a stentorian voice that Meche stared at him in fright.

"No, he had to go to—"

"Well, give 'im a message, will ya? Tell 'im Torcuato wuz here, and he betta not mess with me 'cuz it won't be the first time I kill summun. . . ."

"What's my husband done to you?" Caridad managed to mumble.

"He takin' away my customers. And I ain't gonna let 'im. . . ."

"My husband doesn't take away anybody's customers. He just works—"

"He takin' away my customers," the black man repeated. "Ain't nobody get a leg up on Green Jug."

And he left just as he had arrived, leaving Caridad with her heart in her mouth.

"Be careful," she heard. "That man is dangerous."

She hadn't noticed Doña Cecilia standing by the door.

"My husband didn't do anything to that man."

"That doesn't matter to Green Jug. It's enough that he thinks so."

She turned her back, lingering for just a moment before the child, who was staring at her, wide-eyed.

"She's very cute," she remarked before leaving.

That night, when Florencio returned from his errands, Caridad had already fed their little girl and was anxiously awaiting him.

"I have a message," she started to say, but stopped short when she noticed the expression on his face. "What's wrong?"

"The Count of Fernandina is having a party. Do you know where?"

His wife shrugged her shoulders.

"In the Melgares country house."

"He finally bought the hacienda?"

"Uh-huh! Now he wants to pay his respects to those princes he always talks about."

"Eulalia of Bourbon?" inquired Caridad, who was up-to-date on the latest social events.

"And her husband, Antonio de Orléans. . . . The count wants it to be a full-fledged soiree. And who do you think is going to sell him the order of candles and beverages he needs?" He bowed. "Yours truly."

"We don't have enough candles for a house like that. And I don't think the casks are—"

"I know. Tomorrow at dawn I'll go to the port."

Caridad began dishing out his dinner.

"Torcuato came looking for you."

"Here?"

"He's furious."

"That Negro! . . . He's already sent me several of his little warnings. I didn't think he'd dare come here."

"You have to be careful."

"He's a windbag. He won't do anything."

"Well, I'm afraid of him."

"Don't think about it," he said, stuffing a piece of bread into his mouth. "Did anyone else come?"

"Yes, a lady who ordered five dozen soaps. . . ."

"Miz Ceci. She always buys the same thing."

"Why does she need so much soap? Does she own a laundry?"

"How's Mechita?" Florencio interrupted.

Caridad forgot about her line of questioning in order to relate the progress her daughter was making with the alphabet. Caridad couldn't teach her much, but it was enough to help the girl begin to spell her first words.

The party at the count's was one of the grandest events Havana had seen. The china and the decorations' elegant touch, the guests' attire, the sumptuous dishes served—all the elements that make such a memorable event—had been scrutinized to the last detail. And with good reason. Two representatives of the Spanish court were the honorees. The selfsame Princess of Bourbon would later write in her private diary: "The party given in my honor by the Count and Countess of Fernandina greatly impressed me with its elegance, taste, and majesty, all far more refined than in Madrid society." And later she would recall how she had met them when she was a girl, in her mother's house, when they were frequently invited to the palace in Castile. The Creole women's beauty had especially impressed the princess: "I had heard much praise of Cuban women's beauty, their majesty, their elegance, and most of all their sweetness; but in this case, the reality has greatly surpassed my imagination."

Amid so much luxury, the Infanta might have missed the glimmer of the hundreds of candles illuminating the most distant rooms and corridors of the mansion. But Florencio observed their effect before leaving. From the sidewalk one could see the colorful shimmer of the stained-glass windows. The main entryway, flanked by Cyclopean columns, was ablaze with radiance, as if the stone itself had begun to shine. And perhaps the princess might have also missed the ciders and red wines that intensified the flush on the rosy cheeks of the Havanese women as they drank them by the barrel.

Florencio had spent two days transporting casks and candles. Now, with just a few violet streaks of remaining sunlight, he began the return journey home. A few carriages crossed his path as he drove away, and he traveled for quite some distance before he could no longer hear the music. The coins weighed heavily in the little bag he tucked underneath his shirt. He stroked the edge of his machete and spurred on his horse.

Since he knew the way by heart, he rode along thinking about what he would do with that money. For a while now he had toyed with an idea, and he thought that at last the moment had arrived: he would sell his place and buy another one in a better part of the city.

The light of the street lamps guided him along the final stretch once inside the city walls. Back again in familiar surroundings, after traversing such inhospitable territory, he began to hum as he got out of the carriage and struggled to coax the horse into the makeshift stall beside his store. An unusual squeaking sound caught his attention. And then he noticed that the door to the grocery was open.

"Cacha?" he called. No reply.

He left the horse harnessed and cautiously approached, holding the carriage lantern.

Caridad heard the clatter, the struggle, and the sound of a shelf falling. Running down the stairs, candle in hand, she neglected to grab the machete that Florencio always left under the bed. She barely noticed the chaos in the store because almost instantly she tripped over something blocking her way in. She raised the candle and leaned over. The floor was covered in glass, but she could only see the dark puddle that was beginning to spread beneath Florencio's dying body.

Part Two

GODS WHO SPEAK A

HONEYED TONGUE

From Miguel's Notebook

There's a Chinaman behind me:

A common Cuban expression to indicate that bad luck is pursuing someone. It might originate with the belief that Chinese witchcraft is so strong that no one can counteract or destroy its "work," unlike African witchcraft.

On the island it is also said that someone "has a dead man behind him" to indicate that misfortune is pursuing a person, although "having a Chinaman behind you" is an even more sinister fate.

WHY I FEEL SO ALONE

Cecilia entered by the old road, now paved, leading to the little beach at Hammock Park. To her left, a pair of swans floated weightlessly on the green waters of a lagoon, but she didn't stop to admire them. She continued on to the admission booth, paid the entrance fee, and drove straight toward the beach. When she saw the restaurant's sign, she looked for a parking space and then headed for the door.

A sudden impulse had brought on the excursion. Instead of going to the bookstore as Gaia had recommended, she decided to investigate the site of the second apparition. She had no trouble finding the information she was looking for: Bob, the oldest worker in the place, had started out as a waiter. Now he was almost sixty and the supervisor.

Not only was the man familiar with the legend of the phantom house, but he had spoken to several employees who had also come across it. The strange thing was that the oldest neighbors in the area couldn't recall having heard of the apparitions until relatively recently.

"Something must have triggered the phenomenon," the man affirmed. "When these things turn up, it means they're searching for something."

Although he had never managed to see the house or its occupants, he was convinced of their existence. Otherwise, how could so many people agree on the same details? They all described the apparition as a two-story beach chalet, crowned by a slanted roof, similar to the earliest constructions built in Miami a century ago. But its mysterious occupants wore clothing of a much more recent era. And it was only in this that the stories differed. Some reported seeing an old couple: she, in a floral dress; he, with an empty cage in his hands. Others added a second woman. Whoever had seen them together insisted they were mother and daughter, or perhaps sisters. The man, however, seemed to have no connection with them. He didn't even acknowledge their presence. The same was true of the women. Intrigued, Bob had spent more than one night's vigil in hopes of seeing something, but without luck.

"I believe there are some who can see the Beyond, and others who can't," he said before leaving. "Unfortunately, I'm in the second group."

Cecilia simply nodded, recalling her grandmother Delfina. She sighed as she went out to the terrace; at last she had some new material she could use.

The breeze hit her nostrils, a violent whiff of iodine and salt. In the distance a couple strolled along the wall separating the beach from the open sea. Two or three hours still remained until sunset.

She approached the water's edge, aware of the stirring of the coconut trees. There was no one else around, and she began to walk toward the little grove, thinking once more of her grandmother Delfina. If she were still alive, she would have known the entire story just by being near this place. Her grandmother could will herself to see past or future events. Delfina wasn't like Cecilia or the old gringo, creatures blind to visions. Loneliness, Cecilia suspected, was the only phantom that constantly assailed her.

After meandering through the little grove for a while with only a crab and a few jumping lizards for company, she decided to go home. Tomorrow she'd have to go back to the office to put her notes in order.

She felt a certain suffocation creeping in when she thought about the empty apartment that awaited her. The sky had turned purple as she drove back along the streets. In a few minutes nightfall would envelop the city, a dark background for its countless, glittering signs. The clubs, movies, restaurants, and cabarets would fill with tourists.

Suddenly she couldn't bear the idea of locking herself within four walls, alone with her books and her memories. Her thoughts returned to Amalia. Unlike this strange house that ambled around Miami, the story Amalia had begun telling had a beginning and certainly an end. She felt that those characters, lost in time and distance, were much more real than her own life or the elusive mansion that kept slipping through her fingers. Without a second thought, she turned her car around toward Little Havana.

"The past lurks around every corner," she thought.

And in that same spirit, she plunged into the crowded streets.

WEEPING MOON

Kui-fa's spirit was divided between sadness and joy. Every afternoon she would sit with her son next to the folding screen depicting scenes from the life of Kuan Yin, protector of mothers; and every afternoon she would pray for Siu Mend's return. The goddess floated above a mother-of-pearl water lily as she drifted toward her marvelous island of origin. Kui-fa would smile at the image. She felt safe by the goddess's side. How could it be otherwise when the Goddess of Mercy had rejected an eternity in heaven for an eternity of aiding the earth's afflicted? Other immortals were feared, but this one was beloved; many gods wore frightening expressions, but Kuan Yin emitted a radiant lunar clarity. So Kui-fa confided in her all her fears.

Every so often, Weng would go to the city to handle the legal complications of his export business, and sometimes he brought news of Siu Mend. Little Pag Li, whom his mother had nicknamed Lou-fu-chai, or "little tiger cub," was growing up, spoiled and doted upon by everyone. Mei Lei, the nursemaid who had raised Kui-fa, had taken over his care as if he were her own grandson. And while his mother prayed and waited for news of her missing husband, the little boy lived for the stories of gods and heavenly kingdoms that Mei Lei told him every afternoon by the fire. At five, he had the vocabulary and intelligence of an older child, nothing unusual for someone born under the sign of the Tiger.

Pag Li's favorite story was the legend of the intrepid Sun King who ate only flowers.

"*Ayii,*" the child begged almost daily, "tell me about the time the Sun King wanted to take the pill of immortality."

And Mei Lei would clear her throat as she stirred the soup where vegetables and chunks of fish swam.

"Well," she began, "it seems that the pill belonged to a goddess who guarded it jealously. Nothing in the world would make her give it up. Even though the Sun King begged her and begged her to hand it over to him, his pleas were in vain. One day the king had an idea. He went to the Mountain of the White Jade Turtle, and there he built a beautiful castle with a crystal roof. It was so magnificent and radiant that the goddess immediately wanted it for herself. And so the Sun King offered it to her in exchange for the pill. She accepted, and the Sun King brought the pill home, as happy as could be—"

"You forgot the part where he couldn't swallow it right away," Pag Li interrupted.

"Oh, yes! The goddess told him not to take it right away because he had to fast for twelve months beforehand, but the Moon Queen discovered the hiding place where—"

"You forgot again!" the child burst out. "The King went out and left the pill hidden on the roof. . . ."

"Yes, yes, that's right," Mei Lei said, adding more spices to the broth. "The Moon Queen discovered the pill by accident. The Sun King had gone out, and as she wandered through the palace, she noticed a bright spot shining way up high. It was the divine pill. That's how she discovered it and she—"

"First she climbed up on a piece of furniture."

"Exactly. She scrambled up on a piece of furniture because the palace roof was very high. And as soon as she swallowed the pill, she began to float—"

"She had to grab the walls so she wouldn't bump into the roof," Pag Li corrected. He adored that detail.

"When her husband returned and asked for the pill, she opened the window and flew away. The Sun King tried to chase after her, but she flew and flew until she reached the moon, which is full of cinnamon trees. Suddenly, the Moon Queen began to cough, and she coughed up part of the pill, and it turned into a pure white rabbit. This rabbit is the ancestor of the *yin,* woman's spirit."

"But the Sun King was furious," Pag Li continued, too excited to wait for the rest of the tale, "and he swore he'd never rest until he punished the Moon Queen. The God of the Immortals, who hears everything, heard his threats and appeared before him, ordering him to pardon her."

"So it was. And to calm him, he offered him the Sun Palace and a magical sarsaparilla cake. 'This cake will protect you from the heat,' he told him. 'If you do not eat it, you will die consumed by the palace's fire.' And finally, he gave him a moon talisman so that he could visit the Moon Queen."

"But she couldn't visit the Sun King because she didn't have the magic cake to protect herself."

"Uh-huh. When the Moon Queen saw him coming, she tried to run away; but he grabbed her by the hand, and to show her that he didn't hold a grudge, he knocked down a cluster of cinnamon trees. With their fragrant trunks, he built the Palace of Immense Cold and decorated it with precious stones. Ever since that time, the Moon Queen has lived in that palace, and the Sun King visits her on the fifteenth of every month. And that's how the union of *yin* and *yang* takes place in the heavens."

"And that's why the moon gets all round and shiny," shouted Pag Li. "Because she's so happy!"

The next afternoon, the child burst into the kitchen again, after spending hours frolicking among the plantings, with a request for another story that he knew better than the old woman.

The rains came, and Pag Li watched the fields grow flooded. His mother confined him to the house so that he could begin his studies with a teacher Weng had found. He could no longer play with his friends. He spent long hours among papers, fingers ink-stained, as he struggled to copy the complicated characters, but he took comfort in the promise that someday he would be able to decipher all the hidden stories for himself. And when his chores were done, he still had the tales that Mei Lei continued regaling him with every afternoon by the fire.

One cold autumn morning a letter arrived, announcing Siu Mend's return. It was not in vain that the altar of the Three Origins had always been the most carefully tended of all. Mei Lei was too old and forgot things easily, so Kui-fa cared for it herself in order to hold on to good fortune, which could not, after all, be left to chance.

For the first time in five years, Kui-fa was sent into a flurry of activity. Accompanied by a maidservant, she went into town and bought several packets of incense, a pot of the best honey, and hundreds of candles. She also ordered new clothes for herself, Pag Li, her husband, and Mei Lei.

Long before the Winter Festival preparations began, the Wong family altars were dotted with flowers and sparkled with the glow of candles. The women's supplications scattered in the chilly air as they prayed for another year of good health and prosperity. Kui-fa approached the altar of the God of the Hearth, and smeared his lips with nectar from the northern hives. This was the language the gods spoke and understood: sweet honey and fragrant flowers, incense smoke, and the brightly colored clothing that humans offered them every year. She gave plenty of honey to that deity, who would ascend to the celestial regions carrying their gossip and petitions. With so many proffered attentions, she was sure that Siu Mend would return safe and sound.

All that activity gave Pag Li a breather. His classes were suspended, and on top of that, none of the adults had time to fret over him. Together with his friends, he ran through the fields, setting off rockets and admiring the fireworks that exploded in the streets. And best of all, it was the season for those sugary cakes Mei Lei prepared, treats that the children pilfered at her slightest distraction, even knowing that the old woman would scold them for it. Half the pleasure was in stealing the treats and relishing them in secret.

Every night, Kui-fa went to the altar and smeared more honey on the god's lips.

"Tell the ruler of the First Heaven how I've raised my boy. I'm all alone. I need his father."

And through the smoke that escaped from the aromatic incense, the god seemed to half-close his eyes and smile.

One night, unexpectedly, Siu Mend showed up. He looked sunburned, but with a relaxed air that surprised the whole family. While he was on the island, he had been in daily contact with his grandfather Yuang and was charged with distributing the first shipments of candles, statues, prosperity symbols, incense, and other cult objects that Weng sent to Havana.

Dazzled by that city of light, he had almost forgotten his homeland. Siu Mend blamed his grandfather, whom he had stayed with in Cuba. The old man received a pension from the republican government for having been a *mambí*, as the Cubans called the rebels who fought against the Spanish army. His grandfather's dangerous life had made the island seem even more enchanting.

Every afternoon, the family sat down to hear Siu Mend's tales, tales of an island that seemed as though it came from a Han dynasty legend, with its exotic fruits and its infinite variety of fascinating beings. The most interesting stories were the ones told to him by his own *mambí* grandfather, who had arrived there when he was very young and had met an extraordinary man. He was a sort of sage who spoke with such conviction that Yuang joined him in his fight for the island's freedom. That was how he became a *mambí* and had dozens of adventures that he described to Siu Mend, smoking his long pipe in the doorway of his house. Five years after Siu Mend's arrival, the time came for him to return. Torn between his reluctance to abandon that country and his desire to go back to his family, Siu Mend once again launched himself seaward.

As time passed, Siu Mend still could not forget the salty, transparent air of the island. His nostalgia stayed trapped in the silent nets of his memory, suppressed by his more urgent duties. New winds blew, and with them, news of a civil war that threatened to change the country. It was rumored that the Japanese were advancing from the east. But these were vague whisperings that came and went like the rainy season. No one in the district paid any attention.

And thus they prepared to welcome a new Year of the Rat. In two more years, a complete cycle would have transpired since Pag Li's birth, and another Year of the Tiger would arrive. The difference was that the boy had been born under the sign of fire, and this next cycle would come into the sign of water. In any case, Siu Mend thought that it was time to begin looking for a wife for the boy. Kui-fa protested, it was too soon, but he paid her no mind. After much hesitation and a few secret consultations with his uncle, he decided to speak with the father of one of the young candidates. Gifts passed between the families along with vows of a future betrothal, and everyone returned to their business as usual, waiting for the time to be right.

And then, one afternoon, war broke out.

The sugarcane rose generously beneath the sun, and the fields swayed like an ocean, whipped by the breeze. Kui-fa was embroidering a pair of slippers in her bedroom when she heard the cries:

"Here they come! Here they come!"

Out of sheer instinct she dashed to the hiding place where she kept her jewels, grabbed the bundle, which fit into her fist, and concealed it in her clothing. Before the cries could be repeated, she was already dragging Pag Li toward the door. Her husband bumped into her. He was sweaty, his clothes in disarray.

"Run to the fields!" he exclaimed nervously.

"*Ayii!*" shouted Kui-fa in the direction of the kitchen. "*Ayii!*"

"Leave her alone," her husband said, dragging her outside. "She must have run away with the others."

The first shots burst out when they were still about a hundred paces from the fields. Then came the screams, distant and terrible. They dove into the sugarcane, whose stalks scratched their faces, cutting their skin, but Siu Mend forged on. The farther they ran, the safer they would be. The hail of gunshots grew louder behind them as they made their way into the thick of the fields. Pag Li suffered from the stalks scratching his skin, but his father wouldn't let him stop. Only when the shooting became a distant, dull sound did Siu Mend allow them to rest.

They arranged themselves as best they could among the foliage, but no one slept all night. At times they could hear shouting. Kui-fa wrung her hands anxiously, imagining the faces to whom those voices might belong, and the boy groaned, half in panic, half in annoyance.

"At least we're alive," Siu Mend said, trying to calm them. "And if we are, it's possible the others are too. . . . We'll find them."

The moon rose above their heads, a moon as moist as the dew that soaked their clothing. The cold dampness penetrated their bones. Embracing her son, Kui-fa raised her eyes to the silvery disk that so reminded her of the face of Kuan Yin, the Goddess of Mercy. She felt the whole sky weeping along with her. Or was it just the weeping moon that covered the fields? Siu Mend drew closer to them. And so they remained till morning.

The shooting grew less frequent and finally ceased altogether. Kui-fa sighed with relief when she spied the solar disk between the long, jagged stalks, but Siu Mend would not let them leave their refuge. They stayed all day, despite insects, hunger, and thirst. Only when the sun once again hid its face and the stars shone in the sky did Siu Mend decide that the time had come.

Filled with fear, they retraced their steps to the edge of the field, where Siu Mend ordered them to stop.

"I'm going out," he announced to his wife. "If I don't come back, turn around and run. Don't stay here."

Kui-fa waited anxiously, afraid of hearing her husband's dying cries at every turn, but she heard only the crickets chirping as they once again took over the silence. She remembered the jewels she had hidden in her clothing. She would have to find a more secure place for them. Her husband's absence reminded her of something. Yes, there was a place where no one would discover them. . . .

The insects silenced their voices with the cool breeze just before the dawn. The disk of the full moon moved slightly. The weather grew colder and damper. An interminable, teary fog rose above their heads. The ghost of the wind blew, followed by the sound of footsteps approaching through the sugarcane. The woman pressed her sleeping child against her breast. It was Siu Mend. In spite of the meager light, the expression on his face spoke more than words. She fell to her knees before her husband, no strength left to hold on to her sleeping child.

"Let's go," he said, his eyes filled with tears as he helped her stand up. "There's nothing more for us to do."

"But the house . . ." she stammered. " . . . the fields."

"The house doesn't exist. The land . . . it would be better to sell it. The soldiers have left, but they'll be back. I don't want to stay. Anyway, I promised Weng."

"Did you see him?"

"Before he died."

"And Mei Lei? And the others?"

Instead of replying, Siu Mend took the child by one hand and her by the other.

"We're going someplace else," he announced in a choked voice.

"Where?"

The man looked at her for a moment, but she knew that he didn't see her. And when he replied, it didn't sound like his voice but like that of a mortal anxious to return to the Kingdom of the Jade Emperor.

"We're going to Cuba."

I HATE YOU,
AND YET I LOVE YOU

Just like every other Saturday, Cecilia went walking by the docks. She watched the skaters, young families, cyclists, and runners all crowded into the park. It was a bucolic, but disturbing, image. Far from lifting her spirits, all those happy faces left her feeling isolated. It wasn't just the park that pained her, but the whole world: everything they called civilization. She wondered if she wouldn't have been happier off in the wilderness, free from the social pressures that only added to her anxiety. But she had been born in a warm, seaside Latin city, and now she lived in another warm city by the sea, albeit an Anglo one. This was clearly her destiny.

She had always been a stranger to her time and place, a perception that had grown in the last few years. Perhaps this was why she returned time and again to the bar, to hear Amalia's stories and lose herself in the past.

All her life Cecilia had been interested in exotic people, unlike her mother, who had loved everything that had to do with her own island. That's why she had named her daughter Cecilia, in homage to Cirilo Villaverde's novel *Cecilia Valdés,* a classic. But Cecilia hadn't inherited even a shadow of that passion. She was indifferent to her past. In school they endlessly retaught the island's social history. It had always consisted of the hungry and the powerful, those who had everything and others who had nothing, throughout different stages of history: the same story of the exploiters and the exploited, ad infinitum . . . until La Pelona, the Grim Reaper, arrived, as her prescient grandmother had immediately baptized him, to the great consternation of the neighbors, who cheered his triumphal entrance.

What happened then was worse than anything that had come before, although that story wasn't taught in school. Brandishing his scythe, La Pelona trampled property and human life alike; and in less than five years, the country had become the anteroom to hell. Once more Delfina had foreseen what no one else was able to anticipate, and ever since then her doubters recognized that she had a mouth that was close to God. She became the local oracle, and later on, when the family relocated to Sagua, the entire town went into mourning.

But her grandmother wasn't wholly devoted to forecasting the future. After marrying, she moved to Havana to raise her daughter and grow flowers. She was so clever at producing roses and carnations that many neighbors wanted to pay her for them, but she always refused to mutilate her bushes. Only once in a while, for some special occasion, would she give away little bouquets, gifts that were received like jewels.

Cecilia walked along the winding path through the grass, dotted here and there with clumps of wild bluebells and oleander. Her grandmother's house had been a sort of garden too. Her porcelain dishes, her furniture, her Baccarat crystal, even her clothing, had a floral cast. Now, surrounded by nature's bounty, Cecilia couldn't help evoking her grandmother's memory.

The ring of her cell phone jarred her from her reverie. It was Freddy.

"What are you doing?" he asked.

"Going for a walk."

"Got anything on for tonight?"

She left the path, turning toward the coast.

"There's a program about pyramids on the Discovery Channel I want to see."

"Why don't we go to the bar?"

She walked a little farther before replying.

"I don't know if I feel like going out."

She started to take off her shoes.

"C'mon, *mi china,* you need to get moving! Last year you spent your whole vacation locked up inside."

"You know how I am."

"Antisocial."

"A hermit," she corrected him.

"With a nun's calling," he added. "And the further misfortune of not being Catholic, so you can't even join a convent. Although to tell the truth, it really would suit you perfectly. You're not even trying to catch a man."

"And I have no intention of trying, either. I'd rather be an old maid, dressing up statues of saints."

"See? Saint Cecilia of Havana in Ruins. When Bluebeard dies, they'll build a hermitage in your name in Monte Barreto, right by your house, and people will make pilgrimages there, sliding downhill from the Tropicana in carriages and on palm-frond toboggans, all of them drunk and in sequins. They might even award a prize: the one who makes it to the bottom alive without breaking his head could be declared saint of the month. . . ."

She stopped listening to Freddy, absorbed by the sea crashing against the rocks. She was a hermit here. Here she had no past. It was left behind in a city she struggled to forget, along with her happy childhood, her lost adolescence, her dead parents. . . . Or maybe there was another reason she tried to put it out of her mind. She didn't want to be reminded that she was utterly alone.

Suddenly she thought of her great-aunt, her grandmother's only sister. She had been living in Miami for thirty years, after leaving Cuba at Delfina's suggestion. Cecilia had visited her only once and hadn't seen her since.

"Are you listening to me?" Freddy shouted.

"Yes."

"Then, are you coming or not?"

"Let me think about it. I'll get back to you later."

The loneliness had grown thick around her, like one of Dante's circles. She looked for her address book in order to phone Lauro. She had been meaning to transfer the numbers to her cell phone, but kept forgetting; that's why she carried a dog-eared little directory. Her glance fell on another number on the same page. . . . Yes, she still had family: an old lady who lived right in the heart of the city. Why hadn't she ever gone back to visit her? The answer dwelled in her pain, in her fear of remembering, her fear of perpetuating something that, in any case, she could never have again. But why was she being so selfish? Which was worse: to avoid the memory or to confront it? Making a great effort, she started punching in the number.

Loló lived in a neighborhood of broad sidewalks and newly mowed lawns, very close to those two bastions of Cuban cuisine, La Carreta and Versailles, where the late-night crowd gathered. While nearly all the other businesses closed before midnight and lost money hand over fist, those two restaurants stayed open well into the wee hours.

Cecilia tried to let her memory guide her, but all those buildings were identical. She had to pull out the piece of paper and look at the numbers. It was the wrong corner. She walked a few more blocks until she found it. After climbing the stairs, she pressed a buzzer that didn't work. The squawking of a parrot interrupted a mysterious hum emanating from within.

"*Viva Fidel!*" the parrot shrieked.

Footsteps scuffled toward the door. Cecilia saw the shadow through the glass in the peephole.

"Who is it?"

Cecilia sighed. Why did old folks do these things? Couldn't she see who it was?

"It's me, Auntie. . . . It's Ceci."

Was it her insecurity that compelled her to verify that the person she saw was who she claimed to be? Or was it that she didn't remember her?

The door swung open.

"Come in, child."

The parrot kept up its din.

"*Throw them out, throw them out . . .*"

"Quiet, Fidelina! If you keep it up, I'll feed you parsley."

The shrieking ceased.

"I don't know what to do anymore. The neighbors are all ready to declare war on me. If Demetrio, bless his soul, hadn't left her to me, I'd give her away."

"Demetrio?"

"My bingo partner for nine years. He was here the day you came to see me."

Cecilia didn't recall.

"He left me this damn parrot when he died, and she doesn't stop chattering all bloody day long."

The bird squawked again.

"Viva Fidel! Traitors go to hell!"

"Fidelina!" she screamed.

The cry shook the apartment.

"Even worse, any day now they'll accuse me of being a communist."

"Who taught her to say that?"

Cecilia recalled that slogan, chanted throughout the island against thousands of refugees who had sought shelter at the Peruvian embassy shortly before the *Mariel* exodus.

"That devil learned it from a video they brought over from Havana. Every time someone comes to visit, she repeats the refrain."

"Viva Fidel . . ."

"*Ay,* the neighbors are going to burn me alive."

"Do you have a cloth?"

"What for?"

"Do you have one?"

"Yes."

"Bring it to me."

The old woman left the room and returned with a folded, perfumed sheet. Cecilia spread out the cloth and laid it over the cage. The shrieking stopped.

"I don't like to do that," said the woman, wrinkling her brow. "It's cruel."

"What she does to people's eardrums is even crueler."

The woman sighed.

"Do you want some coffee?"

They went into the kitchen.

"I don't understand why you don't get rid of her."

"Demetrio left her to me," the old lady replied stubbornly.

"I don't see what would be so bad about giving her away."

"All right, I'll ask him. But I'll have to wait till he feels like showing up because I'm not Delfina."

Although Cecilia had been busy with the coffeepot, the last sentence made her look up.

"What?"

"If I were Delfina, I could summon him right now and find out what to do, but I'm going to have to wait."

Cecilia stared at the old woman. She'd never doubted her grandmother Delfina's gifts; there were too many stories about it circulating in her family. But now she couldn't determine if what her great-aunt was telling her was real or the result of old age.

"I'm not crazy," the woman said impassively. "Sometimes I feel he's nearby."

"Do you see things too?"

"I told you, I'm not like my sister. She was an oracle, like the one at Delphi. I think Mama had a premonition when she gave her that name. Delfina could speak with the dead whenever she felt like it. She would summon them and they would show up in droves. I can speak to them, too, but I have to wait for them to appear."

"Can you speak with my mother?"

"No, only with my sister and Demetrio."

Cecilia sweetened her coffee. She still couldn't decide if all that was true. How could she get the answer without offending her great-aunt?

"How long have you been able to talk to the dead?"

"Ever since I was a child, when I chatted with my grandmother in the garden, thinking she had come to pay us a visit. The next day I found out that, at precisely the same time, she was dying in a bed in the Covadonga Hospital. The only one I told was Delfina, who comforted me and told me not to worry, that worse things had happened to her. That's how I learned about her ability."

"But she never predicted that death. And no one in the family ever spoke a word to me of your visions!"

"Mine weren't important. Far more amazing things happened to Delfina. She always knew both good and bad news ahead of time: some plane that was about to crash, who would marry whom, how many children a couple would have, natural disasters that would kill thousands of people anywhere in the world . . . things like that. Delfina knew your mother was pregnant with you before she herself found out, because your grandfather, may he rest in peace, informed her from the Beyond. Ever since she was four or five years old, she would chat with members of the family who had lived long ago. At first she thought they were visitors. And since nobody said anything about it, she assumed she shouldn't let on. But when she grew up and began asking questions, she realized she'd been talking to people who weren't real . . . or rather, who weren't alive."

"And wasn't she scared?"

"The ones who were scared were Mama and Papa when she mentioned 'the visitors.' They thought she was crazy or making things up. My sister tried to convince them otherwise and told them what our great-grandparents had revealed to her about their childhoods . . . secrets that would've been impossible for Delfina to learn. That's what frightened them even more."

Cecilia put her cup in the sink.

"I don't know why we're discussing these things," Loló muttered. "Let's go into the living room."

They left the kitchen and headed for the other room, where they sat down beside the open door.

"Tell me about yourself," the old lady asked.

"There's nothing to tell."

"Impossible. Such a pretty young girl must have boyfriends."

"With my job, I have no time."

"People make their own time. I can't believe you don't go out anywhere."

"Sometimes I go to the beach."

She didn't dare mention the bar, imagining that the woman wouldn't appreciate knowing that her sister's granddaughter frequented such seedy establishments.

"When I was your age, I had a couple of favorite little hideaways."

"There's nowhere to go in this city. It's the most boring place in the world."

"There are some very nice spots here."

"Like what?"

"Vizcaya Palace, for example. Or Coral Castle."

"I don't know them."

"Well, one of these weekends I'll call you so you can see them. And, mind you"—she shook a finger at Cecilia—"these aren't just empty words."

Half an hour later, as she walked downstairs, Cecilia again heard the parrot squawking, apparently freed from its prison.

Her great-aunt was right. There was no reason to shut herself indoors like an eccentric. She thought of the bar, where she had gone several times but where she had never danced, and the fact that it was so dark no one would even notice that she didn't know where to put her feet. Besides, among all those Swedes and Germans, who wouldn't recognize a *gua-guancó* if it bit them, she could practically be queen of the dance floor. But Amalia's story was so fascinating that she forgot everything else as soon as she arrived.

She started her car. There was still time to change clothes and hunker down at a table, a martini in her hand. She felt a tickle in her heart. Really, how important was her loneliness when all the past awaited her in an old woman's reminiscences?

SOUL OF MY SOUL

The village was near Villar del Humo, slightly to the west, on the way to Carboneras de Guadazaón. It was like many other such places scattered throughout the Cuenca highlands, yet at the same time it was different. To begin with, it didn't even appear on the maps. Its inhabitants called it Torrelila, although the name had no connection to the clusters of bluebells that spread through the foothills like a carpet leading to the river, nor did it have anything to do with the color of the crocuses that bloomed throughout the region.

Torrelila owed its name to a fairy. According to legend, she was a spirit older than the village itself, and she had resided in a spring for centuries. They called her "the Moor of the Fountain," and many people swore she could be seen on Saint John's Day, when she left her watery abode to sit alongside a partially crumbled watchtower, combing her hair. Some old women believed she was related to the Galician *mouras,* who also emerge to comb their hair on that day; others maintained she was a cousin of the Asturian *xanas,* denizens of creeks and rivers, who suffer the same obsession with grooming themselves. In any case, the fairy of the foothills wore a lilac-colored tunic, unlike her northern relatives, who dressed in white.

Angela knew nothing about this when she arrived in Torrelila, and even if she had known, it wouldn't have interested her in the least. She and her parents were too busy refurbishing the tiny dwelling located about a hundred paces from Uncle Paco's house. Years ago, the hut had been a storage room. Now sunlight streaked through the holes in the roof, and the morning chill filtered through the paned windows.

Luckily, it was the slow season for fieldwork. The tiny shoots were just beginning to emerge, and all that needed to be done was to keep the weeds from choking the sprouting plants. Pedro, Uncle Paco, and two other locals were busy fixing up the house, while the women embroidered bedspreads and curtains. Between stitches, Uncle Paco's wife, a plump villager with a red nose, informed Angela about regional customs and practices.

"Don't stray too far from the paths," Doña Ana warned her. "All sorts of creatures wander through these mountains. . . . And don't trust strangers, no matter how harmless they may seem! Heaven forbid you should go through something like what happened to poor Ximena. . . . She ran into the devil himself while he was playing his flute in the cave of the wall paintings, and ever since then she's been as crazy as a loon. . . ."

Angela only half-listened, wondering intermittently what had become of Martinico. The imp hadn't returned since they passed through Ciudad Encantada, where they had stopped to rest awhile, fascinated by the beauty of the surroundings. The region owed its name to a group of rocks that had been carved by the water's ageless hand. Wandering among them was like strolling through a ghost town or through the gardens of some mythical castle.

The imp Martinico, who had pursued them, making all sorts of noises and breaking branches with each step, fell as silent as death when they spied the outline of the peaks. At least, thought Angela, the vexing creature wasn't indifferent to certain acts of God. Hours later, she noticed that he seemed to have vanished. She didn't take it too seriously, for she suspected he was probably exploring some of the niches—steps, slides, paths—that were so abundant there. Just two nights after arriving in Torrelila, she realized she hadn't seen him again. Could she have finally gotten rid of him forever? Maybe he was just an imp looking for a more beautiful place to live. . . .

". . . but she remains in that state for just a few hours," Doña Ana continued, checking the edging of a flounce. "And so she keeps waiting for a young man to break her spell, and whoever does will marry her and earn great riches . . . and, some say, even immortality."

Angela couldn't tell if the woman had been narrating a fairy tale or a local legend, but she didn't bother to find out. No matter, she wasn't interested. Absorbed in her labors, she didn't even notice that the men had already returned home until her mother asked her to help take the roast out of the oven.

Every morning she listened to the quiet moaning of the mountains, as if some ancient suffering were burning there. In the afternoon, her chores concluded, she would wander around nearby in search of herbs for cooking, after loading her knapsack with bread, honey, and fruit that she would eat along the way. She walked along the barely trodden paths, losing herself amid the multihued foliage of the mountain range. Little by little she felt her melancholy return: it was the same sadness she had suffered months earlier, but now it was fraught with anguish. Maybe it was the expectant silence of the forest. Or that omnipresent, constant, painful beating of her heart.

And so several weeks went by.

One morning she slipped out of bed earlier than usual and decided to go out looking for herbs. All night long she had felt a peculiar anxiety, and now her chest throbbed as she climbed up toward an area she hadn't explored before.

Propelled by instinct, she climbed toward the cloud-darkened peak. The wind howled strangely, and soon she discovered where the sound came from: the air was playing in the cracks of a ruined turret next to a fountain. Exhausted from the ascent, she sat down to rest.

Despite summer's imminent arrival, the areas surrounding the mountain range radiated their morning chill. Angela lifted her head toward the sun to feel its rays, which were already warming her face. Behind her, the swish of delicate gauze obscured the voice of the breeze. Startled, Angela turned around. Next to the fountain, a young woman, her feet submerged in the water, was combing her hair.

"Hello," said Angela. "I didn't hear you coming."

"You didn't see me," the creature explained, without interrupting her toilette. "I was already here when you appeared on this path."

Angela didn't reply. She noticed the golden strands that fell over the stranger's shoulders and felt a stab of anxiety, but then the young woman finished her steady strokes and smiled at her.

"You shouldn't walk around these places."

"I've already been warned," Angela admitted, recalling Doña Ana's words.

"A young girl is vulnerable to many dangers in these mountains."

"You're young, too, but here you are, as large as life, combing your hair in the woods."

The stranger stared at Angela for a few seconds before pronouncing:

"Something's happening to you."

"To me?"

But the other girl just watched her, waiting for a response. Angela's feet idly brushed a dew-drenched fern.

"I don't even understand it myself," she finally admitted. "Sometimes I feel like crying, for no reason."

"Lovesickness."

"I'm not in love."

"Pick that fern and take it home," the girl recommended. "It will bring you luck."

"Are you a witch?"

The stranger laughed, and her chirp was like the babbling of the streams that flowed down from the peaks. Angela felt a premonition as she noticed the comb that the young lady once again buried in her hair.

"I'll tell you something else," the maiden went on, studying the clouds that had begun to enshroud the morning. "Today is an especially dangerous day. . . . Did you bring any honey?"

"Do you want some? I've got bread too."

"It's not for me. But if you meet anyone else, offer him whatever you've got with you."

"I've never refused anyone food."

"No one will ask you for anything; you're the one who has to offer first, today or any of these days of early summer." The maiden's eyes began to darken. "If you don't . . ."

She stopped in mid-sentence, but Angela didn't want to hear anything that might frighten her even more. She had just noticed the strange limb peeking out from under the violet gauze tunic immersed in the fountain, an appendage that was quite different from the maiden's blushing complexion—a scaly green tail that twisted beneath the liquid surface.

"And you," Angela added, trembling, "don't you need anything?"

The young lady smiled again.

"Yes, but it's not in your power to offer it to me."

"I know who you are," she whispered, torn between sadness and terror.

"Everyone knows who I am," the maiden replied impassively.

"Excuse me, but I'm a stranger around here. . . . Are there others like you?"

"Yes, but they live far away," the young woman continued, staring fixedly at her. "Here you can find other creatures that aren't human, either."

"Imps?" Angela ventured, thinking of her Martinico.

"No. Some of them have been here since long before people arrived; others came with them. I'm a stranger myself, but I feel like a part of this place and can hardly remember my own." The young woman stretched her neck, apparently sniffing the air. "Now go. I don't have much time left."

Angela didn't want to see what would happen to the maiden when her time ran out. She pulled out the fern, turned, and began her return trip without looking back.

"Where were you, child?" Doña Clara scolded, standing by the fireplace, where she was roasting a quartered goat.

Angela hurriedly removed the flowers she had picked but, unsure what she would do with it later, hid the fern behind some jugs.

"Uncle Paco has a guest waiting to eat, and you're out wandering who-knows-where. Why did you take so long?" she repeated, and, without waiting for a reply, added: "Go serve the bread and wine. We've set the table under the arbor."

"How many are we?"

"Let's see: Ana and Uncle Paco, two neighbors, the three of us, Doña Luisa and her son."

"Doña Luisa?"

"The widow who lives on the outskirts of town."

Angela shrugged. She had met many people since her arrival, but she had no memory for so many new faces. Before leaving, she picked up the bread basket and the carafe of wine. Doña Ana distributed dishes and cutlery around the table, which was occupied by men and a woman dressed in black.

"Angelita, do you remember Doña Luisa?" her father asked as soon as he saw her approaching.

The girl nodded, thinking to herself that she'd never seen her before.

"This is Juan, her son."

"You can call him Juanco," the woman suggested. "That's what his father, may he rest in peace, used to call him, and that's what I call him too."

Angela turned toward the young man. A pair of dark eyes, like the bottom of a well, stared up at her, and she felt herself falling into that abyss.

The afternoon went by in discussions of the best way to dry the stigmas, how to fight off the worms that were eating the plants, how one farmer in the region was ruining the others' reputation by adding carbonate to his saffron, and scandals of that sort. The roast disappeared amid full glasses of red wine. The men continued drinking while the women, including the widow, went into the house with the dishes and leftover food.

". . . It's just that I want to do it before it gets dark," said Doña Luisa. "I wouldn't dare go alone right now, even though it's still afternoon."

"Angela can go with you," Clara said. "Let the boy stay with the men for a while. . . . Child, go with Doña Luisa and help her find some ferns."

For the first time, the girl seemed to emerge from her stupor. She remembered her hidden fern.

"What for?"

"Why do you think, child?" her mother reproved, lowering her voice. "Today is Saint John's Day."

"Those ferns cure constipation and fever for the rest of the year," Doña Luisa explained. "Come on, hurry—it's getting late."

Angela picked up her knapsack and followed the widow outside.

"And you should gather some too," Doña Luisa advised her as she walked away. "They also bring love and good luck."

Angela blushed, afraid that the woman had discovered what was already lodged in her heart, but the widow seemed absorbed in examining the shrubs that grew along the paths.

The girl guided her down a trail branching off the main road that she had traversed hours earlier. She didn't want to frighten the good woman with the sight of a fairy combing her hair at the edge of a fountain. So she guided her in the opposite direction, toward a particularly woodsy area. They had walked for half an hour when Angela stopped short.

"I'll look on this side," the girl said. "There are a few caves behind that tree."

"All right, I'll look over here, but I'm warning you, I won't go more than twenty paces by myself. If I don't find anything, I'll wait for you right at this spot."

Each one took a different trail. Angela walked a short distance and almost immediately stumbled upon a clump of ferns, still damp with dew. She gathered plenty for the widow and for herself. She had decided that just one fern wouldn't be enough to bring her what she so greatly needed now. . . .

A whistle pierced the trees, and she stopped to listen. It wasn't a repetitive sound, like that of some ordinary mountain bird, but rather a harmonious, constant clamor, the fleeting cadence of a music she had never heard before. She turned her head to see where it was coming from and, possessed by a sudden urgency, went to search it out.

The melody echoed from rock to rock and from tree to tree, until it reached the entrance of a cave. There it burst forth with the cadences of a pristine, tumbling waterfall; a summer storm; ancient, chilly nights . . . Within that song vibrated the entire mountain range and all the creatures in it. Angela entered the cavern, unable to resist its call. At the back, beside the flames that illuminated the place, an old man was playing an instrument made of different-size reeds. The breath from his lips drew a wave of tones, bass and treble, tremulous and harsh. She gazed at the drawings adorning the rocky walls: enormous beasts of some remote time, with little human figures skittering around them. But she didn't move until the musician stopped playing and lifted his gaze.

"They're very old," he explained, noting her interest.

Then he gestured as if he were trying to work the stiffness out of his legs. And she saw that he had the feet of a goat, and two little horns half hidden beneath his tangled hair. Even as she instantly recalled the story of the devil of the mountains, her intuition told her that this old man with hooves must be one of those creatures the lilac fairy had told her about.

Instinctively she opened her knapsack, looking for the pot of honey that was left over from breakfast, and offered it to him. The old man sniffed the contents and looked at her, surprised.

"It's been centuries since anyone offered me honey," he sighed.

He stuck a finger into the syrup and sucked it with delight.

"Are you from around here?" Angela asked, more curious than terrified.

The old man sighed again.

"I'm from everywhere, but my roots are in an archipelago that can be reached by crossing the sea," he said, and pointed toward the east.

"Did you arrive with the humans?"

The old man shook his head.

"The humans threw me out, although not on purpose. It's more like they forgot about me. . . . And when people forget their gods, there's nothing to do but hide."

Angela began to feel a little tickle in her nose, the kind she often got when she felt confused. The spirits of the mountains—whose existence she had learned to accept after Martinico's arrival—were one thing, but the existence of multiple gods was quite another.

"Isn't there only one God?"

"There are as many as humans want. They create us and they destroy us. We can endure loneliness, but not their indifference; it's the only thing that makes us mortal."

The girl suddenly felt sorry for that lonely god.

"My name is Angela." She held out her hand.

"Pan," he replied, extending his own.

"I haven't brought anything to cook with," she said, pointing to her knapsack.

"No, no!" the old man explained. "Pan is my name."

The girl was dumbfounded.

"You should change it. You'll confuse everybody."

"No one remembers," he sighed.

"Remembers what?"

The old man's face lit up.

"It doesn't matter. You've been very kind to me. I can help you with anything you want. I still have some powers left."

Angela's heart started to beat wildly.

"There's something I want more than anything."

"Tell me—" he began to say, but he cut himself short, as something behind her caught his eye.

She turned around. Standing by the entrance to the cave, Martinico leaped about, making grotesque faces and carrying on behind her back.

"I can't believe it!" Angela groaned. "I thought you had gone to hell!"

She bit her tongue, looking at the old man from the corner of her eye, but he seemed to take no offense. On the contrary, he asked with genuine astonishment:

"Can you see him?"

"Of course I can! It's a curse."

"You can get rid of it."

"And would you help me do something else?"

"I can help *you* with only one thing. Although if one of your descendants should ever need me, even without knowing about our pact, I could offer him whatever he wanted . . . twice."

"Why?"

"It's the law."

"What law?"

"Orders from above."

Apparently, there existed a power stronger than the mountain gods. And now it had restricted her choices.

Torn, she watched Martinico's antics and thought about those eyes awaiting her in the foothills of the mountains.

"All right," she decided. "I'll have to keep living with my curse."

"I don't understand," he replied. "What could be better than getting rid of *that*?"

And the girl told the god Pan about the pain of a soul that has discovered its own soul.

Juan assured her that he had loved her from the moment he saw her, but she suspected that his conviction was a creation of the exiled god—the perfect work of an ancient spirit. Every month she visited the cave to leave him honey and wine, confident that the old man would gobble up the treats with delight, although she never saw him again.

The courtship, however, didn't last very long, just long enough for Juan to finish building their new home, with the help of a few villagers, on an empty parcel of land near her parents' house. While the men busied themselves cutting, planing, and nailing boards, the women helped the bride with her trousseau, spinning and weaving all sorts of tablecloths, curtains, bed linens, and rugs.

The first few months of wedded life were idyllic. For some reason Martinico disappeared again. Perhaps, understanding that there was someone more important in her life now, he had retreated to a remote corner of the mountain range. She didn't miss him. He was an ill-mannered imp who only made trouble, and he soon faded from her memory. Besides, other problems were beginning to arise.

On the one hand, worms were devouring the crops in the area, and Juanco racked his brains trying to think of a solution. As if that weren't enough, Angela surprised him on several occasions reading a mysterious piece of paper that he hid every time she came near. Who could be writing to her husband? And why so much secrecy? Besides, her own health seemed to be declining. She was always tired, and she vomited all the time. She didn't say anything to her mother because she didn't want her to call in a healer again. Only when she noticed that the laces on her dress barely closed did she suspect what was going on.

"Now we'll really have to do it," Juan said on hearing the news.

"Do what?"

The man took the wrinkled paper from his pocket and held it out to her.

"What's that?" she asked, without trying to read it.

"A letter from Uncle Manolo. He's written me several times, saying he needs an assistant. He wants us to go there."

"Where?"

"To America."

"It's very far away," the young woman replied, stroking her belly. "I don't want to travel in this condition."

"Listen to me, Angelita. The harvest is lost, and we have no money to replant. Many of the neighbors have already moved away or are starting new businesses. I don't think there'll be any more saffron around here. We could move farther south, but I have no money and no one to lend me any. Uncle Manolo is offering a good opportunity."

"I can't leave my parents."

"It's just for a little while. We'll save some money and then we'll come back."

"But how will I get by alone in a foreign country? I need someone who knows about children."

"Mama will come with us. She always says she'd like to see her brother before she dies."

Angela sighed, almost defeated.

"I'll have to talk to my parents."

The news struck them like a bolt of lightning, and Juan couldn't say much to comfort them. Pedro himself had spoken to his wife about the possibility of moving to the city, but Doña Clara wouldn't hear of it. And now, suddenly, they discovered that not only would they be separated from their daughter but that they wouldn't even see the birth of their grandchild. They were only slightly comforted when they learned that Luisa would accompany them. At least their daughter would not be alone during the delivery.

Among the six of them, they packed all the necessities. Since the journey to the coast was long and Juan didn't want his in-laws to make the return trip alone, he convinced them to say good-bye right there. With tears and advice, they all said their farewells. The memory of her parents' silhouette at the edge of that dusty trail ending at their door would never leave Angela. It would be her last image of them.

From the stern of the ship, she watched the horizon disappear. Lost in the mist of the gray waters, her home looked like a fairyland, with its little towers and medieval palaces, its reddish roofs and the bustling port that now faded away.

The young woman remained on deck for a long time, together with Juan and Doña Luisa. Her husband chattered endlessly, making plans for their new life. He seemed eager to take on something new, and he had heard so much about the Americas, a mythical place where everyone could get rich.

"I'm cold," Angela complained.

"Go with her, Juanco," Doña Luisa encouraged. "I'll stay here a little while."

Lovingly, he bundled her up in her shawl, and together they went downstairs to their stateroom. Juan struggled a bit with the rusty lock of their modest room. Then he stepped aside to let her pass. Angela groaned.

"What's wrong?" he asked, afraid that her labor had begun.

"Nothing," she whispered, closing her eyes to erase the vision.

But her ploy didn't work. When she opened them again, Martinico was still sitting amid the jumbled clothes, mischievously covering his head with her best mantilla.

DESTINY PROPOSES

Freddy and Lauro had dragged their friend to see the Renaissance fair that was held every year at Vizcaya Palace. Tugging her from one kiosk to another, they made her try on all sorts of clothing until they managed to transform her look into—according to them—something worthy of the event. Now the young woman walked among artisans and fortune-tellers, letting the breeze whip her Gypsy skirt against her legs. On her head she wore the wreath of flowers that Freddy had crowned her with.

The revelry was contagious. Children and adults alike showed off their masks and brightly colored costumes; harp music floated in the air; troubadours meandered among the fountains with their mandolins, flutes, and drums; and Cecilia rubbed elbows with princesses who wandered through the perfectly trimmed gardens. The masquerade also included the vendors and craftsmen. Here, a blacksmith hammered a horseshoe over the coals of his forge; there, a fat, smiling weaver spun on a wheel that looked like it came from a Perrault fairy tale; farther down, an old man with a silvery beard and a Merlin-like expression sold shepherd's crooks inlaid with semiprecious stones and minerals: quartz for clairvoyance, onyx to combat psychic attacks, amethyst to learn of past lives . . .

"Where have I been all this time, and why didn't I know about this?" Cecilia murmured.

"On the moon," Lauro replied, trying on a feather-accented hat.

"And imagine, you haven't even seen the Broward Fair," Freddy commented. "It's much bigger."

"And they hold it in an enchanted forest!" Lauro interrupted. "There are lovely things there: even a medieval joust where the knights charge at each other on horseback, like King Arthur's. If you saw them take off their armor, you'd have a heart attack."

But Cecilia wasn't listening anymore. Her attention turned to a stand full of little wooden boxes.

"Melisa!"

Lauro's cry shook her from her trance. A young woman turned toward them.

"Laureano!"

"Girl, don't call me that," he whispered, looking all around.

"Did you change your name?"

"Here I'm Lauro," he said, adding in a throaty voice, "but my closest friends call me La Lupe: *'It's over, our love is gone. . . . It's over, I swear it's true. . . .'*"

The stranger burst out laughing.

"Melisa, this is Cecilia," Lauro said. "Do you know Freddy?"

"I don't think so."

"Sure you do, girl," Freddy reminded her. "Edgar introduced us in Havana. I'll never forget because you looked divine in that white dress. And when you read your poems, we all practically fainted. . . ."

"I think I remember," said Melisa.

"What are you doing here?"

"I always come to buy things." She looked down at the two shepherd's crooks she held. "I don't know which one to get."

"Don't you like this one?" Cecilia interjected, offering her a different one.

For the first time, Melisa fixed her gaze on her.

"I've already tried it—it's no good."

She turned her back, still holding both staffs.

"Well, I'm almost tempted to buy it," Cecilia insisted. "It looks so pretty."

"What it looks like doesn't matter," the other girl replied. "The crook I need has to *feel* different."

Lauro pulled Cecilia toward a stand farther down the walkway.

"Don't argue with her," he whispered.

"Why not?"

"She's a witch. Has been ever since she lived in Cuba. Celtic magic, or something like that. Be careful."

"If that's the case, there's no need to worry," Freddy assured them as he approached. "Those people believe things come back in threes. So the last thing they want is to do harm. They're even careful with their thoughts."

"A witch is a witch. They have all those weird energies around them. If you don't watch out, you might be struck by lightning just from being close."

"For God's sake!" Freddy exclaimed. "How ignorant!"

Cecilia didn't pay them any attention. Slowly she approached the kiosk where the girl was bargaining with the artisan.

"Can I ask you something?"

Melisa turned around.

"Uh-huh."

"Why do you need a shepherd's crook?"

"It's a long story, but if you're interested"—she looked in her purse and pulled out a card—"come see me at this address on Friday. We're starting a class. . . ."

There was a name on the card—Atlantis—and under that a list of products: books on mysticism, candles, incense, quartz crystals, music . . .

"What a coincidence!" Cecilia exclaimed.

"Why?" she questioned with a distracted expression, taking out some money to pay with.

"A few days ago someone told me to go see Lisa, the owner of that bookstore. I'm a reporter and I'm looking for information about a house—"

"You have a shadow on your aura," the girl interrupted.

"What?"

Melisa finished paying.

"You have a shadow on your aura," she repeated, but she didn't look her in the eye, appearing to focus instead on something floating above her. "You should protect yourself."

"With something you can sell me at your class?" Cecilia asked, unable to mask her sarcasm.

"The protection you need can't be bought. It's something you have to do in here," she answered, and touched her temple with her finger. "I don't want to scare you, but something bad will happen to you if you don't start with what's *inside your head*."

She turned and plunged into the crowd. Leaning on her staff, she looked like a druid enchantress about to embark on a journey as her tunic fluttered around her body.

"What did she tell you?" Lauro asked.

For a moment Cecilia watched the figure withdraw.

"I'm not sure," she muttered.

She stared at the display window from the sidewalk: pyramids, tarot decks, quartz crystals, Tibetan bells, incense from India, crystal balls . . . and, like the absolute monarch of such a mystical kingdom, a coppery Buddha with a diamond-shaped eye in his forehead. All around him hung webs fitted inside rings with dangling feathers: dream catchers. The Navajo placed them over their beds in order to trap benevolent visions and destroy nightmares.

She pushed the door open to the jangling of bells. Immediately she smelled a scent that stuck to her hair like the sweetest molasses. Inside, it was frigid and fragrant. Fairy music filled the air. Atop a counter, colored stones squeaked like insects as two women rubbed them together. One woman was a customer; the other Cecilia figured for the owner.

Silently, so as not to cause a disturbance, Cecilia investigated the shelves filled with books: astrology, yoga, reincarnation, Kabbalah, theosophy . . . Finally the customer at the counter chose three stones, paid for them, and left.

"Hi," Cecilia said.

"Good morning. How can I help you?"

"My name is Cecilia. I'm a journalist, and I'm writing an article about a phantom house."

"I know. Gaia called me. But today's not good because in a little while there's going to be a lecture, and I have to finish up a few things first."

The doorbells jingled. A couple waved as they came in and headed toward the theosophy corner.

"Why don't you phone me and we'll get together some other time?" Lisa suggested.

"When?"

"I can't tell you right now. You can call me tomorrow or . . . Oh, hi! How great you're here!"

Melisa had just arrived.

"How are you?" Cecilia greeted her.

At first Melisa looked at her as if she were a stranger, and then she raised her eyes and stood looking at the air above her head.

"Sorry, I didn't recognize you in those clothes."

"I'll get the room ready," Lisa said, disappearing behind a curtain.

"Can I ask you a question?" said Cecilia when they were alone.

Melisa nodded slightly.

"The day we met, you said I had a shadow on my aura."

"You still do."

"But you never told me what I should do about it."

"Because I don't know."

Cecilia stared at her in astonishment.

"Really, I have no idea. With auras, it's a matter of energies, sensations. . . . You can't always be sure. Why don't you stay for my lecture? Who knows—it might help you later on."

Cecilia didn't believe in it, but she stayed because she had nothing else to do. Besides, she needed to speak to the owner about her article. And so she learned in the course of the lecture that people emit all kinds of vibrations. According to Melisa, anyone could give off—consciously or otherwise—harmful or healing charges toward others. With appropriate training, it was possible to perceive these energies and also to protect oneself. There were many tools for channeling energy: water, crystals, sharp objects like daggers, swords, or shepherd's crooks. . . . At her next lecture, those who were interested could practice some exercises to see their auras. That was one of the first steps toward recognizing the presence of a psychic episode.

Later on, at home, as she listened to Bob and Gaia's recorded testimonies, a spark of intuition—perhaps passed down from her grandmother Delfina—suggested to her that she shouldn't reject anything in her investigation, not even a bizarre talk like that one. Recently her points of reference seemed to coincide, as if everything were connected. Besides, who was she to doubt? Her grandmother had been a sibyl, after all.

For a moment she thought of Amalia. What would she have thought of all those auras and energies? Cecilia had no idea what really went on in that woman's mind. She had barely even spoken to her of anything that wasn't connected to Amalia's story. She listened with the hope that some episode would spill over into her own life. That's why she kept returning to the bar. Those reminiscences had become her vice. The more she found out, the more she wanted to know. It was impossible to avoid Amalia's enchantment. And tonight, she told herself, would be no exception.

FORGIVE ME, CONSCIENCE

Caridad looked out the window and watched the first passersby. Dawn left a trace of dampness on the wooden windowsill. It was her last day in that house where she had arrived with so much hope, dreaming that her life would be different and imagining many outcomes, but none like this one.

After Florencio's burial, she returned to the store, ready to forge ahead with the business. Although she didn't know her numbers and could barely recognize a few letters, she did her best to keep the import-export business afloat, but the selection of products dwindled quite a bit without her deceased husband's bargaining expertise. Besides, the suppliers didn't seem to respond to her demands as they had done to Florencio's. She had to find a go-between, but still it wasn't the same.

She might have been able to stay, eking out a meager living, or perhaps even trying to develop the business, but at last she decided to leave for a reason she would never confess aloud to anyone: her husband's specter pursued her. Every so often, she heard his footsteps. Other times she felt his breath behind her, on the back of her neck. Or his scent would reach her, carried by the wind. A few nights she noticed her mattress sinking beneath the weight of a body in bed beside her. . . . She couldn't bear it, and she decided to sell. With the money she would buy another place and start a new business. Maybe a store specializing in items for ladies.

The morning of the sale, she got up earlier than usual. The notary would arrive at noon in order to have her sign some papers. Shivering with cold—the tropical winter, which can be wet and piercing, was approaching—she picked up the kerosene lamp. It was still dark inside the house, although the streets were growing bright with a gleam that left a golden halo on everything. In that glow, the city seemed like a ghostly vision. The tropical light impregnated the island with its magic, something the inhabitants barely noticed, too absorbed in their own problems . . .

And Caridad's main problem was her daughter, a child who was eager to find out everything but was strangely silent. The woman never knew what thoughts were passing behind those eyes in which—ah, yes!—there shone the same passion that had once filled her father's gaze.

Caridad placed the kerosene lamp on the ground and bent down to light the wood stove to heat some water. She watched as the flames licked the reddening coals, until they grew white-hot and finally turned gray. She was contemplating that metamorphosis when some fingers brushed her shoulders. Thinking her daughter had awakened, she turned around. The image of her husband, chest destroyed by machete blows and his face streaked with blood, rose before her. She screamed and drew back, knocking the kerosene lamp into the flames. The metal burst in the fire, and the fuel intensified the flames, which leaped from their stone enclosure, igniting the kitchen walls and singeing her legs. For a few desperate seconds she tried to put out the flames, swatting at them with a piece of cloth she had found nearby, but the fire grew, fed by the dry wood.

"Mercedes!" she shouted, running to the room where her daughter slept. "Mercedes!"

The child, not understanding what was happening, opened her huge, frightened eyes.

"Get out of bed!" Caridad roared, pulling off the sheets. "The house is on fire!"

By the time the firemen arrived, La Flor de Montserrat was a pile of smoking ruins. The neighbors stared at in horror and fascination. Many women went over to Caridad, offering her water, coffee, and even little sips of liquor to boost her spirits, but she could do no more than stare emptily at the remains of her greatest wealth.

At midday she was still there, sitting on the edge of the pavement, rocking with her hands wrapped around her legs, while her daughter stroked her hair, cradling Caridad against her chest. And that's how the notary found them, with a quick glance at the rubble and the two huddled on the sidewalk, unable to comprehend what possible relationship might exist between him and the disaster. At last he sighed and, seeing that there was nothing else to be done, turned and walked away.

Miz Ceci woke up feeling very perky. The eternal summer heat that always put her in such a foul mood had finally broken. At home, everyone was asleep. She decided to use her early-morning vigor to visit La Flor de Montserrat and place her usual order. She ignored the empty carriages that passed beside her, preferring to walk. It was delicious to stroll in the fresh air, enjoying that cool breeze, refreshing as a hailstorm. At her sixty-odd years of age, she barely looked fifty, and some even took her for a woman of forty or so. She had an alluring presence that was the envy of many twenty-year-olds. In a land where beauty abounded, she was a paragon of loveliness.

She stepped lightly, skirting the puddles that dotted the paving stones. Long before she arrived, the air began to bring Cecilia a whiff of something ominous. She ignored it until she turned the corner and came upon the disaster. For a few seconds she regarded the remains of the fire, shocked and motionless. Then she saw the two crouching figures in front of the building and approached them almost furtively.

"Doña Caridad," Cecilia whispered, not daring to wish her good morning.

The woman lifted her eyes but couldn't muster a response. Only when she was able to look at her old house again did she manage to mutter: "There's no soap today."

Cecilia bit her lip and observed the youngster, still clinging to her mother.

"Do you have anywhere to go?"

Caridad shook her head.

Cecilia gestured toward a carriage that was parked on the corner.

"Let's go," she said, bending to help her. "You can't stay here."

Without resisting, Caridad allowed herself to be guided to the coach. Miz Ceci shouted out an address, and the coachman spurred his horses, which started running toward the sea, but they stopped short. After a few blocks, they turned off to the left and came to a halt in a deserted area.

A man, spotting them from across the street, crossed over.

"How much for your stuff, honey?" he asked, leaning over toward Caridad.

For the first time since the fire, Caridad reacted. She gave the man a shove that nearly knocked him down. He, in turn, lurched toward her as if he were about to strike her, but Miz Ceci intervened.

"We're not open at this hour, Leonardo. And she's not for sale."

Cecilia's haughty attitude was enough to make the man turn back.

"I'm sorry," Cecilia muttered, opening the door.

Caridad hesitated a few seconds before finally crossing the threshold. Once inside, she saw no living room or dining room but rather an enormous patio framed by four covered corridors with doors along their entire length. Several intimate feminine garments rested on haphazard furniture. And then it came to her how she had met that woman.

"So the soaps . . . ?" she began, not knowing what to ask.

Doña Cecilia gazed at her for a few seconds.

"I thought you knew," she said. "I own a brothel."

She had no choice. It was either the street or the bordello. Doña Ceci let her move into the last empty room, which had been recently vacated by a pupil who disappeared without a trace. Every afternoon, mother and daughter locked themselves in their room. Only in the morning would Caridad allow the child to play outside on the patio, while she worked as the brothel's maid. But Cecilia already had a woman to do the cleaning. Caridad took advantage of her every slip, sweeping, washing any clothing that was left around, or cleaning a little. The woman, fearful of losing her job, complained to Doña Ceci.

"Why don't you do some real work?" she suggested one afternoon. "I'll let you choose your clients. I can tell you come from a different sort of background and aren't used to this."

"I could never do it."

"You're prettier than all the others. Do you realize what you could earn?"

"No," Caridad repeated. "Besides, what kind of example would I be setting for my daughter? She's practically a young lady now."

Cecilia sighed.

"I'm sorry to have to tell you this, but if you don't work, you can't stay.

I haven't used this room in months, and I'm losing money. I've already got two girls interested in it."

"As soon as I get a job, I'll pay you for the room. People need maids . . ."

"No one wants other people's children in their homes," Doña Cecilia assured her.

Caridad looked at her, terrified.

"I could . . . I could . . ."

"I'm offering you something I don't offer anyone: choosing your own clients. . . . Believe me, that'll raise your price."

"I don't know," she stammered. "Let me think about it."

"Don't be afraid. I've spent my whole life in this profession. It's not as bad as they say."

"Your whole life?"

"Since I was a child."

"How?" she asked skeptically. "How did it happen?"

"I lived near La Loma del Ángel, and I used to play half-naked in the streets, with no house and no family, surviving however I could. I was starting to develop breasts, but I didn't realize it. A woman picked me up and sold my virginity for a fortune, and here I am: I'm not dead yet," she laughed softly. "Imagine, it's worked out so well for me that I'm even in a novel."

"In a novel?" Caridad repeated, not quite understanding how a person could really be in a novel.

"When I was still running around the streets, I was discovered by a lawyer who had left his practice in order to become a professor. Whenever he saw me, he would call me over and give me a few coins or candies. I think he fell in love with me, even though I was only twelve and he must have been around thirty. After they took me to the brothel, I stopped seeing him, but later I found out through a client that the professor had written a novel and that the heroine had my name."

"He wrote your story?" Caridad asked, suddenly interested.

"Of course not! He didn't know the first thing about me. His Cecilia Valdés and I only shared a name and the fact that we were both from La Loma del Ángel."

"Did you read the novel?"

"A client told me about it. My God! The things Don Cirilo invented! Imagine, in the novel I was an innocent girl, seduced by a rich white boy, and at the end it turns out he's my half brother. How perverse! Finally, the rich boy pays with his life, because a jealous black man shoots him outside a church just when he's about to marry an aristocratic woman. I go crazy and end up in a madhouse. . . . How can writers make up such nonsense?" She furrowed her brow, lost in thought. "I've always thought they must be half out of their minds."

"Did you ever see him again?"

"Don Cirilo? I ran into him by chance one day. He'd been in prison, I think for some political scandal, and he left the country, but he returned after being pardoned. It seems he considered me the great love of his life, even though we never even exchanged a single kiss. He wouldn't let me leave until I gave him my address. And would you believe he came to the brothel several times, asking for me?"

"Did you see him?"

"Not on your life. I had already told the story to the previous owner, who was even more frightened than I was. Every time he showed up, she told him I was busy. I never wanted to get mixed up with lunatics," she sighed. "But one day we bumped into each other on the street, and I felt sorry for him. And so I accepted his invitation to dinner. He came to see me before he left for New York. Then he returned to Havana a few times, always bringing me flowers or candy, as if I were a great lady. The last time was three years ago. He was more than eighty, and he still knocked on the door of this house with a bouquet of roses."

"Did he go back to New York?"

"Yes, and he died almost immediately after. . . . But life is strange. Do you remember that young man who came up to us when we arrived at this house?"

"Yes."

"His name is Leonardo, just like the white gentleman in the novel. A few days after Don Cirilo died, he showed up at my door. He wanted me to take care of him, but at my age, I'm not up to those tasks. He's come around several times already, and he always leaves furious at my rejections. The other girls don't interest him at all. Sometimes I think he's Don Cirilo's ghost, or a curse he left me with that novel of his. . . . Well, now he's become obsessed with you."

Emerging from her trance, Doña Cecilia smacked herself in the forehead.

"Why didn't I think of it before? Do you know who your ruling *orisha* is?

"Oshún, I think."

"Let me make an offering to her. You'll see how you'll lose your fear of men."

Caridad hesitated for a few seconds. She didn't know whether to continue refusing or to let the woman do with her as she pleased. Caridad didn't believe that any *orisha* could take away her scruples, but she said nothing. Perhaps the ceremony would give her a few more days to decide what to do. Though one thing worried her.

"I don't want Mechita to find out anything."

"We'll do it at midnight, when she's asleep."

But Mercedes didn't sleep that night. A monotonous, pulsing thrum drove away the dreaminess that had begun to settle on her eyelids. She slipped from her bed and saw that her mother's was empty. Carefully she opened the door, but all she saw was the gleam of the moon bathing the deserted patio. Following the sound, she advanced along the corridor until she reached a window that shielded a flickering, yellowish light. In a corner, a toothless old woman was rocking to the rhythm of her own chant while Miz Ceci poured an oily liquid over a naked woman's head. The piercing smell of honey assaulted her nostrils. The *oñí*, as her mother called it, the same word her slave grandmother had used, was making her skin glow.

"Oshún Yeyé Moró, queen of queens, I pour this honey over the body of your daughter, and I pray in your name to let her serve you," said Miz Cecilia, walking around and around the motionless figure. "She wants to be strong; she wants to be free to love without commitments. And so I implore you, Oshún Yeyé Karí, free her from embarrassment, render her fearless and without shame."

The candle flames flickered in an invisible breeze, as if someone had opened a side door. The woman, who until that moment had remained still, seemed to tremble with a chill and slid her hands down her thighs, spreading the *oñí*. Despite the moon twinkling over her from outside the window, Mercedes couldn't see the woman's face.

"Oshishé iwáaa ma, oshishé iwáaa ma omodé ka siré ko bará bi lo sóoo . . ."

sang the old black woman in a muffled voice, while the woman started to laugh gently and move in a strange, voluptuous dance.

The girl felt a tickling sensation between her legs. Secretly she wished the honey would drip on her as well, mixing with the dew that dampened the city and its inhabitants. She wanted to lose herself in the same trance that held the woman, laughing madly and shaking her hips with an earthy shudder.

Miz Ceci withdrew. Now the ancestral African voice had acquired a sensual, agitated rhythm, like the galloping of a beast. The naked woman bent over, moaning.

"She's yours, Leonardo," Doña Cecilia said.

A figure emerged from the shadows. Mercedes immediately recognized the man who had frightened them. The woman turned her back on the approaching man, and for the first time, the girl saw her mother's face. The man rubbed up against her, but this time, instead of rejecting him, her mother welcomed his caresses.

The patio suddenly began to spin around Mercedes, and everything grew darker than the night. The moon disappeared, and the world as well.

Leonardo took Caridad's naked body in his arms and led her into a nearby room. The night throbbed to the incessant chanting. Doña Cecilia opened the door to the patio, where she found the girl unconscious. She understood instantly what had happened. Lifting Mercedes, she carried her to bed. She looked for water in the washbasin, but there wasn't any left. She remembered the jar of honey she had left by the door and went searching for it. Taking a bit on her finger, she moistened the child's temples and lips. The pungent sweetness of the *oñí* appeared to revive her.

"It seems you've been dreaming," Doña Cecilia told her when her eyes met the girl's. "You fell out of bed."

Mercedes said nothing. She closed her eyes so she might be left alone, and that was exactly what Doña Cecilia did.

As soon as the door closed, she sat up in bed and discovered the pitcher of honey. Without thinking, she stuck her hand in the jar. Outside, the drums continued worshiping the orisha of love, while Mercedes anointed all the nooks and crevices of her body with honey. *Oñí* for her burning, fire for her impatience. . . . She had been pierced by Oshún's spell.

Part Three

CITY OF ORACLES

From Miguel's Notebook

To stay in China:

In Cuba, when someone says, "So-and-so stayed in China," it doesn't mean that the person decided to remain in that country, but rather that he understood nothing of what he saw or heard.

The expression probably originates with the poor communication or confusion that newly arrived Chinese immigrants experienced, without any knowledge of the language and confronted with a culture so different from the one they left behind.

CUBAN NIGHT

The most beautiful men in the world passed through South Beach. She and Lauro had escaped from the newspaper office to have lunch in an area filled with boutiques and open-air cafés.

As she devoured her arugula, blue cheese, and walnut salad, she thought about her strange destiny: without parents or siblings, she languished alone in a city where she never imagined herself. It wasn't so unusual, then, that she'd gone for those aura classes. After the first one, she returned for a second, and then a third. . . . Lauro made fun of her, saying that a boyfriend would cure her of that quirk. She ignored him, although deep down, she wondered if he was right. Couldn't she just be inventing something esoteric in order to block out more earthly needs?

She was still busy with her salad when Lauro, bored with waiting, opened the newspaper.

"Look," he said. "Since you're into mysticism, this might interest you."

He handed her the page.

"What am I supposed to look at?"

The young man pointed to an ad before returning to his reading. It was an announcement of another lecture at Atlantis, Lisa's shop: "Martí and Reincarnation." She nearly laughed at its audacity.

"Want to go?" she asked.

"No, I've got better offers for the evening."

"Your loss."

A waiter took away the empty plates, and another brought coffee.

"God!" exclaimed Lauro, glancing at his watch. "Let's get the check. We've been here nearly an hour, and I still have three articles to translate."

"We've got time."

"And I need to call the travel agency about the cruise. I wouldn't want to miss seeing the wall come down for anything in this world."

"The wall that was about to fall has already fallen."

"I'm talking about the Malecón wall. When the old Roman lands in Havana in his filmy whites, you'll see what an uproar there'll be on the island."

"Nothing's going to happen."

"Dream on, but I want to be in the front row when the trumpets of Jericho sound."

"Unless there are Chinese cornets at the carnival, I don't know what you'll hear on that island full of lunatics."

The sun was setting. Half an hour after arriving home, she was ready for her exercises. She began turning off the lights until she walked in shadows, where objects were barely distinguishable. It was what she needed. Or, at least, it was what Melisa had recommended at her lecture.

She dragged the dwarf palm from its corner and positioned it against the wall. She sat down a few steps away from the flowerpot, closed her eyes, and tried to compose herself. Then she peeked out from beneath her half-open lids and observed the plant without really staring at it. She recalled the instructions clearly: "To look without seeing, as though you're not interested in what's before you." She thought she could discern a milky outline around the leaves. "It might be an illusion," she mused. The halo grew. It seemed to be beating gently. In, out, in, out . . . like a heart made of light. Could this be the aura of a living being?

She closed her eyes once more. When she opened them again, a lunar radiance surrounded the palm, but it clearly didn't come from an external source. It flowed from the leaves, from the fine, delicate trunk that bent in reverence, even from the earth where its roots were anchored. Cuba, her homeland, her island. . . . Why was she remembering it now? Because of that milky luminescence? In her mind's eye, she saw the moon over the sea at Varadero, over the fields of Pinar del Río. . . . The moon shone differently there, she thought, as though it were alive. Or perhaps she had been influenced by those old folks who insisted that in Cuba everything tasted different, smelled different, looked different . . . as if the island were paradise and she was on another planet. She tried to shake off those thoughts. If her island had once been a paradise, now it was cursed—and curses weren't to be carried in one's heart. At least not in hers.

Exhausted, she opened her eyes. The halo diminished without disappearing altogether. She stood up and turned on the light. The plant, no longer a phosphorescent specter, became, again, an ordinary potted palm. Had she really seen something? She felt like an idiot.

"Luckily no one saw me," she said to herself.

She looked at her watch. In one hour the fourth lecture of the series would begin. She dragged the plant back to its place and turned out the light, then went to her room. She didn't stay long enough to witness the silver clarity still floating around the leaves.

Lauro grumblingly went with her, disappointed at his change of plans for the evening. When they arrived at the bookstore, some forty people buzzed around like frantic bees.

"That gossipy bitch . . ." Lauro muttered, pulling her to the other side of the room and surreptitiously pointing at a young man who was chatting with two women. "I don't want him anywhere near me."

"Hi, Lisa," Cecilia said.

The girl turned around.

"Oh, hi! How're you doing?"

"I brought my tape recorder today. There's a place over there where—"

"I'm sorry, Ceci. We can't talk today, either."

"But I've been leaving you messages for three weeks. I came to the last two lectures but I didn't see you there."

"Sorry, I was sick, and I still don't feel good. If not for a friend who's been helping me out . . ."

A commotion by the door announced the speaker's arrival. At first Cecilia couldn't differentiate her from the group that had just walked in. To her surprise, an ancient woman, nearing the century mark, made her way to the table with the microphone, barely supporting herself on her cane.

"I'll see you later," whispered Lisa as she walked away.

There were no seats left, but the carpet looked new and clean. Cecilia sat down near the door with Lauro.

"Do you believe how he always manages to make trouble wherever he goes?" Lauro whispered into her ear. "When I was in Cuba, he got two of my friends into a fight because . . ." He trailed off. "Oh, I can't believe it! Is that Gerardo?"

He leaped up and shot toward the other side of the room. Cecilia laid her purse on the empty spot, but a few seconds later Lauro motioned to her that he would stay where he was.

The old woman began her lecture by reading from several texts in which Martí spoke of the soul's return after death to pursue its evolutionary apprenticeship. Then she quoted a poem that seemed to attribute her country's suffering to the law of karma, as if the extermination of the indigenous people and the killings of the black slaves demanded a purge, a reincarnation of those souls in the future. Cecilia listened, astonished. It seemed that the apostle of Cuban independence was practically a spiritualist.

When the lecture was over, she tried to approach the old woman, but the throngs of people waiting to speak to her seemed greater than those who had been listening. She gave up and went over to the counter where Lisa was waiting on customers. She couldn't get near her, either. She decided to wait and explore the bookshelves.

Miami had become an enigma. She was starting to suspect that a kind of spirituality remained, which the elders had lovingly tried to rescue from the sacrificial pyre: the glow was just hidden in forgotten little corners of the city, often far from the beaten path. Maybe the city was a time capsule, an attic where the remains of a splendid past were stored, waiting to return to their place of origin. She thought about Gaia's theory of a city's multiple souls.

"Listen, girl, I've been talking to you for half an hour and you're not even looking at me," Lauro huffed indignantly.

"What?"

"Don't even dream of making me tell you the whole story again. What's the matter with you?'

"I'm thinking."

"Yeah, about everything but my story."

"Miami isn't what it seems."

"What's that supposed to mean?"

"It seems cold on the outside, but inside it's not."

"Ceci, *por favor,* I've already had my dose of metaphysics. Now I want to go to Versailles and have my *café con leche,* eat a few *masitas de puerco,* and catch up with the gossip on the Havana Ballet Festival. Wanna come?"

"No, I'm tired."

"Then I'll see you tomorrow."

Cecilia realized that it was just a few minutes until closing. She grabbed a copy of the *I Ching* from the shelves, and, turning around, bumped into a girl.

"Sorry," Cecilia said.

"You're like me," murmured the young woman by way of reply. "You carry the dead with you."

And without another word, she walked away, leaving Cecilia stunned. Another crazy on the loose in Miami. Why was she always the one to find them? Well, that's what you get for frequenting places that attract such types.

"Do you know the girl who just left?" she asked Lisa when she went to the register to pay for her *I Ching.*

"Claudia? Yes, she's the friend who's been helping me. Why?"

"No reason."

She watched her find a bag for the book.

"We could meet Wednesday at noon," Lisa suggested, a bit embarrassed at not keeping her word.

"Are you sure? I mean, the last time I stood around waiting."

"We'll talk at my house," Lisa said, scribbling an address on the sales slip. "Don't bother calling unless you can't make it. I'll be there."

Once outside, Cecilia sighed with relief. At last she might be able to finish her article.

Her car was parked at the end of the block, but she didn't have to get very far down the street to see she had a flat tire. Was it just low, or did it have a puncture? She squatted to examine it, although she had no idea what to look for. A hole? A slash? Or the air could be escaping through an invisible opening. How was she to know what was wrong with the goddamn tire?

A shadow fell over her.

"Do you need help?"

Cecilia blinked. The street lamp behind the stranger obscured his face, but she could tell immediately that he was no criminal. He was wearing a suit that looked elegant, even against the light. She moved aside to glimpse his face. Something about his appearance told her he wasn't American. And in that city, if you weren't a gringo, there was a ninety-nine percent chance you were Latino.

"*Creo que tengo una rueda ponchada,*" she ventured in her Cuban-accented Spanish.

"*Sí, tienes razón.* It's flat, all right. Do you have anything to change it?" asked the man, comfortably leaping from one language to another.

"There's a spare in the trunk."

"Do you want to call Triple A? *Digo,* if you don't have a cell phone, you can use mine."

Lauro had warned her a thousand times: a woman needs to join an auto club for road service. What would she do if her car broke down right on the expressway or in the middle of the night, like now?

"I don't have Triple A."

"Well, don't worry. I'll change it for you."

He wasn't an exceedingly handsome man, but he had his charms. And he exuded masculinity from all his pores. Cecilia watched him as he changed the tire, an operation she had witnessed many times but couldn't imitate if she tried.

"I don't know how to thank you," she said, handing him some cleansing lotion that she always kept in her purse.

"It was nothing. By the way, *me llamo Roberto.*"

"Cecilia. *Mucho gusto.*"

"Do you live nearby?"

"Fairly close."

"Are you Cuban?"

"Yes. And you?"

"Me too."

"I'm from Havana."

"I was born in Miami."

"Then you're not Cuban."

"Yes, I am," he insisted. "I was born here by accident, because my parents left . . ."

It wasn't the first time Cecilia had witnessed this phenomenon. It was as if the genes of the island were so strong that it took more than one generation to disavow them.

"Can I take you to dinner?"

"Thanks, but I'm not sure that . . ."

"If you decide, call me. . . ." He extracted a card from his pocket and gave it to her.

A few streets farther on, Cecilia took advantage of a red light to read it: Roberto C. Osorio. And a line in English that she had to read again. Owner of a car dealership? She'd never known anyone involved in anything like that. It could be an interesting change, the start of an adventure. . . . She had a moment of panic. Change terrified her. The changes in her life had never been good.

She returned to her apartment with no desire to cook. She helped herself to a can of sardines, another of pears in syrup, and a few crackers. She ate standing by the kitchen counter before sitting down to read the *I Ching.* While reading, she thought of consulting the oracle, just to see what it would say. After tossing three coins six times, the hexagram 57 came up: *"Sun"/the gentle (the penetrating) wind.* The message read: "It is auspicious to have somewhere to go. It is auspicious to see the great man." She didn't bother to read the rest of the lines separately. If she had, she might have decided to do something different from dialing the number on the card.

She left a message and hung up. Now all she had to do was wait . . . but not in the loneliness of her retreat.

IF ONLY YOU UNDERSTOOD ME

They boarded the ship, shoved along by the tide of humanity that crammed the docks, but first they had to pay an exorbitant sum: some gold earrings and two silver bracelets. Thanks to the handful of jewels that Kui-fa had rescued, the family managed some space on deck. Before setting sail, they had sold their land and the house, although at a much lower price than they were worth. Jostled by the furious waves, husband and wife made plans, counting the money and jewelry that might help them begin a new life. The other refugees were quite seasick and slept nearly all the time. Or so it seemed.

Two days before they arrived, someone stole their little stash. Although the authorities searched many of the passengers, the overcrowding was so great that it was impossible to carry out a full-fledged investigation. Panic flooded through Siu Mend. He could depend on his grandfather's assistance, but he was terrified at the thought of landing in a strange country with nothing to offer. He commended himself to his ancestors, thinking of the city that awaited him and his family.

The smell of the sea had changed, now that the vessel was rocking gently on the dark waters of the Caribbean.

"Look, Pag Li, there's a full moon," Kui-fa whispered into her son's ear.

They were on deck, leaning against the railing and gazing at the clarity on the horizon. Every so often, a flash of light gleamed amid that resplendence.

"What is that, Father?"

"El Morro." And, anticipating the question in his son's eyes, he explained: "A giant lantern that guides ships in the night."

"A giant lantern? How big?"

"Like a pagoda. Maybe even bigger. . . ."

And he described many wonders to Pag Li. The boy listened in amazement to tales of creatures with black skin, of deities who entered men and women's bodies, making them perform savage dances . . . Ah! And the music. Because music was everywhere. The islanders gathered with their families and listened to music. They cooked to the sound of music. They studied or read, and music accompanied anything that should have been performed in silence or contemplation. These were people who seemed unable to live without music.

Kui-fa stared at the moon, which appeared surrounded by a supernatural halo. Its misty gauziness intensified her sense of unreality. She understood that her former life had disappeared forever, as if she, too, had died along with the rest of her family. Perhaps her corpse now rested in the rice fields, and it was her spirit that sailed toward an unknown island. Perhaps she was approaching the mythical island where Kuan Yin had her throne.

"Goddess of Mercy, lady of the afflicted," pleaded Kui-fa, "calm my fears; watch over my dear ones."

And she continued to pray as dawn broke, and the ship, with its exhausted cargo, drew near the island where gods and mortals coexisted beneath a single sky.

But none of Siu Mend's tales could have prepared her for the vision that appeared at mid-morning, glittering on the horizon. A narrow white barricade, like the Great Wall in miniature, protected the city from the pounding of the waves. The sun tinged the buildings with all the hues of the rainbow. And she saw the docks. And the port. An entire multi-colored, supernatural world. What a bunch of strange people! As if the ten regions of hell had spilled out all its denizens there. And the shouting. And the garments. And that guttural language.

After disembarking, Siu Mend led them through the intricate web of alleyways, guided by his memory. From time to time he would run into a countryman and would ask directions in his own tongue. Kui-fa made note of everyone's expression, including those of the other Chinese. It didn't take long for her to realize her garments were inappropriate for the humid heat of a city where women shamelessly flaunted their legs and wore dresses to reveal, not conceal, their figures.

But it was Pag Li who showed the greatest enthusiasm for such a feast of the senses. He had already noticed how the children tossed coins from one sidewalk to another, and sometimes from the street itself, with the intention of hitting or touching others. He didn't understand the game, but he intuited the pastime's feverishness, repeated on street after street, erupting in shouts and arguments from the players.

At last the family entered a neighborhood filled with their countrymen. The fragrance of incense and boiled vegetables floated in the air, more consuming than the scent of the sea.

"I feel like I've come home," sighed Kui-fa, who hadn't opened her mouth during the entire walk.

"We're in Chinatown."

Kui-fa wondered how she'd ever find her way back to this neighborhood if she had to leave. On every corner was a metallic plate with the street name, but it didn't do her any good. With the exception of the signs in the area, the rest of the city posted an unintelligible alphabet. She took comfort in recalling the number of Asian faces she'd seen.

"Grandfather!" shouted Siu Mend, spying an elderly man, placidly smoking on a step.

The old man blinked twice and adjusted his glasses before standing and throwing his arms open wide.

"I thought I'd never see you again, son."

They embraced.

"I've come back, as you can see . . . and I've brought your great-grandson."

"So this is your firstborn."

He observed the boy with reserve, although his desire to kiss him was obvious. Finally he settled on stroking his cheek.

"And that's your wife?"

"Yes, honorable Yuang," she said, bowing slightly.

"What did you say her name was?"

"Kui-fa," he replied.

"You are lucky."

"Yes, she's a good woman."

"That's not what I meant—I meant her name."

"Her name?"

"You'll have to find Western names in order to deal with the Cubans. There's a very common one that means the same thing as her Chinese name: Rosa."

"Losa," she repeated with difficulty.

"You'll soon learn to pronounce it." He stared at them in delayed surprise. "Why didn't you let me know you were coming? *The People's Voice* published something about some disturbances, but . . ."

Siu Mend's face darkened.

"Grandfather, I have bad news."

The old man looked at his grandson. His chin quivered slightly.

"Let's go inside," he murmured in a thread of a voice. Siu Mend lifted the water pipe that rested by the door, and the four of them entered the house.

That night, while little Pag Li slept in a makeshift bed in the living room, the couple said good night to the old man and went to the room that would be their quarters until they could afford to have their own place.

"Tomorrow I'll go see Tak," whispered Siu Mend, remembering the merchant who had done business with the deceased Weng. "I won't be a burden to Grandfather."

"You're part of the family business."

"But I've come empty-handed," Siu Mend sighed. "If they hadn't taken everything . . ."

Kui-fa's expression caught his eye.

"What's going on?"

"I'm going to show you something," she whispered. "But promise me you won't cry out. . . . The house is small and you can hear everything."

Siu Mend nodded, mute with astonishment.

Deliberately his wife lay down on the bed, spread her legs, and began foraging with her finger in the opening that he himself had penetrated so many times and through which their son had entered the world. A pearly sphere materialized from the reddened flower of her sex, like an insect magically emerging from within its petals. From that cavity, a woman's natural hiding place, came the pearl necklace that Kui-fa had carried with her ever since Siu Mend had left her alone in the sugarcane fields. With that inside her, she had endured that long crossing. They had lost everything except the necklace and something else that she didn't show him. Now she laid the pearls before her husband, like an offering that he received in awe and amazement.

The man looked at Kui-fa as though she were a stranger. He knew he would never have had the imagination—and perhaps the courage—to carry out such an act, and he thought his wife an extraordinary woman, but needn't say this aloud. As he fingered the necklace, he simply murmured:

"I think we can have our own business now."

His wife realized the depth of his emotion only when he turned off the light and flung himself on top of her.

Thus began a completely different life for Pag Li. In the first place, he had a new name. He was no longer called Wong Pag Li, but rather Pablo Wong. His parents would now be known as Manuel and Rosa. And he began to pronounce his first words in that fiendish language, with the help of his great-grandfather Yuang, who for the Cubans was the respectable *mambí* Julio Wong.

The family had moved to a little room nearby. Early every morning, Pablito would go off with his parents to set up the small shop they had bought near Zanja and Lealtad, with the intention of converting it into a laundry. Still half asleep, the boy skipped down the dark streets, tugged along by his mother, awakening only when he started moving things from one side to the other.

They worked until well into the afternoon. Then they would go to an inn and eat white rice and fish with vegetables. Sometimes the boy would order *carita* balls, delicious fritters made of mashed beans. And once a week his father would give him a few coins to take to the Chinaman Julio's ice-cream shop, in order to sample one of his fruit sherbets—*mamey*, coconut, guava—famous for being the creamiest in the city.

When they returned home in the afternoon, they would find Yuang sitting in the doorway, watching the frenetic neighborhood life and smoking.

"Good afternoon, Grandfather." Pag Li greeted him respectfully.

"Hello there, Little Tiger," Yuang replied. "Tell me, what did you all do today?"

And he listened to the boy's tales as he stroked his bamboo pipe. He had fitted that artifact with an enormous tin can, whose top part he cut off. After filling it halfway with water, he sat down on a step. At the other end of the cut-off tin, he placed the smoldering embers. The pipe was a thick bamboo stalk into which he had inserted a narrow tube on one side. Inside that hollow cylinder, he introduced a little balled-up wad of tobacco, lighting it with a rolled newspaper that he ignited from the coals. It was a ritual Pablito wouldn't have missed for the world, despite his fatigue on returning from the store. He didn't change his routine even when school began.

Now that he had to traverse the neighborhood alone, his great-grandfather instructed him about dangers the boy thought imaginary:

"When you see a Chinese man dressed like a rich white, run away from him: most likely he's one of those gangsters who extort money from respectable businesses. And if you see someone shouting and handing out papers, don't go near him: the police might be nearby and they could arrest you for being involved with the union bosses . . ."

And thus the old man listed all possible worldly disasters that lurked in wait. Pablito noticed, though, that his great-grandfather used gentler words when referring to the agitators or union leaders—the "revolutionaries," as he sometimes called them. But even though he tried to ask several times what sort of work those people were engaged in, the old man just replied:

"You're not old enough to worry about such things yet. Study first, and then we'll see."

So Pablito sat down among the children and tried to guess what the lesson was about by looking at the slides and drawings, but his fractured Spanish was an object of ridicule. And although two of his Cantonese classmates helped him, daily he returned home very upset. Despite all this, he painstakingly filled his notebook with symbols and tried to sputter out his half-learned lessons.

In the afternoons, as usual, he went to chat with the old man. More than anything, he enjoyed the stories that seemed like Han dynasty legends. In those tales, there was one character that the boy especially liked. His great-grandfather called him "the Enlightened Buddha." He must have been a great wizard, for although Yuang insisted that he frequently didn't understand what the Buddha was talking about, he never failed to follow him everywhere, and there was always a certain light whenever the man was near.

"*Akún,*" the boy would ask almost daily, in his usual mixture of Spanish and Cantonese, "tell me about the Enlightened Buddha that you fought with side by side."

"Ah! The honorable *apak* José Martí."

"Yes, *Maltí,*" the child prodded, struggling with his *r*'s.

"A great saint . . ."

And his great-grandfather told him about the apostle of Cuban independence, whose portrait hung in every Cuban classroom, recollecting the night when he met him at a secret gathering where he was brought by other coolies, when freedom was still a dream. And he described how, when Martí was still a boy, he had been imprisoned and forced to drag a chain with an enormous ball; and how he had taken that chain and used it to make a ring that he wore always, so that he would never forget the affront to his dignity.

"What else?" the boy would urge whenever his great-grandfather began nodding off.

"I'm tired," he protested.

"All right, *akún,* do you want me to turn on the radio?"

Then they would sit down to listen to the news from their distant homeland, a place Pag Li was beginning to forget.

As the boy became familiar with his new country, Manuel and Rosa grew swamped with customers who, attracted by their laundry's reputation, requested more and more services. Soon they had to hire another countryman to deliver the clean clothes to the clients' homes. Sometimes Pablito helped out, and since neither of his parents could read or write Spanish, he was the one to memorize the descriptions with which they had labeled their clients.

"Take the white suit to the mulatto with the birthmark on his forehead, and the two bundles go to the crafty old lady."

And so he would look for the suit bearing the paper that read in Cantonese *Mulatto with Mole* and the two tied-together bundles with the legend *Old Witch* and deliver them to their owners. Similarly, he would jot down names of the customers whose dirty clothing he had picked up. And right before Don Efraín del Río's very eyes, he wrote *Dumb Fairy,* and on Señorita Mariana's receipt (she always carefully enunciated her name, Ma-ri-a-na, so that the Chinese kid would understand it), he scribbled, with a very serious expression, *Young Lady with One-Eyed Dog,* and on the baker's wife's receipt, he put *Talky Lady.* And so on.

Those first days were times of discovery. Little by little, his classes started making sense. The teacher, realizing his interest in learning, took pains to help him, but that meant assigning him extra homework.

Now he had less time for chatting with his great-grandfather. When he returned home from school, he leaped along the sidewalks, to the songs escaping from the bars where musicians went to play or to eat. Pag Li didn't stop to listen, although he would have liked to hear more of the contagious music that stirred his blood. He kept on going, passing old Yuang's door, and immediately plunged his nose into his notebooks until his mother called him to supper and a bath.

Thus passed many months, a year, then two . . . and one day Pag Li, the firstborn son of Rosa and Manuel Wong, whose friends also began to call him Little Tiger when they found out the year of his birth, irrevocably became young Pablito.

In some other country in the hemisphere it might have been autumn, but not in the capital of the Caribbean. The breeze whipped its residents' hair, lifted the ladies' skirts, and fluttered the flags on public buildings. It was the only sign that the weather was beginning to change. The sun's heat still punished people's skin.

Little Tiger was coming back from the inn on the corner, after running an errand for his father: the weekly *bolita* wager, a clandestine lottery played by everyone, especially the Chinese. Their passion for the game was practically in their genes, and in fact their famous Chinese puzzle, or *chiffá,* which the first immigrants had brought to the island, had permeated and infected the rest of the population. There wasn't a single Cuban alive who hadn't memorized the symbolism of the numbers.

A figure of a Chinese man whose body was covered by all kinds of pictures accompanied by numbers represented the puzzle: at the top of his head he had a horse (number one); on one ear, a butterfly (two); on the other, a sailor (three); on his mouth, a cat (four) . . . and so on, up to thirty-six. But the *bolita* had one hundred numbers, and that's why new symbols and numerals had to be added.

The night before, Little Tiger's mother had dreamed that a tremendous downpour carried off her new shoes. With those two elements—water and shoes—the Wongs decided to play number eleven—which signified *rooster*, but also *rain*—and number thirty-one—which meant *deer*, but could also denote *shoes*. The variety of meanings had to do with the fact that other puzzles had already been invented: Cuban, American, Indian. . . . But the most popular—and the one everyone could recite by heart—was the Chinese version.

Before arriving at the bar where Chiong the numbers runner collected the bets, the boy saw him chatting with a curious character: a countryman wearing a Western suit and tie and with a fine, trimmed mustache, something quite unusual for a Chinese man—at least the ones Pag Li knew. Chiong wore a frightened expression and glanced around in all directions. Was he looking for help, or was he afraid someone would see him? Instinct told Pag Li to keep his distance. While he pretended to read the movie posters, he furtively watched Chiong open the drawer, take out some peso bills, and hand them to that individual. The scene reminded him: "When you see a Chinese man dressed like a rich white, run away; most likely he's one of those gangsters who take money from respectable businesses . . ." Yuang had warned him. Well, the *bolita* wasn't exactly a respectable business, but Chiong hadn't done anyone harm. You could always find him in that corner, greeting his fellow Chinese and offering directions to passersby who asked for them.

The boy sighed. In any case, he mustn't become involved in politics. As soon as the man walked away, he crossed the street and paid the bets like someone who hadn't seen anything.

"Hey, Tiger!"

He turned in the direction of the voice.

"Hi, Joaquín."

Joaquín was Shu Li, a classmate who had been born on the island, the son of Cantonese parents.

"I was just about to look for you. Want to go to the movies?"

Pablo thought it over for a moment.

"When?"

"In half an hour."

"I'll pick you up. If I'm not there on time, it's because they didn't let me go."

Yuang was sitting in the doorway. He greeted the boy with a wave of his hand, but the child ran inside the house.

"Mommy, can I go to the movies?" he asked in Cantonese, as he always did whenever he spoke to his parents and sometimes to his great-grandfather.

"With whom?"

"Shu Li."

"All right, but first take these clothes to the retired teacher."

"I don't know him."

"He lives next door to the man who makes phonograph records."

"I don't know him, either. Why don't you send Chiok Fun?"

"He's sick. You'll have to go. You can go on from there to Shu Li's. . . . And be glad your father's not back yet, because he might not let you go at all!"

The boy regarded the bundle of clothing.

"What's the address?"

"Do you know where Meng's inn is?"

"That far?"

"Two or three houses beyond. There's a door knocker that looks like a lion."

Pablito bathed, dressed, and grabbed a bite to eat before dashing out the door. Along the way, Pablito asked each passerby for the time. He'd never make it. Seven blocks later he passed the inn and looked for the lion door knocker, but he found three identical doors on that block. He cursed his luck and his parents' unfortunate habit of never writing addresses on the tickets. So many years living in Havana, and they still hadn't even learned the numbers. . . . Had his mother said it was two houses past the inn? Or four? He didn't remember. He decided to knock on one door after another until he found the right one. And it was pure luck that he did. Or perhaps misfortune. . . . Or maybe both.

The Rusty Pelican was a restaurant surrounded by water, located at the entrance to Key Biscayne. As soon as she saw the red letters on the unpainted wood, Cecilia recalled it as one of the places her aunt had mentioned. From the immense bridge, it wasn't very attractive. Only the ships and yachts all around it suggested that it wasn't abandoned. But when she entered the cool interior and regarded the sea beyond the glass walls, she realized her aunt had been right: there *were* some dreamy places in Miami.

They watched the sun set from a crystalline fishbowl that isolated them from the summer heat. In the distance, ships trailed their wakes of warm foam on the darkening waters as the buildings began to light up. After dinner, over two glasses of Cointreau, they spoke of a thousand things.

Roberto told her about his childhood and his parents, two immigrants with no knowledge of English who had made their way in a generous but harsh country. While his buddies all found girlfriends and went to parties, he and his brothers worked in an auto repair shop after school, changing tires, taking merchandise out of the storeroom, and answering phones. Somehow or other, he managed to get to the university, but he never finished. One day he decided to invest his school funds in a business . . . and it worked. For the first two years he worked twelve hours a day, sleeping only five or six, but at last he achieved his goal. Now he was the owner of one of the most prosperous auto dealerships in Florida.

Cecilia realized how far apart their worlds and lives were, yet she was fascinated by that smile, his passion for an island he didn't know yet still considered home. And so she decided to keep seeing him.

The following night they went to a club, and when he kissed her for the first time, she had already made up her mind to gloss over his mania for auto races and his obsession with calling the dealership manager every two hours to see how sales were going. "Nobody's perfect," she told herself. She had almost forgotten about her interview with Lisa the next day. That night she excused herself early and went home with a lighter heart.

Lisa lived on the border of Coral Gables, very close to Calle Ocho, but the din of the traffic didn't reach her cozy ochre-colored house. There were plants everywhere, and old, dark wooden furniture. Cecilia turned on her tape recorder, placing it on a table shaped like a chest as she listened to Lisa's explanation. Through the glass door, she could see some blue birds bathing in the patio fountain.

"Generally ghosts come back for revenge or because they're seeking justice for an unsolved crime," Lisa said, "but the inhabitants of that house seem happy."

"So . . . ?"

"I think they've come back because they miss something they don't want to leave behind. The strange thing is that the ghosts always return to the same place, but the house travels all the time."

"Maybe there are other details no one has noticed. Where's that thing you promised me?"

Lisa went over to a sideboard and took out a well-worn notebook.

"Everything's here," she said, handing her the book. "Take a look at it while I go to the kitchen."

The notes were irregular. Some were perfectly legible; others, barely comprehensible; but every page documented a different sighting, with the date, time, and place. The oldest sightings had occurred in Coconut Grove, not very far from the studio apartment where Cecilia had lived when she arrived from Cuba. The most recent noted a section of Coral Gables bordering on Little Havana.

Cecilia was about to copy the name of the first witness when she noticed the date: the dawn of January first, five months after the year of her arrival.

The second one took place seven days later: January 8. Then another report, July 26. And another after that: August 13. Cecilia observed the dates and, despite the air-conditioning, felt a drop of sweat running down her back. No one had remarked on that.

"Do you take a lot of sugar in your coffee?"

"Why didn't you tell me about the dates?"

"What are you talking about?"

"The dates when the sightings took place."

"What for, when there's no coherent sequence? The intervals are irregular."

"There's a pattern," Cecilia emphasized, "but it doesn't have to do with time."

Lisa waited in suspense, afraid she was about to hear something unthinkable.

"They're national holidays . . . or, rather, *bad* national holidays."

"What do you mean?" the girl asked, sitting down beside her on the sofa.

"July twenty-sixth. Don't tell me you don't know what happened on July twenty-sixth."

"How could I not? It was the assault on the Moncada barracks."

"Worse than that: it was the start of what came later."

"And what about the other dates?"

"January first—the triumph of the revolution. January eighth, the rebels enter Havana. August thirteenth, you-know-who is born . . ."

"There are some obscure ones too."

"No, not one."

"Yes, there are," Lisa insisted.

"Which?"

"July thirteenth."

"The killing of those who tried to escape on the *13 de Marzo* ferry."

"April nineteenth."

"Defeat of the exiles at the Bay of Pigs."

"April sixteenth."

"The people who died in the truck."

Lisa tried to recall.

"Which people who died?"

"They were left to suffocate in a locked truck. They were prisoners of war, captured at the Bay of Pigs. Not too many people remember the date."

"And how do *you* know?"

"I interviewed two of the survivors."

Lisa remained silent, still not comprehending what could be inferred from that chronological sequence.

"It doesn't make any sense," she said at last. "Why the hell would a house that appears on unlucky days for Cuba materialize in Coral Gables?"

"I haven't got the slightest idea."

"We should consult Gaia."

"Why?"

"She has experience in this ghost-house business."

"Oh, that's right. She told me she saw one in Havana. Do you know anything about what happened there?"

"No," Lisa insisted, averting her gaze as she said it.

Cecilia knew she was lying, but she didn't insist.

"I'll talk to her. Will you lend me the notebook?"

"Are you leaving already?" Lisa asked, taken aback.

"I've got a date tonight."

"What about the coffee?"

"Another time."

"Please, don't lose the notebook. Make a copy, won't you?"

Cecilia watched the front light go out before she started her motor. On the way home she tried to organize the knot of jumbled ideas pounding in her temples, but only managed an unconnected montage of scenes and faces. She had never taken that stuff very seriously, but now everything had changed: the Miami ghost house had its roots in Cuba.

A TEMPEST GOING NOWHERE

Angela watched the street from her balcony. The morning dampened her nostrils with a frozen taste that reminded her of shadowy mountain vegetation. How distant those days seemed, when she had roamed forests filled with immortal creatures. Now, as she observed the passersby, her youth felt like the shadow of a different life. Had she really spoken with a nymph? Had she been blessed by a sad, forgotten god? If not for the persistence of her imp, she might have believed it had all been a dream.

Two decades is a long time, especially living in a strange land. Anguish beat in her chest whenever she heard the songs of her homeland: "If the songs I breathe here—*ay!*—reach you, sadly, on those shores; they hold my heart, a prisoner of your nearness." Yes, she missed her country, the accent of her people, the placid, eternal life of the hills, where tomorrow didn't exist, only now and yesterday.

Her parents had died beside those foothills. She had promised them she would return, but she hadn't yet, and she carried that broken promise with her like an ancient, heavy bundle.

Juanco, luckily, had turned out to be a good husband. A little irritable, to be sure, especially after he inherited the grocery from Uncle Manolo . . . or the *bodega*, as the locals called it. While she raised their son, Juanco collected money in the hope of opening the only sort of business that excited him: a record company.

"It's madness," she confided to Guabina, a mulatto woman with reddish curls who lived next door. "Can you imagine? He can hardly keep a *bodega* going in this damn neighborhood and he still thinks he can compete with that gringo with his little dog, Nipper."

Juanco had explained to her why it would be so advantageous to open a record company in Havana: the musicians wouldn't have to travel to New York anymore. But she didn't want to hear any of his foolishness.

Angela grew to hate the gringo and his little dog so much that Guabina, an expert in magical matters, suggested doing some witchcraft . . . not on the man but on the beast.

"No more dog, no more frothing mouth," she said. "And afterward the owner will have a fit, for sure. You can tell he loves him a lot: he includes him in all his commercials."

"Oh, Jesus," Angela replied. "I don't want a dead dog on my conscience. Besides, it's not the poor dog's fault—it's those Victrolas they've put everywhere. They're a curse!"

"Not so, Doña Angela. Music is a blessing from the gods, a haven in this vale of tears, a little sip of spirits that sweetens our lives . . ."

"Well, it makes mine bitter, Guabina. And to be honest with you, I think it's driven my son a little crazy!"

"Pepito?" repeated the mulatto woman. "How's it going to drive that boy crazy? He's more alert than ever."

"You're not kidding. Some bug's bitten him, and it has something to do with those songs you hear on every corner all day long."

Angela sighed. Her Pepito, the light of her soul, had been living in another world for weeks now. It all started shortly after he returned home early one morning, half drunk, leaning on two friends' shoulders. She'd nearly had a heart attack when he came home, and she threatened to keep him in at night, but her son played dumb. He smiled in his drunkenness, even though Angela shook her hand before his face like a fan, threatening to slap him.

Suddenly, as might be expected with so much commotion, the imp Martinico appeared in the middle of a Lilliputian cloud, leaping onto a display case full of glazed pottery. At the sight of him, Angela became hysterical, which set Martinico off even more. The furniture started shaking as she screamed—half at Martinico, half at her son—until Juanco left the room, frightened by the uproar.

"The boy's a man now," he said when he learned the original cause of the disturbance, although unaware of Martinico. "It's normal for him to come home a little tipsy. Come on, let's go to bed. . . ."

"A little tipsy?" Angela shrieked, with no concern for the hour or the neighbors. "He's completely smashed!"

"In any case, he's of age."

"A fine thing!"

"Leave him alone," Juanco said in a tone he rarely used, one that halted further discussion. "Let's go to sleep."

And both of them went off to bed, after tucking in their son and leaving the imp frustrated for lack of an audience.

The next day Pepito got up and showered for half an hour until Angela started yelling to find out what was taking him so long. The boy emerged haughtily from the bathroom and left the house without breakfast— something unusual for one who never did anything before quaffing his *café con leche* and devouring half a slice of bread and butter and three fried eggs with ham—leaving his mother in a nauseating wake of cologne.

"He's on vacation," Juanco would explain whenever she complained about her son's sloth. "When he goes back to the university, he won't even have time to blow his nose."

But classes were still two months off, and every morning the young man spent hours in the shower, singing at the top of his lungs: *"For her I sing and weep, for her I feel such love; for you, darling Mercedes, you who ease my pain. . . ."* Or that other song whose whiny rumba plaint drove her crazy: *"Don't cry for her, don't cry for her; she was the great bandoleer; oh, grave digger, don't cry for her. . . ."*

Now, more than ever, she hated the gringo and his little dog. She was sure the army of Victrolas on every corner would drive all of them crazy. Her son had been one of the first victims, and she, no doubt, would be next. How could she enjoy music when it was something she listened to by force, not for pleasure? For the last few years a biblical plague of itinerant troubadours and infernal jukeboxes had invaded the city.

"Master Pepe's problem isn't the music," Guabina interrupted her friend in mid-diatribe one afternoon. "Greater forces are at work here."

Angela fell silent. Each time her friend began to speak like an oracle, some new revelation was produced.

"It isn't the music?"

"No. There's some skirt business going on."

"A woman?"

"And not a good one."

Angela's heart skipped.

"How do you know?"

"Remember that I, too, have my Martinico," the mulatto woman replied.

Guabina was the only person, besides her husband and son, who knew of the imp's existence. Juanco, who had witnessed many inexplicable events, accepted his presence but never referred to him. Her son scoffed at that story, accusing her of being superstitious. Only Guabina respected her curse without fuss or surprise, just another daily annoyance. Angela had confessed to her one afternoon when the mulatto woman spoke of a silent spirit who would appear whenever something evil lurked nearby.

"A woman?" Angela repeated, trying to comprehend the idea: her son was no longer a boy; he was capable of falling in love; he could marry and move far away. "Are you sure?"

Guabina turned her eyes toward a corner of the room.

"Yes," she confirmed.

And Angela knew that the answer had come from someone she could not see.

Leonardo had gone out earlier than usual. Doors opened before him like jewel boxes in a shop of dreams: the neighborhood brothels prepared to greet their customers.

When he reached Doña Ceci's house, the entry door already stood wide open.

"Come in," the owner greeted him, wrapped in the black stole she always wore. "I'll tell the girls."

Leonardo grabbed her arm.

"You know who I came for. Just tell her."

"I don't know if she'll let you in today."

Leonardo looked at the woman with disgust, wondering how she had ever appealed to him. That had been long ago, of course. His blood had run so wild then that his brain hardly ruled his decisions. But now he was looking at the ruins of what had once been one of the most beautiful women in the city. She was just an old lady slathered in makeup who tried to hide the tremors in her hands with the same prideful gestures of her youth.

"I've come because she promised to see me this afternoon."

Cecilia wriggled out of the man's grasp.

"With Mercedes, a promise is no guarantee," she assured him, straightening her shawl. "She's flightier than her deceased mother, may God keep her in His glory."

Leonardo smiled sarcastically.

"In glory? I doubt there's room for women like you there."

Cecilia's icy stare pierced the man's face.

"You're right," she replied. "We'll end up in the same place as men like you."

Leonardo was about to give her back what she deserved, but he shrugged his shoulders instead. The memory of that young girl held his entire attention. He had first seen her when her mother was still alive. Caridad had driven him mad ever since she offered herself to him, bathed in honey. In those days Mercedes was just a little girl who emerged from her mother's bedroom, sometimes half asleep, whenever he came to visit his lover. He never saw her any other way until Caridad died in the fire that had nearly ruined the business. But Leonardo didn't notice her at first. He nearly forgot she even existed because he stopped coming to the brothel. And when he finally returned two years later, his visits were sporadic, always during the early-morning hours, so their paths never crossed.

"She says she can't help you right now."

Doña Cecilia's voice behind him shook him from his reverie.

"But she told me—"

"It's not that she won't see you at all tonight, but she's busy right now."

Leonardo fell onto a sofa and lit a cigarette.

Months before, at barely midday, a friend had insisted that he accompany him to Doña Cecilia's.

"Doña Cecilia's not in," a golden-haired girl informed them as she opened the door, "but you can wait if you like."

The girl wore a nightgown that did nothing to conceal her splendid figure. Leonardo watched her walk away, vanishing through one of the doors. Her appearance seemed familiar to him, but his stunned reverie kept him from recognizing her. Only when he emerged from a room hours later and saw her by the lamplight illuminating the dark patio did his heart leap back to the past. The girl was the very image of her late mother, with a paler complexion and an angelic face. It was already quite late, and he had no time to linger . . . but he came back the following night, requesting to see her.

"The lover wants to rekindle an old passion," Doña Ceci joked. "The mother's not here anymore, but the daughter is . . . and she's much more desirable, incidentally."

"Enough talk . . . go and get her."

"I'm sorry, but Mercedes is with someone."

"I'll wait."

"Don't get your hopes up. Onolorio came to see her today."

"Who?"

"Her protector, her number one man. . . . When he shows up, she has to be at his disposal."

"It's not as if he's her owner," Leonardo began, but Cecilia's expression cut him short. "What's the matter?"

"He *is* her owner."

"What do you mean?"

"He bought her."

"What are you talking about?"

"How do you think I managed to rebuild my house after the fire? Don Onolorio had been drooling over her for a while, but her mother wouldn't have permitted it for anything in the world. When Caridad died, Onolorio offered me a fortune to let him become the girl's 'mentor.' I had no choice but to accept."

"You handed that little girl over to a man?"

"She wasn't a little girl anymore, and besides, Mercedes was thrilled. She always struck me as half-bedeviled."

"Mercedes?" he insisted, recalling the young woman's face. "It can't be."

"I'm just warning you."

Leonardo left at dawn without having seen her. But he came back the next day, and the next, and the day after that. At last, around midnight, Mercedes emerged from a room, accompanied by a man. He was a mulatto with Chinese features, dressed in an impeccable white suit. She kissed him good-bye and went back inside, leaving the door ajar. The mulatto passed by Leonardo's side.

"I know you're infatuated with her," he told him. "Lots of men would get fed up and go off with someone else, but you're persistent."

"Who told you . . . ?"

"That doesn't matter. You can see her tonight, but be careful, and don't get carried away."

Leaving Leonardo with his mouth agape, he crossed the main threshold, followed by a sinister figure who appeared to be waiting for him at the entrance.

"Your sweetheart is free now," Doña Ceci said.

"You're an old snitch," Leonardo accused her. "You didn't have to go around saying who I came for."

"I'm not the one that gives out information. Onolorio has his own ways of finding out what's happening, especially when it concerns his mistress."

At that exact moment someone stepped out of the shadows and bumped against him, practically knocking Leonardo to the floor.

"Good evening," said the boy with a humble expression. "My name is José, but my friends call me Pepe. . . ."

He was obviously drunk.

"Sorry, sir," another young man interjected, struggling to drag his friend away. "We didn't mean to disturb you."

Leonardo turned his back on them, anxious to be with Mercedes, to complete what had already been too long delayed.

"We'll arrange the price later," he whispered to the woman as he walked toward the half-open door.

She had never thought of men as anything but little beasts that were put on earth to satisfy her desires. Other women might dress up to attract them, but for Mercedes, it was they who should adorn her with dresses and jewels. No one ever told her that she'd gotten it wrong; and she never discussed the matter either, believing that such was the natural order.

She didn't know where those ideas had started. After losing consciousness that night, her mind had become a jumble. Only Cecilia noticed the change. She understood her mistake in trying to revive the child with the same honey she had used in the ceremony, but the damage had already been done.

First came that certain expression on Mercedes' face whenever she saw a man. Several times Cecilia had caught her peeking in on what was going on inside the rooms, and later she found her thrashing strangely between the sheets. The girl painted her lips with coffee liqueur, applied sugar to her eyelids to make them sparkle beneath the red lanterns, and wandered naked up and down the halls, wrapped in a golden silk shawl. Cecilia concluded that Oshún's spirit had touched her and she was under her grasp.

But the main problem was that Mercedes wasn't such a girl anymore. Although Mercedes was nearly fifteen, her mother needed to scold her to get dressed. And she had to fend off the customers who offered money for her. Onolorio was the most dangerous. Cecilia felt threatened every time the man walked into her house with those shadowy bodyguards lurking behind him.

Caridad's death two years later was providential. Although the fire had almost destroyed her business, Doña Cecilia saw a way out of her dilemma when Onolorio offered her twice the amount it would have cost her to repair everything in exchange for lifetime rights to that nymphet. He wasn't trying to buy her, of course not. He just wanted to be a priority and have unlimited access to her bedroom whenever he wished to see her.

Cecilia didn't hesitate. The girl seemed anxious to get started in such a life . . . something she'd surely turn to sooner or later, now that her mother was dead. According to the agreement, Mercedes would receive no money for those visits, but Onolorio was pledged to her, and the young woman did with him whatever she pleased.

Very soon, men became instruments to fulfill her whims and to calm what burned inside her night and day. No one awakened anything but pure instinct within her. Not even Onolorio, who never left her side for the first few months, or all the others who came later, including Leonardo, that dandy who always brought her gifts.

Onolorio's visits, which had become more infrequent, picked up again when Leonardo appeared. She suspected that a silent battle for her affection was going on. Onolorio asked her to go away with him, but she refused. She liked her life and the house, which she considered her own, and she wasn't prepared to submit to the will of a single man who might not treat her so well if she were to become his and his only. But her comfortable existence would not last long.

The first inkling of change came about in an unexpected way, like one of those dreams that one later confuses with reality. It happened, as luck would have it, the first night Leonardo spent with her.

At dawn, when nearly all the customers had gone home, there was a lunar eclipse over Havana. Mercedes didn't know what an eclipse was. She just heard the women's racket on the patio, shouting that the moon was growing dark and it was the end of the world. But when she went out to look, she didn't see anything unusual. It was the same old moon, only a piece of it was missing. A few young men, probably students, were trying to calm the women. Mercedes, unamused with the spectacle, went back to her room.

She never found out if the eclipse had unchained some magical powers or if other strange forces were at work.

As she returned to her bedroom, a different sort of creature passed by her side, its face leaving the trace of something that compelled her more than the spirit of Oshún. She didn't think of the apparition as human, although it was, because of the shadowy quality of his gaze. The man fixed his eyes on Mercedes, with an expression like no other. Her inner demon—the succubus that had penetrated her when the goddess's honey wet her lips—withdrew before the gentleness of that face. With all its might, this spirit within her latched onto the beautiful body it had inhabited for years, refusing to relinquish it. The young woman fought against that power, almost suffocating, and it was as if a veil over her eyes had fallen to her feet. For a few moments the world seemed transformed. She repeatedly struggled to throw off the alien will that tied her to a dark, desperate universe, but at last she succumbed to the entity that had dominated her, and she walked past the man, distant and indifferent, as though he did not exist.

Pepe made fun of his mother's superstitions, but only in public. The young man had inherited a sixth sense that, although it didn't allow him to see creatures beyond the world, enabled him to sense omens and premonitions. However, he wasn't even aware of his gift's existence. Rather, he perceived them on a distant, hidden level.

He would dwell on this years later as he reviewed the events that had changed his life the afternoon Fermín and Pancho invited him to a play at the Teatro Albisu. The zarzuela was about the victory of the now-extinct

Spanish army over the *mambí* troops, and although the Republic had already been in place for several years, the boy took the Cuban bloodshed very much to heart. It didn't matter that he was the son of Spaniards. He had been born on the island so he was Cuban.

During intermission, Fermín and Pancho remarked on his grave expression.

"Don't take it so seriously," Fermín whispered in his ear. "It's all history."

"But it lives on here," Pepe answered, touching his temples.

"Cheer up, man," Pancho said. "Look at all the women around you."

José shrugged.

"The truth is, God gives a handkerchief to a man without nostrils," Pancho sighed.

After the show, they invited him to dinner.

"Don't come home too late," his mother had pleaded.

He got home not only very late, but completely drunk and accompanied by his friends in more or less the same condition. Maybe if they had told Angela immediately the reason for his behavior, she wouldn't have been so angry: her Pepito was in love. But falling in love doesn't usually come with the frenzy that Pepito experienced.

After dinner, they had gone for a few drinks. Four were sufficient for young José, who never drank, to want to make friends with every passerby. The world now struck him as a place filled with kind, lovable people. He had never noticed before.

At ten in the evening, and without understanding how, he found himself wandering through an unknown part of the city, escorted by his friends. They stumbled across the threshold of an unfamiliar house. Immediately, the boy noticed a gentleman chatting with a mummy. The mummy wasn't dead, which would have been normal. It was smiling, and when it did, it grew even more wrinkled. Everything was quite dark, except for the red lanterns that filled the patio with shadows. He drew a little closer to see more clearly. The gentleman looked very distinguished, worthy of being a part of such a gala evening. Despite the frustrated expression that hardened the man's features, Pepe felt a sudden desire to count on his good graces.

"Good evening," he said, extending his hand. "My name is José, but my friends call me Pepe. . . ."

The stranger stopped speaking and turned to him.

"Sorry, sir," said Fermín, approaching. "We didn't mean to disturb you."

And he grabbed Pepe by the arm to pull him away.

"If you're going to stay, you'd better shut up," Fermín whispered. "You could get us into a mess."

But José was in no condition to decide whether to stay or go home, so Fermín and Pancho left him with a woman while they went off with others.

"My name is José," he repeated when she sat him down on a bed. "But everybody calls me Pepe. . . ."

He closed his eyes and his speech trailed off. The woman understood that she could expect nothing of him, but, as she had already collected the fee, she let him sleep.

He awoke one hour later, startled by the commotion around him. His head didn't hurt too much, but the world was spinning endlessly. He went over to a basin of water and wet his face. Staggering, he opened the door. The cold dawn air awoke his senses. Where was he? Some red lights illuminated the patio. He leaned against a wall, trying to get his bearings.

And then he saw her. An angel. A creature sent to him by God to lead him to any kind of heaven imaginable. He was astonished at the fragility of her features, but especially by her eyes: the eyes of a sorceress . . . The creature stopped, scrutinizing him with wonder. Her wings moved behind her shoulders with a slow, aquatic quality. Unreal. She must be a water nymph, like the one his mother had seen before he was born.

But the miracle was fleeting. The nymph returned his gaze, afflicted with an old pain, and assumed her previous, hermetic expression, as she walked on by. Only then did José realize that she didn't have wings but a filmy tunic that the night air had lifted above her shoulders.

Half an hour later, when his friends came by to pick him up, he was drunker than ever, after having downed several shots of rum.

Mercedes might have forgotten him, but the man with the shadowy expression returned, and with an unusual gift: roses, and a trio of troubadours who serenaded her on the patio, a first in the history of the bordello.

The devil within her, bewildered by such an homage, abandoned her body for several hours: enough time for Mercedes to be able to speak to José, find out his name and from what mysterious universe he—so unlike any other—had sprung.

José told her of his dreams and of the thoughts buzzing in his head; of impossible images, like those that appear in moments of romantic ecstasy, when one's humanity is transformed. . . . She listened, enraptured, and then, in turn, she told him her dreams as well: dreams that differed from all those she had harbored until then and that emerged from some deeper place within her.

She felt transported to her infancy, to the time when her parents would rock her to sleep, when Doña Cecilia ordered dozens of bars of soap from her father, who was still alive. Because José spoke to her, she became a child again. With him by her side, all the men—with their harsh expressions, cruel jokes, and the smells of the bordello—dissipated into thin air. She was happy—a new kind of happiness—until he went away, and she was once more in the company of mortals and demons. Could she have dreamed it?

That night Leonardo visited her. And Onolorio too. But she had long left her body during those visits. She was detached, indifferent to the ruby necklace that Onolorio had bought for her . . . and it didn't pass unnoticed.

Without her knowing, Onolorio ordered his escorts to stand guard in front of the bordello. Although he hadn't seen Leonardo, he suspected that dandy was to blame for Mercedes' attitude. This was a matter that had to be resolved. It was one thing for the guy to bed her, but quite another for her to be distracted with thoughts of him when they were together. Everything had its limits, and Onolorio had warned him.

Twice he met with Leonardo, who claimed not to have noticed the changes in Mercedes. Onolorio didn't give up. Something strange was going on, and he would watch and wait from four in the afternoon on, when the clients began to arrive.

Luckily, José wasn't one of them. He visited Mercedes at the noon hour, when she seemed relaxed and hardly any clients were in the bordello. But he had already determined to fill his nights with her memory.

It didn't take long for the story of the serenades to reach Onolorio.

Every night a solitary troubadour—or a duo or a trio—would approach Mercedes' window to croon a bolero for the occasion. The first week, Onolorio tried to find the perpetrator's identity. The second week, the thugs went after the wretched crooners, beating them with their own guitars. The third week, he destroyed three bouquets of roses—from an unknown sender, but with the addressee clearly marked—that a messenger had left in Doña Cecilia's hands. The fourth, he threatened to beat Mercedes if she didn't tell him her suitor's name. The fifth, when Pepe arrived just after noon, Mercedes had a black eye.

"Collect your things," José told her. "We're getting out of here."

"No," the demon inside her replied. "I'm not leaving."

His expression pained her so greatly that, for the first time, she explained herself.

"Your parents would never accept me."

"If I accept you, so will they."

The girl fought against the spirit that controlled her will.

"Onolorio won't ever stop looking for us," she insisted. "He'll kill us—"

José gave her a quick kiss on the lips, and the demon withdrew, stunned.

"Trust me."

She nodded, shaken by a deadly anguish.

"Go collect your things," he said. "Wait for me by the back door, but don't worry if I'm a little bit late. . . ."

Because, before he could pick up the suitcases, he had to go see his parents.

Guabina handed her a glass of ice water that Angela gulped down between sobs. Pepe had told her the news, and the poor woman didn't even want to think about what would happen when her husband found out. A prostitute in their home—how had such a thing happened? A well-brought-up boy who was studying for a profession . . . How could the good Lord allow it?

Guabina sat down beside her, unable to offer any comfort. She didn't dare, especially since, right next to the corner where her saints rested, that spirit who alerted her to danger had reappeared. She was struck dumb with fear. There it was, crouching in wait. Something would surely happen if she didn't take measures.

She went over to the white soup tureen belonging to Obba, one of the three "death-dealing" goddesses and the mortal enemy of Oshún. Only she would be able to help her snatch a victim away from that ghost.

She stood before the tureen, banged on the stones, and prayed before the images of the Catholic and African saints that filled the altar. Angela watched her over the top of her handkerchief, trusting in the mulatto woman's powers. The sound of the stones exploded in the room and ricocheted off the walls like crazed, clucking laughter.

An hour had already passed since Pepe had left. Maybe he'd had a change of heart. What man would think of bringing a prostitute to his parents' home? No, José was different. Mercedes was sure he'd return. Some mishap had delayed him. Too nervous to wait in her room, she dragged her two suitcases along the corridor toward the back door. She was returning for the third one when a hand bent her arm, forcing her to her knees.

"I don't know where you think you're going." Onolorio pointed an open razor at her cheek. "No woman—do you hear me?—*not one,* has ever left me. And you're not about to be the first."

He grabbed her by the hair, shaking her so violently that Mercedes screamed, imagining her neck would break.

"Leave her alone!"

The voice came from the patio. Out of the corner of her eye, she saw Leonardo approaching.

"If you don't leave her alone, I'll call the police."

"Now it's all clear!" Onolorio said without releasing her, wielding the razor sharp against her belly. "So the turtledoves were about to fly the coop."

Mercedes prayed that José wouldn't come walking in.

"I don't know what you're talking about," Leonardo assured him, "but you're going to hand that woman over to me right now or you'll end up in jail."

"I'll hand her over, all right . . . as soon as I'm finished with her."

Mercedes felt a chill on her side. Terrified, knowing that she had nothing to lose except her life, which was already beginning to escape, she dug her elbow with all her force into the side of the man, who, surprised, let her go.

With a reaction closer to instinct, Leonardo charged the other man. Both of them were so tangled in each other that Mercedes, too dizzy now, couldn't keep track. As she tried to stanch the blood, something shot out of her insides as if it, too, wanted to escape through the wound. But it wasn't her soul grudgingly separating from her body. Her eyes clouded over. She heard screams—a woman's piercing, terrified screams—but the world was spinning so fast that she fell to the floor, relieved to find a spot where the ground would support her.

Before José reached the door, he knew something terrible had happened. Several women were screaming hysterically in the street, and the police were everywhere.

When he went inside, he had to lean against a wall to keep from falling. Two men were bleeding to death in the middle of the patio. One of them, whose face looked familiar, lay motionless on the cement. The other, an unsavory-looking mulatto, was still crawling on his belly, but José knew he wouldn't live much longer.

The patio was momentarily empty. Women were still screaming in the street, and the police had gone looking for help. José walked over to the only person he cared about. Mercedes was still breathing agitatedly, but quietly.

"For God's sake, what happened?" he muttered, not expecting a response.

The mulatto's vibrating breath reached him from the other side of the patio.

"If I die from this, I swear I'll take revenge on all the whores from the other world," he spat in Mercedes' direction, although she didn't hear him. "They'll find no peace, even in hell."

The man lowered his head, vomited a mouthful of blood, and lay still, nose nailed to the ground.

"José," Mercedes whispered, feeling a warm wave in her chest, and she realized that the cold that had inhabited her for years had left forever with the blood that flowed from her wound.

. . .

Guabina prayed, banging Obba's stones together. Angela had fallen asleep, as though the power of the spell had exhausted her strength. Suddenly, Guabina stopped her prayer. She heard a noise behind her, a guttural sound, and then an unrelated creaking like the vibration of a piece of paper tossed by the wind. She turned around to face her spirit messenger. There it was, squatting as usual, a mute, scar-crossed Indian, assassinated centuries ago, whose soul still clung to that bit of city for reasons she did not comprehend. The apparition began to tremble as if a hurricane were trying to demolish it, and Guabina intrinsically knew that this would be the last time she would see him. The Indian had come to warn her of tremendous danger ahead, but that danger had passed. She gave a deep sigh of relief and she turned back to wake her friend after she bade farewell to the gradually fading silhouette.

While it's true that she never saw him again, it wouldn't be the last time the Indian appeared to someone in that city.

It was raining buckets when she parked her car next to Gaia's house. It was barely five p.m., but the storm had swallowed up the meager light, and changed the sky to night.

Inside, in the dry, cozy living room, Circe and Polyphemus were napping on a cushion that their owner had placed at the foot of the sofa. The cats' purring was audible above the sound of the rain beating pleasantly against the wood. Gaia served tea and opened a tin of biscuits.

"My grandmother used to like to make hot chocolate in weather like this," she said. "At least, that's what she always told me whenever a hurricane was approaching; but since hot chocolate was already an unknown luxury when I was a kid, we'd fry a little bread in oil and eat it while we listened to the squall."

Cecilia recalled how her grandmother Delfina also used to mention drinking hot chocolate whenever a hurricane threatened, but since Cecilia belonged to the same generation as Gaia, her grandmother couldn't offer her a cup of chocolate, either.

"What do you make of the dates?" she asked, after tasting her tea.

"Same as you: that it's no coincidence. There are eight dates, and all of them represent different misfortunes in Cuba's history. Some are repeated more than once. In order to discover why the house's appearances coincide with those dates, I'd check out its inhabitants."

"Why's that?"

"Because the house is a symbol. I've already told you that these phantom mansions revealed certain aspects of a place's soul."

"But which place? Miami or Cuba? Because this house appears in one place, on certain dates related to another . . ."

"That's why we need to find out who's occupying it. Usually it's the people who move from one place to another. I think the house is following the impulses of its inhabitants. That's the link we have to look for: the people. Who were they? What did they do? Who or what did they lose on those days?"

"They might be relatives of any one of the thousands of Cubans who live in Miami," Cecilia ventured, squeezing more lemon into her tea.

"And hasn't it occurred to you that they might be famous people? Actors, singers, politicians . . . people who symbolize something."

Cecilia shook her head.

"I don't think so. No one has recognized them. According to the testimonies, they seem like ordinary people."

Polyphemus was snoring at his mistress's side. He had rolled off the cushion without realizing it, displaced by Circe, who was now sleeping with her paws in the air.

"There's something else you can do," Gaia said when she saw Cecilia getting up to leave. "Mark down the locations on a map. It might give you another clue."

"I don't know if I should keep investigating. I have to actually write my article sooner or later."

Gaia walked her to the door.

"Cecilia, listen to me: you're not interested in the article anymore, but the mystery of the house. Don't impose limits on yourself."

They looked at each other for a moment.

"Well, I'll keep you posted," Cecilia muttered, then turned and disappeared among the trees.

But she didn't leave immediately. From the darkness of her car, she observed her surroundings. Gaia was right. Her interest in the mystery went far beyond the article. The phantom house had, in a way, become her Holy Grail. Without realizing, she had turned it into a source of anxiety, as if she could sense the pain of those souls who were buried in the mansion. She didn't need to see it in order to feel the traces of melancholy left behind at the locations where the house had appeared, or the feeling of nostalgia in the air, bordering on sadness, that lingered after the vision had vanished.

She thought of Roberto. What would he have made of this? She'd wanted to tell him about the house but he always avoided the subject. Each time she tried to bring him closer to her world, he had to make a phone call or he remembered a meeting or suggested going for a drink. It was as if they only shared one area of existence: emotion. Cecilia would begin to feel a sort of suffocation, like being trapped, although she didn't know by exactly what or why. Roberto, similarly, seemed distant and withdrawn when they were together.

She decided to stop by the dealership. He had told her he'd be there until eight. She found him in the showroom where some sports cars were on display.

"I need to tell you something," Cecilia said.

"Let's go to my office."

As they walked, she began to tell him of the house, the interviews, and the visions.

"Why don't we go get a drink?" he suddenly suggested.

"Again."

"Again what?"

"Every time I try to talk to you about something personal, you change the subject," she said.

"That's not true."

"I've tried to tell you about the house twice now."

"I'm not interested in ghosts."

"It's part of my work."

"No, you're you, and your work is something else. Tell me about yourself and I'll listen."

"My work is part of me."

Roberto thought for a moment before replying: "I don't want to talk about things that don't exist."

"Maybe the house doesn't exist, but lots of people have seen it. Aren't you even curious to find out why?"

"There are always people who are ready to believe anything instead of getting involved in more productive activities."

She gazed at him with a look that resembled pain.

"Ceci, I've got to be honest with you . . ."

Instead of walking away, as she had planned to do, she remained in her seat and listened to him for half an hour. He confessed that the whole world of specters, auras, and mind reading made him uneasy. Or, rather, it annoyed him. Cecilia didn't understand. She had always found comfort in things she couldn't see; it meant that one could rely on an arsenal of powers if circumstances became too painful or terrible. But such matters filled Roberto with uncertainty. Finally he said that all those stories were stupid, and that only fools could believe in them. And that's when he really hurt her.

They saw each other again three days later . . . and again they drifted apart. She recalled the *I Ching* hexagram she had consulted the night she decided to phone Roberto. She opened to the still-bookmarked page and discovered, beneath the epigraph that read "different lines," the number nine that she had drawn from the third line but had overlooked in her previous reading:

> *This deep and persistent nocturnal analysis must not be taken too far, as it will impede the ability to make decisions. Once a matter has been duly committed to reflection, it is a question of decision and action. Excessive thought and deliberation will time and again provoke a burden of doubt, and therefore, humiliation, since one will become unable to act.*

That was it. She had been forcing something that was finished. Undoubtedly she had made a mistake, but the realization came too late to console her.

From that moment on, she stopped putting on makeup, eating, and even going out, except to the office. And that was how Lisa found her, slumped on the sofa and surrounded by cups of lime tea, one afternoon when she stopped by to bring her another testimony she had just recorded. Contrary to Lisa's expectations, Cecilia showed no enthusiasm. Her pain over Roberto had shifted the mystery of the house to second place.

"This isn't healthy," Lisa said as soon as she found out. "You're coming with me."

"I haven't missed anything from the outside world."

"We'll see about that. Get dressed!"

"What for?"

"I want you to come with me somewhere."

Only when they had completed half the journey did Lisa tell her that she was taking her to see a fortune-teller who lived in Hialeah. The woman bought products in Lisa's store, and whenever Lisa recommended her, the customers spoke wonders of her.

"And don't even think about complaining," Lisa added, "because the consultation is on me."

Annoyed, but resolved to endure it as best she could, Cecilia leaned back in the passenger seat. She'd pretend she was at a show or something.

"I'll wait for you in the living room," Lisa whispered as they knocked at the door.

Cecilia didn't answer, but her skepticism was shaken when the fortune-teller, after shuffling the deck of cards and asking her to divide it into three parts, revealed the first card and asked:

"Who's Roberto?"

Cecilia jumped in her chair.

"A former boyfriend," she muttered. "The relationship's over."

"But you're still in it," the sibyl affirmed. "There's a redhead who's also connected with that man. She's put a spell on him to bind him to her because she's still obsessed with him. Don't stop calling him; don't let him go."

Cecilia couldn't believe what she was hearing. Roberto had told her of that relationship, which had ended before they met, and it was true that the woman continued calling him because he himself mentioned it to her, but the whole bewitched business . . .

"It can't be," she dared to contradict her. "That girl was born here, and I don't think she knows anything about witchcraft. She works in a company that—"

"*Ay, m'hijita,* how innocent you are," the old woman said. "Women will go to any lengths to get their men back, no matter where they were born. And this one"—she consulted her cards again—"if she hasn't bound him with witchcraft, then she's done it with her mind. And believe me, thoughts are very harmful, especially when they're filled with anger."

The woman threw the cards again.

"What a strange man!" she said. "Deep down he believes in the beyond and in spells, but he doesn't like to admit it. And if he does think about these things, he immediately changes the subject. . . . Very strange!" she repeated, looking up to gaze at her. "You love him very much, but I don't think this one is the man for you."

Cecilia returned her glance so desolately that the old woman added:

"Well, do whatever you like. But if you want my advice, you should wait for something different that will appear in your life."

She picked up the deck again and asked Cecilia to divide it.

"See? Here it is again," she said, pointing out the cards as she read them. "The redhead . . . the devil. . . . There's the job I told you about. . . . Jesus!"

The woman crossed herself before returning to the cards. "And this is the man who will appear, someone who has to do with papers: tall, young, maybe two or three years older than you. . . . Yes, he definitely works with papers."

The woman shuffled the cards again.

"Choose three piles."

Cecilia obeyed.

"Don't worry, *m'hijita*," the mystic added as she studied the outcome. "You are a very noble person. You deserve the best man possible, and he'll appear sooner than you can imagine. The one who will lose what he seeks is the man you're crying over now. Unless his guiding spirits illuminate him in time, he's the one who'll come out the loser." She raised her eyes. "I know you're not going to like this, but you should wait for the second man. He's the one for you."

Nevertheless, when Roberto called, she accepted his invitation to go to dinner with two other couples. She was still tied to him, as he was to her . . . or that's what he told her, anyway: the past few days he hadn't been able to get her out of his mind. Why didn't they go out together again? They could go to that Italian restaurant Cecilia liked so much because its walls reminded her of the Roman ruins at Caracalla. They'd order that dark, rich wine, with its scent of cloves that pierced her nostrils. . . . Yes, Roberto had thought about her when he chose that place.

At first, everything went quite well. Roberto's friends brought their respective wives along, bedecked with jewels but with blank faces. By the time dinner ended, Cecilia was excruciatingly bored, but she was resolved to salvage the evening.

"Do you guys like to dance?" she asked.

"A little."

"Well, I know a place where you can hear good music . . . that is, if you like Cuban music."

The bar was a madhouse that night. Perhaps it was due to the body chemistry–altering heat, but the clientele seemed even more outrageous than usual. When they walked in, a Japanese girl—the soloist of a Nipponese salsa group—was singing in flawless Spanish. She had come to the bar directly after a performance on the beach, but ended up playing with a band of musicians that had assembled gradually over the course of the evening. Three Canadian concert performers joined in the merriment. On the dance floor and at the tables, total delirium reigned. A group of Italians at the next table shouted, some Argentines chatted loudly at the bar, and even a bunch of Irish people were dancing some new variation on the jig.

Roberto decided there were too many people on the dance floor. They'd dance when there was more room. Cecilia sighed. That would never happen. While he went on talking with the men, she withdrew into herself more and more. She felt out of place, especially among those women who seemed sculpted out of ice. She tried to get involved in the men's conversations, but they were speaking of things she was unfamiliar with. Bored, she thought of her old friend. But at the table where the woman usually sat, some Brazilians were shouting like madmen. A cocktail waitress walked by.

"Listen," she whispered, tugging at the waitress's sleeve. "Have you seen the lady who usually sits at that table?"

"Lots of ladies sit at the tables."

"The one I'm talking about is always there."

"I didn't notice," the girl said dismissively, continuing on her way.

Roberto tried to divide his attention between Cecilia and his friends, but she felt lost. It was like tiptoeing through uncharted territory. Three new acquaintances of Roberto's walked over to the table, all of them very elegant and surrounded by women too young for them. Cecilia didn't like the feeling she got from them. It reeked of phoniness and greed.

The song ended, and spirits grew somewhat calmer. The musicians left the stage for a break as the dance floor lit up again. A recording, famous on the island when she was a little girl, played over the loudspeakers: *"Wounded by the shadows of your absence am I, darkness is my only companion now. . . ."* She felt something in the atmosphere, a vague impression in the air. She couldn't figure out what it was. And suddenly she saw her, this time sitting at the end of the bar.

"I'm going over to say hello to a friend," she excused herself.

As she made her way among the dancers who were returning to the floor, she looked around in the darkness. There was Amalia, crouching like a solitary animal.

"A martini," she called to the barman, immediately changing her mind. "No, make that a *mojito.*"

"Lovesickness," Amalia observed. "The only thing that persists in the human heart. Everything ends or changes, except for love."

"I came here because I want to forget," Cecilia explained. "I don't feel like talking about myself."

"I thought you wanted company."

"Yes, but just so I can think about other things," the young woman said, trying a sip of the cocktail just placed in front of her.

"Like what?"

"I'd like to know who you wait for every night," Cecilia insisted. "You told me about a Spanish woman who sees imps, a Chinese family that escaped slaughter, and a slave's daughter who ended up in a brothel. . . . I think you may have forgotten your own story."

"I haven't forgotten," Amalia reassured her gently. "Here comes the connection."

LIKE A MIRACLE

For four months, her injury held her between life and death. But that wasn't the worst of it: the chill penetrating her body since infancy was once again fighting to possess her. It was as if two women lived within her. When José went to the hospital in the daytime, he found himself in the presence of a sweet, timid young woman who hardly spoke; at night Mercedes' crazed eyes refused to recognize him.

The most difficult part was facing his parents' opposition. Juan stopped speaking to him, and his mother complained of chest pains, the consequence (as she said between sighs) of her suffering. But José would not be intimidated by that sort of blackmail.

His credentials as a medical student won him a loan, with which he paid the hospital bills. Nothing would deter him from his goal, and he took comfort in noting that, despite her mood changes, Mercedes was recovering . . . not only from her injury, but also from the sufferings of her soul.

Little by little, her confusion withdrew to a dark corner of her subconscious, revealing an innocent young girl who seemed to be viewing the world for the first time. José was taken aback by her questions: Where was God hiding? Why did it rain? What was the very biggest number of all? It was as though he were speaking to a little child. And maybe that was the case. Perhaps some incident, unknown to him, had forced her spirit out during her childhood, and now that spirit was returning to help her see the world anew.

One night, shortly after he left the hospital, a nurse walked into the room with some water. The girl awoke on hearing the sound of the liquid filling the glass. The light—moonlight—was reflected in it, and the liquid spilled interminably. Suddenly, she remembered everything: the nocturnal ceremony, the honey bath, her fainting spell. . . . She realized that she had been possessed since infancy, and that the spirit possessing her was as cold as an iceberg. She had barely recalled the memory for a few moments when a merciful hand covered it over forever. Her mind flooded with calming thoughts. Her father's assassination became a sudden illness; her mother's ghastly death, a benevolent accident; and her life in the brothel, a long sojourn in the country, where she had lived surrounded by female cousins.

José, the only witness to her previous life, said nothing, not even to her, preferring to keep the real story to himself.

Before he became her husband, José was the father and brother she'd never had, the friend who took care of her and taught her genteel manners; he was also the teacher who taught her to read.

After graduating, he opened his own practice. And she, with nothing to do, took up reading. José was surprised by the books he discovered at their bedside every night: about heroes of the past and impossible loves, mythical journeys and miracles . . . like the one Mercedes herself had wished for. Because the years were beginning to pass, and she understood that, in spite of her husband's love, nothing would make her as happy as having a child. But the ugly scar across her abdomen seemed like a divine prohibition. Could it be punishment for some sin she didn't recall?

After much praying, the miracle finally happened. One autumn day her womb began to swell. And then she knew that her life and her sanity depended upon the bundle that throbbed inside her. . . .

Mercedes stroked her belly and watched the reddish cloud moving through the Havana sky, fleeing a hurricane that threatened the island. With a sigh, she abandoned the balcony.

Lately she had hardly been able to take a siesta, riveted as she was to the radio and the latest soap operas. Today's episode might turn out to be decisive for Father Isidro.

"I love you, María Magdalena," said Juan de la Rosa, her husband's rival, "but I cannot leave Elvira. If she hadn't sacrificed herself to save little Ramiro. . . ."

María Magdalena, so understanding at first, was plotting an assassination that only Father Isidro, her confessor, knew about—Father Isidro, the same man who had been in love with Elvira since childhood and who had entered the priesthood when he learned of her marriage. Now that his beloved's life was in his hands, it seemed he could do nothing to save her, for he was obliged to respect the secrecy of the confessional. And yet . . . would he dare reveal what he knew? Or, at least, would he be able to find some way to do it without breaking his oath?

Mercedes fell asleep. On that windy, overcast day, troubling dreams shook her spirit: icy talons seized her belly and stifled her breathing. She brought her hands to the old wound, but an even sharper sting told her that the pain was coming from somewhere else. She awoke, feeling dizzy. The ceiling vibrated with a muffled sound, as though many bare feet were running across it. Then the windowpanes rattled together in dissonant arpeggios. Mercedes lifted her eyes and saw an outrageous dwarf hanging from the chandelier, the same one she had seen running down the hotel corridors on her wedding day. At that moment it had struck her as very odd that she was the only one who saw him. When, more than a little upset, she reported it to her husband, José, he told her a fantastic story. The dwarf was an imp that only the women in his family were able to see, including the women who joined the family through marriage. But the imp had never shown up again. She had almost forgotten about him . . . until now.

"Get down from there, you fiendish thing!" she shouted furiously. "If you break that lamp, I'll kill you."

But the manikin pretended not to notice; quite the contrary, he duplicated himself so that he could swing from the balcony. Now there were two imps in the house.

"Damned devil," Mercedes muttered, trying to ignore him.

A piercing stab forced her to lean against a small table where she often placed flowers. She heard shrieking behind her and turned around. Now there were four imps. The third one was balancing on top of a painting of the Sacred Heart of Jesus. And the fourth was leaping from one rocking chair to another.

At that moment José opened the door and stopped in his tracks, perplexed. The flowerpots on the balcony were spinning like tops. The painting and the lamp vied with the clock's pendulum in a swinging competition. Four chairs rocked all by themselves, suggesting a convention of ghosts. Then the cause of that carnival-like commotion hit him.

Mercedes' moan roused him from his daze. He ran to pick her up while the apartment trembled with the thud of the painting falling to the floor. Oblivious to everything else, he lifted her in his arms and ran downstairs to the car, forgetting to close the door.

Mercedes was moaning with her eyes shut, and long before they arrived at the clinic, a warm liquid soaked her legs. The pain was agonizing, as if an internal force threatened to split her in two. At that moment she didn't think of the child she had so ardently desired. She wanted to die. At the hospital she ignored the doctor's recommendations and the nurses' exhortations. She just screamed as though they were killing her.

After many long, confusing hours—hands touching her, squeezing her, or comforting her—she heard the cry of a new voice. Only when they brought her a little girl who was bawling like the dickens did she notice the nurses with their enormous nuns' wimples coming and going along the corridors. It took her a few moments to understand that her child had been born in the Católicas Cubanas Clinic, formerly the country estate of José Melgares and María Teresa Herrera, where her mother had worked as a slave until she met Florencio, the coachman who would become her father. Florencio had left that same mansion one night, after delivering his shipment of candles and wine, just before he was murdered. . . . Mercedes closed her eyes to stave off the forbidden memory.

"José," she whispered to her husband, who was leaning over the newborn, entranced, "hand me my purse."

The man obeyed without questioning why she might need a purse just then. She rooted around in the lining and pulled out a tiny package.

"I bought it a long time ago," she said, before revealing what the package concealed.

It was a shiny, little black stone, mounted in a hand-shaped hoop. With a safety pin, Mercedes affixed it to the blanket that swaddled her daughter.

"When she's older, I'll hang it around her neck on a gold chain," she announced. "It's to protect her from the Evil Eye."

Pepe didn't comment. How could he refuse such a strange request when his own mother had spent her life seeing imps and had bequeathed that curse to his wife, possibly even to the little one now sleeping beside them?

"Are you ready to inscribe her birth?" asked a voice from the doorway.

"We prefer to have her baptized."

"Of course," replied the little nun, "but first you must inscribe her. Have you thought of a name yet?"

They looked at each other. For some reason they had always thought they'd have a son, but Mercedes remembered a woman's name that she'd always liked: a sweet name, yet filled with strength.

"We'll call her Amalia."

Part Four

PASSION AND DEATH IN THE YEAR OF THE TIGER

From Miguel's Notebook

Not even the Chinese doctor can save him:

This expression is still used in Cuba for cases of incurable illness, and, by extension, for those who find themselves in very grave situations. It's assumed that the phrase alludes to one of the Chinese doctors who arrived on the island during the second half of the nineteenth century—according to some, Chan Bombia, who landed in 1858, while for others it was Kan Shi Kon, who died in 1885. In any event, it's a sort of popular homage to the Chinese Galens who achieved astonishing and inexplicable cures in colonial Cuba.

AH, LIFE!

After the car pulled up to the curb, the driver got out to open the door. The woman emerged, wrapped in a very tight-fitting green suit, and the man was about to bow, but he contained the impulse, bending only slightly.

"How much do I owe you?" she said, opening her purse.

"Don't even mention it, Doña Rita. I'd go straight to hell if I charged you a single cent. It's been my honor to drive you."

The woman smiled, accustomed to such displays of admiration.

"Thanks, dear," she said to the taxi driver. "May God brighten your day."

And she crossed the sidewalk, heading toward the door whose sign read: THE IMP, RECORDING STUDIO.

The bell startled the young girl who was drawing next to a shelf stacked with musical scores.

"Hello, sweetheart!" The woman smiled.

"Papa, look who's here!" the child shouted, running toward the newcomer.

"Be careful, Amalita!" Pepe scolded as he emerged from the back of the store with some records. "You'll ruin her hat!"

"Isn't it pretty?" the girl shrieked, spreading the tulle across the visitor's face.

"Come, try it on," the woman said, removing the garment.

"You spoil her too much," the man protested, delighted. "You'll ruin her for me."

The actress, normally suspicious of such fawning, shared a special bond with this twelve-year-old creature, and she was transformed before the young girl. The girl's mother also piqued her interest, albeit for different reasons. If the child throbbed like a cloudburst, ready to sweep away mysteries and shadows, Mercedes was the enigma that generated them. She would never forget the night when José introduced them during a performance of *Cecilia Valdés*.

With a vacant expression Mercedes had remarked: "Who could ever have told me that such a pretty lie could come from such an ugly truth?"

The actress was dumbfounded. What was she referring to? When she tried to probe more deeply, Mercedes didn't seem to recall what she was talking about, as if she had never made the remark at all. Rita ran into her again on other occasions, but they barely exchanged a few words. Mercedes lived in her own world.

Amalia, on the other hand, radiated a special charm. Sometimes she acted as though she harbored an invisible friend within her that only she could see. She invented conversations filled with incomprehensible phrases, which Rita attributed to her imagination, although she was fascinated by such creativity nonetheless. It had been only during the past few months that the girl seemed to have forgotten those games. Now she paid much more attention to other details, like Rita's outfits.

"Has Ernesto arrived yet?"

"He called to say he'd be late," Pepe replied, arranging the records in alphabetical order.

"Every time I have a rehearsal, he does the same thing to me."

"Which theater are you going to perform in?" Amalia asked, with an expression halfway between innocence and shamelessness.

"No theater, darling. We're going to make a movie."

Pepe looked up from the records.

"Are you about to leave us for the States?"

"No, my boy." Rita smiled. "Can you keep a secret for me? We're doing a musical comedy."

The man swallowed hard.

"In Cuba?"

She nodded.

"Well, this *is* the event of the century," he uttered at last.

"Let's see if I can guess what's being cooked up behind my back."

Everyone turned toward the man who had just arrived.

"Something you already know about," Rita replied, unperturbed. "The first Cuban musical comedy."

"Maestro Lecuona!" Pepe exclaimed.

"Ah!" the man sighed. "*Now* we're all excited about the project, but these experiments will be the downfall of creativity. They'll squelch talent. . . ."

"The same old story, Ernesto!" Rita cried. "A few of these motion pictures have already been made; we can't be left behind."

"I hope I'm mistaken, but I think this mess will lead to the creation of false idols. True art must be live, or at least it mustn't have so much technical mumbo jumbo. You'll see, soon they'll feature singers with no voice at all. Oh, well . . . Is everything ready?"

"Yes, Don Ernesto."

"Can I go in, too, Papa?"

"All right, but once you're inside, not even one breath out of you."

The girl nodded in silent anticipation. With Rita's hat still perched on her head, she followed the adults into the studio at the back of the store, insulated from noise by acoustical panels. The technicians stopped joking around and took their places in the booth.

Amalia adored those recording sessions. She had inherited her father's passion for music. Or, rather, her grandfather Juanco's, the true founder of the business that he later passed on to his son. José didn't hesitate for a moment before abandoning his medical career in favor of that world full of surprises.

Father and daughter alike were fascinated by the parties that came out of those recording sessions, where they learned all the gossip of a bohemian Cuba at the turn of the century. They heard about the historical gaffe made by Sarah Bernhardt, who, enraged by her Cuban audience's whispering during a performance, tried to insult them by screaming that they were a bunch of Indians in frock coats, but since there weren't any Indians left on the island, no one took it personally, and they all kept chatting away without a care. Or else they'd laugh at the antics of the local journalists, who every night placed a microphone on the roof to broadcast the firing of the nine o'clock cannon, which had been discharged in Havana

since the days of the pirates, reverberating throughout the entire island. . . .
Those were joyful days whose memory they would treasure in years to
come.

Amalia liked going out with Doña Rita, and vice versa; and of late,
whenever Doña Rita felt the urge to go shopping, she would stop by the
store, where the girl helped sort records after school.

"Lend her to me for a little while, Don José," the actress pleaded with
a tragic air. "She's the only one who doesn't torment me and who helps
me find what I'm looking for."

"What choice do I have?" the father agreed.

And the two of them went off arm in arm like schoolgirls, exploring the
elegant shops and admiring the window displays that even the Europeans
envied. Gossiping and laughing, they tried on piles of clothing. The actress
took advantage of the adoration she provoked everywhere she went, asking
the clerks to bring her more and more boxes of hats and shoes, shawls, fur
coats, and all sorts of accessories. Afterward they'd snack on ice cream
and syrup-drenched sponge cake, and sometimes they'd end up at the
movies.

One afternoon, after making a few purchases—including a pair of dainty
shoes for the girl—Rita proposed something new.

"Have you ever had your cards read?"

"Cards?"

"Yes, a deck of cards. Like the Gypsies do."

"Oh! You mean my fortune!"

"And your future, my child."

Amalia didn't know what Gypsies were, but she was sure no one had
ever predicted her future.

"There's someone around here who can do it," said Doña Rita. "Her
name is Dinorah, and she's a friend of mine. Would you like to go
with me?"

But of course. What little girl wouldn't have adored it?

They walked three blocks, crossed a park, climbed some narrow stairs,
and, two doors past the last step, rang the bell.

"*Mi negra,* how are you?" Rita greeted the woman who came out to
receive them, a short blonde dressed all in white like an angel.

"You picked a good time to come. There's no one else here."

Amalia sensed that the actress visited her often.

"Wait for me here, darling," Rita told her as she followed the woman.

Twenty minutes later she poked her head into the living room.

"Come on, it's your turn."

A candle illuminated the darkened room. The woman sat at a little table with a glass of water on it. Before shuffling the cards, she sprinkled them with the liquid and murmured a prayer.

"Cut," she said, but Amalia didn't understand what she was talking about.

"Pick a pile of cards," Rita whispered.

The woman began arranging the cards from top to bottom and from right to left.

"Hmm. . . . Your birth was a miracle, little one. And your mother escaped from quite a. . . . Let's see. . . . There's a man here. . . . No, a boy. . . . Wait. . . ." She chose another card, and then another. "That's strange. There's someone in your life. It's not a lover, not your father. . . . Do you have a special friend?"

The child shook her head.

"Well, there's a presence watching over you, like a spirit."

"This child has always seemed different to me."

Amalia said nothing. She knew who it was, but her parents had warned her not to speak of such things to anyone, not even to Doña Rita.

"Yes, you have a very powerful guardian."

"And very annoying," the girl thought to herself, recalling the imp Martinico and the ruckus he created.

"Ah . . . I see some love affairs. . . ."

"Oh, yes?" Rita grew as excited as if the news was for her. "Go on, tell us."

"I don't want to deceive you," the seer revealed with a somber air. "They will be very difficult love affairs."

"All great loves are like that," the actress declared optimistically. "Cheer up, little one! Good times are coming."

But Amalia didn't want any kind of love, no matter how big, if it would complicate her life. She swore to herself that she'd always remain in her father's store, helping him put his discs in order and listening to the stories of the musicians who came there to make recordings.

"Hmm . . . Let's see: you'll have children. Three of them." She looked at the girl, hesitating to continue. "No, just one . . . a girl." She selected three more cards from the deck. "Be careful. Your man will get into trouble."

"With another woman?" Rita inquired.

"I don't think so. . . ."

Amalia stifled a yawn, uninterested in a man she would never marry.

"My God, look how late it is!" Rita suddenly exclaimed.

"What about my tickets?" asked the woman, accompanying them to the door.

"Don't worry," Rita assured her. "I promise you'll be there on opening night."

José threw an "intimate, cozy" party, according to the note in the society column, for the artists and producers involved in the film. He also sent invitations to a few musicians who were up and coming, in order to establish new contacts.

For the first time he was glad his wife had suggested moving to a house. Initially he had rejected the idea—he'd always preferred high places—but even his mother had supported Mercedes' decision. The old woman was growing tired of climbing those interminable stairs.

"If climbing is hard for you two," Pepe had insisted, "thieves will feel the same way. This apartment is safer."

"Rubbish!" Angela said. "It's your mountain heritage that makes you want to live high up, but we're not in Cuenca anymore."

"I'm talking about safety," he replied.

"It's in your blood," Angela insisted.

But Mercedes was fed up with stairs, and at last he gave in. Now he was pleased with the change. He had a large space for parties at his disposal: a patio that his wife had decorated with earthenware jars crammed full of jasmine.

Under the chill of the stars they set up a table laden with liquor. A gramophone filled the air with melodies. The aroma of the dishes—meat pies, deviled eggs, cheeses, hors d'oeuvres piled high with red and black caviar, spiced eel rolls—piqued the appetites of the attendees. But the most excited one of all was Amalia, who asked permission to stay up till midnight, when the adults planned to leave for the Inferno, an all-night cabaret located at the intersection of Calle Barcelona and Amistad. The child would stay with her grandmother, who was now fussing about in the kitchen, preparing punch for the guests.

Almost everyone had arrived, anxious to share the evening with the great Rita Montaner, who hadn't yet made her appearance, and with Maestros Lecuona and Roig, whose imminent arrival was expected. The clock chimed nine times, and, as if waiting for that signal, the doorbell rang. When Amalia went to open it, there was a suspenseful pause where some people finished the last sip of their drinks or polished off their sandwiches.

The night breeze blew through the jasmine. A discernible change came over the atmosphere, and some looked around to determine the cause. A spontaneous gasp rose from the multitude. Draped in a pearl-gray gown, with a silvery shawl around her shoulders, the silhouette of a goddess appeared on the threshold. Flanked by the two musicians, the actress crossed the room.

Amalia was as amazed as the others, savoring the enchantment, but she soon realized that the magic didn't originate in the diva. Her glance was drawn to an object: the mantle covering her shoulders. She had never seen anything so beautiful. It didn't look like cloth, but rather like a piece of liquid moonlight.

"Oh, what *is* that you're wearing?" the girl whispered to her when she finally managed to make her way through the crowd of admirers.

Rita smiled.

"Mexican blood."

"What?"

"I bought it in Mexico. They say that silver flows from the earth there as blood does from the people."

And, noticing Amalia's expression, she removed the amorphous bit of quicksilver and placed it over the child's head.

A deadly silence spread throughout the patio. Even Don José, who had been about to reprimand his daughter for monopolizing the guest of honor, was speechless. As soon as the shawl covered Amalia, an otherworldly clarity radiated from her skin.

"It's so heavy," the girl whispered, feeling the weight of hundreds of small metallic scales.

"It's pure silver," its owner informed her. "And it's bewitched."

"Really?" the child inquired, interested.

"With a spell from the time when the pyramids were covered with blood and flowers. 'If the mantle of light comes in contact with a talisman of shadows in the presence of two strangers, they will love each other forever.'"

"What's a talisman of shadows?"

"I don't know," the woman sighed. "I never asked the person who sold it to me. But it's a very lovely legend."

The girl fingered the shawl, which draped obediently between her fingers. She felt a force emanating from the garment and penetrating her body, making her feel both frightened and euphoric.

"Dear God, what is this?" she thought.

"How pretty you look," Rita said, pushing her toward the mirror in the entryway. "Run, go and look."

As Amalia turned her back on Rita, the guests caught their breath after witnessing the metamorphosis.

In front of the mirror, Amalia recalled the story of the runaway princess who hid beneath a donkey skin during the day but kept one suit of sunlight and another of moonlight that she secretly donned every night. That was how she met the prince who would fall in love with her. . . . She enveloped herself in that icy beauty, feeling more protected beneath the weight of the cloth.

The doorbell rang twice, but no one seemed to hear it. Amalia went to open the door.

"Does the retired schoolteacher live here?" asked an unfamiliar voice.

"Who?"

She drew a little closer to make out the shadow lurking in the doorway, but all she saw was a Chinese boy with a bundle of clothing in his hands. The jet amulet she wore around her neck came loose from its setting and fell at the young man's feet. He hurriedly picked it up. Accidentally, his fingers brushed the silvery fabric.

He raised his face to look at her, and at that moment he saw none other than the Goddess of Mercy herself, she whose features all mortals adore. She took back the stone with trembling hands. She had just met her prince.

Coral Castle: a magical name for a forgotten corner of misty Miami. That's what Cecilia thought as she gazed at the horizon. Her great-aunt had convinced her to go there in order to see "the eighth wonder of Miami." And as they traveled south, she noticed the flocks of ducks on those man-made rivers that paralleled the streets, kissing the patios of the houses. "Miami, city of canals," she mentally baptized it, thus endowing it with a certain Venetian, and even vaguely extraterrestrial, quality that reminded her of Schiaparelli's *canali.* Not such a far-off comparison for that quasi-tropical city that hosted Renaissance fairs where anything could happen.

She awoke from her daydream when her aunt pulled in beside a rough, medieval-looking wall guarding what resembled a tiny fortress more than one of the castles of Ludwig II, the mad king of Bavaria. The structure looked undeniably surreal, like one of Lovecraft's visions, with all their esoteric, astronomical symbols. And that energy . . . it was impossible not to feel it. It flowed from the ground like a current that could rise to the top of one's head. Who the devil could have built such a thing? And for what purpose?

She glanced at the brochure. It had been built by Edward Leedskalnin, born in Lithuania in 1887. The day before his wedding, his fiancée had informed him she wouldn't marry him, and he fled, brokenhearted, to other lands. Suffering from tuberculosis, and after much travel, he decided to move to Florida, where the climate was good for his health.

"He was obsessed with her," Loló said, sitting down in a stone rocking chair and observing the interest with which her niece studied the brochure. "That's why he built this place. Some said he was crazy, others that he was a genius. I think it's possible he was both things at once."

Crazy or not, the man had sought a spot in which to build a monument to his love. Thus, he devoted himself to the task of raising that fortress during the 1920s. The rocks, carved in the shape of household or architectural objects, lent it a peculiar, dreamlike appearance. In the bedroom there was a bed for him and his lost sweetheart, two little beds for children, and even a stone cradle that actually rocked. Nearby was a gigantic sculpture known as the Obelisk, as well as a sundial that marked the hours from nine in the morning until four in the afternoon. And there was the Nine Ton Door: an irregular rock that revolved—through a miracle of engineering—like the door of a modern hotel. But the two places that most fascinated Cecilia were the Fountain of the Moon and the Northern Wall. The first had three sections: two lunar-shaped sickles and a fountain in the shape of the moon, with a little island in the form of a star. The Northern Wall was crowned with several sculptures: the crescent moon; Saturn, with its rings; and Mars, with a tiny tree carved on its surface, a tribute to the life that might exist there. Observing the Heart Table, where a jungle geranium bloomed, Cecilia suspected she understood the origin of his obsession with carving immense rocks: perhaps the only way that man could deal with his anguish was by turning his love into stone.

"These are his tools," the old woman remarked, entering a room.

Cecilia saw a jumble of iron, pulleys, and hooks. Nothing heavy or particularly large.

"It says here," Cecilia observed, reading from her brochure, "that there are more than one thousand tons of rock, including the walls and the tower. The average weight of the stones is six and a half tons, and some of them weigh more than twenty tons. It would be impossible to move all this without a crane."

"But he did," Loló affirmed, "and nobody could figure out the secret. He worked at night, in the dark, and when visitors showed up, he wouldn't go back to work until they'd left."

Cecilia wandered around the place, mesmerized by the stones' radiance. She could almost see it gleaming from every rock, surrounding them with a translucent, slightly purplish, halo.

"What's wrong?" her aunt asked. "You're silent all of a sudden."

"I'd better not say. You'll think I'm crazy."

"I'll be the one to decide what I think."

"I see a halo around the stones."

"Oh, is that all?" The old woman seemed disappointed.

"Aren't you surprised?"

"Not at all. I see it too."

"You do?"

"It always appears in the afternoon, but hardly anyone notices it."

"What is it?"

Loló shrugged. "Some sort of energy. It reminds me of Delfina's aura, bless her soul."

"My grandmother had a halo?"

"Just like that one." Loló pointed toward the Fountain of the Moon. "Quite strong, because Demetrio's is lighter—a little diluted, I'd say."

"Well," Cecilia remarked, doubting her own sanity for taking her aunt seriously, "it's not so strange that you can see it, but what about me? The family's gift of sight ended with you and with my grandmother."

"These things are always inherited."

"Not in my case," Cecilia assured her. "Maybe it's the exercises."

"What exercises?"

"For seeing the aura."

Cecilia assumed that the old woman didn't know what she was talking about because she remained silent for a few seconds.

"And where exactly did you learn that?" she asked at last, in a tone that left no doubt of her understanding.

"In Atlantis. Do you know the place?"

"I didn't know you were interested in esoteric bookstores."

"It happened by chance. I was doing research."

And as they approached the Florida Table, Cecilia told Loló about the phantom house.

When Cecilia crossed the threshold, setting off the bells in the doorway, the fragrance of roses overcame her. The young woman behind the counter wasn't Lisa, but rather Claudia, the one she had bumped into after the lecture on Martí. Cecilia was about to turn and leave, but she remembered what she had come for and headed to the shelf where she had seen several books on enchanted houses. She chose two and went over to the cash register. Maybe the cashier wouldn't remember her. Without saying a word, she handed her the books and watched Claudia's hands as she wrapped them.

"I know you were frightened the other night when I told you that you were walking among the dead," Claudia said without raising her eyes, "but you don't have to worry. Yours aren't like mine."

"And what are yours like?" Cecilia boldly ventured.

Claudia sighed.

"I had one that was especially awful when I was living in Cuba: a mulatto who hated women. It seems he was murdered in a brothel."

"And they say there's no such thing as coincidences," Cecilia said to herself.

"He was a very disagreeable dead man," Claudia went on. "Luckily, he stopped stalking me after a few months. When I left the island, I also stopped seeing a mute Indian who warned me of misfortunes."

Cecilia was speechless. Guabina, Angela's friend, also had a spirit that warned her of danger, although she couldn't remember if it was an Indian. Once more she recalled Mercedes' mulatto lover, the one who was so jealous . . . but what was she thinking? How could they be the same spirits?

"Don't worry," Claudia insisted, noting her expression. "You have nothing to fear from yours."

But Cecilia didn't much like the idea of walking among the dead, not even if they were her own or if they had good intentions. And less so if suddenly the whole matter was about to turn into something even more mysterious when similar dead people appeared to women who didn't know one another. Or did they?

"Do you know a woman called Amalia?"

"No, why?"

"Your dead . . . do you know anything else about them?"

"Only Ursula and I could see them. Ursula's a nun who's still in Cuba."

"Were you a nun?"

The other woman blushed.

"No."

For the first time, Claudia seemed to lose her desire to talk and brusquely handed over the books to Cecilia, who now felt perplexed by her demeanor. What had she done to bring about such a change? Maybe her question had awakened some memory. Many painful stories resided on the island.

Corners of her childhood sprang to mind: the feel of the sand, the wind whipping along the Malecón. . . . She had struggled to forget her city, to exile a memory that was half nightmare, half longing, but the effect Claudia's words produced in her proved she hadn't really succeeded. All roads led to Havana, she thought. It didn't matter how far she might travel: one way or another, her city managed to catch up with her.

Good God! Could she be a masochist without knowing it? How could she hate something and long for it at the same time? So many years in that inferno must have burned out her brain. But didn't people go crazy when they were so alone? Now she was beginning to feel nostalgic for her city, that place where she had known only an agonizing fear that never abandoned her. *"You are always with me, in my sadness. You are in my agony, in my suffering. . . ."* She must really be out of her mind, thinking in boleros! Whatever happened to her, good or bad, was set to music. Even her memories of Roberto. That's how she'd been living lately, with her soul split in two parts she couldn't forget: her city and her lover. And so she carried them, as the bolero went, very close to her heart.

LOVE ME DEEPLY

The paper lion moved along like a serpent, attempting to bite an old man who walked ahead of it, making faces. It was the second year in which the traditional Lion Dance had branched out of Chinatown and joined the Havana Carnival festivities. But the Cubans saw a different sort of creature in the lion that twisted and turned to the sound of cornets and cymbals advancing toward the sea.

"Mama, let's go see the Dragon Parade," Amalia begged her mother.

It wasn't that she was so interested in seeing the gigantic puppet that sometimes jumped convulsively when one of the Chinese men underneath it got caught up in the distant rhythm of the drums. All she knew was that Pablo was waiting for her on the corner of Prado and Virtudes.

"We can go tomorrow," her father said. "The parade must have already left Zanja."

"Doña Rita told me it was more fun to see it on Prado," Amalia insisted. "That's where the Chinese people forget to follow the maracas when they start to hear the congas at the Malecón."

"They're not maracas, child—" corrected her father, who couldn't stand it when musical instruments were called by the wrong names.

"It's the same thing, Pepe," Mercedes interrupted. "In any case, that Chinese music makes an infernal noise."

"If we keep arguing, I won't get to see anything," Amalia shrieked.

"All right, all right . . . Let's go!"

They walked down Prado, sweating profusely. February is the coolest month in Cuba, but—unless a cold front comes along—Carnival crowds could melt an iceberg in seconds.

They approached Virtudes, surrounded by a throng of people dancing and blowing whistles. Amalia dragged her parents in the direction of a signal that was audible to her heart. She herself didn't know where it was coming from, but her instinct seemed to guide her. She didn't stop until she saw Pablo, eating an ice cream in the middle of the street.

"We can stop here," she decided, letting go of her mother's hand.

"There are too many people," Mercedes complained. "Wouldn't it be better to go over toward the bay?"

"It's worse there," the girl assured her.

"But, child . . ."

"Pepe!"

The shout came from a doorway where several men were drinking beer.

"It's the maestro," Mercedes whispered to her husband, who seemed more bewildered than she was.

"Where? I don't see him."

"Don Ernesto!" she waved, walking toward him.

Only then did Pepe see him. Amalia followed her parents, annoyed at the coincidental meeting keeping her from her goal.

"Can you guess who's written me from Paris?" the musician asked, after an effusive handshake.

"Who?"

"My old piano teacher."

"Joaquín Nin?"

"It seems he's planning to return next year."

Amalia's gaze wandered among the multitude, searching for those dark, slanted eyes that had stayed with her since that night at her front door. She saw their owner, absorbed in studying the convertibles that joined the parade of carriages a few blocks farther down. Taking advantage of her parents' distraction, and before anyone could notice, she ran up to Pablo.

"Hi!" she greeted him, tapping him lightly on the shoulder.

The surprise on the boy's face turned into a joy he couldn't conceal.

"I thought you wouldn't come," he said, not daring to add anything more.

The three adults who were with him turned around.

"Good afta-noon," said one of the men in a tone that was supposed to be friendly but which didn't hide his distrust of the white young lady.

"Papa, Mama, *akún,* this is Amalia, the record maker's daughter."

"Ah!" the man said.

The woman uttered something that sounded like "Aha!" and the oldest man simply scrutinized her with a displeased expression.

"Who'd you come with?" Pablo asked.

"With Mama and Papa. They're over there, with some friends."

"And they leave girl alone?" the woman asked.

"Well, they don't know I'm here."

"That not good," said the Chinese woman with her terrible accent. "Parents must watch daw-tah."

"Ma!" the boy hissed.

"We came to watch the Dragon Parade," she said, in the hope of making them forget their obvious displeasure.

"What's that?" the boy asked.

"You don't know?" she asked incredulously, and as they all continued to stare at her with a vacant expression, she continued, "A few people move an orange dragon . . . like that . . ." And she tried to imitate the swaying of the paper creature.

"It not dla-gon, it lion," the woman replied.

"And it not pa-lade, it dance," the old man grumbled, even more annoyed now.

"Amalia!"

The call couldn't have come at a more opportune moment.

"I've got to go," she muttered.

And, anguished, she escaped to the doorway where her parents stood.

"*Now you see* what these Cuban girls are like," said his mother in Cantonese after Amalia had disappeared among the crowd. "They're not raised properly."

"Well, we have no reason to worry," commented Great-grandfather Yuang in his language. "Pag Li will marry the daughter of genuine Cantonese . . . right, son?"

"There aren't many of those on the island," the boy dared to reply.

"I'll send for one from China. I still have many contacts there."

Pablito felt a knot in his throat.

"I'm tired," Kui-fa complained. "Grandfather, wouldn't you like to go home?"

"Yes, I'm hungry."

Far from lessening, the crowd grew along the route. The city swarmed during those days, the air swelled with parades, and Chinatown was no exception. The arrival of the Lunar New Year, which almost always fell in February, had contributed to the grand commotion. The Chinese joined the city festivities while also organizing their own celebration.

Nearly everyone had finished their preparations for the close of another Year of the Tiger. Even more than in previous years, Pablo's mother had taken great pains with every detail. New suits hung on their hangers, ready to be inaugurated. Crisp strips of red paper dangled from the walls, with letters that invoked good fortune, wealth, and happiness. And days ago she had rubbed the God of the Hearth's lips with plenty of molasses, sweeter than honey, so that her words would arrive in heaven sufficiently sweetened.

Throughout the entire neighborhood, little colored lanterns waved in the winter breeze. They were everywhere: in the doorways of businesses, on the clotheslines strung from one sidewalk to another, on solitary lampposts . . . Rosa had also hung some of them from two posts at the threshold of the front door.

The old man smiled at the lanterns and breathed the familiar odors of the neighborhood where he had lived for so many years. He recalled his wanderings through the countryside of that island where he had risked his hide in the company of other *mambises,* throwing themselves on the enemy, their bare machetes in the air.

"Good night, Grandfather," said Siu Mend, waiting for the old man to enter.

"Good night. . . ."

The squeal of tires on asphalt interrupted their leave-taking. The Wongs turned and saw a black car that had stopped at the corner. From the open windows, two white men began firing at three Asians who were chatting beneath a street lamp. One of the Chinese men fell to the ground. The others shielded themselves behind a fruit stand, shooting back at their assailants.

Siu Mend grabbed his wife and son, forcing them to lie on the sidewalk. The old man was already huddled in a corner of the doorway. The screaming throughout the neighborhood could be heard above the exchange of gunfire. A few passersby, too terrified to think, ran from one side to the other in search of a hiding place.

At last the car disappeared around the corner with another squeal of tires. Little by little, the people began to peer out of their hiding places. Siu Mend helped his wife stand up. Pablito went over to help his great-grandfather.

"They're gone now, *akún* . . ."

"Goddess of Mercy," the woman cried in her language. "Those gangsters will bring tragedy to the neighborhood."

"Akún?"

The old man was still huddled on the sidewalk. Manuel went over to pick him up, but the effort made him groan. Wong Yuang, who had so often defied danger, had just been struck down by a bullet not even intended for him.

The Lunar New Year arrived without celebrations for the Wong family. While the old man was dying in the hospital, the entire neighborhood paraded through the house with gifts and miracle cures. Despite their generosity, the hospital bills were excessive. Two doctors offered their services free of charge, but even that proved insufficient. Then Siu Mend, alias Manuel, thought they could use an extra salary at home. He remembered the kitchen at El Pacífico, a restaurant filled with the most delicious aromas in the world, and went to ask humbly for the lowliest possible job for his son. Any questions about the boy's commitment were just a formality, since the whole community already knew about his dying grandfather. He would begin work the next day.

"Hurry up, Pag Li," his mother chided him that morning. "You can't be late your first week."

Pablito scurried over to the table and sat down. He quickly said his prayers and attacked his bowl of fish and rice with chopsticks. The boiling tea burned his tongue, but he liked that sensation early in the morning.

Siu Mend had never been especially religious, but now he prayed every morning before the image of San-Fan-Kon, a saint who didn't exist in

China but who was an omnipresent figure on the island. And so Pag Li left him to his devotions as he went to his room in search of his shoes. As he fastened them, he recalled the story his now dying great-grandfather had told him about the saint.

Kuan Kong was a brave warrior who had lived during the Han dynasty. When he died, he turned into an immortal whose reddish face reflected his proven loyalty. When the first Chinese arrived on the island, an immigrant who lived in the central area affirmed that Kuan Kong had appeared to him to announce he would protect anyone who shared his food with his unfortunate brothers. The news spread throughout the country, but in Cuba there already lived another holy warrior named Shangó, who dressed in red and had arrived on the ships coming from Africa. Soon the Chinese believed that Shangó must be an avatar of Kuan Kong, a sort of spiritual brother of a different race. Shortly thereafter, the saint became the dual figure Shangó–Kuan Kong. Later he turned into San-Fan-Kon, who protected everyone equally. Pablo had also heard another version of the story, in which San-Fan-Kon was the badly pronounced name of Shen Guan Kong ("the ancestor Kuan, who is venerated in life"), whose memory some of his compatriots had vulgarized. The young man suspected that, at this rate, even more versions of the mysterious saint's origins might appear.

He thought about all this as he listened to his father's prayers. When he left the room, his mother was just finishing breakfast. Siu Mend drank a little tea, and then they all put on their jackets and left.

His parents walked in silence, their mouths puffing vapor. The boy tried to forget the cold, peeking curiously into doorways that allowed a glimpse of their interior patios. Sheltered from intrusive glances, early risers moved with the slow motion of the morning exercises Pablo had practiced so often with his great-grandfather.

On any other day Pablo would have gone to school in the morning and worked in the afternoon. But on this particular Saturday the family said their good-byes in front of the building, and the boy went upstairs to begin his first day of work. He was to light the ovens, clean and chop vegetables, wash kettles, take merchandise out of boxes, and do anything else that needed doing.

By mid-morning, a cloud floated over the kitchen with the aroma of steaming, sticky rice, pork cooked in wine and sugar, shrimp sautéed with dozens of vegetables, and the pale green tea that accentuated all these flavors on one's palate. . . . Heaven must surely smell like this, Pablo thought: a bewitching, delicious mixture that squeezes your insides and unleashes an enormous appetite.

From the corner of his eye, the young man observed the cooks' skill and efficiency, constantly squabbling and whipping the most sluggish ones. Pablo never had problems, except for one day, when he had already been working there for several months. Normally he carried out his tasks with the greatest dedication, but that morning he seemed more distracted than usual. It wasn't his fault. He had received a note from Amalia, which he read standing by the kettles where the soups were cooking:

Dear Friend Pablo:

Well, I guess I can call you a friend now, right? I was very happy to meet your family. If you're free one afternoon, maybe we could get together and talk for a while, if you want to, because I'd like to know more about you. Today, for example, my parents won't be home after 5 p.m. It's not that I'm trying to invite anyone when they're not home (since there's nothing wrong with talking to a friend), but I think we could talk better without adults around.

Affectionately,
AMALIA

He read the note three times before putting it away and going back to his chores, but his mind was in the clouds and, at the height of his daydreaming, he dropped a load of fish in the kitchen. His supervisor delivered a blow to his head that knocked away any further desire to dream.

No one was home when he arrived. He remembered that his parents had planned to go to the hospital to look in on Grandfather, who had been readmitted the night before due to complications from the wound, which never seemed to heal altogether, but he didn't wait around for news. He bathed, changed clothes, and left. He couldn't avoid glancing at the doorway where the old man used to sit, and he felt a burning in his heart. He revived somewhat at the idea of seeing that strange girl again, the same one who occupied his thoughts both night and day.

Once more, he was confused by the doors with identical knockers; he stood there, uncertain, not knowing what to do. The third door on his left opened up right in his face.

"I *thought* you'd get lost!" Amalia greeted him, adding candidly, "That's why I was watching."

Pablo entered shyly, although his embarrassment didn't show.

"And your parents?"

"They went to meet a musician who's arriving from Europe. My grandma went along with them. . . . Sit down. Want some water?"

"No, thanks."

Instead of calming him, the girl's cordiality made him more nervous.

"Let's go into the living room. I want to show you my music collection."

Amalia went over to a box from which a sort of giant horn emerged.

"Did you ever hear Rita Montaner?"

"Of course," said Pablo, almost offended. "Do you have any of her songs?"

"Yes, and also the Trío Matamoros, Sindo Garay, the Sexteto Nacional . . ."

She kept on reciting names, some familiar and others that he was hearing for the first time, until he interrupted her:

"Play whatever you want."

Amalia placed a record disc on top of the box and carefully lifted the mechanical arm.

"Love me deeply, my sweet love, for I'll always adore you. . . ." rang a clear, tremulous voice through the speaker.

For a few moments they listened in silence. Pablo watched the girl, who, for the first time, seemed inhibited.

"Do you like movies?" he ventured.

"A lot," she replied, perking up.

And they began comparing films and actors. Two hours later, neither one of them could control their amazement at the other creature before them. When she lit the lamp, Pablo realized how late it was.

"I have to go."

His parents didn't know where he was.

"We could see each other again," he suggested, brushing the girl's arm.

And suddenly she felt a wave of heat spreading through her body. The boy, too, noticed that headiness. . . . Ah, the first kiss. That fear of losing oneself in dangerous lands, that whiff of the soul that could easily die if destiny were to take an unforeseen turn. . . . The first kiss can be as terrifying as the last.

Above their heads the lamp began to sway, but Pablo didn't notice it. Only the crash of something smashing into pieces jolted him back to reality. Beside them lay the ruins of a broken piece of porcelain.

"Are they home already?" Pablo whispered, terrified at the possibility that the aggressor might be his girlfriend's father.

"It's that idiot Martinico, up to his old tricks."

"Who?"

"I'll tell you another time."

"No, tell me now," he insisted, staring at the inexplicable destruction. "Who else is here?"

Amalia hesitated slightly. She didn't want this dream before her to evaporate because of some ghost story, but she could tell by the boy's face, he wouldn't tolerate excuses.

"There's a curse on my family."

"A what?"

"An imp that pursues us."

"And what's that?"

"A kind of spirit . . . a dwarf who appears at all the most inconvenient times."

Pablo remained silent, not knowing how to digest her explanation.

"It's like a spirit that's inherited," she explained.

"Inherited?" he repeated.

"Yes, and damn that inheritance. Only our women are affected by it."

Contrary to what she had expected, Pablo took the news quite naturally. Among the Chinese, stranger things were thought to be true.

"Go on, explain it all to me," he asked, curious.

"I inherited it from my papa. He can't see it, but my grandmother can. And Mama can, too, since she's his wife."

"Do you mean any woman can see the imp if she marries a man in the family?"

"And even before she marries. That's what happened to one of my great-great-grandmothers: she saw the imp appear as soon as she was introduced to my great-great-grandfather. She was awfully frightened."

"Just from meeting him?"

"Yes. It seems the imp can figure out who's going to marry whom."

Pablo stroked her hand.

"I have to go," he muttered again, spurred to action by an anxiety even greater than anything an invisible imp might provoke. "Your parents might come home, and mine don't know where I am."

"Will we see each other again?"

"Our whole lives," he assured her.

On the way back home, the boy forgot about Martinico. His heart had room only for Amalia. He bounced along, light and happy, as if he himself had turned into a spirit. He tried to think of how he'd explain his tardiness to his parents. He had just enough time to invent an excuse before pushing the half-open door.

"Papa, Mama . . ."

He stopped short in the doorway. The house was filled with people. His mother was crying in a chair, and his father, head hanging, remained by her side. He saw the coffin in a corner of the room and then he noticed that everyone was dressed in yellow.

"*Akún* . . ." the boy whispered.

He had returned from the Isle of the Immortals only to face a world where people died.

I'LL REMEMBER YOUR LIPS

Despite the card reader's warning, Cecilia refused to end her relationship with Roberto. Although she couldn't shake the apprehension she felt when she was with him, she decided to attribute it to insecurity rather than instinct. It was true that everything the oracle had said surprised her with its accuracy, but she had no plans to follow the advice of a fortune-teller.

Roberto introduced her to his parents. The old man was a pleasant guy who talked constantly about the businesses he would set up once Cuba was free. He'd establish a paint factory ("because everything looks gray in the photos people bring over from the island"), a shoe store ("because those poor people over there go around practically barefoot"), and a bookstore where they'd sell inexpensive editions ("because my countrymen have spent half a century not being able to buy the books they'd like"). Cecilia was amused by that combination of investor and Good Samaritan, and she didn't try to slip away when the man called her over to tell her about some new project he'd dreamed up. His wife scolded him for his crazy insistence on creating more work for himself when he had retired over ten years ago, but he told her it was a temporary retirement, just a little respite before undertaking the last part of the journey. Roberto didn't get involved in those discussions; he seemed interested only in finding out more about the island he had never set foot upon. But, after all, that was a common obsession for those of his generation, whether or not they were born in Cuba, and she didn't stop to give the matter any further attention.

The Christmas festivities of the past few weeks had revived their relationship. Cecilia's spirits, which were always stirred up during the winter months, now bubbled. She went shopping for the first time in ages, eager to adopt a younger, fresher look. She tried on new makeup and bought herself some new dresses.

On New Year's Eve, Roberto came by to pick her up for a party that was being given on a private island filled with mansions owned by actors and singers who spent half the year filming or recording in some remote corner of the planet. The host was an old client of Roberto's who had invited him before.

They got slightly lost on the dark, leafy streets before arriving. The patio, with its recently mowed lawn, ended at a dock from which one could see the large downtown buildings and a slice of sea. Strangers came and went, passing through the rooms, poking around among the works of art that complemented the minimalist décor. After greeting the owner of the house, they escaped the commotion and went out to the dock and, chattering away, took off their shoes and awaited the arrival of the New Year.

Cecilia was sure her romantic problems were over at last. Now, splashing her bare feet in the cold water, she felt completely happy. Behind her, the countdown on TV had begun as the East Coast of the United States watched the shiny ball fall in Times Square. Fireworks began bursting over the Miami bay: white clusters, spheres ringed with green, willows with red branches . . .

When Roberto kissed her, she yielded to her sensations, intoxicated with pleasure, savoring the grape juice in his mouth like a divine, supernatural delight. In the last season of that romance, it was a sensual, unforgettable, almost religious experience.

A week later Roberto showed up at her apartment at dusk.

"Let's go get a drink," he said.

From a little outdoor table by the bay, one could see a sailboat—a combination of pirate ship and clipper—full of people who had nothing to do but sail along the calm waters and watch the bustling activity onshore. Between one martini and the next, Roberto announced:

"I don't know if we should keep seeing each other."

Cecilia thought she'd misheard. Little by little, stumbling on his words, he admitted that he had started seeing his old girlfriend again. Cecilia still didn't understand. He was the one who had insisted that they get back together; he had assured her that there was no one else. Now he appeared confused, as if struggling between two forces. Was there really a spell on him? He confessed that they had talked, trying to clarify what went wrong in their past relationship. And Cecilia died a little with each of his words.

"I don't know what to do," he concluded.

"I'll make it easy for you," Cecilia said. "Go to her and forget about me."

He looked at her, surprised . . . astonished, maybe. Her tears blinded her. Now she was behaving with that sort of irrational, slightly suicidal instinct that had always surfaced whenever she found herself in an unfair situation. If perseverance and love weren't enough, she'd rather step aside.

"I need for us to talk," he said.

"There's nothing to talk about," she murmured, without a drop of bitterness.

"Can I call you?"

"No. I can't go on like this, or you'll kill the little bit of sanity I have left."

"I swear I don't understand what's happening to me," he whispered.

"Find out," she replied, "but do it far away from me."

When she reached Freddy's house, she was at the point of collapse. Unaware of what was going on, the boy invited her in amid a chaos of cassettes and compact discs. A plaintive bolero could be heard coming from the tape recorder. Cecilia sat down on the floor, on the brink of tears.

"Did you hear that the pope has arrived in Havana?" the young man inquired, piling discs in various heaps.

"No."

"Luckily, I remembered to tape the reception ceremony. It was spectacular," he said, trying to decide where to put Ravi Shankar. "Oh! I've got a joke for you. Do you know why the pope is going to Cuba?"

She shook her head indifferently.

"To get to know hell up close, see the devil in person, and find out how to live on miracles."

Cecilia managed a faint smile.

"They're going to broadcast all the Masses live," he added, "so don't miss them. Maybe Troy will burn right in front of you-know-who's beard."

"I can't stay home watching TV," she muttered. "I've got to work."

"That's what recorders were invented for, my dear."

A female voice began to sing: *"They say your caresses are not for me, that your loving arms will not embrace me. . . ."*

The knot in Cecilia's throat was cutting off her air.

"I'm going to record everything for posterity," Freddy remarked, stacking several cassettes of Gregorian chants. "So no one will be able to tell me some story. . . ."

And when that mid-century bolero moaned, *"Give me a kiss and forget you've kissed me; my life is yours for the asking. . . ."* her sobs startled Freddy. He dropped the cassettes and two whole columns tumbled over.

"What's wrong?" he asked, alarmed. "What's the matter?" He'd never seen her like this.

"Nothing. . . . Roberto . . ." she stammered.

"Him again?" he exclaimed. "Damn him to hell."

"Don't say that."

"What happened now? Did you break up again?"

She nodded.

"And why this time?" he asked.

"I don't know. He doesn't know. He thinks he might still be in love with her."

"The one you told me about?"

She nodded.

"Well, listen carefully to what I'm about to tell you," he said, positioning himself in front of her. "I know who that woman is. I've made some inquiries. . . ."

"Freddy!" Cecilia started to reprimand him.

"I know who she is," he continued, "and I'm telling you she doesn't even measure up to your ankle. If he wants to stay with that boring, miserable little woman, let him. You're worth more than any other girl in this city. What am I saying—in this city? On the whole planet! If he wants to give up the last wonder of the modern world, he's a real fool and he doesn't deserve a single one of your tears."

"I wish I were somewhere else," she sobbed.

"This will pass."

Freddy stroked her head, not knowing how to console her. That was Cecilia's dilemma: a sensitive nature that always caused her to flee. Most of the time she tried to appear distant, as though she were running away from her emotions, but he knew it was a defense against getting hurt . . . like now. He also suspected that her parents' early deaths were responsible for a temperament that sought refuge in hidden corners, seeking escape from the pain of the world. But his suspicion wasn't enough to know how to help her.

"I hate this country," she said at last.

"Come on! With you, it's always the country's fault. First it was Cuba, because you didn't like Bluebeard. Now you're picking on this one, just on account of some girl, some nobody. It's not a country's fault when horrible people live in it."

"Cities are like the people who live there."

"Excuse me, but you're talking nonsense. Millions of people live in a city: good and bad, wise and stupid, heroes and murderers."

"Well, I've drawn the shortest straw. I don't even have friends. I have no one to talk to, just you and Lauro."

She was about to mention Gaia and Lisa, but she quickly decided not to include them in her list of confidants.

"It's about time for you to make some new friends," Freddy advised her.

"Where? I like walking, and you can't walk anywhere around here. Everything's a thousand miles away. You don't know how I'd love to lose myself on some street and forget about everything. . . . Go on, tell me where I can find anything here like the parks of El Vedado or the Malecón wall or the benches on Prado, or Teatro Lorca during a ballet festival, or the entrance of Cinemateca when they're showing a Bergman series . . . ?"

"If you keep on talking like that, I just might move back to Cuba . . . with Lucifer in power and everything. And don't confuse things! Your problem is romantic, not cultural. You love to mix everything up so you don't have to face the hard stuff."

The last accusation hit its mark, snapping her back to reality. She was convinced she'd never see Roberto again, but how would she get over him? No one had found a cure for that kind of pain, nor would they ever.

Since her parents left her . . . Cecilia shook her head to get rid of the memory and tried to find a more comforting thought: Amalia's tale. It was a consolation to know she wasn't alone. She felt a breath of hope. She wasn't about to let it be trampled.

"I'm leaving," she said suddenly, drying her tears.

"Want me to go with you?" Freddy asked, surprised at the sudden change.

"No, I'm going to see a friend."

And, without so much as a good-bye, she walked out into the blue Miami night.

I CAN'T FIND HAPPINESS

"Amalia, is the coffee ready?" her father called.

She jolted from her daydream in front of the sink, noticing that the tap water was overflowing the rim of the coffeepot.

"Get out of here," her grandmother told her, walking into the kitchen. "I'll do it."

With weary gestures, quite different from the agile leaps and bounds she had once used to climb mountains in search of ferns, her grandmother Angela turned off the faucet and put the pot on the burner to boil.

Amalia returned to the living room. Standing next to the window, her father was chatting with Joaquín Nin, that pianist with a Chinese name. Or did everything sound Chinese to her these days? She'd been seeing Pablito secretly for three years now and couldn't stop thinking about him.

"When's the premiere of the ballet?"

"In less than a week."

"Won't you miss Europe?"

"A little, but I've wanted to return for so long. This country is bewitching. It drags you back, it always calls you. . . . As I was telling my daughter the last time we spoke, Cuba is a curse."

Another one, Amalia thought. Because she was cursed too. And with a burden worse than carrying the shadow of an imp around for all eternity.

"Maybe the hardest part of returning is being far from your children," Pepe remarked.

"Not for me. Remember, I was separated from their mother when they were very small."

"I've heard that Joaquinito turned out like you: a brilliant musician."

"Yes, but Thorvald went into engineering, and Anaïs is obsessed with literature and psychiatry. . . . That girl is different from everyone else. She attracts people like flies."

"Some people are touched by an angel."

"Or by an imp," the musician replied, "as Lorca would say. But I tell you, just between us, Anaïs is bedeviled." Amalia shuddered.

"Excuse me," the young woman interrupted, emerging from the shadows.

"Ah, the lovely Amalia!" exclaimed the pianist.

With a slight smile, she passed between the two men on the way to the dining room, where other musicians were smoking by the open windows—so wide open that she immediately spied Pablo, nervously pacing on the corner.

Her mother stopped her as she opened the door. "Where are you going?"

"Grandma asked me to buy some sugar."

And she left without giving her time to respond.

He spotted her right away: a vision, hair curling at the slightest wisp of breeze, eyes like liquid sparks, and pale copper skin. For Pablo she was still the reincarnation of Kuan Yin, the goddess who moved with the grace of a golden fish.

"I'm so glad you came!" she greeted him. "Friday we won't be able to see each other. Papa wants to take me to the premiere of a ballet, and I can't get out of it."

"We'll have to find another time." He looked at her for a few seconds before breaking the news. "Did you know my parents are going to sell the laundry?"

"But they're doing so well!"

"They want to open a restaurant. It's better than a laundry."

"Will you quit your job at El Pacífico?"

"As soon as the business is open. We'll have to figure out another way to communicate."

"Amalia!"

The shout reached her through the window grating.

"Gotta run," she interrupted him. "I'll let you know when we can see each other."

Her father's expression left no room for doubt: he was furious. Her mother's glare was identical. Only her grandmother looked worried.

"I went to buy sugar . . ."

"Go to your room," her father whispered. "We'll talk later."

For half an hour Amalia bit her nails, working on her alibi. She'd say she couldn't find sugar for the coffee and had gone out to buy more. Just by chance she ran into Pablo and—

Someone knocked.

"Your father wants to talk to you," Mercedes said, poking her head in the doorway.

When she got to the living room, the guests had already gone, leaving ashes and empty coffee cups everywhere.

"What were you doing?" her father asked.

"I went to get—"

"Don't think I haven't noticed how that boy's been following you around for some time now. At first I played dumb because I thought it was just a childish crush, but you're almost seventeen now, and I'm not going to allow my daughter to go out with any riffraff—"

"Pablo's not riffraff!"

"Amalita," her mother intervened, "that boy is way beneath us."

"Way beneath?" the girl repeated, her indignation growing. "Tell me, what class do we belong to that's so different from his?"

"Our business—"

"Your business is a recording studio," she interrupted, "and his parents have a laundry that they're going to sell in order to buy a restaurant. Tell me, what's the difference?"

Amalia's agitated breathing clouded the silence.

"Those people are . . . Chinese," her father said at last.

"So?"

"We're white."

A dish crashed noisily in the sink. Everyone except Amalia turned toward the empty kitchen.

"No, Papa," the girl corrected, feeling the blood rush to her face. "You're white, but my mother is a mulatto, and you married her. That leaves me out of such refined categories. And if a white man can marry a mulatto woman, why can't a mulatto woman who passes for white marry the son of Chinese parents?"

And she bolted from the living room, heading for her room. The bang of her door slamming was followed by the crash of a vase full of fresh flowers. Above their heads, the crystal chandelier began to sway furiously.

"I'll have to take some measures," Pepe said, composing himself.

"Take all you like, son," Angela muttered with a sigh, "but the girl is right. And forgive me for saying so, but you and Mercedes are the last people who should object to such a match."

And with labored little steps, the old woman went off to her room, leaving a faint trail of mountain dew on the marble tiles.

The cream of Havana society wandered up and down the corridors of the theater. All sorts of individuals—estate owners and marquises, politicians and actresses—rubbed elbows that night at the premiere of *The Little Countess,* a ballet with music by Joaquín Nin, "Cuba's glory and favorite son, now back from his fruitful artistic exile in Europe and the United States," according to a newspaper from the capital. And just in case there was any doubt about his musical pedigree, the addendum stating that he had been the piano instructor of none other than Ernesto Lecuona was enough to attract even the most skeptical.

Amid the bustle, Amalia, despite her pink tulle dress and the bouquet of violets on her bodice, looked like the picture of desolation. The girl clutched her little silver purse tightly as she scanned the crowd for the one person who might help her. At last she spotted her, lost in a flurry of handsome admirers.

"Doña Rita," the girl hissed, rushing to her when her parents weren't looking.

"But what a beautiful girl!" the woman exclaimed when she saw her. "Gentlemen," she said to the male public surrounding her, "I want to introduce you to this adorable creature, who, allow me to add, is single and unattached."

Amalia, all smiles, had to greet the coterie.

"Rita," Amalia implored, whispering in her ear, "I need to speak to you urgently."

The woman looked at the young girl and, for the first time, felt alarmed by her expression.

"What's the matter?" she asked, leading her away from the group.

Amalia hesitated a few seconds, not knowing where to begin.

"I'm in love," she burst out.

"Blessed Saint Barbara!" the diva cried, about to cross herself. "Anyone would've said . . . You're not pregnant, are you?"

"Doña Rita!"

"Forgive me, child, but when love makes you look like that, anything's possible."

"The problem is, my dad doesn't like my boyfriend."

"Oh! So, there's a courtship going on already?"

"My parents don't want to have anything to do with him."

"Why not?"

"He's Chinese."

"What?"

"He's Chinese," she repeated.

For one moment the actress regarded the girl, mouth agape; suddenly, unable to contain herself, she let out a guffaw that made everyone nearby turn their heads.

"If you think it's so funny . . ."

"Wait," Rita begged, still laughing and grabbing her arm to keep her from running away. "My God, I always wondered how Dinorah's prediction that night would turn out. . . ."

"Who?"

"The card reader I took you to see a few years ago—don't you remember?"

"I remember her but not what she said."

"Well, I do. She warned you that you'd have complicated love affairs."

Amalia was in no mood to discuss oracles.

"My parents are furious." She swallowed hard before opening her purse. "I need a favor, and you're the only one who can help me."

"Ask away."

"I have a note I've written to Pablo. . . ."

"So it's Pablo," the woman repeated, savoring the story as if it were a sweet.

"He works in El Pacífico. I know you go there sometimes. Could you make sure someone gives him this note?"

"Gladly. Look, I have such a craving for fried rice that I think I'll run right over there after the performance."

Amalia smiled. She knew that this alleged yearning for Chinese food had nothing to do with appetite and everything to do with curiosity.

"May God bless you for this, Doña Rita."

"Hush, child, hush—you're only supposed to say that for noble actions, and what I'm about to do is madness. If your parents find out, I'll lose a lifelong friendship."

"You're a saint."

"Enough with the church! You're not thinking of becoming a nun, are you?"

"Of course not. If I did I couldn't marry Pablo."

"Jesus! This girl moves fast!"

"Thank you, thank you so much," said Amalia, touched, as she embraced the woman.

"Why such enthusiasm, if one might ask?"

Pepe and Mercedes approached, smiling.

"We were planning a little excursion."

"Whenever you like. For me it's always been an honor to consider you a member of the family," and he pressed the woman's hands between his own. "If I were to die, I'd hand my daughter over to you with my eyes closed."

The actress smiled, a little uncomfortable at that display of confidence she was about to betray, but then she thought, "Everything for love," and felt slightly less guilty.

A bell resounded throughout the corridors.

"See you later." Amalia kissed her, and the girl's smile erased any remaining hesitation on her part.

"Ah, how beautiful it is to fall in love like that," the actress sighed to herself, as she might in one of her own films.

"*If they catch you,* I don't know anything," Rita warned.

And so, when she asked her father's permission to go shopping, she knew what she was in for.

The couple didn't even go to the movies, as they had agreed. They took a walk around El Vedado, had lunch in a cafeteria, and ended up sitting on the Malecón wall to carry out the sacred ritual of every lover or would-be lover in Havana.

Years later an architect would remark that not since the building of the Great Pyramid at Giza had an architectural work been more carefully constructed than that seven-mile-long wall. No sunset in the world, the engineer affirmed, had the transparency or duration of those Havana nightfalls. It was as though every afternoon a careful mise-en-scène was staged, so that the Almighty could sit down and delight His eyes with the stars emerging from the golden halo of the clouds and the turquoise sky, like the landscape of another planet. . . . At such moments the spectators suffered momentary amnesia. Time acquired a different physical quality, and then—some people swore—it was possible to see certain ghostly shadows from both the past and the future strolling by the wall.

Therefore, Amalia wasn't too surprised to spy the imp Martinico, who, after leaping tirelessly over sea foam–sprayed rocks, stood motionless before the strange mirage that she, too, could see, knowing that it was not a real, present image but rather something from another era: hundreds of people launched themselves into the sea on rafts and anything else that would float. Pablo also fell speechless at the sight of a young woman in a scandalously short dress, walking alongside the wall, as his great-grandfather's favorite saint looked on. He didn't understand what the spirit of *apak* Martí was doing there, or the sadness with which he regarded the young woman, whose natural rhythm bore the marks of a life of bought and sold love.

Visions . . . phantoms . . . The entire past and future came together along the Havana Malecón during moments when God sat there, at rest from ruling over the universe. At any other time the young couple would have been taken aback, but those who witness Malecón sunsets understand their effects on the spirit, which momentarily accepts such metamorphoses without hesitation. Absorbed in contemplation of the many specters around them, neither young lover noticed Pepe in his car, spying from a distance on his daughter's unmistakable silhouette.

A gust of wind knocked over the carnations that Rosa had just placed on Wong Yuang's tomb. Carefully she lifted the flowerpot once more, moving it closer to the niche to protect it from the wind, while Manuel and Pablito finished pulling the weeds around the gravestone.

Havana's Chinese cemetery was a sea of burning candles and incense sticks. The breeze was filled with sandalwood smoke rising up to the nostrils of the gods, perfuming that April morning when the immigrants visited their ancestors' tombs.

For two hours the Wongs cleaned the site and shared rations of pork and sweets with the deceased, but most of the food was left behind on the marble slab so that the departed could help himself to his favorites: chicken, boiled vegetables, tea, spring rolls filled with shrimp . . . Before leaving, Rosa burned a few bills of fake money. Then they left, a little sadder than before.

Pablo had many more reasons than anyone else to feel depressed. Amalia hadn't called or written. The boy sniffed around the neighborhood, but his habitual rounds earned him only a couple of slammed windows when Don Pepe surprised him peeking through the blinds.

"I could go for some tea," Manuel said, hailing a taxi.

"Well, I'm hungry," Rosa replied.

"Why don't we go to Cándido's inn?" the young man suggested. "They make the best tea and the best fish soup in this city."

But his real motive was to keep watch on the girl's house.

"All right," his father said. "On the way, I'll buy a couple of lottery tickets."

"You should bet on 68," his wife recommended. "Last night I had the strangest dream. . . ."

And while Rosa related her dream about a large place full of dead people, Pablo gobbled up the streets with his eyes, as if he expected Amalia to appear at any moment. Ten minutes later they climbed out of the taxi and entered the restaurant that smelled of cod fritters.

"Look who's here!"

The Wongs went over to the table where Shu Li's family was chatting over bowls of pork and rice.

"Where've you been hiding?" Pablito whispered into his friend's ear. "I've been looking for you for days."

"School is driving me crazy. I've had to study like mad."

"I need your sister to take a message to Amalia," Pablo murmured, looking at the girl out of the corner of his eye.

"Elena doesn't study with her anymore."

"Did she change schools?"

"Not Elena, Amalia . . ."

Pablito was stunned.

"Where is she now?" he asked finally.

"I don't know; it seems they've moved."

"That's impossible," Pablo cried, feeling panic rush through him. "I've seen her parents several times."

"Maybe they took her to another city. You told me they didn't want . . ."

Pablo couldn't listen anymore; he had to sit down with his parents and order tea and soup. Now he understood why Amalia had disappeared. How would he find her? He racked his brain, imagining acts of heroism that might endear him to Amalia's parents. A Victrola blared the strains of a proclamation: "Peanuts! We'll meet again! Peanuts! This street again!" Pablo gave such a violent start that his mother turned around to look at him. Feigning a slight cough, he covered his face to hide his excitement. Why hadn't he thought of it before?

A hint of breeze brushed his cheeks, lessening the oppressive heat. Above the rooftops, the clouds swiftly dissipated. And the sky became so blue, so bright . . .

No matter how he tried, Pablo couldn't get to see the actress . . . and not for lack of leads, either—who didn't know the great Rita Montaner?—but rather because her crazy schedule made her hard to pin down.

He decided to ask his parents to speak to Don Pepe, since the weeks were flying by. Sadly but firmly they advised him to forget about the matter; another girl fit for marriage would come his way. His pleas had no effect on Mercedes, either; she closed the door and threatened to call the police if he didn't leave them alone. He had no choice but to keep looking for the actress.

After many failed attempts, he managed to find her leaving a performance, surrounded by spectators who wouldn't let her escape and protected from the downpour by an admirer's umbrella. Pushing and shoving, he made his way to her side. He tried to explain who he was, but it wasn't necessary: Rita recognized him at once. It was impossible to forget that bony face, the square, masculine jaw, and those slanted eyes that gave off sparks like two knives clashing in the darkness. She vividly recalled the night when she had slipped the note into her purse, acceding to Amalia's pleas. One glance was enough for her to understand why that boy had the young woman so charmed.

To everyone's surprise, the actress seized him by the arm and pushed him into a taxi with her. She slammed the door in the faces of all present, including the admirer with the umbrella, who stood there in the rain, watching the car pull away.

"Doña Rita . . ." he began, but she interrupted him.

"I don't know where she is, either."

More than disappointment, the woman felt his anguish, but there was nothing she could do. Pepe hadn't told anyone of his daughter's whereabouts, not even Rita, who was like her second mother. She'd only managed to send her a note. In return, she had received another in which the girl explained that she had enrolled in a small school and didn't know when she would see her again.

"Come over Saturday at the same time," was all she could offer him. "I'll show you the note."

Three days later she met again with Pablo, who kept the note as though it were a sacred relic. The woman watched him walk away, sad and despondent. She would have liked to say something to cheer him up, but she felt bound, hand and foot.

"Thank you very much, Doña Rita," he said as he was leaving. "I won't bother you again."

"Don't mention it, child."

But he had already turned and disappeared into the darkness.

The young man kept his promise not to return, a mistake, since some weeks later Pepe phoned, inviting her to visit his daughter. The couple and the actress traveled to a small town called Los Arabos, about two hundred kilometers from the capital, where some relatives who were caring for their daughter lived. Amalia nearly cried when she saw Rita, but she contained herself. She had to wait more than three hours, when everyone went to the kitchen for coffee.

"Take this to Pablo for me," the girl whispered, handing her a small, wrinkled piece of paper from her pocket.

Rita hid it in her bosom, briefly recounting her conversation with Pablo and promising to return with a reply.

But Pablo no longer worked at El Pacífico. A waiter informed her that his family had opened a restaurant or an inn, but no matter how she tried, she couldn't make him tell her where it was; no Chinese person would give her that information, no matter how famous an actress and singer she might be. Those Cantonese immigrants didn't trust their own shadows.

Following instructions provided by Amalia, who had an approximate idea of the place where Pablo lived, she attempted to find his house; but she had no luck there, either. She sent several messengers to make inquiries, all with the same results. Amalia's hopes went up in smoke when Rita returned her undelivered letter.

Pablo never learned of these tormenting events. During vacations, and also on some weekends, he kept continued surveillance on his girlfriend's house. Pepe, seeing that he hadn't given up, abandoned the idea of bringing her back. And so the months and years went by. And as time passed, Pablo visited the neighborhood less and less, until at some point he stopped going altogether.

The young man looked indifferently at the clothing his mother had prepared for his first day at the university: a suit made of fine, light-colored cloth.

"Aren't you ready yet?" Rosa asked, peering into the shadowy bedroom. "I just have to heat some water for tea."

"Almost," Pablo muttered.

The restaurant's success had allowed Manuel Wong to fulfill his dream. His son, Pag Li, would no longer be the little Chinaman who delivered clothing or the kitchen helper in El Pacífico—not even the owner of the Red Dragon. He would soon become Dr. Pablo Wong, medical specialist.

But the young man felt no emotion; nothing had mattered since Amalia's disappearance. His enthusiasm belonged to another time, when he was able to imagine the fiercest battles, the most delirious love. . . .

"Did you wake him?" his father whispered from the hallway.

"He's getting dressed."

"If he doesn't hurry, he'll be late."

"Calm down, Siu Mend. Don't make him more nervous than he needs to be."

But Pablo wasn't nervous. In any case, he felt furious when he realized that Amalia had disappeared forever. Alternating bouts of rage and tears had caused his parents to find a reputable Chinese doctor to examine him. But aside from prescribing some herbs and poking him with dozens of needles that slightly calmed his spirit, the physician could do nothing.

"Let's go, son, it's getting late," his mother urged, flinging open the door.

When Pablo left his room, shaved and dressed, his mother gasped. There was no more handsome man in the entire Chinese community. It wouldn't be difficult for him to find a young lady from a good family who would make him forget that other girl. . . . She knew her son was still sad; in spite of all the time that had passed, nothing seemed to brighten him.

"Do you have money?"

"Did you check your briefcase?"

"Leave me alone," Pablo replied. "It's not like I'm going to China."

His mother wouldn't stop stroking his cheek or brushing off his suit. His father tried to display more composure, but he felt an uncontrollable itch on the tip of his nose, something that happened only when he was extremely nervous.

At last Pablo freed himself of their ministrations and walked out into the crisp morning. The neighborhood was shaking off sleep as it had done every morning since his arrival on the island. As he looked for the right streetcar to the university, he observed the shopkeepers placing their boxes of merchandise along the sidewalks, old folks practicing tai chi in their interior courtyards, students walking to class, their eyes still heavy with sleep. It was a peaceable, familiar landscape that for the first time slightly relieved the ennui that had accompanied him these past few years.

His separation from Amalia had caused him to fail a course, in addition to the one he had failed because of his ignorance of the language when he first came to the island. But he had graduated with honors from the Instituto de Segunda Enseñanza de Centro Habana. And now, after so much effort, he was about to tread the campus of the university itself.

The streetcar passed through San Lázaro, stopping two or three blocks from the university, near a cafeteria. Pablo noticed how the shop owner furtively accepted money from a passerby and understood that he was taking *bolita* bets. Under the counter with its packs of cigars was the notebook where the amount and the name of the bettor were jotted down—quite a familiar scene for Pablo, and one that triggered his memory. He had dreamed something. What was it? Suddenly he felt an urgent need to remember.

A ghost . . . no, a dead man. He recalled the silhouette of a corpse advancing through an open field, heading toward the moon, a full, powerful moon that had dipped dangerously close to the earth. Now the memory became clear. The dead man had raised his hand, and when his fingers brushed the surface of the disk, it began to crumple like a burning piece of paper, ultimately turning into a sort of cat or tiger. . . . That was all he could recollect. Let's see, a dead man. The dead man was number 8. And the moon was 17. And the cat? What number was the cat? He walked over to the *bolitero*. A moon that turned a dead man into a cat or a tiger. Of course the man knew. Wouldn't the gentleman like to bet on some other combinations? Because 14, which was the tiger cat, was also marriage. But the first number for marriage was 62. And sometimes images in dreams aren't exactly what they seem to be. He knew it from experience. . . . But Pablo didn't let himself be seduced. He played number 17814, and he kept the tickets in his briefcase while he watched the time on the wall clock. He'd have to hurry.

Dozens of students headed toward the university hill for their first day of classes. Groups of girls greeted each other extravagantly, as though they hadn't seen one another for a lifetime. Young men in suits and ties embraced or argued.

"They're communists in disguise," said one of them, his face purple with indignation. "They're trying to disrupt the country with all those speeches."

"Eduardo Chibás is no communist. All he's doing is criticizing government fraud. I have faith in his party."

"Well, I don't," said a third. "I think he's going too far. You can't go around every day making accusations of this and that without proof."

"Where there's smoke—"

"The main problem here is corruption and the murders committed by gangsters disguised as police. This isn't a country, it's a slaughterhouse. Look at what happened in Marianao. And President Grau hasn't done anything to solve it!"

He was referring to the latest national scandal. It had been such a hair-raising story that even Pablo's parents, not at all inclined to political discussions, had been outraged. Someone had given the order to detain one commander who was visiting another's house. Instead of obeying, the police—a bunch of official thugs—had filled him and several others with bullets, including the innocent wife of the owner of the house.

Pablo was about to retrace his steps in order to get in on the conversation, but he recalled his father's advice: "Remember, you're going to the university in order to study, not to get mixed up with troublemakers."

"Pablo!"

He turned around, surprised. Who could possibly know him here? It was Shu Li, his old schoolmate.

"Joaquín!"

They had stopped seeing each other two years before, when his friend moved to a different neighborhood and another school.

"What are you studying?"

"Law. And you?"

"Medicine."

They climbed the staircase and crossed the threshold of the rectory to go out into the central plaza, where the commotion was even greater. Near the library they met up with a friend of Shu Li's . . . or rather Joaquín, since neither of them used his Chinese name in public.

"Pablo, this is Luis," Joaquín introduced them. "He's studying medicine too."

"Nice to meet you."

"Where's Bertica?" Joaquín asked the new arrival.

"She just left," Luis said. "She told me she couldn't wait anymore."

"Bertica is Luis's sister," Joaquín explained.

"That's her former title," Luis said, winking at Pablo. "Now she's Joaquín's girlfriend."

"If I don't leave now, I'm not going to get there on time," Joaquín interrupted.

And he said good-bye to the two medical students, but not without reminding them of their coffee date after class.

It was a tiring day, even though none of the professors really gave a lecture. It was just lists of grading standards and exams, a repertory of books they'd need to buy, and a description of university activities.

By the time class was over, Luis and Pablo had already become great friends and had exchanged addresses, telephone numbers, and their real Chinese names. Luis warned him that his line was always busy, because of his sister.

"What courses did she register for?" Pablo asked as he waited for Joaquín and Berta.

"Arts and Letters. . . . Look, here she comes. And, as usual, Joaquín's not here yet! Get ready for a fight."

Pablo glanced toward the corner, where a trio of young women had just appeared, laden with books. One of them, with Asian features, had to be Luis's sister. The blondest one was giggling madly, choking on her own laughter. The other, golden-skinned, smiled silently, her gaze fixed on the ground.

When they were just a few paces away, the golden-skinned girl raised her eyes, and her notebooks fell to the floor. For an instant she stood motionless, while her friends picked up the trail of papers at her feet. Pablo understood then that his dream had been a coded message from the gods: death, caressing the moon, had turned into a tiger. Or, in other words, his deadened spirit, in the presence of a woman, had come back to life. And if he gave it a different reading? The number 8—corresponding to death—meant tiger; the number 17—belonging to the moon—could be a good woman; and 14—the key for *tiger*—also signified marriage. It was a heavenly formula: even the order didn't affect the result. In any case, he had come within reach of Kuan Yin, the Goddess of Mercy, whose outline shines as brightly as the moon, in order to touch a face he had never stopped dreaming about. And there she was before him: more beautiful than ever, after his many years of fruitless searching.

YOU, MY DELIRIUM

Was it an epidemic, or was it something that had happened always but that no one noticed? Finally Cecilia had to admit it: Cuban women were dying in droves, like whales that beach themselves en masse.

First it was that actor's girlfriend, a girl she had spoken to a few times. Someone told her that, after a heated discussion, the girl headed out to the street, mad with rage. Dozens of witnesses testified that it hadn't been the driver's fault. The girl saw the car, but she threw herself beneath the wheels. . . . Then it was a friend she used to get together with when they both still lived in Havana. Trini was a brilliant woman, an eloquent professor, a tireless reader. Many times they had sat together, discussing a literary work both of them worshipped: *The Lord of the Rings.* Cecilia would always remember their conversations about the forest of Lothlórien and their mutual love for Galadriel, the Elf Queen. . . . But Trini was dead now. After breaking up with her last partner, with whom she had lived in some city in the United States, she sat down on a park bench, pulled out a revolver, and killed herself. Cecilia couldn't understand it. She didn't know how to connect the Elf Queen with a gunshot suicide. It was one of those things that turned her universe upside down.

Soon she stopped questioning herself. And, as though she shared the karma of the deceased, she began to plunge into a depression, finally taking to her bed with an inexplicable fever. Worried, Freddy and Lauro went to her house, accompanied by a doctor.

"I don't know if my insurance . . ." she began.

"Don't worry about the money," the man reassured her. "I came because I was a good friend of Tirso's."

That name didn't mean anything to Cecilia.

"Tirso was my cousin," Lauro said.

From his tone of voice, Cecilia deduced that his cousin had died, but she didn't want to find out how or of what.

"Do you have hypertension?" the man asked, after watching the needle jump.

"I don't think so."

"Well, your pressure's pretty high," he remarked, rummaging for something in his valise.

The man examined Cecilia's arms and legs.

"You can't allow your pressure to go up. Look at those black-and-blue marks. With your fragile capillaries, your arterial walls could burst. I don't want to alarm you, but that combination of high blood pressure and vascular fragility could cause a stroke."

"Both my grandfathers died of that," she muttered.

"Oh, God!" said Lauro, fanning himself with his hand. "I think I'm going to faint. These things really affect me."

"Goddamn it, Lauro," Freddy admonished, "quit screwing around for a change, will you?"

"I'm not screwing around," Lauro protested. "I'm a very sensitive person."

"Keep this," the doctor went on. "When you're better you can return it to me."

It was a digital blood pressure monitor. The numbers appeared on a screen.

"Take two pills right now," he recommended, removing a bottle from his valise. "And one every morning when you get up. But I recommend seeing a specialist for a complete checkup. . . . How's your cholesterol?"

"Normal."

"It's possible that your hypertension is emotional. . . ."

"Of course it is!" Freddy agreed. "This woman keeps everything inside. Every time something happens to her, she hides in a corner, crying her eyes out."

"Emotions can kill faster than cholesterol," the doctor warned her as he left.

But her emotions weren't under Cecilia's control, and the medications didn't manage to lower her blood pressure. Besides, she still had that fever, a fever the doctor couldn't explain. She underwent all sorts of procedures. Nothing. It was a mysterious, isolated fever that didn't appear to be associated with anything but her depression. The doctor ordered complete rest. Two days later, when someone called to tell her they had seen Roberto at the beach with a redhead, she plunged into a lethargy that was almost welcome. She had dreams and visions. At times she thought she was talking to Roberto, and the next moment she found herself alone. Or else she was leaning over to kiss him and suddenly was with a stranger.

An endless downpour began falling on the city. It rained for three days and three nights, to the alarm of the authorities. Classes were suspended, as were nearly all jobs. The news proclaimed it was the greatest rainfall in half a century. It was a strange storm, hallucinatory. And while Miami turned into a new Venice, Cecilia was delirious with fever.

On the last night of the flood, she felt she was dying. She had taken several aspirins, but her high fever continued. Despite her test results, she was shriveling up like an old woman. Suddenly she understood why people in other eras died of love: a deep depression, a compromised immune system, emotions that shot your blood pressure up to the stars, and . . . everything could go to hell. The heart's fragility can't withstand the burdens of the spirit.

The dawn of the third night, she awoke suspecting her end was near. Her eyes still closed, she felt a hand brushing her burning forehead. She turned her head, trying to locate the source of that caress. There was no one in her bedroom. For some reason she thought of her grandmother Delfina. Her gaze rested on a book she hadn't yet begun to read. Acting on impulse, she opened it at random: "Our minds carry the power of life and death." She had barely read that line when she recalled Melisa's words: "You have a shadow on your aura." She shuddered. "Something bad will happen to you if you don't start with what's *inside your head.*"

She checked her pressure: 165/104, and again she felt the icy touch of a nearby invisible being. She had an idea. She closed her eyes and visualized the numbers 120/80. She held on to that image for a few moments until she could see it in her mind, feeling—more than wishing—it would be there when she looked again. She took her pressure once more: 132/95. The numbers had fallen. She concentrated and closed her eyes for a few minutes, focusing on the image "120/80 . . . 120/80" until the figures shone clearly in her head. A breeze blew through the stuffy room, refreshing her skin. Three minutes passed, then four, then ten. She relaxed and pumped one more time until she read: 120/81. She could hardly believe it, but there was no doubt she had done it. She decided to do the same thing with her fever. After several attempts, her temperature began to fall until she herself fell . . . into a deep sleep.

She awoke the next morning with the sunlight filtering through her window. She peered out onto the balcony and saw a few cars parked on the sidewalk. Their owners had tried to rest them on whatever elevated surface they could find, fearing they'd be washed away. Dozens of people milled around in the street, barefoot and in shorts. For the first time in many hours, the sun shone brilliantly above their heads. From still-drenched telephone wires, birds shook their feathers and sang at the top of their voices.

Life was returning for everyone, including Cecilia.

Part Five

THE SEASON

OF THE

RED WARRIORS

Go find a Chinaman to take you in:

A popular expression indicating rejection. When a man fought with a woman, he might say: ". . . and go find a Chinaman to take you in," meaning that she could go to hell if she liked, because the last thing a decent woman would do was live with a Chinese man. The later mixture of the Asian population with blacks and whites proved that, despite the taboo, many women really did follow this advice.

MY ONLY LOVE

She still shuddered to think of how she had gotten there. Countless times she had defied her parents, seeing Pablo secretly at the university, even running off to the movies with him. In fact, she had been eluding her parents' authority for the last four years of her studies. But this . . . ?

"You've got to help me," she had begged Bertica. "I've always covered your back with Joaquín."

"This is different, Amalia. My parents know yours."

"You owe me this favor."

Grudgingly, her friend went with her to ask permission to go on a "trip" to Varadero. Don José and Don Loreto had been classmates in medical school, and they still exchanged patients and postcards. Musicians who knew Don José went to the doctor's clinic, and Don Loreto's patients bought records at Pepe's store.

That connection hurt Amalia because she didn't understand how her father could be such a good friend of the Cantonese doctor's and still refuse to accept her relationship with Pablo. That's why she felt no scruples about disobeying him by making crazy plans, like this three-day escapade they had planned.

Walking along the orchid-lined path, she noticed how her feet sank into the carpet of leaves. Indifferent to the chill, and with her gaze lost in that ossuary of skeletal vegetation, she felt as though she were in another time, thousands of years earlier, when human beings did not yet exist, just strange and mythical creatures like her imp.

A dense fog hovered over the Viñales Valley. The peace and silence were omnipresent, as though civilization had ceased to exist. She listened carefully for some familiar sound but heard only an indefinable murmur. Instinctively she clutched the jet amulet that dangled from her chain, looking up. Was it the rush of the breeze or the voice of the water? A little frightened, she clung to Pablo.

The icy wind blew over the heights of the sierra where that ancient, Jurassic valley was set. Hummocks—that's what they called those peaks where one-of-a-kind snail species had resided since time immemorial.

Millions of years ago, Viñales had been a woodsy plain that nature's whimsical hand had gradually shaped into those rounded masses. The mollusks entrapped in each one of the promontories encouraged the growth of independent species that, in time, would transform the valley into a mecca for scientists.

But Pablo and Amalia knew nothing of this. Their glances passed right over the dwarf palms and clumps of ferns. Among the orchids they discovered hummingbirds that plowed through the atmosphere like flickers of light, stopping to sip their sustenance and beating the air with frenzied wings before disappearing. It was a vision of Paradise. Awed and mute, the young couple took delight in those marvels; and just behind them, also reveling in all that beauty, Martinico followed.

Ever since Angela had left her village half a century earlier, the imp had not fully enjoyed a forest or a hill. Now he found himself in the midst of the Cuban hills, relishing the plumage of the *tocororos*, the fragrance of the tobacco plantations, the outline of the cork palm—more ancient than the imp himself—the red clay of the fields, and the prehistoric mountain range encircling the valley.

A delicate music pierced the fog. Amalia looked up as if she had caught the sound of it . . . to the surprise of the imp, who knew that the sound was inaudible to human beings. But perhaps it had been a coincidence—or a premonition—because she immediately turned to Pablo and they plunged again into an intimate conversation.

As they advanced, the mysterious sound grew closer. The young couple had fallen silent again, deep in their own thoughts. To his right, the imp Martinico spied a tiny bird, almost like a toy: a black hummingbird. He leaped forward in order to catch it, but it slipped from between his fingers. "May God always preserve this," he heard his mistress's silent voice in his head. "May we love each other unto death, even beyond death." Then suddenly the melody ceased. The imp turned his gaze from the humming-bird he had just caught and, startled, let the winged jewel escape, twin-kling before it disappeared in the mist.

At the end of the path, Pablo kissed Amalia. But that wasn't what had frightened the imp. Atop a nearby rock, with his dark hooves and his horns, the old god Pan held the reed instrument that Martinico had seen years before in the mountains of Cuenca.

The imp and the god stared at each other for a few seconds, equally disconcerted. The question "What are you doing here?" wordlessly passed between them. And in the same way their explanations crossed from one to the other: "Unto death," Amalia's thoughts resounded. "Beyond death." And he knew then that the god had stopped playing his pipes because he, too, had heard Amalia's longing for eternity.

How could it be? The creatures of the Middle Kingdom could hear human thoughts only if there was a special link between them. The imp then remembered the promise Pan had made to Amalia's grandmother: "If one of your descendants should ever need me, even without knowing about our pact, I could offer him whatever he wanted . . . twice." The god was bound to her by the favor she had granted him over honey on a certain Midsummer's Night. "Let it be forever, then," he felt the god concede in his silent tongue. "Until beyond death."

Pablo and Amalia began walking, preceded by the god who impercep-tibly led the way. The imp followed them from a certain distance, too intrigued to think of mischief. Soon they reached the foot of a peak where the mountain range began. The whole terrain was covered by the densest weeds, as if no one had ever trod there. The god made a gesture that nei-ther of the young people saw, but they both suddenly came upon an open-ing in the middle of the foliage. It was the start of a spiral path leading to the summit. The imp knew that no human being of those times had ever traversed it. It belonged to another era, designed by creatures who, fleeing an ancient catastrophe, had taken refuge in the then-uninhabited island before continuing to other lands. Now, thousands of years later, Pablo and Amalia were about to repeat a ritual which no one could recall, except a few dying gods in a world that had lost its magic. . . .

They made their way among the curtains of ferns, toward the heights. Dew hung from the leaves, falling like frozen rain over their heads.

Upward . . . upward . . . toward the clouds, toward the soul's dwelling place, following the ever-curving path around the hill. First toward one side and then the other. Never in a straight line. Only in this way would their spirits remain united: bound together by invisible twists and turns.

A voice recited a magical incantation that they didn't hear, immersed as they were in a cloudbank that barely allowed them to see. The psalms, chanted in an ancient tongue, seemed to them like the chirping of unfamiliar birds. . . . They could perceive nothing more. The peak stood awaiting the ceremony that would mark their souls. Such a ceremony had already taken place countless times, and so it would occur again and again as long as the world existed and the gods—forgotten or not—retained their power over humankind.

Lulled by a silent liturgy, Pablo and Amalia surrendered to the most ancient of acts. And it was as if a divine finger, emerging from the void, had blessed them. A light descended—or perhaps emanated—from their bodies. It surrounded them like gauze and adhered to the edges of their souls like a mark of love, visible only to their spirits, that would last for all ages.

"*This chicken and rice* tastes like heaven," remarked Rita, with that movement of her eyebrows that could signify both admiration and flattery.

"It comes from nearby," José commented, stabbing a piece of white meat. "Mama learned to cook in the mountains."

Doña Angela smiled slightly. With her seventy-some years behind her, she had the placid expression of someone who was waiting only for the end. But her son was right: The house of her childhood was closer to heaven than earth. The image crossed her mind of that immortal damsel combing her hair beside a pond as well as the sound of the music that flooded the mountains. She thought of how close those creatures might be to the Supreme Authority she would soon seek in order to join her Juanco.

"Child, watch where you're putting things!"

Mercedes' cry shook her from her reveries. Her granddaughter had just spilled a glass of water on the tablecloth. Mercedes leaped up, napkin in hand, to stem the flow that threatened to spread. It was practically a family dinner. Besides the four members of the family and Rita, only an impresario they called El Zorro and Bertica's parents were in attendance.

Amalia nearly fainted when she learned that her parents had invited Don Loreto and his wife.

"What will we do if they catch us?" she asked Pablo as they ate their ices. "They might even send me to Los Arabos again."

"Nothing will happen," he reassured her, stroking her hair. "That was three months ago. There's no reason to mention it."

"And if he does?"

"If your father finds out and wants to send you to Matanzas again, you'll phone me, and that same night we'll run away."

But Amalia was very nervous anyway.

Pepe observed his wife's efforts to control the spill and, for the first time, noticed the girl's appearance. She looked paler, different . . . Could she be anemic? As soon as he finished the recording session with the *soneros*, he'd take her for a checkup.

". . . but what's happening in Japan is unbelievable," El Zorro was saying. "They've gone crazy over our music."

"In Japan?" José repeated.

"There's a new band called the Tokyo Cuban Boys."

"Is it true that over there they commit suicide by slitting their bellies open?" Mercedes asked, unable to imagine anything worse than to die under the blade of a knife.

"I've heard something along those lines," Loreto recalled.

"It doesn't surprise me," Rita sighed. "With that sad music they play on those stringless mandolins, they must go around feeling very depressed."

"Well, now they're all dying to dance the *guaracha*," El Zorro said cheerily.

Amalia's chair jumped. Her parents and her grandmother looked at her, alarmed, although the guests simply thought that the girl had moved abruptly.

"Is something wrong?" whispered Angela, noticing her pallor.

"I don't feel well," the girl replied, feeling a cold sweat overcome her body. "May I go . . . ?"

But she didn't complete the sentence. She covered her mouth and bolted to the bathroom. Her grandmother and mother followed.

"At that age, the same thing used to happen to me," Rita said. "Whenever it was hot, I couldn't eat much because I ended up emptying my stomach."

"Yes, young ladies today are more delicate than men," Loreto commented. "And Amalia has turned into a very pretty young lady. Who would've guessed? The last time I saw her, she had that talking doll—"

José choked on his water. Loreto had to slap him on the back a few times.

"Hey, my only experience with cases of drowning was in medical school," the doctor joked. "I can't guarantee anything."

José stopped choking.

"I don't remember that Amalita had a talking doll," her father commented, feigning great composure.

"Well, it was a few years ago. You used to buy her all sorts of toys. . . . I don't think you remember. . . ."

"Well, I remember," Loreto's wife, Irene, interjected, "because for months Bertica hounded us to buy her one just like it."

Something was happening. Rita discreetly observed Pepe as she asked for more lemonade. What connection could that doll have with such tension? She heard a muffled sound and realized that Amalia was vomiting. . . . Oh, Jesus, Mary, and Joseph! Not that. Anything but that.

Mercedes' footsteps caught the attention of the guests.

"She seems a little better," she remarked with the greatest innocence, but when she raised her eyes and saw her husband's expression, her heart stopped.

Thirty years of living with someone is a long time, and Mercedes had been with José for somewhat longer than that. For one moment she held her fork suspended halfway between her plate and her mouth, but her husband's gesture indicated that she should dissemble.

"The one I'd love to hear in person is Beny Moré," said Don Loreto. "I've only heard a few recordings he made in Mexico with Pérez Prado."

"That mulatto sings like the gods," Pepe began, making an effort. "Mercedes and I went to see him a month ago."

"Well, let's arrange to go all together . . . including Doña Rita, if she's willing to accompany us."

"I'd love to," she replied, giving a smile and the best performance of her life, because the fear she felt for Amalia right then was worse than facing the flames of hell.

"Well, it's settled, then," José exclaimed, without anyone's suspecting that his tone concealed a different intention.

But when Angela returned to her seat, he decided to postpone the discussion until the next day. He didn't want to upset his mother, whose eerie calm worried him more every day.

The old woman hadn't noticed her son's anxiety, nor did she take in her granddaughter's panic or Mercedes' fear. A new bit of joy was beating in her heart. Unaware of the tension surrounding her, she finished her dinner and cleared the dishes. As usual, she refused help from Mercedes, and she stayed in the kitchen, cleaning up.

Behind her, a pot rattled, announcing Martinico's arrival. For several weeks now he had been showing up every night. It was as if he wanted to provide her with his uninvited company. She didn't turn to look at him. That noise, like a little bird at her back, reminded her of the murmur of the mountains on summer afternoons, when she and Juanco would go walking in the foothills and return to the fountain where the water nymph had given her the advice that joined her with the love of her life.

She missed Juanco. Not a day went by when she didn't think of him. At first she had tried to keep busy with mundane tasks, attempting to forget his absence, but largely she had begun to feel his presence close to her again.

She turned off the kitchen light and went to her room, dragging her feet, shivering as though she were still slipping on the damp, tangled weeds of the sierra. She undressed without lighting the lamp. Her bones creaked when the mattress sank to receive her. In the darkness she saw him. Beside her lay Juanco, with his same lovely, youthful face. She closed her eyes to see him better. How her husband would laugh! How he would take her face in his hands and kiss it! And she would dance with her ribboned skirt that swirled at each turn. . . .

The imp went over to the bed and looked at the old woman's face, her eyelids trembling from the dream. Patiently he waited at the head of her bed until dawn, and in her dream he leaped and danced through the hills with her to the rhythm of the panpipes in the magical afternoon, and he watched her embrace the young man she had loved so madly.

Angelita, the visionary maiden of the sierra, smiled in the darkness of her dream, as innocent as when she played among the pottery of her father's kiln. And when at last her breathing ceased altogether and her spirit floated toward the light where Juanco awaited, the imp leaned over her and, for the first and last time, kissed her on the forehead.

. . .

When Pablo spied his friends without their seeing him, he stopped beside the Victrola as it launched its plaintive bolero into the wind. It was an obstacle. For a moment he thought of spying on the house from the barber shop across the street, but it didn't take long for the boys to discover him.

"Tiger!"

He had no choice but to go over to them.

"It's about time!" Joaquín greeted him. "We were about to order another round of coffees."

"Do you know Lorenzo?" Luis asked, pointing to a chubby guy with thick glasses.

"Nice to meet you."

"Pupo!" Joaquín shouted to the mulatto working behind the counter. "Another coffee."

"That business about Manolo's assassination gave me a bad feeling," said Lorenzo, who seemed to be leading the discussion. "I think gangsterism has taken hold in the university, and it's all Grau's fault. If he hadn't appointed thugs as the chief of police, we'd be singing a different tune."

"You're acting like Chibás: making accusations has become your favorite sport."

"Chibás has good intentions."

"But his obsession is driving him crazy. I'm telling you, the problem with this country isn't economic, it's social . . . and maybe psychological."

"I agree," said Pablo. "We just have a lot of political corruption and senseless violence. The change in government hasn't accomplished anything. Grau went out, Prío came in, and everything's still the same."

"That's more or less what Chibás says."

"Yes, but he's blaming the wrong person, and he's creating confusion that people take advantage of to—"

"Taw-king about gull-friends?"

The boys turned around. Pablo was startled, but he kept his composure.

"What are you doing here, Papa?"

"Señor Manuel," asked Luis, not giving him time to react, "don't you think they should change leadership in the police departments where there's been suspicious activity?"

Manuel's smile evaporated. The boys, far from discussing their future wives, were filling their heads with nonsense.

"I don't t'ink you should be taw-king about dat," he replied very seriously, with his noticeable accent. "Student should finish college and t'ink about family."

Pablo tried to redirect his father's discourse.

"See you tomorrow," he said, standing up.

They took their leave of the group.

"I didn't know Shu Li and Kei were involved in politics," his father scolded in Cantonese as soon as they left that place.

"We were just talking."

"Of things that don't concern you and that you know nothing about."

Pablo didn't respond. It was useless to debate these issues with his father. Besides, he had something more important to think about.

"I forgot to give Joaquín a message."

"Call him when you get home."

"But I don't know if he's on his way home, and it's urgent. I should go now."

"Don't take too long."

But the boy didn't go back to the café. He turned the corner, looking for a phone booth. He hadn't finished dialing when a car pulled up alongside him.

"Pablo," a woman's voice called.

Thinking it probably was Amalia, he went over to the car, but he stopped short, surprised. It was Doña Rita. Something had happened.

"Get in, son, I don't have all day."

The boy entered the car and the driver sped up to get away from the corner.

"How's Amalia?"

"She can't come," the woman said, dabbing at her eyes with a handkerchief. "Doña Angelita died last night, and José knows everything."

Pablo felt his knees melting like sugar on a flame.

"What?" he stammered? "How . . . ?"

"We were eating at her house, and Amalia had to go to the bathroom to throw up. . . . And this morning they found Doña Angela dead."

"Oh, God."

The woman leaned back in her seat. The young man's serious nature had always made her feel a little uneasy, but now she was terrified by the abyss reflected in his eyes.

"Amalia begged me to look for you," she went on. "Her father will take her to Santiago in a few days. From there, they plan to put her on a ship for Gijón with some relatives."

"Amalia never told me. . . ."

"She didn't know, either, until yesterday."

"What will I tell my parents?"

"You'll have to figure that out later on," the woman said. "But if you want to see her again, you must go look for her at midnight."

"Doña Rita, don't get me wrong. I love Amalia more than my life, and of course I'll go with her to the ends of the earth. The problem is that I have nowhere for us to stay. I have enough money to rent a room for a few days, but after that I don't know what we'd do. I can't count on my parents. It would be better just to die. . . ."

"What foolishness!" screeched Rita with such fury that the boy bumped his head against the roof of the car. "Death doesn't solve anything. It only creates problems for the living."

"What do you suggest?"

"Go get her tonight. . . . No, not tonight—they'll be at the wake. Tomorrow would be better, at dawn. Come straight to my house. She knows the address."

"Thank you, Doña Rita." He took her hand to kiss it.

"Not so fast," she said, pulling it back in annoyance. "Amalia can stay there, but you'll go to your parents' house and behave as if nothing is wrong so they don't suspect anything. And I'm warning you, if you don't get a job and marry her right away, I'll talk to her parents and have them come take her back."

"I swear to you, Doña Rita, I promise you—"

"Don't swear to me because I'm no altar saint or virgin. Do what you have to do and then we'll see."

"Tomorrow, then," he whispered, choked up, as he got out of the car.

And only when she saw him disappear in the crowd, in his wrinkled suit, running like someone who'd seen the devil, did Doña Rita breathe a sigh of relief.

ABSENCE

She had forgotten to lower the shade the night before, and now the sun was hitting her full in the face. She walked toward the window, groping for the canvas, which she unrolled with a gentle tug. Then she went to make some coffee. She vaguely recalled Gaia's message. She had heard it from her bed, when she was feeling too weak to care about the rest of the world. Now, however, she went over to the answering machine to listen one more time. Gaia had seen the house again. She didn't provide too many details, but she sounded excited.

With her toast half-eaten, she began to dial the number. She didn't stop to wonder if the other woman would be awake on a Sunday at eight in the morning, but Gaia picked up immediately, as if she had been next to the phone, awaiting her call. In fact, she had hardly slept. Could Cecilia guess where she'd seen the house? Well, in the empty lot on Douglas Road . . . Cecilia stopped chewing. That was on the same corner as *her* house. You could see the lot from her balcony. She ran to look out the window, the telephone stuck to her ear. No, it wasn't there anymore, of course. The house only appeared at night. What time had she seen it? Well, it was very late, almost one a.m. She was driving by in her car and hit the brakes so hard that everyone in the neighborhood probably heard. There wasn't a soul in the street, perhaps because of the cold.

"How did you recognize the house from inside your car, and in the dark?"

"I'd already seen it twice before; it's not the kind of house you find so often around here. Besides, it was impossible not to notice: all the lights were on. So I got out of the car and walked over."

"I thought you didn't like phantom houses."

"I don't, but it was the first time I'd seen it so close to other houses. I thought if something happened, I could scream. Besides, I was just going to watch it from the sidewalk. I was about ten steps away when the door opened and I saw the old lady in the flowered dress, along with a young couple. The woman's face looked familiar, but I have no idea where I might've seen her. The man was tall, in a dark suit and a very old-fashioned tie with light-colored polka dots. The couple didn't even look at me; only the old lady smiled at me. For a minute I thought she was about to walk down the front stairs, and it scared me so much that I turned around and got back in the car."

With the telephone pressed between her ear and her shoulder, Cecilia began to clear the breakfast leftovers.

"When was that?" she asked.

"What difference does it make?"

"Remember the national holidays?"

"Oh, yeah. It was Friday the thirteenth. . . . No, it was already after midnight. Saturday, the fourteenth."

"What happened that day?"

"What planet are you living on, girl? February fourteenth: Valentine's Day!"

"No," Cecilia said, as she stacked the last plate in the dishwasher. "It has to be a national holiday."

"Wait, I think I have a Cuban almanac."

As Gaia searched her house, Cecilia poured in the detergent, shut the door, and pressed the button. The dishwasher began to hum.

"I found it, but it doesn't say anything about that day."

"Then the theory doesn't hold."

"Maybe it has to do with something that's not listed here."

Cecilia felt annoyed. Her discovery of the national holidays had intrigued her because it had provided her with a point of departure. Now the parameters had been broken: a single date was enough to scrap the whole thing.

"I'll keep looking," said Gaia before she hung up. "If I find anything, I'll call you."

Cecilia went to the bathroom to take a shower. Lisa had suggested that she draw a map with the sightings, in order to see if there was a different pattern, but she had forgotten. The theory of fateful events had seemed so solid. . . . But what if Gaia was right and it was a question of a minor event that didn't always appear on calendars? Where could she find more information? In general, the older generation treasured those sorts of oddities. Her great-aunt had a closetful of magazines and yellowed newspapers.

She dried her hair and dressed quickly. She phoned ahead but only reached the answering machine. Maybe she'd gone to the market. It was ten a.m. To kill time, she turned on the TV and flipped through the channels. She saw some horrible cartoons with monsters, a few sports programs, two or three newscasts, some dull films, and the like. She clicked off the TV. What should she do next?

She got up to look for the city map she kept among her travel brochures, unfolded it on the table, and began checking her notes. With a red crayon, she went about marking the spots where the sightings had taken place and, beside each one, the date in very small print. Half an hour later the map was sprinkled with red dots. She turned it around and around, studying it from all possible angles, but she didn't see any special pattern or anything else that indicated a logical sequence. Suddenly she remembered something: the constellations. She tried to draw random figures but didn't accomplish much. There were no squares there, no stars, no triangles, no creatures of any kind. She attempted to cross the lines, with still no results.

Exhausted, she stepped out on the balcony. From her position she could observe the empty lot on the corner where the house had appeared. To think it had been so nearby . . . which didn't mean much, because she might not have seen it anyway, even if it had popped up right under her nose. Maybe she needed mediumistic gifts in order to see it. She vaguely recalled Delfina, her prescient grandmother, with that floury apron, surrounded by bees that always followed the fragrant trail of her desserts. She would have solved the mystery in the blink of an eye.

She returned to the dining room and stared at the speckled map; she had the feeling she was missing something. A hazy, shapeless idea floated into her mind. The premonition grew stronger when she looked at the dates again. The answer was there, before her eyes, but she just couldn't see it . . . yet.

. . .

Like an oasis in the desert, she was alone. And in a city where lovely young things abounded. Never before had she worried about her appearance, but lately her surroundings seemed to demand that she look in the mirror. "I'm devolving," she said every time she surprised herself with such vain indulgences. "I'm becoming superficial." And she left her bedroom in a hurry, filled a kettle with water, and stepped out onto the balcony to water her plants.

Now here she was again, caught in one of those moments. Barefoot, hair matted with sweat, she pulled some weeds that were growing around the roots of her carnations. After spending two hours with the map, she decided to pluck her eyebrows and examine imaginary wrinkles around her eyes until she was sufficiently horrified with herself and her behavior, and remembered her flowers. . . . The telephone rang. She dipped her hands into the bucket of water, dried them off, and picked up the receiver. It was Freddy.

"Are you up yet?"

"Since eight."

"But it's Sunday! What are you doing?"

"Watering my plants."

"I'll drop by for a minute."

She barely had time to change her blouse when he knocked at the door.

"I'm dying of thirst," he complained, shrugging off an enormous backpack.

Cecilia gave him some water.

"Where are you coming from?"

"Why don't you ask me where I'm going, instead?"

"Where are you going?"

"I have to visit some friends."

She was about to ask him the reason for all the mystery when the doorbell rang again.

"How strange!" she muttered, peering through the peephole.

"Gaia!" she exclaimed, opening the door. "What are you doing here?"

"I thought you'd probably still be thinking about the dates, and it occurred to me. . . . Oh! I didn't know you had company."

After the appropriate introductions, Cecilia suggested, "I'm hungry. Why don't we order in something to eat?"

While Gaia phoned a pizzeria and she put some sodas on ice, Freddy decided to inspect her CD collection.

"They'll be here in fifteen minutes," Gaia announced, sitting down on the sofa.

Cecilia looked for a bottle of pills.

"What's that for?" Freddy asked.

"Antidepressants. I forgot to take them this morning."

The boy gestured his disapproval.

"It's just temporary," she explained.

Freddy was about to put up an argument, but Gaia cut him off, saying, "Have you thought of anything yet?"

"I made a map with the locations of the sightings, but I didn't figure anything out."

"Did you try to see if the points formed figures?"

"There aren't any."

"What are you two talking about, if I might ask?"

Cecilia quickly explained the details about the house and its appearances to her friend. When the pizzas arrived, they were still arguing over the significance of the dates, especially the last one. Without a doubt it was the most puzzling because it broke the golden rule that had seemed to work before. They finished eating without reaching any conclusions. Freddy glanced at his watch and said it was getting late. He was practically out the door when he exclaimed:

"I forgot the most important thing!" He opened his backpack and took out several videocassettes. "I came to lend you these. They're the tapes of the pope's visit. Don't lose them."

"Thanks, really, but I'm fed up with everything having to do with that country."

"It's not true," Freddy thought. However, what he said was, "Me, too, but you learn to love the place where you've suffered."

"It's not true," Cecilia contradicted him. "You learn to love the place where you've loved. Maybe that's why I'm beginning to like Miami."

"If you're right, then you'd have to love that damn island. We've loved too many things there. Things that deserved it and things that didn't. . . ."

Cecilia felt something begin to melt inside her, like a fortress crumbling, but she refused to yield.

"I don't want to remember anything. I want to forget. I want to think I'm someone else. I want to imagine I was born in a dark, peaceful place where the only things that change are the seasons, where a stone I lay on my patio will still be there a thousand years from now. I don't want to have to adapt to anything new. I'm tired of being attached to someone only to lose him at the first turn. I can't take any more loss. My soul hurts; my memory hurts. I don't want to love because I don't want to die later from the pain."

Freddy understood her anguish, but he refused to support her desire for solitude. He couldn't allow her to cut herself off from everyone again. Lack of outside interaction is sanity's worst enemy.

"Well, I miss my friends, the walks, my adventures," he insisted, "and I don't mind admitting it."

"Absence means forgetting," Gaia warbled.

Freddy glared at her.

"When people leave a place, they mythologize it," Gaia pronounced.

"That's right!" Cecilia said. "The Havana you miss surely doesn't even exist anymore."

"Look who's talking!" Freddy grumbled. "The one who just a month ago was sighing over the lines in front of the Cinemateca."

"Sometimes people say dumb things," Cecilia admitted, slightly irritated. "A few months ago I wanted to disappear from here."

"Well, when you were in Cuba . . ."

Cecilia let him talk. Unlike her friend, she didn't pursue every echo of the island. Even though she might have felt the same pain, her spirit was far from that sort of blind surrender.

She noticed the breeze stirring the vine on a nearby wall, the birds chasing each other among the branches of the coconut palm. . . . She recalled her old city, her lost country. She hated it. Oh, God, how she hated it! It didn't matter that her memories filled her with torment. It didn't matter that the torment now resembled love. She'd never admit it, not even to her own shadow. But from some corner of her memory, the bolero burst forth: *"If all those dreams were lies, why do you complain when my heart so deeply sighs?"*

SWEET ENCHANTMENT

"*Good morning, neighbor,*" the woman greeted her from the garden, without interrupting her stirring. "I'm out of sugar. Could you lend me two cups?"

Amalia was unperturbed by the stranger in her doorway, beating that meringue. Two days earlier she had watched her through the blinds as she flitted around the men who were hauling furniture and boxes out of a truck.

"Of course," Amalia replied. "Come in."

She knew who the woman was because fat Fredesvinda, who lived near the corner, had already spoken of her.

"Here you are."

"What's your name?" the newcomer inquired, momentarily interrupting her mixing.

"Amalia."

"Thank you very much, Amalia. I'll return it tomorrow. I'm Delfina, at your service."

Her fingers brushed the hand that extended the package, and she almost dropped the sugar.

"*Ay!* You're pregnant!"

Amalia was startled. No one knew but Pablo.

"Who told you?"

Delfina hesitated.

"It shows."

"Really?" Amalia asked. "I'm only two months along. . . ."

"I didn't mean in your body—in your face."

Amalia didn't respond, but she was sure that the woman hadn't been looking at her face when she took the package of sugar. Only her hands.

"Well, see you later. I'll send you a piece of *panetela*. So your little girl will grow up with a sweet tooth."

"My little girl . . . ?" Amalia began, but the other woman had already turned her back and was walking away, beating her dessert with renewed vigor.

Amalia was dumbstruck. She had that same shocked look on her face when Fredesvinda found her a few minutes later.

"What's wrong?"

"Delfina, the new neighbor . . ."

She didn't finish the thought because she didn't want to reveal her secret.

"Don't mind her. I think she's a little crazy, poor thing. Just yesterday, when the newspaper vendor came by yelling something about some Peruvians who took asylum in the Cuban embassy in Lima, do you know what she did? She put on this Sphinx-face and said this country is cursed; then she said in ten years it'll be upside down and in thirty years the same thing that happened in the Cuban embassy in Peru will come to pass here in Havana, only backward and multiplied a thousand times over. . . ."

"What did she mean?" Amalia asked.

"I told you she's slightly touched in the noggin," the fat woman affirmed, pointing a finger to her temple. "I heard she got married recently and that she miscarried in a car accident. Guess she couldn't predict that, huh?"

"Is she married?" Amalia asked, prepared to side with the madwoman after hearing the news.

"Her husband is coming soon. They were living in Sagua, I think, but she arrived first to get the house ready while he closed the business."

"How are you, Doña Freddy?" called a voice from behind them.

Amalia ran to greet Pablo with a kiss.

"Well, I'll leave you turtledoves alone," the fat woman excused herself, walking down to the garden.

Pablo closed the door.

"I got everything done. I won't have to go back to the port anymore."

"How—?"

"I saw my mother."

Now, *that* was really a bit of news! Ever since they eloped, only Rita had stood behind them, but she couldn't offer them very much except advice.

"You spoke with her?"

"Not only that."

He took a package out of his pocket and extracted two objects that gleamed like pearls in the afternoon light. Amalia held them in her hands. They *were* pearls.

"What's this?"

"Mama gave them to me," Pablo replied. "They belonged to my grand-mother."

"What will your father say when he finds out?"

"He won't find out. Mama managed to save a few items when they left China. On board ship, they were almost all stolen, but she had hidden a necklace that she handed over to my father when they arrived, and these earrings that she never showed him because she planned to keep them for an emergency."

"They must be worth a lot."

"Enough for us to think about opening the business we talked about."

Amalia stared at the earrings. Her dream was to have a shop where she could sell instruments and musical scores. She had spent her childhood among recordings and those who made them, and that passion, which was her father's and her grandfather's, had been transmitted to her as well.

"In any case, we'll need a loan."

"We'll get one," she assured him.

She opened her eyes and, even before getting out of bed, saw Martinico sitting on the cedar display case, swinging his little legs against the strange-smelling wood. She felt the kick and placed her hand on her belly. Her baby was moving inside her. She noticed the imp's expression and felt a strange tenderness.

From the bed she could hear Pablo praying before the statue of San-Fan-Kon. That devotion to his ancestors was a sign of love that reassured her. The fragrance of incense reminded her of the day they had exchanged marriage vows. Accompanied by Rita and other friends, they had gone to the cemetery where the remains of his *mambí* great-grandfather rested.

Pablo lit some incense sticks, which he waved before his face, murmuring phrases alternately in Spanish and Chinese. Finally he stuck the incense into the ground so that the smoke would carry his prayers. That night the bridal couple and their friends gathered at El Pacífico for dinner. Beer accompanied the sweet-and-sour pork, and rice wine was served along with Cuban coffee.

Rita gave them a contract for the desired amount of their loan, with her own signature as guarantor. Thus it was that they opened their shop near the busy intersection of Galiano and Neptuno. From then on, Pablo awoke at six every morning, stopped at a warehouse to pick up the preordered merchandise, and, when he arrived at his business, phoned the interested customers. The rest of the day was devoted to selling and jotting down special orders, and he returned home at seven in the evening, after the day's business was sorted out.

"Honey, I'm leaving," Pablo said from the hall.

Pablo's announcement roused her from sleep. She needed to get dressed so she could fill in for her husband, who was going to the port to pick up an important shipment. When she leaped out of bed, Martinico vanished from the display case, reappeared by her side, and held out the sandals she was looking for. The woman couldn't help being surprised at the attentions the imp had extended to her ever since the start of her pregnancy. She dressed hurriedly and ate breakfast. A little while later she was walking toward the corner.

Luyanó was a humble neighborhood inhabited by laborers, teachers, and professionals just starting their careers or businesses and waiting for time—or good fortune—to allow them to move elsewhere. Amalia enjoyed those sunny, peaceful streets. Traveling half an hour to downtown Havana, where her store was located, didn't bother her. She was happy. She had married Pablo, she was awaiting her first child, and she had the business she'd always dreamed of.

She boarded the bus, which left her off near the Malecón, and half an hour later she unlocked the metal bolt, opened the glass door, and turned on the air-conditioning. Guitars and bongos hung from the walls. On the black satin-lined counters, musical scores displayed their cardboard and leather covers. Two grand pianos—one black and the other white—filled the available space to the left. Stringed and metal instruments were arranged along the shelves. A jukebox was wedged into the right-hand corner. She pressed a button, and Beny Moré's voice flooded the morning with passion: "Today, as yesterday, I keep on loving you, my darling . . ." Amalia sighed. The man sang like an angel drunk with melancholy.

The door chimes sounded the arrival of her first customer, or rather two: a couple looking for sheet music of Christmas carols. Amalia showed them half a dozen scores. After much deliberation and bargaining, they bought three. Almost immediately a young man came in and tried several clarinets, finally taking the cheapest one. The chimes rang again.

"Doña Rita!"

"I stopped by to check up on you, my dear. I remembered today is the day Pablo picks up merchandise at the port, and I figured you'd be alone. Besides, last night I had a dream, and that's why I want to look at some music."

"Go on, tell me."

"I dreamed we were in Dinorah's house. . . ."

"The card reader?"

"Yes, but I was the one reading the cards, and I could predict the future. I saw it all so clearly! And I'm sure everything will come true. . . . You were in the dream too."

"And what did you see?"

"That's the worst part: I don't remember anything. But I was like a clairvoyant. I looked at the cards, and everything went through my mind. Suddenly I felt a hand grab me by the throat, cutting off my breath. When I was just about to suffocate, I woke up."

"But what does that dream have to do with the music?"

"It's just that a while ago I read about a new opera by Menotti. I think it's called *The Sibyl,* or something like that. I don't know, but I felt an impulse to read the libretto."

"I have an index of composers and another one of recent titles. . . ."

"Let's look for it by title."

And with the gasping "Crazy for Mambo" and the mournful "Ah, Life" by the Great Sonero playing, they sifted through the inventory of titles.

"This is it!" Rita exclaimed. "*The Medium,* by Gian Carlo Menotti. How much is it?"

"For you, free of charge."

"Absolutely not. If you start giving things away, soon you'll have to ask for money, and that's not why I signed for you at the bank."

"I couldn't charge you after all you've—"

"If you don't charge me, I won't take it, and I'll have to go somewhere else to buy it."

Amalia told her the price and went in search of wrapping paper.

"I'm not sure why I want this," Rita confessed as she paid. "Maybe the dream has to do with this bronchitis that keeps me up at night."

The actress walked out with her score under her arm, and Amalia set to organizing the catalogs. A chime alerted her that Pablo was entering through the back door, but she was already attending to another customer. When he left, Amalia went to the back of the store.

"Pablo."

Her husband gave a start, dropping the pamphlets.

"What's that?"

"Joaquín asked me to hold on to them for a week." He hurriedly stuck them in a box.

"It's political propaganda, isn't it?"

Pablo remained silent as he continued putting the pamphlets away.

"If they catch us with those things, we'll be in trouble."

"No one will ever guess that in a music shop—"

"Pablo, we're about to have a child. I don't want trouble with the police."

"I can assure you, it's not dangerous at all; just a call for a strike."

Amalia observed him silently.

"If we don't take action against Prío," he said, "the situation will get worse for everyone."

He hugged her, but she didn't return his embrace.

"I don't want you getting involved in politics," Amalia insisted. "That's for people who wheel and deal instead of getting real jobs."

"I can't abandon Joaquín. That's what friends are for."

"If he's such a good friend of yours, ask him to take this stuff away."

He stood there staring at her, not knowing what else to add. Amalia knew about all the disappearances and imprisonments that filled the pages of the newspapers every day. He didn't need to convince her that things were going badly. It was precisely her awareness of the danger that made her back away from the bigger picture.

"This country is a disaster," he insisted. "I can't just sit around twiddling my thumbs."

"Do you want your child to be born an orphan?"

The bell rang again.

"Please," whispered Amalia.

"All right," he sighed. "I'll take them someplace else."

He gave her a kiss to calm her.

"How did things go this morning?"

"Rita stopped by," she replied, relieved at the change of subject.

"Someone told me she was sick."

"She has a touch of bronchitis."

"Well, she ought to be in bed," Pablo said, heading toward the back door. "I'm going to the club for a little while."

"Where?"

"The sports club at Zanja and Campanario, don't you remember? I want to find out about that *wushu* business. A little exercise will do me good."

"All right, but don't be late," she agreed, walking out into the showroom.

A tall, ungainly man in a gray suit that hung on him like a sheet from a nail was examining an ivory baton, one of the curiosities that Pablo had ordered to give the place a touch of distinction. She put on her nicest smile, but she froze in place when the visitor turned to greet her. Instinctively she looked toward the back of the store. If only Pablo had forgotten something! The visitor was Beny Moré.

"Good afternoon," she said in a thread of a voice. "How may I help you?"

"Do you have anything by Gottschalk?"

"Let me see," she said softly, turning toward an armoire with glass doors. "Nineteenth-century music."

She pulled out a catalog and traced a few lines with her finger.

"Here it is. Gottschalk, Louis Moreau: *Fantasy on El Cocuyé* . . . *Cuban Country Scenes* . . . *A Night in the Tropics* . . ." She muttered a number and looked for it in the armoire. "Look."

She showed him two books.

"I'll take whichever ones you recommend," he said with a candid, almost apologetic smile. "I don't read music, you know? I don't understand this scribbling one bit!"

Amalia nodded. How gauche she was! She suddenly remembered that this man who sang like a nightingale and conducted his orchestra like a genius had never learned to read music and had to dictate his compositions. He was a sort of tropical Beethoven—not deaf but, rather, blind to the signs of the pentagram.

"I want them as a gift," he added, responding to a question Amalia hadn't posed. "My nephew is studying in a conservatory and always talks about this composer."

Amalia wrapped the scores in silvery paper and tied them with a red ribbon.

"And how much is that?" the singer asked, pointing to the ebony and ivory baton.

Amalia told him the price, convinced he wouldn't go for such extravagance.

"I'll take it."

Amalia could think of just one thing: if only her father could see her . . .

"You haven't been open very long, have you?" the man asked as she took his change from the register.

"Two months. How did you find out about the store?"

"Someone mentioned you at the Imp and I didn't forget the name. It struck me as very unusual."

Amalia had to make an effort to appear unemotional. The Imp was her father's recording company. Who could have mentioned them there?

"Good luck," said the musician, lightly tipping his hat. "Ah! And keep listening to me every once in a while."

For a moment she didn't understand what he was saying. Then she realized that the jukebox was still playing the medley of his songs.

Amalia watched the fragile figure pause a moment on the sidewalk, on the green marble tile, before disappearing into the crowd, but her eyes remained fixed on the ground, on the faunlike creature that was their business logo, the letters that read *Pan's Flute*. Why had they chosen such a ridiculous name? It had occurred to both of them that long-ago night in Viñales as they were making plans for the future. A very strange association of ideas.

A sudden racket shook the windows. Amalia stood motionless, wondering what it could be: a door slamming, a thunderbolt, or a tire that had blown? Only when she saw some people stopping to look, others stumbling, and a few running away and screaming did she realize that something truly serious was happening. She peeked out the doorway.

"What's going on?" she asked the owner of the Stork, who was already locking her shop with a sorrowful expression.

"Chibás committed suicide."

"What?"

"A few minutes ago. He was giving one of his speeches on the radio and he shot himself right there, in front of the microphone."

"Are you sure?"

"My daughter heard it. She just phoned me."

Amalia thought she was dreaming.

"But why?"

"Something he couldn't prove, after he'd said he would."

Amalia noticed the panic around her and heard the commotion rising from every corner of the city. Everyone was running and shouting, but no one seemed able to explain what had occurred. She thought about Pablo. Had he gone to the sports club, or was he involved in some other sort of mix-up? Police whistles and a few gunshots filled her with terror. She went to find her purse and, against her better judgment, closed the door and headed out into the street. She had to find her husband. She attempted to walk calmly, but she was jostled by pedestrians running in both directions.

Two blocks ahead, a crowd, marching and chanting, dragged her along in its current. She tried to take shelter in a doorway on the sidewalk, but it was impossible to escape the avalanching throng. She was obliged to keep up the same pace, practically running, knowing that if she stopped, the deaf and blind mob might trample her.

The tires of two police cars squealed in the middle of the street, and the crowd slowed its pace. Amalia took the opportunity to move forward and clamber up on the stoop of one of the entryways. People were still tripping over her, but it was no longer quite so dangerous. A column blocked her view of what was developing on the corner, so she didn't realize that many people had begun to retreat.

The first shots started a stampede she managed to avoid, protected on the stoop. However, the first gush of water knocked her to the ground. For a moment she didn't comprehend what was happening; she just felt the blow as the pain clouded her vision. She looked at her clothing and saw the blood. She had been hurt when she bumped against the edge of the wall.

Once more the water hit her right in the chest, thrusting her against a cement column covered with flyers. She could see the announcement for the new show at the Tropicana ("The greatest open-air cabaret in the world"), which half-concealed another one that proclaimed the opening of the Blanquita Theatre ("With 500 more box seats than Radio City Music Hall in New York, until now the largest in the world"). And she vaguely considered the destiny of her island, with its obsession with boasting the biggest this or that, or for one thing or another . . . A strange country, full of music and pain.

The water struck her again.

Before falling to the ground unconscious, she saw a flyer for the recent musical hit about a naughty incident that had taken place nearby: "A girl was going to Prado and Neptuno. . . ."

MATTERS OF THE HEART

Half asleep, Cecilia picked up the phone. It was her great-aunt, inviting her to have a proper breakfast, and she warned her she wouldn't take no for an answer. She already knew Cecilia had called her several times that week. If she needed to talk or to ask her for anything, today was the day.

She rinsed her face with cold water and dressed quickly. In her haste she nearly forgot the map. She'd had a week full of work, with two articles for the Sunday supplement, "Grandma's Culinary Secrets" and "Your Car's Secret Life," even though she knew nothing about cooking or auto mechanics. But despite these and other minor distractions, she never stopped thinking about the infamous map. Her aunt had disappeared—or, in any case, she hadn't answered the telephone. Cecilia had even passed by her house a couple of times with the idea of calling the police if she noticed anything unusual. A neighbor informed her that Loló went out very early every morning and came back late. What could she be up to?

From the staircase she could hear the parrot squawking: "Down with the scum! Down with the scum!"

And also her aunt's screams, worse than the bird's: "Shut up, you damn parrot, or I'll stick you in the closet and you won't get out for three days!"

But the parrot paid no attention and continued screaming all sorts of slogans:

"Go, Fidel! Give the Yankees hell! Fidel, thief! You've stolen all our beef!"

"Blessed Christ!" her aunt screamed. "If you keep that up, I'll put parsley in your food!"

Cecilia rang the doorbell. The bird shrieked with fright and the aunt with alarm, thinking perhaps that one of the neighbors was about to lynch her. Then there was a deadly silence, followed by a rapid hammering and a dull thud.

"That's it," Cecilia thought. "She's finished her off."

The door opened.

"How good to see you, my child," the old woman greeted her with her most affectionate smile. "Come in, come in, you'll catch a cold standing there."

While Loló fastened all the locks on the door, Cecilia glanced around.

"Where's the parrot?"

"Over there."

"You've finally done it! You've chopped her to bits!"

"Child, what ideas you have!" her aunt muttered, crossing herself. "Those aren't Christian thoughts."

"What Fidelina does to you isn't very Christian, either."

"She's one of the Lord's creatures," the old lady sighed with a martyred expression. "I forgive her because she knows not what she does."

"I heard screaming and then some noise. . . ."

"Oh, that . . ."

Loló went over to a closet and opened the door. Next to several boxes and suitcases, there was the parrot in her cage. Seeing the light again, she shrieked jubilantly, but her joy lasted only for a moment. Loló slammed the door in her beak.

"I had to drag the cage over; it weighs about ten tons. The iron feet rattle when it moves. That's what was making the noise."

"What a pity," muttered Cecilia, disappointed.

"Let's go into the dining room. The hot chocolate's ready."

Cecilia followed her toward the sweet, tempting aroma. Loló had risen early to buy the freshly made churros at a nearby café. When she returned, she put them in the oven to keep warm and melted a few tablets of Spanish chocolate in a pot filled with milk. Now a brimming pitcher of hot chocolate stood in the center of the table. Next to it, the churros were piled up on an earthenware tray, giving off steaming cinnamon fumes.

"What did you want to see me about?" her aunt asked as she served.

"I haven't visited you for a while."

"I could be your mother twice over, so don't tell me any tales. What's going on?"

Cecilia told her about the phantom house again and the historical dates on which it had appeared.

". . . but now it's been spotted on a day that has nothing to do with those events," she explained, "and I don't know what to think."

The girl dipped the end of a churro in her hot chocolate, and when she brought it to her mouth, a dark drop fell on the tablecloth.

"I almost forgot!" she cried.

She ran out into the living room, pulled the map from her purse, and returned to the dining room to spread it out on the table; but her aunt refused to look at anything until both of them had finished breakfast. After clearing the dishes, Loló began to examine the map, while Cecilia watched her every move. A couple of times she noticed that she would frown and stare quietly into space, to see or hear something that only she could perceive. Then she silently shook her head and went back to the map.

"You know what I think?" the old woman suddenly said. "That house could be a reminder."

"A what?"

"A sort of monument or sign."

"I don't get it."

"Until now, most of those dates have coincided with Cuba's recent history. But it's possible that the house might also want to show its special relationship with someone."

"What's the meaning of that?"

"Nothing. It's just establishing its coordinates."

"Can you explain more clearly?"

"Child, it's very simple. All this time, the house might have been announcing: 'I come from such-and-such a place, or I stand for a certain thing'; now it's saying 'I'm here for such-and-such a person.' I think the house started out in Cuba, but it's also associated with something or someone in this city."

Cecilia didn't reply. She found the theory rather disconcerting. If the house was the repository of some individual history that ended up in Miami, why did it keep showing up haphazardly in such unlikely parts of the city?

The clock chimed, stirring her from her reverie.

"I'm sorry, dear, but I've got to go to Mass, and afterward . . . Goodness! Just look at your skirt."

A chocolate stain stuck out from underneath her blouse.

Loló went to the refrigerator, opened it, and took out a piece of ice.

"Go to the bathroom and rub it with this."

The girl left the dining room.

"*Tía,* why did you go out so many times this week?" she asked as she passed through the bedroom. "I thought something had happened to you. You're not going to tell me you were stuck in church all these days . . ."

She trailed off when she saw the photos on top of the dresser. There was her grandmother Delfina, sporting one of her customary floral dresses and her usual smile, surrounded by roses in her garden. In another picture was a man Cecilia couldn't identify except for the unmistakable parrot he carried in a cage. When she saw the third photo, she felt the floor shift beneath her feet. With a combination of tenderness and horror, she recognized her parents as bride and groom: she, with her hair pulled back and in a long gown; he, with his actor's face and that tie with light-colored polka dots that Cecilia had long since forgotten. At the bottom of the photo was a dedication: *To my aunt Loló, souvenir of our wedding in the Sacred Heart Parish of El Vedado* . . . and a date . . . a date . . .

"February is the only month of the year when I go to church every day," the old woman said from the kitchen. "I always go to pray to the memory of your parents, who were married on February fourteenth to show how much in love they were. May God always keep them in His glory!"

I WAS MISSING YOU

When Amalia found out she had lost her baby—a girl whose sex Delfina had predicted—she didn't cry. Her eyes fixed on Pablo's face, as he sat in a chair in the hospital where she was born and where her grandmother had worked as a slave when the Marquis of Almendares's daughter had lived in the mansion. The stained-glass windows still reflected their colors over the walls and on the floor. The ferns on the patio still whispered beneath the rain, filling all the rooms with the fresh fragrance of the Cuban countryside.

"Those bastards," Pablo muttered between clenched teeth. "Look what they've done to us."

"We'll have another one," she said, stifling her tears.

With damp, reddened eyes, Pablo leaned over to embrace her. And it was as if Delfina had transmitted her sibylline powers to her, because a few months later she was pregnant again.

During the period that followed, Amalia thought a great deal about Delfina, who had moved again, although not without filling her head with prophecies beforehand. Her predictions continued to give Amalia nightmares.

One day, as they were discussing Chibás's suicide, she had asserted: "His death didn't prove anything, and it's left us worse off than before. In a few years this island will be hell's waiting room."

Before leaving, Delfina had stopped by to borrow some rice.

"There will be death after the deluge," she told Amalia.

At first Amalia thought she was referring to her baby, killed by the hosing . . . until the 1952 coup d'état took place, led by General Fulgencio
Batista, all very civilized and without firing a single shot. The dead, in
effect, began to show up later. The prophecies didn't stop there. Worse yet
would be the arrival of La Pelona, the Grim Reaper, a mythical being who,
supported by an army of red devils, would become the Judas, Herod, and
Antichrist of the island. Even small children would be massacred if they
tried to escape his clutches, Delfina swore.

Anxious to banish negative thoughts, she returned to her embroidery as
her mind wandered. Many things had happened of late. Her mother, for
instance, had appeared at the store. Did her father know? Of course not,
Mercedes had reassured her. And he mustn't find out under any circumstances. Resolute in his refusal to see her after her elopement and sub-
sequent marriage, he had become antisocial and didn't even laugh like
before.

Amalia didn't like to think about him because she always ended up crying. She had a husband who adored her and a mother who now lived only
for her, but she missed her best friend. She longed for his irreplaceable
affection, that of an old, faithful companion.

Pablo did his best to relieve his wife's sadness. From the time he was an
adolescent, he had been aware of the strong bond between this father and
daughter, two creatures as alike as they were hardheaded. Now nothing
seemed to cheer her up. After a great deal of thought, he decided to use
one of the strategies he knew to make her stop worrying: he'd bring her
some problem—the more complicated, the better—that would require her
direct intervention.

That night he had arrived home, complaining about his job. Sales were
booming, and he couldn't meet his customers' demands. Besides, the
business's reputation was like a social calling card. What a pity they
couldn't attend all the events to which they were invited. He hadn't said
anything because he didn't want to upset her, but how could they accept
so many courtesies if they had no way to reciprocate? They couldn't ask
anyone over . . . unless they decided to move to a more appropriate place.
Where? He wasn't sure. Maybe an apartment in El Vedado?

Although she was due in a month, Amalia gave up her idle chats with
fat Fredesvinda and, newspaper in hand, went to look at more than twenty
apartments in two weeks. Pablo was pleased, although somewhat puzzled.

Never before had he seen his wife so eager to get involved. He didn't know if her enthusiasm was due to wanting to help or to some other, secret desire. He suspected the latter when a real estate agent handed him the keys to an apartment.

The day of the move, Amalia stopped at the entrance, as though she still doubted this could be her new home. The apartment was small but clean, and it had a smell of imminent wealth. There was a balcony from which one could glimpse a slice of sea, and ample picture windows that let the light pour in. The bathroom's blinding whiteness mesmerized her, as well as the gigantic mirror in which she could see herself reflected full-length if she stepped back a little. She walked around the whole place, reveling in such brightness and so much blue. After her big old house near Chinatown and the modest dwelling in Luyanó, the new apartment left her breathless.

It soon became obvious that their old furniture wouldn't work there. The bed looked like a medieval beast against the light-colored walls, and the sofa was a faded monstrosity beneath the sunlight that filtered through the balcony.

"We can't invite anyone over like this," Pablo concluded, half annoyed and half satisfied. "We need new furniture."

It was then he discovered that furnishing their house was the real passion lurking behind her enthusiasm.

With the help of loans and credit, Amalia found a leather sofa with two matching armchairs and two wooden lamp tables for the living room. In the dining room she placed a cedar table that could expand to accommodate eight guests, and chairs made of the same wood, upholstered in wine-colored fabric. Above the table she hung an amber crystal chandelier. In addition, she bought wineglasses, silver cutlery, kitchen utensils . . . Little by little, she added more details: fine, filmy curtains, porcelain plates for one wall of the dining room, a seascape above the sofa, a ceramic bowl filled with decorative snail shells.

In less than two weeks she had transformed the apartment into a place that cried out for the admiration of guests. Wasn't that what Pablo had hinted at when he complained about the old junk? As she spoke, she unpacked the case she had just bought: two silver candleholders that she adorned with red tapers. It was the finishing touch for her dining room.

That night after dinner, Rita called to let them know about the premiere of her new play, *The Medium*.

. . .

It had been a disturbing performance, filled with shadows moving across the stage. But they weren't theatrical shadows; they weren't fake ghosts that Doña Rita, in her role as Madame Flora, brought back to life before her guests to preserve her reputation as a clairvoyant.

Madame Flora brought her hand to her throat, insisting that phantom fingers had attempted to strangle her, which was impossible because she, more than anyone else, knew that such ghostly apparitions were pure invention. . . . Amalia felt a contraction. Now the medium accused the two children who had helped her stage the fabrication, saying that one of them had tried to give her a scare. Nobody—they both swore—had done any such thing. They were too busy playing with puppets and imitating voices to frighten the guests.

Amalia tried to ignore the pulsing in her belly. She remained very still, hoping it would quiet down. Uncharacteristically, she didn't get up during intermission. She asked Pablo to bring her some candy and, quite distressed, waited in her seat until the lights went down once more. Was it the music or that eerie world that occupied the stage? Madame Flora turned to the boy, Toby, enraged. He had to be the one who had touched her again, but the mute boy couldn't reply; despite her daughter's protestations, Madame Flora threw him out of the house.

Ay, her child, dead in that hosing . . . and Delfina's demons . . . and the Chinese pearls rescued from the massacre . . . What magic did the actress use to attract so many specters to her? Anything could happen when she performed, and now her Madame Flora had turned out to be more than Amalia could bear. Onstage, the medium had gone mad with fear. And one night, convinced that some noise was a ghost trying to kill her, she fired a shot, killing poor Toby, who had returned in order to be with his beloved Monica.

But Amalia saw something no one else had seen. The hand that Rita brought to her throat gave off a reddish glow like a lunar eclipse. Blood . . . as if her throat had been slit.

The audience rose, bursting into applause. Pablo barely managed to keep Amalia from falling as a clear, warm liquid dampened the carpet in the corridor.

. . .

And now the baby girl was gurgling on the tile floor. The imp Martinico, tired or bored, was out on the balcony, amusing himself by throwing seeds at the passing cars three stories below. The noise of the door startled him. Pure reflex caused him to vanish, although only the child and her mother noticed, just as Pablo's flushed face appeared in the doorway.

"My God! What a fright you gave me!" the man cried with a start. "Weren't you supposed to be going shopping?"

"I was tired. What are you doing here?"

"I forgot some papers."

She recalled that, two weeks earlier, she had surprised him leaving the apartment as she was arriving, and he had been startled then too.

"Tonight the contract will be settled," he said. "We need to be at Julio's by seven."

Pan's Flute had grown into a chain of four stores that sold not only musical scores and instruments but also recordings of foreign music. Julio Serpa, the main record importer on the island, had asked Pablo to be his distributor, but first he would have to open three more stores. When Pablo replied that he didn't have enough money, Julio offered to become the co-owner, buying out fifty percent. That way, Pablo could double his capital and both could invest an equal share. But Pablo didn't accept. That would mean having to consult him on every decision. The impresario raised the ante and offered to buy out forty percent, but Pablo didn't want to own only sixty percent of his dream. He told him he'd sell him just twenty. Finally the man invited him to dinner with a consultant, someone with enough experience to serve as go-between in cases like his. He wanted to propose another plan that he just might like.

"I'll pick you up at seven," Pablo said, kissing his wife before leaving.

Amalia put the baby, who had fallen asleep, to bed. Only then did she realize that her husband had forgotten the papers he had come home for.

Amalia wanted to make the best possible impression, but Isabel's fussing exploded into a tantrum, distracting her from getting dressed.

"Do you think she's sick?" asked Pablo, rocking the child, whose face was contorted, in his arms. "Maybe we should cancel the dinner."

"Absolutely not. You can go by yourself if you have to. I'll take care of . . ."

Martinico poked his head out from behind the curtain, and the girl smiled. While the imp and the little one played peekaboo, the woman finished dressing. The whimpering started up again when Martinico waved his hands to say good-bye, grew more insistent when the family walked into the hallway, and reached its height at the front door of the Serpa mansion.

"Come in," said the impresario, opening the door for them. "Vivian!"

His wife's complexion was stark white, almost translucent.

"Would you like something to drink?"

Isabel was still crying in her mother's lap, and for a moment the adults looked at each other, not knowing what to do.

"Go to the library with Pablo," Vivian suggested to her husband. "I'll look after Amalia and the baby."

From the door, Amalia noticed the warm golden glow from the mahogany bookshelves, stacked with leather-bound volumes.

"Let's go into the kitchen," Vivian said. "I'll give her something."

"I don't think she's hungry. She ate before we left," Amalia replied, as they walked down the hall. "And even if she is, I don't know if you'd have anything for her. She still doesn't eat lots of things."

"Don't worry, Freddy will see to it."

Amalia thought about the distance that separated her family from this one. She didn't even dare dream of the luxury of a cook.

Isabel was no longer crying, perhaps because of the sweet aroma of *panetela* cake that filled the kitchen. Amalia stopped short when she saw the cook.

"Fredesvinda!"

The fat woman was astonished too.

"Amalita!"

"You two know each other?" Vivian asked, with a new inflection to her voice.

"Of course," Amalia began. "We were—"

"I worked for the lady's aunt and uncle when she was just a little girl," the cook interrupted. "Doña Amalia visited the house quite often."

Amalia didn't dare correct her. Freddy's eyes held a glint of warning.

"Is this your little girl?" the woman asked.

"Yes," Vivian answered. "What can we feed her?"

"I've just baked a cake."

"A little warm milk would be good," Amalia said.

"Do whatever the lady wants, Freddy. . . . You're in good hands, Amalita."

The tapping of heels receded down the black marble hallway.

"Why did you make up that story?" Amalia whispered.

"What did you expect me to do?" Freddy said, reverting to her intimate tone as she heated a little milk. "Admit we were neighbors?"

"Why not?"

"*Ay,* Amalia, you're too innocent," her friend chided, slicing a piece of cake. "If you and Pablo hadn't improved your social standing, Don Julio wouldn't have invited you over for dinner. Saying you used to be a cook's neighbor isn't going to help you get ahead, and Pablo needs to close that deal."

"How do you know?"

"We servants hear lots of things."

While Freddy talked, the child filched a slice of cake and held out her little hand for another.

"No, Isa," Amalia said. "That's not for you."

The girl began to whine.

"Try a little *panetela* before you go," urged the fat woman. "I'll give her some milk and try to get her to sleep. . . . *Ay,* how cute she is!"

She began walking back and forth with the child in her arms, humming softly. By the time Amalia had finished eating the *panetela,* she realized her baby had fallen asleep, rocked by Fredesvinda while she hummed in her beautiful contralto.

"I didn't know you sang so well. You should do it professionally."

"Anyone would think you have no eyes. Who'd want to hire a three-hundred-pound singer?"

"You could lose a little weight."

"Don't you think I've tried? It's a sickness. . . ."

The echo of voices reached them.

"Hurry, go," Freddy scolded her. "A lady shouldn't spend so much time talking to the hired help. If the baby wakes up, I'll come and look for you."

Amalia walked down the hall, guided by the sound of laughter. She couldn't remember if she should turn right or left, but the voices reverberating off the walls guided her to the parlor.

"What would you like to drink, Amalia?"

Before she could respond, two chimes rang in the entryway.

"That must be him," Julio said. "Vivian, offer Amalia something. I'll get it."

Pablo leaned over to get more ice, and Amalia sipped her liqueur as the voices in the hallway grew closer. All of a sudden the conversation stopped abruptly. It was Pablo's sudden tension, rather than the prolonged silence, that made Amalia turn toward the door. There stood her father, with a completely shocked expression on his face.

"Are you all right, Don José?"

"Yes . . . no . . . ." Pepe muttered, as if he couldn't breathe.

A vague, undefined groan could be heard in the hall.

"We could have the meeting another day," Julio proposed.

"Excuse me," said the plump Fredesvinda, struggling to hold Isabelita, who was trying to clamber down from her arms. "Señora Amalia, the child was calling for you."

"Sorry, Don Julio," murmured José.

And to the astonishment of his hosts, he turned and walked out of the parlor. He groped for the door and tried to open it but was impeded by the complicated lock.

He felt a tug on his pants.

"*Tata.*"

The little girl, not much more than a baby, was toddling over to look at the gentleman who couldn't open a door. José took two steps backward to get away, but the little one wouldn't let go of his pants.

"*Tata,*" she called, with unusual persistence.

It was his own expression and his daughter's too. Weakened, overcome, and conquered, he bent down, scooped her into his arms, and began to cry.

It was as though no time had passed, except now her father had more gray hair, and his eyes glowed in a new way whenever he played with his granddaughter. If José had been fascinated by his daughter, Isabel had an almost hypnotic effect on him. He never tired of picking her up, or telling her stories, or showing her how to open the instrument cases. Amalia took advantage of every opportunity to leave the child with him while she attended to other errands. Now, on a hot afternoon in that eternally humid city, the jangling bells again announced her arrival at the store where she had played so many times as a little girl.

"Hi, Papi," she greeted the man who was leaning over the counter.

José raised his head.

"We're losing her," the man uttered softly.

His terrified expression paralyzed her.

"Who?"

"Doña Rita."

Amalia left her daughter on the floor.

"How? What happened?" she asked, her knees giving way.

"She has a tumor. And on her vocal cords!" her father said, choking on his words. "Good heavens! A woman who sings like the angels."

Images of the Rita who had been her companion since childhood paraded at random through Amalia's mind, and she realized she owed her whole life to that woman: a doll with golden curls; the silvery shawl she wore when she first met Pablo; the letters she carried back and forth for her beloved; the shelter she offered her when they were planning to elope; the loan for their first shop . . .

"It's like vengeance from hell," her father sobbed. "As if the devil was so jealous of that voice that he wanted to shut it down forever."

"Don't say those things, Papi."

"The most unique voice this country has ever had. . . . There will never be anyone else like her!"

Her father's eyes were red, but she didn't want to cry.

"I have to see her," she decided.

"Then don't go anywhere; any minute now she'll walk through that door. She told me she'd stop by after rehearsal."

"She's going to sing? In her condition?"

"You know her."

A loud noise from behind the piano brought them running. Isabelita had knocked over several empty violin cases; she wasn't hurt, but the noise had frightened her and she was screaming at the top of her lungs.

"Good morning, people! What's going on here? Has the world come to an end, or what?"

That unmistakable voice, a voice like fresh, frothy laughter.

"Rita."

"No kissy-kissy right now. Let me see that little angel who's screaming like the devil."

As soon as Rita took her in her arms, Isabel quieted down.

"Take the money, Pepe," she said, rummaging in her purse. "Count it to make sure it's all there."

"Rita."

"Enough with the 'Rita, Rita.' You'll wear it out."

The actress retained her usual expression.

"Amalita," her father said, "go do whatever you need to do, and I'll take care of the little one."

"No, Papa. I'd rather take her."

"But didn't you come here to drop her off?"

"I was going to do some shopping, but I don't feel like it anymore."

"Why don't the two of us go alone, like in the good old days?"

Amalia turned to Rita and noticed the scarf wrapped around her throat. When she looked up, she realized Rita had caught her staring.

"Leave the child with me," Pepe urged her. "I'll keep her till tonight."

Amalia understood that her father was clamoring not just for his grand-daughter but also for an entire world that was collapsing with the weight of the bad news. For the first time she observed how stooped he had grown, and she discovered a shadow of fear in his eyes, an insecurity that appeared to be the beginning of a tremor, but she said nothing. She gave a kiss to her daughter, another to him, and she left with Rita to explore Havana.

They ended up sitting in a café on Prado, watching the passersby strolling beneath the trees where sparrows and pigeons took refuge. They spoke of a thousand trivial things, skirting the one topic that neither of them dared to mention. They reminisced about their old escapades, the first visit to the card reader, Rita's laughing fit when she found out that Amalia's suitor was Chinese. . . . A few pigeons approached the table to peck at crumbs on the ground.

"*Ay, mi niña,*" the actress sighed after a long silence, "sometimes I think it's all a bad joke, as if someone had invented this to frighten me or make me suffer."

"Don't say that, Rita."

"It's just that I don't see myself closed up in a box, with my mouth shut and not even two words to say. Can you imagine? Me, who's never stopped singing out the truth to my people."

"And you'll keep on singing it, you'll see. When you're cured . . ."

"Let's hope so, because I don't believe I'm going to die."

"Of course not, Doña Rita. You never will."

She arrived home depressed and decided to sleep for a while. Her father would bring Isabelita home later, so she took advantage of the opportunity to forget about the world for a couple of hours.

Those high heels were killing her. She entered her apartment and took them off in the living room. A commotion from the bedroom stopped her. Just in case, she calculated the distance between the bedroom door and the exit. With her heart in her throat, she tiptoed toward the room.

"Pablo!"

Her husband jumped, startled.

"What's that?" she asked, pointing to three packages tied with a cord that her husband had dropped on the floor.

"Some copies of the *Gunnun Hushen.*"

"What?"

"From Huan Tao Pay's newspaper."

"You're speaking Chinese to me," she said, but immediately she realized that the expression was too literal to be clever. "What are you talking about?"

"Huan Tao Pay was a countryman who died in prison. They tortured him for being a communist. These are copies of his newspaper, relics . . ."

Amalia remembered her husband's mysterious meetings, how he'd been returning home at unexpected hours.

"Was he a friend of yours?"

"No. That happened years ago."

"Didn't you swear to me you'd never get involved in politics again?"

"I didn't want to worry you," he said, hugging her, "but I have bad news. It's possible they may come to search the house."

"What?"

"We don't have time," he replied. "We'll have to hide the papers somewhere else."

He went over to the window and looked out.

"They're still there," he confirmed, turning to his wife, "and I can't leave because they saw me come upstairs. It wouldn't be good if they knocked at the door and I wasn't here. They'd be suspicious right away."

"Where should I take them?"

"To the roof," Pablo decided, after hesitating briefly.

Amalia put her shoes back on. Pablo arranged the packages in her arms and opened the door for her. The numbers on the elevator panel indicated that someone was calling it from the first floor.

"Take the stairs, and don't move until I come to get you."

Amalia climbed the five flights in less than two minutes. Where could she hide those pamphlets? She remembered a conversation she had overheard between a neighbor and the super. The water tank that supplied apartment 34-B, empty ever since its occupants' divorce, had a leak and was out of service. She began lifting the concrete lids until she found it and threw the three bundles in before replacing the cover.

She waited a few minutes for Pablo, pacing nervously around the roof until the wait became unbearable. Then she ran her fingers through her hair, smoothed her skirt, and took the elevator back down to her floor.

When she saw the door standing open, she felt her legs tremble. One look was enough to reveal the broken lamp, the contents of the drawers emptied all over the floor, the closet in disarray . . . And Pablo? Her eyes clouded over. There was blood on the floor. She ran to the balcony in time to see they were beating him and shoving him into a police car. She tried to scream but it came out a muted cry like that of a dying animal. The world grew dark; she didn't fall. A pair of invisible hands supported her. Her childhood sweetheart, the love of her life, was on his way to some prison.

HAVANA OF MY HEART

Whom could she tell about her discovery? Lisa suspected the phantoms had returned because they had grown fond of someone; Gaia had recommended she find out more about the inhabitants of the house, because she felt the dates were connected with them; and Claudia had told her she walked with the dead. And no wonder! She was up to her neck in investigating the house in which her grandmother Delfina, old Demetrio, and her parents had traveled. Her own great-aunt had suggested the dates might refer to something that had originated in Cuba and was now in Miami. Each theory contained a germ of truth.

Cecilia stopped in her tracks: there was a loose piece to the puzzle. The house and its inhabitants couldn't be related to her because she'd never met old Demetrio, despite the fact that the old lady insisted she'd introduced her to him. Maybe those ghosts weren't there because of her but rather because of Loló, the only link to the four of them. She felt deeply distraught. She'd started to believe that her parents were trying to make contact, but apparently her great-aunt . . . Wait a minute. Why would her father have gone looking for Loló, his mother-in-law's sister, instead of following his own daughter? She had another upsetting thought. What if the specters had family reunions? Were there communities of ghosts? Did their presence become stronger when they all came together?

Struck by yet another possibility, she took out the map and studied the dates again. Although Loló had been in Miami for thirty years, the house sightings had begun only after Cecilia arrived in the city. Was it a coincidence? She looked for the point where the first appearance had taken place and marked the first address where she'd lived. Then she traced the second one. Instead of counting the streets, she decided to measure the distances on the map. It would be easier. She began comparing the spaces between the visions and the places where she had lived. By the time she had finished, she had no doubt. The house always inched a bit closer to the place where she was residing. She repeated the operation with Loló's neighborhood for the last twenty years, but the pattern wasn't the same. The house was connected to Cecilia. It was looking for her.

Now, more than ever, she was glad she hadn't told anyone. This was madness. She still didn't understand what the deceased Demetrio had to do with her. Would the mysteries of that wretched house never cease?

Once more she felt a twinge of pain mixed with the memory of her parents' voices and the beaches of her childhood. The dead who wandered through Miami brought her the scent of a city she now despised more than any other. She was a woman from nowhere, someone who didn't belong. She felt more forsaken than ever. Her glance fell on the videos Freddy had brought. She wasn't interested in seeing them, but she had to write an article on the pope's visit to Cuba. In the hope of forgetting her demons, she picked up the cassettes and went into the living room.

The white vehicle drove through all of Havana. For the first time in history, a pope was visiting the largest island in the Caribbean. And as Cecilia studied the masses, witness to the miracle, she rescued from the oblivion of memory those sidewalks and where they had taken her so many times. "Do you remember the Teatro Nacional?" she asked herself. "And the Café Cantante? And the bus stop in front of the statue of Martí? And the cold that escaped from the Rancho Luna Restaurant when the door opened as people walked by?" She went on listing memories, absorbed in the sunny spectacle of the streets. She could practically hear the hum of the trees and the gentle wind that rose off the Malecón, wafting along Avenida Paseo toward the plaza, and the warm light that intensified the colors of that bucolic urban landscape. For the first time she saw her city through different eyes. Her island seemed a rustic, untamed garden that, despite its dusty buildings and the fatigue etched on its citizens' familiar faces, glowed with beauty.

"Beauty is nothing but the beginning of a terror we are able to endure," she recalled. Yes, true beauty is terrifying and often leaves us in a state of absolute abandon. It hypnotizes through our senses. Sometimes the slightest fragrance—like the perfume emanating from the sex of a flower—can make us close our eyes and leave us breathless. At moments like those, our will is overtaken by such an intense stimulus that it cannot be released until the moment has passed. And if that beauty reaches us through music or through an image . . . ah! Then life hovers in suspense, stunned before the supernatural sounds or the limitless potency of a vision, and we feel the terror begin. But at times it passes so fleetingly that we don't notice it. The mind immediately erases the traumatic event and leaves us with only the impression we have been in the company of an unavoidable power, something that threatens to pull us along and might make us lose our sanity. Beauty is a blow that paralyzes. It's the certainty of finding oneself before an apparently ephemeral phenomenon that will transcend us, nonetheless . . . like the landscape Cecilia now contemplated.

On-screen she saw her city from the helicopter that traced the voluptuous curve of the Malecón. In spite of the altitude, it was possible to distinguish the shaded avenues, the gardens of venerable mansions from the days of the Republic, with their stained-glass windows and marble floors; the perfect design of the streets that led to the sea; the colonial fort that used to be known as Santa Dorotea de Luna; the majestic entrance to the tunnel that dipped toward one side of the Almendares River, emerging on Quinta Avenida . . . The images began to grow confused, and the magic vanished. According to the announcer, Cuban Television had just cut off the transmission. "The same old thing," she thought. "They interrupt the signal because it's not in their interest to show the houses where terrorists and drug dealers are hiding."

She barely realized that she had ejected the videocassette and put in another one. The equestrian statues in the parks, the dried-up fountains, and the crumbling roofs of the buildings all paraded through her mind. Why were ruins always beautiful? And why were the ruins of a once-beautiful city even more so? Her heart was torn between love and horror. She didn't know what she was supposed to feel for her city. She suspected it had been wise to move away. She now had a clearer view of a landscape she'd never really seen because of its proximity. A country is like a painting: you can see it better from a distance. And that distance had allowed her to understand many things.

At once she recognized her debt to Miami. There she had learned stories and sayings, customs and flavors, ways of speaking and working: treasures of a tradition that had been lost in Cuba. Miami might be an incomprehensible city, even for those who lived there, because it reflected the rational, powerful image of an Anglo-Saxon world while its spirit bubbled with stormy Latin passion; but in that contradictory, feverish place, Cubans preserved their culture as if it were the British crown jewels. From Miami, the island was as palpable as the cries of the people on the screen: "Cuba for Christ! Cuba for Christ!" She now knew that a specter floated on the island, or perhaps it was a mystique that she hadn't noticed before— something about Cuba that she could discover only in Miami.

She was furious. She hated her country and yet she loved it. Why was she so confused? Maybe it was the ambivalence the images provoked. The world was spinning backward; the pope was celebrating Mass in Santiago de Cuba. It was as if his visit was a demonstration of Einstein's theories, finally proven on that haunted island. Black holes and white holes. Everything absorbed by one can reappear in the other, thousands of light-years away. Was that Miami or Santiago she was watching on the screen?

In the heart of the island, a throng congregated in front of a replica of the Shrine of Our Lady of Charity of Miami, the most beloved sanctuary of Cubans in exile. In front of the chapel, the dark waters carried vegetation, fragments of bottles, and all sorts of messages back and forth. The sea was the kiss of both coasts, and Cubans on either side gazed out upon it, searching for traces of loved ones who lived on the opposite shore.

The architectural design of the original hermitage, located on the eastern part of the island, was quite different. And so, the image of the Miami temple on Cuban soil was a strange spectacle. Although, when one thought about it, it completed a cycle. The original image of the Virgin stood preserved in her lovely basilica in the mountains of El Cobre, near Santiago de Cuba. The Miami hermitage had been built in imitation of her mantle. The Cuban setting where the pope now found himself also emulated— unwittingly or deliberately reproducing that mantle—the profile of the temple in exile. It was like one of those tricks with mirrors that repeat an image ad infinitum. And beneath the bower that was supposed to represent the union of everyone, the pope crowned the spiritual mother of all Cubans.

The mestiza Virgin's tiny crown was taken from the image, and the pope's trembling fingers placed another, more splendid one on top of her coppery mantle. The Virgin of Charity was proclaimed queen and patron saint of Cuba. The people went wild with enthusiasm, and the congas began: "Dear brother John Paul, don't ever go home." And another one, even bolder: "Dear brother John Paul, please take me to Rome."

Cecilia sighed as the camera panned the landscape. In the distance the blue mountain range rose, along with the sanctuary of El Cobre shrouded in eternal clouds, next to the spot where the visionary archbishop Antonio María Claret allegedly had predicted, in the nineteenth century, the terrible disaster that would befall the island. Cecilia recalled fragments of the prophecy: "A young man from the city will arrive at this Sierra Maestra and will spend a short time committing acts that will be quite removed from Christ's commandments. There will be unrest, desolation, and slaughter. He will wear an unusual uniform that no one in this country has ever seen before. Many of his followers will wear rosaries and crucifixes around their necks, the images of many saints, side by side with weapons and munitions." More than a hundred years before she was born, the saint had seen visions that terrified him: "The young man will govern for about four decades, around mid-century, and during that time there will be bloodshed, much bloodshed. The country will be devastated. . . ." And Cecilia imagined how alarmed the archbishop's companions must have been to see him fall into a trance while traveling through the mountains on his mule. "When this time is over, that young man, who will already be old, will die, and then the sky will become clear, blue, without this darkness that now surrounds me. . . . Columns of dust will rise up, and once more bloodshed will flood Cuban soil. There will be revenge and retribution among the injured, and other, greedy folk, which will cloud everyone's eyes with tears. After these few agonizing days, Cuba will again be the pride of all the Americas, including North America. . . . When this occurs, a state of joy, peace, and unity for Cubans will arrive, and the Republic will flourish beyond anyone's imagination. There will be such great activity of ships on the waters that, from afar, Cuba's noble bays will look like cities piercing the sea. . . ." Cecilia had no doubt that if the archbishop had envisioned the first part of the story with such clarity, there was no reason for him to be mistaken about the conclusion . . . unless God had since decided to alter the plot to confuse the saint with the ending of a different story; but she was confident that wasn't the case.

The girl drank in the images that were now displayed on the screen with greater clarity: the foggy hills of the mountain range, teeming with legends; the mythical sanctuary of El Cobre, full of ex-votos from centuries past; the sacred red earth of Oriente, soaked with minerals and blood. "Beauty is the beginning of terror . . ." Cecilia closed her eyes, unable to bear any more.

She hadn't been to the bar for three weeks, fearful of finding too much comfort in Amalia's tale, which had slowly become an even more agonizing story than her own. But perhaps that was why she kept returning. As she listened, she realized her own life wasn't so unbearable. When she arrived, the darkness throbbed with life amid the bodies that filled the room. She headed for her customary corner, tripping over tables, and long before she got there, she could discern the sparkle of a jet stone in the darkness. Practically groping her way, she moved forward until she was face-to-face with Amalia.

"I've been waiting for you," the old lady said.

Her eyes shot off sparks that seemed to illuminate everything. Or was the light just a reflection of the images on the screen behind her? Images of the Malecón with its statues and lovers, its fountains and palm trees. *Ay,* her lost Havana . . . Cecilia summoned the recollections buried in her memory, and a wild idea struck her. Didn't they say the island was surrounded by submerged ruins? And didn't many people swear that those Cyclopean stones belonged to the legendary continent described by Plato? Maybe Havana had inherited the karma of Atlantis, which lay so near its coasts . . . and probably its curse, as well. If people could be reincarnated, then why couldn't cities? Didn't she know that cities had souls? The phantom house was proof. And if that was true, couldn't they also carry the burden of others' karmas? Havana was like the rest of those mythical lands: Avalon, Shambhala, Lemuria . . . That's why it left an indelible impression on those who saw it or had lived there.

"Havana of my heart . . ."

The bolero throbbed in her ears like a premonition. She looked at Amalia once more. Every time she saw that woman, strange revelations came upon her. But for now she didn't want to think, just learn the ending of the story that had made her forget about her own for a while.

"What happened after the military police kidnapped Pablo?" she asked.

"He was freed a little while later, when the guerrillas took the capital," the woman muttered, playing with the links of her chain.

"*. . . if I gave you my soul, Havana of my heart . . .*"

"And after they let him go, what happened?"

Amalia gave a sigh.

"It turned out my Little Tiger was still the same old rebel as always."

Part Six

CHINESE

PUZZLE

From Miguel's Notebook

To stick someone in China:

In Cuba, the expression alludes to someone who finds himself in a complicated situation or a very tight spot. A student might remark that his teacher "stuck him in China," referring to questions on a very difficult test.

By extension, it has also come to signify the existence of a situation so overwhelming as to render any reaction to it impossible.

I SHOULD HAVE CRIED

People milled around in front of the doors to the Hotel Capri, trying to enter the cabaret where Freddy, that artist of monumental body and voice, was about to sing. She would give two performances that Friday: one in the late afternoon and the other around midnight. The commotion wasn't due only to the crowd's anticipation of Freddy's singing but also to the state of growing unrest since an army of bearded men had poured into the streets and onto the estates, like a relentless tide advancing throughout the island.

A few months after they took power, rumors started to spread about hasty trials, secret executions, desertions by top officials . . . and "intervention" in large companies had already been announced. *Intervention,* a euphemism for a violent concept, used to circumvent more explicit phrases like "stripped of their property" or "robbed of their businesses." After the fat cats, it was said the smaller ones would also fall. Some had begun plotting against the government in fear of what might occur, but their voices were silenced by the effervescence of the majority, buoyed along by a whirlwind of hymns and slogans.

Displaying the same fervor with which it applauded each act of the new government, the bejeweled throng pushed its way into the Red Room, where everyone waited to hear the popular contralto, but the former cook seemed unhappy.

"These people have no respect, Amalia," she confided to her friend in the dressing room. "And without respect, there are no rights."

Amalia, glad to have recovered her husband when the rebels opened the jails and released the former insurgents, did not take her complaints too seriously. After months of agonizing separation, they had been reunited. Pablo was free: that was her only thought. And more important, he wasn't going to get involved in any political movement.

"They're only rumors," she assured Freddy.

For a few weeks now, the singer had become increasingly uneasy, and she gave in to her emotion whenever she sang:

"I should have cried but, you see, what I feel is almost joy. I should have cried in pain, perhaps in shame. . . ."

Sitting at her table, Amalia squeezed Pablo's hand. Ah, the good fortune of hearing a bolero sung stylishly, the pleasure of a cocktail made of rum and liqueur-soaked cherries, the privilege of nibbling fruit with flesh as supple as the tropics . . .

A noise jolted her from her daydreams. Someone was arguing with the doorman, trying to force his way into the cabaret.

"It's your father."

Pablo's announcement startled her. Oh, God—Isabelita! She had left her with him. She never did figure out how she reached his side, but suddenly there she was on the sidewalk, wondering what had happened to her little girl.

"Isa's all right," José said, trying to allay her fears. "I'm not here because of her. It's Manuel."

"My father?"

Pablo froze. Ever since he had committed that act of betrayal that dishonored his family, his father hadn't spoken to him; but Rosa communicated with them in secret.

"Your mother called," José told him. "The rebels are in the restaurant."

"The rebels? Why?"

"Manuel was helping some conspirators."

"That's impossible. My father's never been involved in politics."

"It seems he was hiding a friend at the back of the store for a few days. The man's already gone, but they're inspecting the business with the idea they'll find something."

Without waiting for further explanation, Pablo and Amalia climbed into José's car. No one spoke during the trip to the old section of the city.

When they arrived, the neighborhood seemed deserted: nothing unusual for Chinatown, where the residents preferred to observe the city from behind their blinds. Fear floated in the atmosphere, palpable as a cloud, perhaps because many people recalled similar scenes from the old country they had fled a lifetime ago. Now, as if some surly demon were pursuing them, they again faced the same nightmare in the city that had welcomed them with open arms.

Pablo got out of the car before José could come to a complete stop. He saw the smashed cash register on the sidewalk, the shop doors that stood wide open, the darkness inside . . . Rosa ran to her son.

"They took him away," she said in Cantonese, her voice broken with grief.

And she kept on babbling words too garbled for Pablo to comprehend. He finally pieced together that Manuel was in a station wagon parked at the curb, concealed by tinted windows.

Pablo confronted the man in the olive green uniform as he left the restaurant with a sheaf of papers in his hand.

"*Compañero,* may I ask what's going on?"

The conscript looked him up and down.

"And who are you?"

"The owner's son. What happened?"

"We have reports of a conspiracy here."

"The time for conspiracies ended for us long ago," Pablo explained, attempting to appear friendly. "My father is a peaceful old man. This restaurant is his whole life's work."

"Yes, that's what everyone says."

Pablo wondered if he could maintain his composure.

"You can't destroy an innocent person's business."

"If he's innocent, he'll have to prove it. Right now, he's coming with us."

Rosa fell to the man's feet, speaking to him in a confused jumble of Cantonese and Spanish. The conscript tried to free himself, but she clung to his knees. Another man, coming out of the restaurant, shoved the woman violently aside.

Pablo attacked him. With a quick movement, he threw him to the sidewalk headfirst and immediately immobilized the second man, whom he grabbed from behind. His assault took the soldiers by surprise; they'd never seen anything like it. Two decades would pass before the West became acquainted with the martial art the Chinese call *wushu*.

The soldiers scrambled up from the ground while José and Amalia tried to restrain Pablo. One of them grabbed his revolver, but the other man stopped him.

"Leave it," he muttered, gesturing around them.

As they began to realize how many witnesses had seen the incident, they opted to close the restaurant, placing a seal on the door to indicate an intervention by the revolutionary government. They returned to their station wagon.

"Where are you taking him?"

"To the Third Precinct, for now," they said. "But don't bother going there today or tomorrow. It'll be difficult for us to release him anytime soon. First they'll have to find out if he's a counterrevolutionary or not."

"I plotted against Batista!" Pablo shouted as the vehicle started up. "And I was thrown in prison!"

"Then you'll understand that all this is for the good of the people."

"My father *is* the people, you idiot! And you can't justify revolutions by destroying his property."

"Your father will sleep in jail as a warning," the driver yelled, throwing the vehicle into gear. "And he won't be the only one! Right now there are search warrants issued for the businesses of plenty of conspirators."

Pablo hurled himself against the station wagon, but José held him back.

"I'll file suit in court!" he roared, flushed with rage.

He thought he heard the men laughing as the vehicle disappeared in a dark, fetid cloud.

"I didn't fight for this shit," Pablo said, feeling a new wave of rage rise in his chest.

Amalia bit her lip, as if she could anticipate what was lurking behind his words.

"I have to go to the studio," José muttered, turning pale.

"You have no reason to worry," Pablo began, but he stopped when he noticed his father-in-law's expression. "What's the matter?"

"I . . . kept some papers," José stammered.

"Papa!"

"Just for one night, as a favor for the lady upstairs. They took her husband prisoner, and she was afraid of being searched. I burned everything, but if the man confessed, and if they threatened her. . . ."

They got into the car after convincing Rosa it would be safer to spend the night with her son and daughter-in-law.

The ten-minute drive to the Imp was agonizing. Several nearby streets were blocked by rubble. Jukeboxes, cash registers, tables, and other accessories formed mounds of debris on the pavement. When they arrived at the recording studio, the door had been boarded shut, and the terrifying seal of revolutionary intervention covered the lock. From the sidewalk, Pablo, José, Amalia, and Rosa saw the shattered glass, the broken shelves, the musical scores scattered on the floor.

"My God!" José exclaimed, ready to collapse.

How dare they! This was the universe his father had created. There were Beny's footsteps, La Única's smile, Maestro Lecuona's dances, the Matamoroses' guitars, Roig's *zarzuelas*. . . . Forty years of the best music on the island threatened to disappear in the face of such incomprehensible violence. He ran his fingers across the nailed boards, imagining he would never recover the treasures from a place that his daughter and little granddaughter had filled with their laughter. His life had been taken away.

Amalia noticed her father's pallor.

"Papa."

But he didn't hear her; his heart ached as if a fist were wrenching it.

He closed his eyes so he could no longer see the destruction before him.

He closed his eyes so he could no longer see his country.

He closed his eyes so he could no longer see.

He closed his eyes.

Every morning Mercedes imagined she might find a bouquet of roses on her doorstep. Or a box of chocolate-covered liqueurs. Or a basket of fruit tied up with a red ribbon. Or a letter that someone would have to read to her later, since she still didn't know how. And not just a love letter but an inventory of afternoons that paled in comparison to the sheen of her skin, always signed with the same name, the only one that mattered to her . . . Because Mercedes could not remember that José was dead. Her mind now wandered through the days when her suitor had courted her while she, immersed in a different sort of fog, had barely noticed his efforts to conquer her dark, bewitched heart.

She remembered other things too: she had lived in a brothel; she had been possessed by countless men; her mother had died in a fire that nearly destroyed Doña Ceci's business; her father had been murdered by a rival businessman. . . . But she didn't have to hide it anymore because no one knew what was locked inside memory. The only one who shared her secret had died. . . . No! What was she thinking? José would come to see her, just as he did every day at noon, while Doña Ceci screamed at the cleaning woman. He'd sing her a serenade, and she'd peek out the window toward the corner, fearful that Onolorio's thugs would get there first.

But José didn't come to her. She got out of bed and looked impatiently through the window, at the street . . . the street where armed pedestrians passed by day and night: men with long weapons they brandished even in front of children. She was the only one who realized these were Onolorio's thugs, although they dressed differently now. She had to warn José, or they'd kill him as soon as he rounded the corner. She felt overcome by a sudden panic.

"Assassins!"

The word caught in her chest, emerging a little with each heartbeat. She wanted to pronounce it, even in a whisper, but the nightmarish scene had left her mute.

"Assassins!"

There was a commotion near the corner. Her fear finally overcame the paralysis that had kept her silent.

"Assassins!" she muttered.

The tumult on the corner grew louder. A few people were chasing someone. Mercedes couldn't make out his face, but she didn't need to see him to know who he was.

Like a wandering spirit, like a banshee calling for the death of its next victim, she went out into the street, shrieking:

"Assassins! Assassins!"

And her howls blended with the crowd, which also shouted accusations at a man fleeing from his crime.

But Mercedes neither saw nor understood any of this. She threw herself on the pursuers who were trying to stop her José. In the confusion she heard a gunshot and, for the second time in her life, again felt that numbness in her side, in the same place where Onolorio had stabbed her eons ago. This time the blood gushed forth, much warmer and more profusely. She moved her head a little so she could see the people coming toward her, calling for a doctor, for an ambulance. She wanted to reassure them, to let them know that José was nearby.

She searched all the faces for the only one that was smiling, the only one that could comfort her.

"Do you see him?" she tried to utter. "I told you he'd come."

But she couldn't speak, only sigh, when he held out his arms and lifted her. What tenderness there was in his eyes! Like on those afternoons so long ago . . .

They walked away from the throng still gathered in the middle of the street. Behind them they heard the din and the wail of a siren, coming to save a dying woman whose spirit had already left her body. But Mercedes didn't turn back to look. José had come to take care of her, this time forever.

How her world had changed! "No one is ever prepared to lose their parents," Amalia said to herself. Why hadn't they warned her? Why hadn't they ever explained how to deal with such loss?

She rocked nervously in front of the television. She tried to hold it together on the outside, for her daughter's sake and for the other little one who would soon arrive, but something had shattered in her breast. She would no longer be "someone's daughter"; she'd never again call anyone "Mama" or "Papa"; there would no longer be two people running to her side, shutting out the rest of the world, to embrace her, spoil her, come to her aid.

As if that weren't enough, Pablo had changed too. Not with her. He still loved her madly. But ever since his father's arrest, a new bitterness seemed to gnaw at his soul. Manuel had been given a hasty trial and sentenced to one year in prison. Pablo tried to use his influence. He'd even spoken with several officials whom he had known from the days of his underground activity, but each petition slammed him up against an unscalable wall. Only after Siu Mend had served his sentence did he finally return home, badly injured and fatally ill, so sick that many people thought he wouldn't live much longer. Amalia suspected that Pablo wouldn't just stand around with his arms folded. She'd remembered that same expression from when he was conspiring against the previous government. And he wasn't the only one. Many friends who had previously celebrated the arrival of the new order now came to visit them with outlooks as grim as their own. Amalia knew they whispered whenever she turned her back and fell silent whenever she returned with the coffee.

She tried to think of other things—for example, the masses of refugees fleeing the insurmountable wave of changes. Hundreds of them had escaped. Even Freddy had left for Puerto Rico. . . .

"Isabel!" she called her daughter, attempting to drive those thoughts away. "Why don't you take a bath?"

Her belly weighed a ton, even though she was only five months along.

"Papa's in the shower."

"When he comes out, you'll take your bath."

Isabel was only ten, but she acted fifteen, perhaps because she had already seen and heard too much.

Amalia changed the channel and rocked in her chair, practically suffocating with the effort. Everything bothered her, even breathing.

"And now . . . La Lupe!" announced an invisible emcee, in that throaty voice in vogue during the early sixties.

She tried to ignore the pain in her back and listen to the singer everyone was talking about: a mulatto woman from Santiago, with fiery eyes and the hips of an odalisque, shimmying onstage like a mare in heat. She was beautiful, Amalia conceded. Although, in truth, ugly mulattas were the exception in Cuba.

"Just like on a stage, you act out your pain. . . . Your drama doesn't fool me. . . . You see, I know that play. . . ."

Too theatrical, Amalia decided. Or hysterical. There was none of Rita's suave grace in this new generation. . . . What was she thinking? You can't get pears from an elm tree. There would never be another like her.

"Lying . . . how well you play that part. After all, it seems that's how you are."

There was a slight change in the tone of the music; it grew unexpectedly dramatic. Suddenly, La Lupe seemed to go wild: she undid her bun; her hair spilled all over her face; she clawed at her chest and struck her belly.

"A play, with you it's all a play: rehearsed lies, a perfect simulation. . . ."

Amalia couldn't believe her eyes when she took off one shoe and began attacking the piano with her stiletto heel. Three seconds later she seemed to change her mind, hurling the shoe from the stage and insistently pummeling the pianist in the back while he continued playing, unperturbed.

She held her breath, waiting for someone to come onstage with a straitjacket and take the singer away, but nothing happened. Quite the opposite: each time La Lupe began one of her outbursts, the audience screamed and applauded convulsively.

"This country has gone crazy," Amalia thought.

She was almost glad her father wasn't there. José, who had rubbed elbows with the most exquisite artists, would have died all over again had he seen this farce.

"Can't you change the channel?" Pablo shouted from the bedroom.

"Did you see her?" Amalia asked. "She's like a lion in a cage."

How far would this madness go? Had times changed that much? Was she getting old? She stood up to turn off the television, but she didn't get there. A sharp buzzing made her jump.

"What do you want . . . ?"

She had barely opened the door when four men pushed her inside. Startled, Isabel shrieked and ran to hide against her mother's legs.

Shoving aside the furniture and decorations in their way, the men searched the apartment and discovered some leaflets sandwiched between the mattress and the bed frame. Two of them attempted to remove Pablo by force, but he resisted fiercely. While mother and daughter screamed, they dragged him, semiconscious and bleeding, from the room. Amalia stationed herself between the men and the door and received a kick in her belly that made the vomit rise out of her right there.

The shouting had alerted the neighbors, but only one elderly couple dared approach when the men had finally gone.

"Señora Amalia, are you all right?"

"Isabel," she whispered to the girl as she felt the thick liquid running between her legs, "go call Grandma Rosa and tell her to come right away."

The blood pooled at her feet, mixing with the water that was supposed to protect her baby. For the first time she noticed that the goblin Martinico was looking at her, terrified, and that's when she learned that imps can grow pale. Besides, he was shimmering with a greenish light, the meaning of which she couldn't determine.

Amalia wanted to shout insults, scream, bite into her arms, and rend her clothing like La Lupe. She would have sung a duet with her if only she could spit in the face of the one who had deceived them, promising them the moon with that monkish expression that doubtless concealed—*ay, Delfina!*—the face of a red devil.

"A play, with you it's all a play: rehearsed lies, a perfect simulation. . . ."

She tried to get up, but she felt herself growing weaker. Before she blacked out, she suddenly understood why people were so crazy about La Lupe.

Rosa stirred the fish soup and tossed in a handful of salt before tasting it. In what seemed like another life, there would have been pieces of ginger, oyster sauce, and vegetables to season it, and the fragrance would have wafted up to the clouds like the aroma of the soups her nanny had prepared. She poured part of the broth into a container and went out into the street.

Since Siu Mend's death, she no longer found pleasure in cooking, and less so now that she couldn't indulge those moments of inspiration when adding a few sesame seeds or a splash of sweet-and-sour sauce could make all the difference between an ordinary dish and something worthy of the gods. But despite it all, every afternoon she prepared a little food for Dr. Loreto, the father of Luis and Bertica, her son's former schoolmates.

The doctor had moved nearby after his family left for California. The government had refused him an exit visa without any explanation, but he suspected the reason was a certain influential individual: a former guerrilla leader, recently arrived from the mountains, who had tried to make a move on his wife. The couple had suffered from horrible reprisals for years, until Irene died of cancer. The doctor had forgotten about the matter until he ran into the man again, face-to-face, the day he went to apply for permission to leave the country. His children didn't want to abandon him, but he insisted they leave. Now he looked like the mere shadow of the once striking doctor he had been—a man who always drank a glass of Calvados after those sumptuous meals he ordered at the Red Dragon. They had labeled him a *gusano*—a worm. As his punishment for wanting to pursue the luxuries of imperialism, they had forbidden him to work. Now his clothing hung off his frame like wet rags.

Rosa found him in the doorway of his home and she nostalgically recalled the figure of the *mambí* who had also once sat in a doorway, waiting for Little Tiger, the boy who was always ready to listen to a tale of the days when men fought with honor for justice in the world. . . . Now the old man was dead and her Little Tiger was languishing in prison.

Twenty years. That was what the trial had decreed for his connection with a faction that planned to sabotage the government. Twenty years. She wouldn't live that long. It reassured her to know that Amalia existed. To a woman who saw the world through his eyes, it was a comfort being second place in her son's heart.

She greeted the doctor and handed him the dish. He looked like an old man, and his decrepitude only increased with the anxiety and the tremulous gestures with which he sipped the soup. A dog approached to sniff, but he kicked it away.

Rosa averted her eyes, unable to bear this image of such a man. What would await her, alone and without any resources but a miserable pension?

She returned home, closed the door, and turned off the only light that illuminated the living room, but the glow lingered in the room. There, in a shadowy corner, was her mother, the stunning Lingao-fa, with her almond eyes and that silken skin.

"Kui-fa," the dead woman called, stretching out her arms.

"*Ma,*" she whispered in the language of her childhood, embracing her.

"I've come to keep you company," the spirit murmured in a musical Cantonese.

"I know," she replied. "I've been very lonely."

In her mother's embrace, she luxuriated in the aroma of her childhood—her mother's smell—which brought back so many memories. Then she stepped back and went to the door to her room. From the threshold she turned to her mother.

"Will you stay with me?"

"Forever."

She entered her room, climbed onto the bed she had shared with Siu Mend, and took a rope that hung from the highest beam. Soon she would see her husband, Uncle Weng, the *mambí* Yuang, Mei Lei. . . . From now on she would live with them; she would hear her own language; and she would eat moon cakes all day long. She felt a little sorry for Dr. Loreto, though, so thin and defeated, so worn out. . . . He'd never again have his afternoon bowl of soup.

Out of the corner of her eye, Amalia watched her daughter, who walked alongside her with a bouquet of flowers. On this Day of the Dead, both of them would fulfill the wish of the man who had been imprisoned for seven years. They had wanted to go to the cemetery instead, but Pablo had begged them to take the flowers to the monument built in honor of the Chinese *mambises.* He thought it was a more appropriate place to honor his family. Great-grandfather Yuang was the first on the list of rebel ancestors. His father, Siu Mend, who had died demanding what was taken from him, followed. And his mother, Kui-fa, who had renounced a life shrouded in sadness, deserved the same respect.

The breeze that swept up leaves and petals also carried a familiar tune: a childhood ditty that Amalia hadn't heard in years:

> *A Chinaman fell*
> *into a well,*
> *his guts turned to water,*
> *And started to swell.*
> *Arré, pote pote pote,*
> *arré, pote pote pa . . .*
> *His wife ran away*
> *to a little café,*
> *her socks were on backward*
> *and her slippers were gray.*
> *Arré, pote pote pote,*
> *arré, pote pote pa . . .*

The woman looked around, but the street was deserted. She gazed up at the sky, but all she saw were clouds. The words, sung in a mischievous little voice, spoke of a common form of suicide among the coolies who tried to escape slavery by jumping headfirst into a well. Pablo, who had heard about it from his great-grandfather, had described it to her.

For a few seconds the music kept falling from the sky. Maybe she was imagining it. She looked at her daughter, an adolescent with wavy hair like her grandmother, Mercedes, a pink complexion like her Spanish great-grandmother, and slanted eyes like her Chinese grandmother, but the girl was off in her own world. She had stopped before the inscription engraved on the monument. Without needing an explanation, Isabel knew that no other nationality—among the dozens populating the island—could declare anything similar to what that phrase revealed.

Her mother gently touched her elbow. The girl, roused from her daydream, placed the flowers at the base of the column. Amalia recalled that soon they would mark another anniversary of Rita's death. She would never forget the date because, in the midst of the best-attended wake in Cuba—or had it been at Chibás's wake?—she had bumped into Delfina.

"This April seventeenth won't be the only wretched date in our history," the clairvoyant assured her. "A worse one is yet to come."

"I don't believe it," sobbed Amalia, who couldn't imagine anything worse than the tragedy of losing Rita.

"Within three years, on this same day, there will be an invasion."

"A war?"

"An invasion," the woman insisted. "And if we stop it, it will be the worst misfortune in our history."

"You mean if we *don't* manage to stop it."

"I meant what I said."

Amalia sighed. Where could sweet Delfina be now? She thought about Maestro Lecuona, dead in the Canary Islands; about dear Freddy, buried in Puerto Rico; about so many musical icons of her island who had taken refuge in foreign lands after the defeat of the invasion she predicted. . . . And ultimately Amalia would remain alone with her daughter, while Pablo served his twenty-year sentence.

The last little life she carried in her womb had died of a kick. It would have been her third child, if not for the harshness of the men in her history. Life is like a game of chance in which not everyone gets to be born and others die ahead of their time. Nothing could be done to guarantee a better or worse outcome. It was too unfair. Although maybe it wasn't a question of fairness, as she'd always believed, but of other rules she needed to learn. Maybe life was an apprenticeship. But for what, if after death there was only eternal bliss or eternal damnation? Or was it true what Delfina said: that there were more lives after death? If only that weren't the case. She didn't want to come back, if that meant starting another charade governed by such illogical rules. She would give anything to ask God why he had chosen such a fate for her Pablo, a loving, honest man. . . .

"Mommy," the girl whispered, pointing to the policeman watching them from a distance.

They needed to go. They weren't doing anything illegal, but one could never tell.

Isabel once again read the phrase engraved on the black marble, a phrase she would show the children she would one day bear, when she would tell them about the deeds of her great-great-grandfather Yuang, the tenacity of her grandparents Siu Mend and Kui-fa, and the rebelliousness of her father, Pag Li. The memory of her father filled her eyes with tears. Ashamed of her own weakness, she cast a scornful glance at the policeman still watching them but who couldn't quite decipher her gesture. Then off she went with her mother, her head higher than ever, repeating like a mantra, so she might engrave it in her genes, the phrase on the monument that her future child must never forget: *There never was a Chinese Cuban deserter; there never was a Chinese Cuban traitor.*

DEFEATED HEART

Cecilia felt as if she had been thrown to the bottom of a pit. It seemed to her that Amalia's tragedy formed part of her own life. When she was living in Cuba, her future had been like the horizon surrounding her: a monotonous sea with no possibility of change. Her refuge was in her friends, her family, and her friends' families. Some helping or comforting hand would always appear, even if that hand belonged to another castaway like herself. Now the universe was within her reach. For the first time she was free, but she was alone. Her family was practically extinct, her friends dead or dispersed throughout the world. Several of them had committed suicide, weighted down by life's complications. Others had drowned in the Strait of Florida, attempting to flee. Many were exiles in unlikely places: Australia, Sweden, Egypt, the Canary Islands, Hungary, Japan, or any other corner of the planet where there was a piece of earth to land on. It was a myth that the Cubans had immigrated en masse to the United States; she could name dozens of friends who lived in almost legendary countries as distant and inaccessible as the mysterious Thule. The friendships she had cultivated so lovingly throughout her life were now lost in unforeseen banks of fog. Certain doubts caused by the occasional squabble would never be resolved; misunderstandings would remain misunderstandings for all eternity; and explanations would be left to ponder what might have been but never was. . . . And better not to think about her own homeland, that sick, broken landscape, that ruined geography with hardly a hope of recovery. Nothing had escaped Cuba's dire fate. She recalled every bit of her own history, and her heart was choked with pain. She didn't know a single scenario in which everyone lived happily ever after. That's why, night after night, she ended up in the bar, listening to Amalia's stories in the hope that, in spite of everything, there'd be a happy ending.

That Thursday she had gone to bed very early, but she couldn't sleep. At two a.m., seized with insomnia, she decided to get dressed and go out. As she drove, she tried to see the glittering of the stars through the windshield. The blackness of the sky reminded her of the saying "It's always darkest before the dawn." And it struck her that, perhaps, if the expression was rooted in truth, like all bits of popular wisdom, very soon her life would be tinged with the light of morning.

She pushed open the door to the bar and looked around among the tables. It was so late that she didn't think she'd find her friend, but she was still there, looking dreamily at the photos that flashed across the two screens hanging on either side of the dance floor.

"Hi," Cecilia greeted her.

"My daughter and grandson are coming in two weeks," the woman announced without preamble. "I hope you'll come and meet them."

"I'd love to," Cecilia replied, sitting down opposite her. "Where will you see them?"

"Here, of course."

"But kids aren't allowed in places like this."

Amalia bit into a piece of ice that crunched like a dried shell.

"My grandson's not so small anymore."

Two or three couples moved slowly on the dance floor. Cecilia ordered a Cuba libre.

"What about your daughter's husband?"

"Isabel's divorced. Just she and her boy are coming."

"How'd they manage to get out?"

"They won the visa lottery."

Now, that was luck! To get a visa in that mountain of half a million applications per year was almost a miracle. When would the exodus end? Her country had always been a land of immigrants. People from every latitude had sought refuge on the island since the time of Columbus. No one had ever thought of running away . . . until now.

Cecilia noticed the woman staring at her.

"What's wrong?"

"Nothing."

"Don't lie to me, child."

Cecilia sighed.

"I'm tired of my country's not being a country, with all the opportunities it's had. Now the whole place can explode, for all I care. I just want to live in peace, knowing I can plan what's left of my life."

"It's your anger talking, not your heart. And anger is a sign that you really care about what goes on there."

The waitress brought her Cuba libre.

"Well, it could be," Cecilia admitted, "but I'd give anything to know the future, so I wouldn't keep gnawing on my own insides. If I could find out once and for all what's in store for us, I might know what to cling to, and I'd stop tormenting myself."

"The future isn't just one thing. If you could see the destiny of your country or even of one person right now, that wouldn't mean you'd see the same thing a month from now."

"What are you saying?"

"The future you'd see today would become reality only if nothing changed minute to minute. Even an accident can change the original prediction. At the end of a month, the sum total of all its events would turn the future into something different."

"But what does it matter?" muttered Cecilia. "No one can see what's coming, anyway."

The waiters were cleaning off the tables as they emptied. Two more couples called for their checks.

"Do you like games of chance?"

"I never play the lottery. I have bad luck."

"I'm referring to an oracle to predict the future."

Cecilia leaned over the table.

"You've just said that no predictions are for sure. And now you want to play fortune-teller?"

Amalia's clear, gentle laughter rang through the nearly deserted bar. What a shame she didn't laugh more often.

"Let's say, because of the situation I find myself in, I know certain things that others don't know. . . . But let's not complicate matters. Why don't we consider these predictions like a sort of game?"

Six dice fell onto the table. Two of them were ordinary, hexagonal ones; another pair had eight sides; and the third set had so many that it was impossible to count them.

"Destiny is a game of chance," Amalia went on. "A certain wise man once said that God didn't play dice with the universe, but that man was wrong. Sometimes I think He must even try Russian roulette."

"What should I do?"

"Throw them."

The woman looked at the numbers before picking up the dice.

"Toss them again," she instructed, handing her the tiny cubes.

After seeing the results once more, she scooped up the dice and shook them a second time.

"Again."

Cecilia repeated the steps somewhat impatiently, but Amalia pretended not to notice and made her go through the whole process three more times. Finally she put the dice back into her purse.

"Look up the meaning of the numbers 40, 62, and 76 in the Cuban lottery. Their combination will show you who you are and what you can expect of yourself. Then look up 24, 68, and 96 in the Chinese lottery. They represent a future that concerns us all."

Cecilia remained silent for a few seconds, skeptical about how seriously to take the game.

"I've heard that lottery numbers have more than one meaning," she finally said.

"Just look up the first one."

"How am I going to interpret a three-word message?"

"Not the words, the concepts," Amalia explained. "Remember, fortune-telling systems are more intuitive than rational. Look for synonyms, associations of ideas . . ."

The lights in the bar began to flicker.

"I didn't realize how late it was," Amalia said, rising. "Before I forget, I want to thank you for keeping me company all these evenings when I felt so alone."

"You don't have to thank me for anything."

"And also for your interest in my story. If you're part of what we left behind, I'll go in peace. I believe something better awaits Cuba."

The woman swept her hand across her brow, as if she were trying to drive away an ancient weariness. Cecilia accompanied her to the door.

"And Pablo?" she ventured, finally. "Did he ever get out of jail? When will you see him again?"

"Soon, my child, very soon."

And in her eyes Cecilia found traces of a heart even sadder than her own.

TWENTY YEARS

The ugly gray building stood before her, surrounded by a wall that looked as though it had been designed to fence in dreams. Protruding above the wall were posts that glared like the lights of a sports arena. Amalia tried to calculate how much energy those reflectors consumed, while nearby cities and towns had no power at all.

Someone pushed her gently. She emerged from her daydream, advancing a few more steps in the line of people who were waiting. The moment she had awaited for so many years had arrived. Twenty, to be exact. No pardons for good conduct, no review of the case, no appeals to a higher court. Nothing like that existed now.

During all those years she saw Pablo every time she was given permission. The visits depended on his jailers' frame of mind. Sometimes they'd let her see him month after month; on other occasions she would wait beneath the sun, in the rain, or the cold hours of dawn without arousing anyone's pity. A few times they had held him in solitary confinement for six, seven, or even eight months. For what reason? None that she knew of. Was he alive? Sick? No word. It seemed like a land of the deaf. Or the mute. A nightmare.

But today, yes—today, yes, she repeated. And she wanted to dance, sing, laugh with joy—but no, better to remain calm and put on a repentant face, lest they punish him again. Better to lower her eyes and adopt a humble demeanor she was so far from feeling. She couldn't bear another night without embracing him, without hearing the voice that drove away her fears. When she heard his name called over the loudspeaker, she realized that at some point she must have shown her identification card without being aware of it. She tried to remain calm. She didn't want to tremble; she didn't want to attract the guards' attention. It might look suspicious—anything might look suspicious. But her nerves . . .

She fixed her gaze on the metal door until she was able to identify the frail figure standing in the middle of the corridor as he glanced around, until finally he recognized her. But then two strange things happened. When she reached out to embrace him, he brusquely pushed her away as he advanced with long strides and a tense, unfamiliar expression on his face.

"Pablo, Pablo," she uttered.

But the man kept walking, gripping the bundle of clothing he was taking with him from prison. What had happened? At last the doors closed behind them, and they were alone on the dusty road. And that's where the second strange thing occurred. Pablo turned to his wife and, without warning, began kissing her, embracing her, smelling her, caressing her, until she understood why he had hardly glanced at her before. He didn't want the guards to see what she was seeing now. Pablo was crying. And his tears streamed down into the woman's hair, revealing a passion she feared lost. Pablo sobbed like a child, and Amalia understood that not even her daughter's tears had pained her as much as those of this man, who now looked like a fallen deity. And, in a moment of delirium, she yearned to renounce the blessed serenity of death and become a spirit, caring for the souls of those who suffered. In the distance she thought she heard a delicate sound, something like a flute, hidden in the brush, but she soon stopped paying attention. She and Pablo kissed, and neither of them cared about the other's haggard body or flaccid skin or shabby clothes; nor did they notice the light radiating from within them, ascending toward an invisible nearby kingdom where all promises were one day fulfilled; a light like the one that had emanated from their bodies on a certain afternoon years ago when they made love for the first time in the enchanted valley of the hummocks.

Now it was like living in another world. Amalia watched his stooped figure, barely able to imagine the suffering that had amassed within it. She never dared to ask him about his life in prison; it was terrible enough seeing the scars it had left on his spirit, but the expression on his face reflected its endless loneliness.

They no longer lived in that sunny apartment in El Vedado, either. The government had seized it to hand over to a foreign diplomat.

Pablo still had twelve years of his sentence left to serve when she had moved to one of the three residences she was offered. All of them were pigsties compared to the apartment they had shared together; however, she had no choice but to accept. She moved to a little house in the heart of Chinatown, not because it was better than the others, but because she thought it would please Pablo to return to the neighborhood of his childhood. There she waited for him until his release. But she never imagined his memories would turn into something so burdensome.

Sometimes Pablo would ask about the Mengs' inn or Chinaman Julio's ice cream, as if it was still difficult for him to believe that twenty years of chaos had wiped away the lives of those he once knew.

"It's been worse than a war," he would mutter whenever Amalia would recount the fate of those former neighbors.

Even so, she kept the worst stories to herself, inventing others in their place. For example, she never told him that Dr. Loreto had been found dead on the same stoop where Rosa used to bring him his dinner. She vaguely mentioned something about the doctor having gone to the United States to be with his children.

Amalia was glad just to have him beside her, although her joy was clouded by a sorrow she didn't want to admit: they had robbed her of twenty years of life with this man, years that no one—not even God—could give back to her.

And Pablo? What did he still keep locked inside his head, this man who every afternoon walked up and down the streets of his childhood, now inhabited by men who seemed like shadows? Although he never complained, Amalia knew that a piece of his soul was a landscape of darkness and ashes. He smiled only when Isabel came to visit, bringing his grandson, a little boy with greenish slanted eyes. Then both of them would sit in the doorway of the house, and—just as his great-grandfather Yuang had done with him—he would tell the child stories of the glorious days when the *mambises* listened to the holy words of the *apak* José Martí, the Enlightened

Buddha, dreaming of a freedom that would soon be theirs. And the boy, who was still very small and believed in fairy-tale endings, smiled happily.

Sometimes Pablo insisted on leaving Chinatown. Then he would walk through Paseo del Prado, which still boasted its bronze lions, sparrows twittering among the branches. Or he would go to the Malecón to remind himself of the days when he and Amalia were still courting.

One Day of the Dead he visited the monument to the Chinese *mambises* together with Amalia, his daughter, and his grandson. Isabel's husband didn't go. Years of assault and threats had turned him into a miserable individual, full of fear and very different from the young dreamer whom the girl had met. He no longer went to see his in-laws, because his father-in-law had spent twenty years in prison as a counterrevolutionary. And it was during that outing that Pablo realized the extent of the destruction.

Havana looked like a Caribbean Pompeii, devastated by a Vesuvius of epic proportions. The streets were lined with potholes that the infrequent vehicles, old and run-down, tried to skirt. The sun singed trees and gardens. There was no grass left anywhere. The city was overrun with barricades and billboards calling for war, destruction of the enemy, and merciless hatred.

Only the black marble monument remained intact, as if it were made of the same material as the heroes to whom it paid tribute, the same stuff as the dreams for which those heroes of yesteryear had fought: *There never was a Chinese Cuban deserter; there never was a Chinese Cuban traitor.* He inhaled the breeze blowing off the Malecón, and, for the first time since leaving prison, he felt more himself. His great-grandfather Yuang would be proud of him.

A fine drizzle began to fall, indifferent to the sun that made steam rise from the asphalt. Pablo looked up toward the blue, cloudless sky, allowing his face to receive those sweet, shiny drops. He had never been a traitor, either, and he never would be. And, watching that miraculous rain, he knew that the deceased *mambí* was sending him his blessings.

FREE OF SIN

Cecilia sped through the narrow streets of Coral Gables, streets dappled by trees that shed squalls of leaves over people and houses. Inexplicably, the landscape reminded her of certain hidden corners of Havana, but with its rough walls and Gothic gardens, damp with ivy, Coral Gables more closely resembled an enchanted village than the ruined city she had left behind. Perhaps the association was due to the two different kinds of decrepitude: one cloaked in sham elegance and the other a remnant of past glory. She glanced over the flower-dotted gardens and felt a wave of nostalgia. What an obsessive nature she had, still yearning for the roar of the waves against the coastline, the warmth of the sun over the dilapidated houses, and the fragrance escaping from a soil whose fertility rose to meet you each time it became soaked with the steaming rain.

She couldn't lie to herself. That country *did* matter to her—as much as her own life, or even more. How could it not, when it was a part of her? She wondered how she would feel if it disappeared from the map, if suddenly it were to vanish and land in another dimension: an Earth where Cuba didn't exist. . . . What would she do then? She'd have to look for some other exotic, impossible place, another region where life defied logic. She had read that people stayed healthier if they maintained some connection with the place where they had been brought up, or if they lived somewhere similar. And so she would have to find a country that was elusive and bucolic at the same time, where she could readjust her biological and mental clocks. Without Cuba, what other places might do? Through her mind paraded the megaliths of Malta, the abandoned city of the Anasazi, and the ancient, dark coast of Tintagel, plagued with nooks where the characters of the Arthurian legend wandered . . . mysterious places where the echo of danger resounded and that were, of course, filled with ruins. In essence, that was her island.

She snapped back to reality. Cuba was still in its usual place, within her reach. Its glittering cities could be seen from Key West on the darkest nights. Her mission, for the moment, was something else: to untangle her immediate future. Or, at the very least, to find a clue that would move her in the right direction.

The parrot's screeching was the first response to the door buzzer. A shadow blocked the peephole.

"Who is it?"

"Juana the Mad."

"Who?"

Holy Virgin! Why did she insist on asking when she could see her?

"It's me, *tía* . . . Ceci . . ."

There was the sound of locks sliding open.

"Goodness, what a surprise," the old woman said, opening the door as if she just now could see her.

"The people, united, will never be defeated. . . ."

"Fidelina! That damn parrot is going to give me a nervous breakdown."

"It's your fault for not getting rid of her."

"I can't," Loló groaned. "Every night Demetrio begs me not to give her away to anyone else, because he can only see her through me."

Cecilia sighed, resigned to being part of a family that hovered between insanity and kindness.

"Do you want some coffee?" the woman asked, entering the kitchen. "I've just brewed some."

"No, thanks."

The old woman returned a few seconds later with a demitasse in her hand.

"Did you find out anything about the house?"

"No," Cecilia lied, not able to rehash her newest discoveries.

"And your exercises for seeing the aura?"

Cecilia remembered the whitish cloud surrounding the plant.

"All I saw were illusions," she complained. "I'll never be like my grand-mother. I don't have a single drop of vision."

"It's possible," the old lady murmured, daintily sipping her coffee. "Neither Delfina nor I ever had to do anything unusual in order to speak with angels or with the dead, but things today just aren't like before."

Cecilia waited for the woman to finish her coffee.

"*Tía,* do you know what the numbers in the puzzle mean?"

The woman stared at her with a slightly foggy expression, as if trying to remember.

"It's been years since I heard anyone talk about that, although some-times I use them to play the lottery. And believe me, it works: I've won my little stash of cash."

"And do you play the Chinese or the Cuban puzzle?"

"Why are you so interested in those things? No one your age knows what the puzzle is. Who told you about it?"

"Some woman," she replied vaguely. "She gave me a few numbers to play, but I'd like to know what they mean."

"Which numbers?"

Cecilia extracted a little piece of paper from her purse.

"Look: 24, 68, and 96 from the Chinese puzzle. And 40, 62, and 76 from the Cuban one."

The old woman scrutinized her niece, pondering whether or not to expose her lie. The Florida lottery didn't go up to 68 or 96. So no one in his right mind would want to play such high numbers. She was sure there must be some other reason for the girl's interest in those figures, but she decided to go along with her.

"I think I've got a list somewhere," she said, getting up and heading for the bedroom.

Cecilia stayed in the living room, going over her notes. She had always thought the oracles were elaborate, mysterious entities, with revelations that could produce ecstasy, not some amusement for a private eye. Should she pursue such games?

"I found it," said her aunt, emerging from the bedroom and placing a wrinkled paper on the mantel. "Let's see . . . 24: dove . . . 68: large ceme-tery . . . 96: challenge."

Cecilia jotted down the words.

"Now all I need are the numbers from the Cuban puzzle," she reminded her.

"I've never used that one," Loló admitted. "The Chinese one was the most famous."

"Where can I find it?"

The woman shrugged.

"Maybe . . ." she began, but she stopped short, staring into space. "In which drawer?"

Cecilia's hair stood on end when she understood that her aunt was talking to the lamp.

"In the closet?" the old woman asked. "But I don't remember . . ."

Even though she knew she wouldn't see anyone, the girl turned around, looking for the invisible speaker.

"Well, if you say so. . . ."

Without any explanation, Loló rose from the sofa and went to her room. After a few, unidentifiable sounds, she reappeared with a little box in her hands.

"Let's see if it's true," the woman remarked, rummaging through the container filled with papers. "Well, yes. Demetrio was right. I guess he's not as forgetful as he thinks."

She was referring to a newspaper article she had taken from the little box. It was so brittle that one of its corners flaked off when she tried to smooth it out. It was a copy of the Cuban puzzle.

"Will you lend it to me?" Cecilia asked.

The old lady lifted her face, and once more her gaze wandered off into the distance.

"Demetrio wants you to keep it. He says that if a young girl like you is interested in these relics, we've won the battle. And he says . . ."

Cecilia folded the paper carefully to prevent it from crumbling further.

". . . he'd like to know you better," the old woman sighed.

The girl looked up.

"Me? Why?"

"He was only able to see you once, the first day you came to visit me."

"You've told me that before, but I can't remember."

Loló sighed.

"And to think how important you were to him!"

"Me?"

"I'm going to let you in on a secret," Loló said, sitting in a rocking chair. "After my husband died, may he rest in peace, Demetrio became my greatest support. We'd known each other since we were young. He was always in love with me, but he never told me so. That's why he came here, right after I left Cuba. You were Delfina's only granddaughter, and she never stopped sending us your photos and telling us about you. Your parents had been planning to come here when you were born, although your mother never made up her mind for sure. The truth is, she was afraid of change. Delfina died, but she kept on sending us news about you. Demetrio knew that I spoke with my dead sister, and he found it quite natural. So we kept up with your life, especially after your parents died. I was very worried, knowing you were so alone. It was then that Demetrio declared his love to me and said that if you came here, between the two of us, we would take care of you like the daughter we could never have. You don't know how obsessed he was with the idea. He dreamed of meeting you, going to your wedding, helping to raise his grandchildren . . . because we spoke of your children as though they were our own grandchildren. Poor Demetrio! He would have been such a good father!"

While Loló spoke, Cecilia's knees turned to stone. That was the missing connection. Demetrio had wanted to protect her. She would have been the daughter sent to him by Fate and his link to Loló, the sweetheart of his dreams, with whom he couldn't part even in death. That's why he, too, traveled in the house together with her parents: to protect her, to take care of her. . . .

"I've got to go, *tía,*" she muttered.

"Call me whenever you like," the old lady urged, surprised by her sudden departure.

From the window she watched her climb into the car and pull away. What odd manners young people had! And why did she need to know the meaning of those numbers? She remembered how, when she was young, it had been fashionable to play guessing games with the puzzle. If this had been another time, she would have sworn Cecilia was solving some riddle. She bolted the door and turned around. There were Delfina and Demetrio, like every other afternoon, gently rocking in their chairs.

"You should have told her . . ." Delfina mumbled.

"Everything in due course," Loló said.

"It's true." Demetrio sighed. "She'll find out all by herself. The important thing is that we're here for her."

And they chatted for a long while, until twilight filled the house.

One hour later, night had fallen over the city. Loló bade farewell to her guests, who now had to hurry off to errands more compatible with their present state.

The clock struck nine. When the old lady headed to the kitchen, she noticed that for some time now the apartment had been disturbingly silent. The parrot seemed asleep in her cage. So early? She went to the dining room and poked a hand through the bars, but the little creature didn't move. She had a premonition and opened the cage door in order to feel her feathers. The flesh, stiff and still warm, was rapidly growing cold. She walked around the cage to look at her from a different angle. Fidelina had died with her eyes open.

She felt sorry for the poor parrot and was about to say a prayer for her soul. But—what the devil—that damn bird had driven her, her neighbors, and half of humanity out of their minds. No prayers for Fidelina. Better just to make her disappear—something, she thought regretfully, she should have done long ago, when the beast was still alive. Why didn't she try it earlier? A heavenly design, some inescapable karma. Who knows? But no more. She had freed herself of that miserable wretch and she swore never again to allow anything like it to appear in her life.

"Rest in hell, Fidelina," she said, throwing a rag over the parrot's corpse.

As she drove back to her apartment with the solution to the mystery, Cecilia thought of her adolescence. In those happy times, her greatest adventure was to explore houses that had been barricaded by the government, like that mansion in Miramar, the one they called the Little Castle, where she and her friends used to meet and tell ghost stories on Halloween nights, even though the holiday wasn't celebrated on the island. Every year they would climb to the roof of the haunted house to invoke the spirits of a crazy, sensual Havana, which nevertheless seemed free of sin.

The ocean, the rain, and the hurricanes provided a natural baptism that redeemed the children of the island's Virgin. According to legend, she had arrived by sea on a raft, gliding over the waves, the first account of surfing in history. It was no surprise, then, that this same Virgin, whom the pope had crowned queen of Cuba, struck such a resemblance to the goddess of love that the slaves worshipped, dressed in yellow like the African deity, and had her sanctuary in El Cobre, a place from which the metal devoted to the *orisha* was extracted. Ah, her radiant mestiza island, innocent and pure as Eden.

She recalled the drizzle that had accompanied the pope as he left the sanctuary of San Lázaro—a healing rain, delicate as filigree, spilling over the tropical night—and she remembered the cloudless rain that fell on Pablo before the black marble monument. But by some fluke of memory, she also thought of Roberto. . . . *Ay,* her ill-fated lover, as beautiful and as distant as her island. In her mind, she blew him a kiss and wished him luck.

YOU GOT ME IN THE HABIT

It was as if Yuang's rainy message had reawakened that rebellious, adventurous spirit that characterized his sign. The rain strengthened the spirit he had never lost. His tears on being released from prison hadn't been a sign of defeat, as Amalia had thought, but one of rage. No sooner had he returned to normal life than he recovered his inner voice, the one that demanded justice above all else. He continued to speak his mind, as if he had no inkling that it might earn him a beating or even another stint in jail. In his heart he still felt like a tiger, old and caged, but a tiger nonetheless.

Amalia, on the other hand, feared for him and for her family on that island of draconian justice. And so she began to negotiate—papers passing back and forth; certificates and stamps; interviews and documents—the only possibility if all of them were to stay alive.

One day she came home from running around and stopped in the doorway, trying to catch her breath. She looked at Pablo, her daughter, and her grandson, who was coloring the paper boats his grandfather placed on the table.

"We're leaving," she announced.

"Where to?" Isabel asked.

Amalia heaved an impatient sigh. As if there were any other place one could go!

"Up north. They gave Pablo his visa."

The child turned away from his boats. He had been hearing about the visa for months. He knew it had to do with his grandfather, who was a former political prisoner, although he didn't really understand what it all meant. He only knew that he mustn't mention it at school, especially after the stigma of his parents' divorce.

"When are you leaving?" asked Isabel.

"You mean when are *we* leaving. You and the boy also have a visa."

"Arturo will never give me permission to take him out of the country."

"I thought you'd already spoken with him."

"He doesn't care, but he can't okay it. He'd lose his job."

"That . . ." Amalia began, but she held back on seeing her grandson's expression. "He only thinks of himself."

"I won't be able to do anything until the boy is older."

"Yes, and when he turns fifteen, he'll be old enough for military service, and then they won't let him leave."

The child listened in fear to the battle between his mother and his grandmother.

"I haven't waited twenty years for your father only to lose my daughter and grandson."

"You won't lose us—we'll be reunited," she assured her, furtively eyeing her father, who hadn't said a word, immersed in who-knew-what kind of thoughts. "You're the ones who mustn't wait."

"At least, try to talk to Arturo. Or would you rather I do it?"

"We'll see," she whispered without much conviction. "It's late. We really should go. . . . Say good night, sweetheart."

The little boy kissed his grandparents and hopped out to the sidewalk. There he remained standing on one foot until his mother took his hand and walked him away.

Amalia looked out the window to watch them, and she felt her heart ache as much as it did the day she watched her father die. How could she leave them behind? Not to see her grandson grow up, never to embrace her daughter again: this was just half her fear. The other half was to lose Pablo again, and that was what would happen if she didn't get them out of there.

For that reason, she anxiously awaited the exit permit from the government: the famous white card. Or the "freedom card," as Cubans called it, following the success of a certain soap opera in which a slave woman spent more than one hundred episodes waiting for that document. All those with travel visas had to live through a similar soap opera: unless that card arrived, they could never leave.

The first months were full of hope. When the first year had passed, hope turned to anxiety. After the third year, anxiety became despair. And after the fourth, Amalia was convinced they'd never let them leave. Maybe they thought twenty years of prison weren't enough.

She took comfort in watching her grandson grow: he was as beautiful and sweet a boy as her Pablo had been in the days when they had met. Amalia noted how he took pains to please his grandpa. He always found ways to be near him, as if the threat of separation made him treasure each minute they spent together. The boy's fear seemed increasingly unreal, because time passed, and Pablo remained living in a different prison: the island itself.

Although he still alarmed people with his bold speeches, he never returned to jail. Perhaps the secret police had decided he was a harmless old man after all. In any case, no matter what he said, he couldn't actually take action.

Deprivation is the most effective weapon for containing rebellion. With the exception of a few signs on walls and in certain public restrooms, nothing appeared to be happening. There was no one to conspire with, either. It was the fault of that epidemic that had stuck to everyone's skin like a parasite: fear. Nobody dared do anything. Well, perhaps a few had tried, but they were already in prison. They went in and out of jail regularly, without inciting anything besides protest or denunciation. They were younger men and women than Pablo, as brave as he, although without the means to obtain anything more than what Pablo himself had achieved.

Pablo had no choice but to watch: watch, and try to understand a country that grew stranger by the minute. One day, for example, he went out for a walk very early in the morning and found himself at the Mengs' old inn, now a storage place for folders belonging to the Young Communists' Union. He lifted his face to a cloud-dappled sky, wishing for a little rain, the blessings of his great-grandfather. A mangy, nearly hairless dog passed by, the kind that used to be known as "Chinese dogs" because of their lack of fur. The animal regarded him with fear and hope. Pablo squatted to pet him, thinking of a song from his childhood:

The day I left Havana,
I didn't tell a soul;
The only one who followed me
was a little Chinese dog.
Since he was just a Chinese mutt,
a man who thought him cute
bought him for half a peso
and a pair of leather boots.
The money, well, I spent it,
and the boots soon fell apart.
Ay, doggy of my sorrows!
Ay, doggy of my heart!

He glanced around, as if expecting to hear the Chinaman Julio's bells, announcing his coconut, *guanábana,* and French vanilla ice cream, the best in the neighborhood, but all he could see on the street were three half-naked children playing, and they soon grew bored and disappeared inside a house.

As he was about to leave, he noticed the face of a little girl looking at something around the corner, outside his field of vision. He craned his neck a little, without revealing himself to her, and saw two young women talking spiritedly next to some trash cans. He immediately recognized that one of them was a prostitute. Her clothing and makeup gave her away— a pity, because she had lovely, delicate features and a very distinguished air. The other was a nun, but she didn't seem to be delivering a sermon to the wayward one. On the contrary, both of them were chatting like old friends.

The prostitute had a sweet, mischievous laugh.

"I can imagine the expression on your confessor's face if you told him you talk to the spirit of an African slave," she joked.

"Don't say that, Claudia," the nun replied. "You don't know how bad that makes me feel."

What were those women talking about? He looked around. There was no one else in sight except the little girl, still sitting in the doorway.

The three boys who had been playing on the sidewalk earlier came out again, whooping and striking machete blows against the Spanish conquerors. Pablo couldn't hear the rest of the conversation. He only saw that the nun held a little piece of paper the prostitute had given her before walking away. Then she did something even more peculiar: she glanced at a pile of rubble and crossed herself. Immediately she appeared to blush and, almost angrily, made the sign of the cross in the direction of the trash bins before continuing on her way.

My God, what a strange place the island had become.

Warm days and rainy nights arrived. New slogans were invented and others were forbidden. There were demonstrations organized by the government and silent protests inside people's homes. Rumors of uprisings circulated, as well as speeches denying them. In time, Pablo forgot everything. He forgot his first years on the island, his struggles to understand its language, the endless afternoons of lugging clothing back and forth. He forgot his years at the university when he moved among three existences: studying medicine, secretly seeing Amalia, and fighting for the underground; he forgot that he had once tried to leave a country he'd come to love; he forgot the documents that were growing mildewed in a drawer somewhere. . . . But he never forgot his rage.

On the darkest nights, his breast moaned with an ancient pain. Hurricanes, droughts, floods: he had witnessed it all during those years when his life had less and less meaning. Now the country was going through a new stage that, unlike the others, seemed planned because it even had an official name: Special Period of War in Peacetime. A stupid, pedantic name, Pablo thought, trying to silence his insides, which cried out with loneliness. Never before had he felt such fierce hunger, so absolute, so all-encompassing. Could that be why they had never let him leave the country? So they might kill him slowly?

He opened the door and sat down in the doorway. The neighborhood was dark, plunged again into one of its interminable blackouts. A light breeze blew down the street, carrying with it the muffled sound of the palm trees that whispered in Parque Central. Luminous shadows half-covered the disk of the moon, transforming it in smudged spirals. For some reason he thought of Yuang. He'd been thinking of him quite a bit lately—perhaps because with the years, he'd come to value his wisdom.

"It's a shame I never took more advantage of it when he was alive," he said to himself, "but that must happen to lots of people. We realize too late how much we loved our grandparents, how much they were able to give us, and what we, in our innocent ignorance, didn't know how to receive. But the mark of that experience is undying. It remains with us somehow. . . ."

He enjoyed indulging in such monologues. It was like conversing with the old *mambí* again.

The wind whistled with a ghostly voice. Instinctively he raised his eyes: the stars were turning pirouettes among the clouds. He looked more closely. The points of light drew closer or faded; they joined in clusters and seemed to dance in a circle; then they connected into a single body and suddenly shot out in all directions like fireworks. . . . But they weren't fireworks.

"*Akún,*" he called silently.

The stars moved, forming whimsical figures: an animal . . . maybe a horse. And, riding on it, a man; a warrior.

"*Akún.*"

And he heard the murmured reply:

"Pag Li . . . *Lou-fu-chai* . . ."

The pale vision stirred in the shadows.

Pablo smiled.

"*Akún . . .*"

An eyelid of clouds half-opened, revealing a sliver of moon, whose light spilled over the spirits that walked among the living. From the earth there rose that fragrance of home: it was an aroma like the soups his mother used to make, like the talcum his father used to dust himself with after his bath, like his great-grandfather's wrinkled hands. . . . The night was faltering like the soul of a man condemned to death, but Pag Li felt a new, ecstatic happiness.

The silhouette approached and, for a few seconds, regarded him with an infinite tenderness that even his years as a dead man had not extinguished. With his icy hands, he stroked his cheeks. He leaned over and kissed him on the forehead.

"*Akún,*" Pag Li sobbed, feeling all of a sudden like the most abandoned being in the universe. "Don't go; don't leave me alone."

And he clung to his great-grandfather's lap.

"Don't cry, little one. I'm here."

He rocked him gently, cradling the Little Tiger sweetly against himself.

"I'm afraid, Grandfather. I don't know why I'm so afraid."

The old man sat down at his side and placed his arm around his shoulder, as he had done when Pag Li was a little boy, when he would lean against his grandfather's chest and listen to the deeds of those legendary heroes.

"Do you remember how I met the *apak* Martí?" he asked him.

"I remember," he replied, drying his tears, "but tell me again."

And Pag Li closed his eyes, allowing his memory to fill with the images and cries of those forgotten battles. And little by little, embracing his great-grandfather's shadow, he stopped feeling hungry.

TODAY, AS YESTERDAY

It was so early that the sky still showed some traces of violet, but the bar seemed darker than usual. Guided by memory more than by sight, Cecilia approached the corner where Amalia always sat. She didn't think she'd find her there, but that's where she preferred to wait. When she noticed a shadow moving in the chair, she stopped short. The shadow belonged to a man.

"Excuse me," she said, drawing back. "I thought you were someone else."

"Couldn't you stay for a while?" he asked. "I don't know anybody here."

"No, thanks," she responded frostily.

"Sorry, I didn't mean to offend you. I've just arrived from Cuba, and I don't know the customs here."

Cecilia paused.

"The same as anywhere else," she said, irritated without knowing why. "No woman with even half a brain would sit down at a bar with a stranger."

"Yes . . . of course," he admitted, stammering so sincerely that Cecilia almost felt sorry for him.

At once she understood why she had been annoyed. It wasn't because of the invitation, but rather because the intruder had invaded the hideaway she and Amalia had shared for so many nights.

She looked for a table where she could watch for her friend's arrival, but they were nearly all full, obliging her to choose one close to the dance floor. She was anxious to speak to Amalia and tell her that she had given up on the puzzle. Although she had found out the meaning of the six figures, she still understood nothing. The first riddle, which was connected to her, was still a mystery. *Tavern, vision,* and *illuminations* were the words that corresponded to the numbers, but she didn't have the slightest idea what they might signify. The same thing happened with the second group. She couldn't figure out what to do with a *challenge,* a *dove,* and a *large cemetery.*

She looked up and saw the landscape that filled the entire screen. There it was again: in Miami, Cuba was more omnipresent than Coca-Cola. She tried to see the table where she and Amalia used to meet, but it was too far away and the bar was very dark. Even if Amalia were to come in now, she wouldn't see her, and if she found that stranger in her place, she might even leave. Taking a deep breath, she approached the young man once more.

"My friends will be arriving any minute," she said, in order to justify her boldness. "May I wait for them here for a few minutes? We always meet in this corner."

"Of course. Do you want something to drink?"

"No, thank you."

She looked away.

"My name's Miguel," he said, extending his hand.

She hesitated for a moment before replying.

"Cecilia."

A flicker of light allowed her to examine his face. He was more or less the same age as she, but his features were so exotic that they struck her as almost otherworldly.

"Do you come here often?" he asked.

"Pretty often."

"This is my first time," he admitted. "Do you know if . . . ?"

Several people passed by, tripping over some chairs.

"Gaia!" Cecilia called.

The figure in front stopped short and the others followed, tumbling over one another like a deck of cards.

"Hi! How are you?" the new arrival asked. "Look who came . . ."

But she didn't finish the sentence.

"Gaia!" the young man exclaimed. "I didn't know you were here."

"Miguel?" she sputtered.

There was a hesitation, and almost immediately thereafter a sort of earthquake. The silhouettes that followed behind Gaia rushed to the table.

"Is that you, Miguel?"

"What a surprise!"

"When'd you get here?"

"Claudia, I'd never have guessed! Melisa, it's been so long!" he said, laughing. "God, what a coincidence!"

And they ran their hands through his hair, laughing and hugging him, like people who had found a lost family member.

"Where do you know each other from?" Cecilia asked.

"From Havana . . ." he replied vaguely.

"Has anyone seen Lisa?" Gaia asked. "She's the one who suggested we meet here, but I don't see her."

Lisa hadn't arrived.

"We have a couple of tables reserved," Claudia said. "If you'd like to join us . . ."

Cecilia said she was waiting for someone, and they both stayed there.

"Ah, Beny," murmured Miguel.

The Great Sonero of Cuba appeared on the screen.

"Today, as yesterday, I go on loving you, my darling . . ."

"Would you like to dance?" the man asked, taking her by the hand.

And without giving her time to reply, he led her to the dance floor.

"Too bad you don't know anybody here," she scolded him. He seemed more familiar after the warm reception her friends had given him.

"I never heard a word from any of them again," he whispered, as if he were afraid of being overheard. "I helped them at different points in their lives."

Cecilia observed him suspiciously and resolved not to let herself be taken in by those pure, translucent eyes.

"Helped them how?"

"A friend of mine introduced me to Claudia when she was working in a pizzeria," he explained, "which was kind of strange, because she has a degree in art history. It turned out she had a political problem. I gave her some money when I found out she had a little boy."

"I didn't know she was married."

"She wasn't."

Cecilia bit her lip.

"And I met Gaia because she worked in my office for a while after she left the university. She always went around with a frightened look, like she wanted to run away from everything. I tried to take her to a psychologist, but I never managed to get her to see him because she left for Miami."

"I don't think Gaia is sick."

The screen lit up Miguel's face. Now his eyes looked green.

"Maybe this city's cured her," he speculated. "I've been told that Miami has that power over Cubans. Melisa was seeing a psychiatrist, too, and now just look at her. Although I never thought she had any problem. It was a mysterious business. . . ."

The bolero ended and they returned to their table. The girls sat down at another table with a group of friends. Claudia motioned them over to join them, but Cecilia wasn't ready to lose sight of her corner.

"I don't want to move from here," she confessed.

"Neither do I."

They rejected the invitation with a gesture.

"What did you study?"

"I'm a sociologist."

"And what were you doing there?"

There meant the island.

"I was working in hospitals, helping with group therapy, but I never told anyone about my real dream."

Cecilia listened without comment.

"For a while I've been making notes for a book."

"Are you a writer?"

"No, I'm just researching."

"Researching what?"

"Chinese contributions to Cuban culture."

She looked at him, surprised.

"Hardly anyone ever mentions the Chinese," he continued, "although according to the history and sociology texts, they're the third link in our culture."

A waitress approached the table.

"Would you like to order anything?"

"A *mojito,*" said Cecilia unhesitatingly.

"I thought you didn't drink with strangers," he said when the waitress walked away, smiling for the first time.

They studied each other for a few seconds. The darkness no longer impeded her vision, and Cecilia could distinguish the light coming from his eyes.

"When did you arrive from Cuba?"

"Two days ago."

Cecilia thought she had misheard him.

"Only two days?"

And, as he didn't respond, she ventured another question: "Who told you about this place?"

The waitress arrived with their drinks. When she had left again, Miguel leaned over the table.

"I don't know what you'll think if I tell you something a little strange."

"Try me," she silently challenged, but aloud she said: "I won't think anything."

"I came on account of my grandmother. She's the one who told me about this bar."

Cecilia froze.

A woman draped in a shawl went out to the dance floor, opened her arms as if she were about to perform the Dance of the Seven Veils, and crooned in her soothing voice, a voice made for boleros:

"How could it be? I can't tell you how, I can't explain it, but I fell in love with you. . . ."

"Let's go," Miguel said, tugging her toward the dance floor once again.

How hard it was to talk under those conditions.

"How long has your grandmother lived in Miami?" the girl asked, not daring to pronounce the name that was about to spring from her tongue.

"She was in Cuba, waiting several years for them to give her and my grandfather permission to leave. They finally gave it to her after he died. Then she came here alone, thinking that my mother and I would join her right away, but they didn't let us travel until recently. Look," he said, reaching under his shirt, "this is hers."

The familiar black stone, mounted in its little golden hand, hung from the chain around his neck. It looked like a very delicate jewel, barely visible on the young, strong chest. Cecilia closed her eyes. She didn't know how to tell him. . . . She tried to follow the rhythm of the melody.

"And when will she show up here?"

"Who?"

"Your grandmother."

Miguel looked at her with a strange glow in his eyes.

"My grandmother died."

Cecilia stopped moving.

"What?"

"A year ago."

He tried to keep dancing, but Cecilia was nailed to the floor.

"Didn't you say she told you about the bar?"

"In a dream. She told me to come here and . . . Are you okay?"

"I have to sit down."

Her head was spinning.

"How did you get that amulet of hers?" she managed to ask as she regained her composure.

"She gave it to a friend to give to me. I've had it since last night. Maybe that's why I dreamed about her."

Then Cecilia remembered the first set of clues: *tavern, vision, illuminations*. How could she not have realized it before? *Tavern:* that's what they called bars in Amalia's day. That was what the woman had meant to tell her: she was a vision in a bar, someone who was there in order to be illuminated. She thought about Amalia's words: "Their combination will show you who you are and what you can expect of yourself." She had no further doubts: she, too, was a visionary, someone who could talk to spirits. That's why she carried within her a house inhabited by the souls of her loved ones. Now she was sure she had inherited her grandmother Delfina's gifts. Even Claudia had told her so: "You walk among the dead." But she had been blind.

But there was still the second set of clues. What could the "challenge" be that was related to the future? Amalia had warned her that the oracles were intuitive, that she should look for associations. Fine. The "dove" was a peace symbol. But how could she associate it with the image of a "cemetery"? Did it mean that the future of her island was a challenge, where everyone would have to decide between peace and death, between harmony and chaos?

"Not for one moment can I be apart from you," sang the lady in the veils. *"The world seems different when you're not beside me . . ."*

The sweet, melancholy song seemed to calm her.

"Do you feel better?"

"It was nothing."

"Feel like dancing?"

"I think so."

"There is no lovely melody where you don't appear, and I don't want to hear it if you're not with me . . ."

The bolero seemed meant for her city. Or maybe it was simply that she couldn't hear a bolero without remembering Havana.

"It's just that you've become a part of my soul . . ."

Yes, her city, too, was a part of her, like breathing, like the nature of her visions . . . just like the one she must be having right now in the hazy atmosphere of the place: a crooked little man, dressed in a sort of cassock, rocking himself absurdly on top of the piano.

"Miguel . . ."

"Yes?"

"Am I drunk on half a *mojito,* or is there really a dwarf on top of the piano?"

He glanced over her shoulder.

"What are you talking about?" he began. "I don't see . . ."

He hesitated. And when he lowered his eyes to her face, she could tell that he knew about the legend of Martinico and what it meant for her to see him, but neither of them said a word. There'd be time for explanations later. And there would be time to ask questions of the dead. Now she suspected she'd always have them nearby, because she had just discovered Amalia amid the smoke that swirled like the fog rising off the river.

Cecilia stopped dancing.

"What's wrong?" Miguel asked.

"Nothing," she answered, trembling, as Amalia's shadow passed between them, leaving a sudden trail of cold.

But the girl ignored the chill. She only wanted to know what the woman was after with her fixed, mesmerizing gaze. She turned her head a little and could barely recognize her: a young, adolescent Amalia was dancing with a boy who looked like Miguel, with slightly more Asian features.

"Beyond your lips, the sun and the stars, with you in the distance, my darling, am I . . ."

Her dying Havana, haunted by so many phantoms scattered across the world.

"You learn to love the place where you've loved," she repeated to herself.

She looked up at Miguel and thought of the faces of those beloved dead who lodged in her memory. Her heart was somewhere halfway between Havana and Miami. At which point did her soul breathe?

"My soul beats in the center of my heart," she told herself.

And her heart belonged to the living—near or absent—but also to the dead who remained with her.

"With you in the distance, my darling, am I . . ." intoned Cecilia, watching the image of her city on the screen.

Havana, my beloved.

And, as she rested her head on Miguel's chest, Amalia's ghost turned to look at her, and smiled.

Acknowledgments

This novel is a tribute to many people and facts; also to certain places, and of course, to a city . . . or perhaps to two. My gratitude goes to all those sources that inspired it, especially the composers of the boleros whose words form the title of every chapter. Nevertheless, one essential factor served as impetus for the plot: the desire to tell a story that would re-create the symbolic union of the three ethnicities that make up the Cuban nation, especially the Chinese, whose sociological impact on the island is greater than what many people suppose. From my desire to pay homage to those three roots, this novel was born.

Many books offered me valuable information about the different eras and social customs re-created here, but I must mention three that were essential to an understanding of the immigration patterns and adaptation of the Chinese who arrived in Cuba during the second half of the nine-teenth century: *La colonia china de Cuba (1930–1960)* by Napoleón Seuc; *Los chinos de Cuba: Apuntes etnográficos* by José Baltar Rodríguez; and *Los chinos en la historia de Cuba (1847–1930)* by Juan Jiménez Pastrana.

Among my living sources of information, I would like to recognize the invaluable assistance of the Pong family, especially Alfredo Pong Eng and his mother, Matilde Eng, who shared with me their personal anecdotes and memories of that gigantic migratory journey that was common to those Chinese who emigrated from Canton to Havana more than one hundred and fifty years ago. Without their help, I would not have been able to reproduce the family atmosphere that appears in these pages.

My research into the musical universe of the period would have been impossible to conceive without the historical and anecdotal data provided by Cristóbal Díaz Ayala's book *Música cubana: Del areíto a la nueva trova*.

I have incorporated several historical musical figures into the plot, attempting to respect their personalities and biographies. The dialogue and facts narrated here are fictional, inspired only by my admiration for the musical heritage they have bequeathed us. Nevertheless, I suspect, had they found themselves in those situations, they might have acted in a very similar way.

I would also like to extend my thanks—from this world to the next—to the late Aldo Martínez-Malo, executor of the estate of singer Rita Montaner (1900–1958), who, one day long ago, in a gesture characterized as "unusual" by those friends who witnessed it, draped my shoulders with the legendary diva's silvery shawl, a relic that he loved to show off but would never allow anyone to touch. . . . Did that shawl hold any connection with the soul of the incomparable artist, or was it just my fantasy, enraptured by contact with such an unusual garment, that brought me strange visions of the past? Who knows! The important thing is that, somehow, the experience left such an insistent mark on me that it ended up as a part of this novel.

Miami, 1998–2003